exit here.

More timely reads from Simon Pulse

exit here.

Jason Myers

Simon Pulse
New York | London | Toronto | Sydney

SIMON PULSE
An imprint of Simon & Schuster Children's Publishing Division
1230 Avenue of the Americas, New York, NY 10020
Copyright © 2007 by Jason Myers
All rights reserved, including the right of reproduction in whole or in part in any form.
SIMON PULSE and colophon are registered trademarks of Simon & Schuster, Inc.
Designed by Steve Kennedy
The text of this book was set in ITC Tyfa Book.
Manufactured in the United States of America
First Simon Pulse edition May 2007
10 9
Library of Congress Control Number 2006940468
ISBN-13: 978-1-4169-1748-9
ISBN-10: 1-4169-1748-9

I dedicate this book, with special thanks, to . . .

*My mother, Diana Sash, who told me to be whatever I wanted
and that nobody owed me a thing.*

*My agent, Gary Heidt, who kept the faith, then caught
his second wind.*

*Justin Scherrer, who finally said to me, "Just shut up
and name your book* exit here *already."*

*Nina Asay, who pored over that very first draft again and again and
again in the same night, and called me to tell me
about it each time she finished.*

*And finally my wonderful editor, Jen Weiss, who kept telling me,
"This is really good, but not good enough."*

This is the root of our nature, we hate ourselves and don't know why . . .
This is the root of our nature, we numb ourselves until we die.
                                        —400 Blows, "The Root of Our Nature"

Retire now to your tents and to your dreams. Tomorrow we enter the
town of my birth. I want to be ready.

                                        —Jim Morrison

foreword.

THIS IS NOT A LOVE STORY.

These are the words that have been scraped into the ceiling of my tiny, shit-hole room. My boxlike dungeon. My brand-new fucking home.

Below that,

There are no happy endings.

Sometimes I think about who the fuck carved this shit in here. A lot of times, actually. Because I have a lot of time on my hands to think about everything. Around here this is what passes as entertainment.

You wake up.

Think.

You eat.

Think.

You shower.

Think.

You write some shit down.

Think.

This is what my days and nights consist of.

This is my life.

My life.

I can't wake up and fuck some hot girl anymore and get fucked up on some shit, and it sucks, but I have nobody else to blame except myself. I made all of the decisions that led me to this point, so even if I tried to point a finger, I would only be pointing at myself, and there's no need for that. Not anymore. I'm well past that shit now.

But still, I sometimes catch my mind wandering around. Walking backward. I catch myself thinking about the things that have happened and how if I'd just done this or that differently, I might be in a different place right now. Who knows where. Maybe getting loaded in a room and going off to some wicked Lightning Bolt shit. Maybe booze cruising down some highway smoking cigarettes, jamming out to the Replacements. Maybe lying in some bed next to Laura, bodies covered in sweat, holding on to her, Greg Ashley flowing from some nearby stereo.

Laura.

I always catch my mind racing back to her, especially to this one night in particular, Christmas night two years ago, when I was home briefly from college.

This night jumps out because it was the night before I left for my trip to Hawaii, the trip where everything changed and flipped upside down for me. The night when Laura stood across from me and told me not to go. "Stay here the rest of your break and be with me."

No way, I told her. I've been stoked for this trip since like two months ago.

"Fine," she said. "Just go. Leave again. But get me something awesome."

What do you mean?
"Buy me some cool shit from Hawaii."

Pulling my shirt off, I crawl into bed and look at the ceiling.

This is not a love story.

I look below that.

There are no happy endings.

Travis Wayne

"YOU LOOK KINDA WEIRD, MAN."

How's that?

"You almost don't look like the same Travis," Chris tells me after picking up a small mirror with two lines of blow on it.

I take the mirror from his hands. Set it down on the coffee table in front of me, right next to an issue of *VICE* magazine—the drugs issue—and even though I actually think I know what Chris meant by that, I still ask him:

What's that supposed to mean, dude?

Chris swings his bloodshot, pitch-black-circled eyes over to his roommate and childhood friend of mine, Kyle, then quickly back to me, and says, "You've totally lost your edge, man." He sniffs. Swipes his nose. "Your face looks all worn out and sunken in. You look out of shape. You're pale. Pale, Trav. You've been in the fucking desert for a year and you look pale, man. Unbelievable. I mean, I remember when you came back to the city during Christmas break and you came over here one time in the middle of the night in a fucking limousine, wearing a pair of shades with like three scarves hanging off your neck, a bottle of champagne in your hands, totally name-dropping a couple of the dudes from the Brian Jonestown Massacre that you and Laura were hanging out with after a show. And now look at you, man. You walked off the airplane an hour ago with your shoulders bunched up, looking all timid and shit while you were waiting for your luggage at the bag claim. And no sunglasses. It's June and you weren't wearing any sunglasses. Your swagger's gone. That's what I mean, man," he finishes, before dipping two of his fingers in a glass of water and sliding them up his nose real fast.

"Come on, Chris," Kyle says. "Don't be a dick. You should be happy because our rad friend is back from Arizona. I am."

Thanks, man, I say.

Chris rolls his eyes.

Jamming a blue straw that's been cut in half up my right nostril, I snort—

Once.

Twice.

Breathe.

My eyes start watering.

I go, Do you guys ever feel like you're locked inside a car that's moving really fast?

"What kinda car?" Chris asks.

Like a fucking red Monte Carlo with a black racing stripe cutting through the middle of it, and there's some superintense Fantômas shit jolting from the car speakers, like Mike Patton and Buzz Osbourne just completely losing it, but no steering wheel. The car doesn't have one. And the car is so out of control, right? It's swerving all over the road, and you're crying, pounding your fists against the window trying to jump out of it, trying to bail from it, and then all of these people start popping up on the road, like your parents and your sister and your friends, and the car is playing human dodgeball with them. It's trying not to run anyone over, but it's not slowing down, either, and then some junkie babe pops up in the middle of the road and the car destroys her, leaving her mangled body in its burnt rubber path, and then it keeps on going and going even though it can't maintain anything close to the same speed.

Pause.

You two ever feel anything like that?

"I'm a fucking coke dealer," Kyle says. "All I do is run over junkies. Night after night, again and again."

And Chris goes, "Nah. I never feel like that. But if I was in that car, instead of Fantômas blasting, I think I'd be listening to early Faith No More, the Chuck Mosley days. That shit would really blow your mind during a human dodgeball game."

"You think you'd have a choice?" Kyle snorts. "The car he's talking about doesn't even have a steering wheel, so no way that you'd be able to pick out the music. No way, man."

"I'm just saying," Chris snorts right back. "Early Faith No More would be the better choice to listen to in that particular situation. Don't you think, Trav?"

Maybe.

I lean forward. Wipe a thin line of coke residue off the mirror with my thumb and rub it back and forth against my gums a bunch of times until my mouth goes numb. Then I light a cigarette.

"You gonna be all right?" Chris asks me. "You look like your heart's just been ripped from your chest."

Plugging my nostrils with my other hand, I snap my head back and sniff superhard.

I think I'll be okay.

I look at the clock that hangs crooked on the dirty white wall in front of me, just above this black and white poster of PJ Harvey sitting on a bar stool, legs spread, panties showing. It's five o'clock.

Shit.

"What's up?" asks Kyle.

I gotta meet my parents for dinner soon. Like in an hour.

Chris starts laughing.

The three of us are watching this new Queens of the Stone Age DVD, and when I see Kyle get out of the blue reclining chair he stole from a nursing home recreation room last summer, I say, Yo, Kyle. Will you grab me something to drink?

"What do you want?" he asks.

Water.

And Kyle says, "No problem, dude."

Then he walks back into the living room a few moments later in his blue Dickie pants, his white Death from Above T-shirt, his left arm sleeved, his black hair butched with two thin lines shaved into each side of his head, and hands me a warm glass of water.

I take a drink and light another cigarette and look hard at Chris, who's wearing a pair of dark blue Levi's, a plain black T-shirt, and a pair of Vision Wear high-tops, and I ask him when the last time he slept was.

"This morning. What about you?"

On the plane ride here.

Kyle goes, "What happened to your car? What happened to all the shit you took with you to Arizona?"

I shrug.

Sold most of it. Fucked my car up like two nights after I got back to school from Hawaii.

Both of them smile and then I start asking them about what's been going on since I left. . . .

Not much.

What's new . . . ?

Not much.

I ask about everyone I can think of.

Cliff: *Livin' with his dad. Being a loser. Fuckin Natalie Taylor.*

Michael: *Gettin' wasted. Destroying meatpits. Lurking on Kennedy Street.*

Claire: *Being totally hot.*

I swallow a huge glob of spit.

Laura . . .

Silence.

Laura . . .

Silence.

Laura . . .

Nothing.

Chris starts blushing. He rubs his eyes. Shakes his head slowly from side to side.

Laura . . .

"I don't know," Kyle finally jumps in. "I don't see her that much anymore. She pretty much hangs out with different people now. But the last time I saw her at the Glass Castle, she was still looking good, man. She still had that whole Kate Bosworth thing going for her."

It's not a thing, I say. She really looks like that Bosworth chick. Maybe it's Kate Bosworth who has that whole Laura Kennedy thing going for her.

"Come on, Trav," Chris grunts. "Get real. Why do you even care what she's up to? She probably hates you."

I just wanted to know, Chris. What the fuck.

"What happened to you, anyway?" Kyle asks. "You came back for Christmas, flew to Hawaii, went back to Arizona, and cut everyone off."

Things got, ya know, complicated.

And Chris goes, "Things have always been *complicated* with you, Trav."

Did I do something to you, Chris? Cause you're being a total dick to me right now.

Chris shoots a look at Kyle, and Kyle goes, "You pretty much are, man."

Facing me again, Chris goes, "No, Trav. You didn't do anything. You just look different and talk different."

Pause.

He lights a cigarette. "It's making me a little nervous."

Well, your jaw's sliding around all crazy cause you're tweaking so hard and that's kinda freaking me out.

"I know it is," Chris says back. "It's been doing that every time I get high lately. I should probably chew gum when I do this shit."

Probably.

Kyle dumps some more coke onto the mirror.

Last night I called him and I asked him if he'd pick me up from the airport this afternoon but to not tell anyone that he was, which he didn't. Except for Chris.

And he went, "You're coming back? Do your parents know?"

Yeah. But they already have plans and can't pick me up. My dad sounded pretty pissed off.

"But I thought you wanted to stay out there for the summer," he said. "Maybe even do some traveling."

I need to come back, man.

"Why?" he wanted to know.

And I told him:

Kyle, just pick me up.

He cuts two more lines then he hands me the mirror.

One.

Two.

Goddamn this is some good shit.

Breathe.

And I'm really back.

□ □ □

The restaurant I'm meeting my parents at is called the Red Tie. I'm already a half hour late when Kyle drops me off at the front doors in his '91 Toyota Camry. He pops the trunk, and he, Chris, and I get out of the car, the Bronx album *White Drugs* blasting from the car stereo speakers, and we pull out all the shit I brought home with me.

The two suitcases.

A garbage bag filled with DVDs and CDs.

Some posters.

"What are you gonna do when you're done eating?" Kyle asks me.

Go home.

"What about after that?"

I'm gonna take some Percocet and crash, baby.

"Nice," says Chris, and then I bump fists with both of them and get my things and walk through the tinted doors of the Red Tie. The hostess seems to know who I am right away. She says, "You're meeting the Lance Wayne party?" and I say, Yeah, and she says, "Travis, right?"

I nod.

"Would you like to leave your things up front? We can store them in the coat check room while you dine."

I hesitate.

Sure.

She motions at this guy, who promptly comes over and takes my things. When he begins to walk away, I shout that I know exactly how many DVDs and CDs are in the garbage bag.

"I'm sure you do, sir," he smirks, cocking his head at me. Then he continues walking.

I turn back to the hostess.

"Are you ready?" she asks.

I guess.

"Right this way then," she smiles, leading me through the main dining area, up a short flight of stairs, then through a set of doors labeled PRIVATE.

She stops just short of a large table where my mother, father, and younger sister, Vanessa, are seated, and hands me a menu, and I tell her thank you before taking a seat across from my father, who's all swagged out in the blue Armani suit my mother and sister bought him for his birthday when we were in LA two years ago.

"Well you look like crap," my father immediately snorts. Twisting his wrist to look at his watch, my father, the big real estate GOD, the city's PERSON OF THE YEAR, he says, "But it's still nice that you could finally join us."

"Lance, don't," my mother snaps, in between sips of her red wine. "Let's have a nice dinner."

I don't say anything.

I just stare at Lance. Lance with his chiseled and groomed face.

Lance with his big, successful life.

Lance, who's taking a sip of his scotch, staring right back at me.

I slide my Parliaments out and light one. I'm starting to come down off the coke.

"How was your flight?" my sister asks.

Inhale. Exhale.

Long.

"Who picked you up from the airport?"

Kyle.

"Oh, how is he?" my mother asks, draped in a black Gucci dress.

He's fine, Mom.

"That's nice," she says. "Have you lost weight? You look like you have. Like you've lost a lot."

"Oh come on, Scarlett," my father barks. "Look at the boy. He looks like a shadow of his old self."

"Like a total junkie," my sister smirks. "Totally worse than Casper from that movie *Kids*."

"Who?" my mother asks.

And I say, I don't look that bad. Jesus. Give it a break. People still think I look good. Real good.

There's a long pause.

All of us look at each other. We all look around the room. I look at my sister again, and I start thinking that my sister looks a lot older than the last time I saw her.

"What are you staring at, Travis?" she asks, adjusting the strap on the pink halter dress she's wearing.

Nothing.

My sister rolls her eyes. Runs a hand through her shiny blond hair, parted down the middle.

Nothing, I say again, whispering it this time, and I flick some ashes into a nearby crystal ashtray.

From behind me, our cute waitress emerges in a white button-up shirt, a black miniskirt, and a pair of black tights. She has jet-black hair and a she-mullet and looks at my mother and father and says, "Now who's this handsome gentleman?"

See, I blurt out, throwing my arms up. Some people think I still look good.

"Like she knows anything," my sister snorts.

"Okay, that's enough," my mother smiles. "Maggie, this is our son, Travis."

"Nice to meet you," Maggie tells me.

My mother sets her empty glass down and goes, "He just flew back from Arizona."

"Wow," Maggie grins. "That's neat."

Yeah.

I smudge my smoke out and open my menu.

Neat.

"Would you like something to drink?" she asks me.

Whiskey sour. A double.

My father smiles.

"Sure," Maggie says. "I just need to see your ID."

I pull out my fake one and hand it to her.

"Thank you," she says. "I'll be right back with that."

My sister goes, "I'm gonna tell her you're really only nineteen."

Shut the hell up.

"I am," she hisses, sliding the tip of her tongue between her lips. "I'm gonna bust your ass."

You're such a bitch.

"Hey, you two," my mother snaps, jumping in. "I want to have a pleasant dinner, all right? *All right?*"

All right.

"I was just giving you shit, Travis. Jesus," my sister snorts. "Calm down."

I light another Parliament.

"So, Travis, did you pass any of your classes last semester?" my mother asks, lighting a clove cigarette.

I swallow a little water.

I think. Maybe one.

"Really," my father says, folding one arm over the other. "Which one?"

Inhale. Exhale.

Maybe economics.

"Jesus Christ," he snorts. "Economics." He says, "You don't even know what you're talking about, son."

I look at my mother as my father continues, "You call me out of the blue to tell me that you flunked out of a school I didn't want you to attend in the first place, and then you show up here, at this beautiful restaurant, late as hell, looking like a zombie, lying about passing a class you didn't take."

"Lance," my mother quickly interjects. "Not here."

"What the hell happened to you? Where did my son disappear to?"

I'm right here, Dad.

"We'll see," he says. "We'll see."

Maggie returns with my drink. "So what are your plans while you're back?" she asks me.

Glancing at my father, I tell her, I don't know. I haven't thought about it. I've been . . .

My voice fades. And I stop because I don't know how to finish the sentence.

"He'll be getting things in order," my father jumps in. "Maybe the two of you could hang out sometime. You seem to be well adjusted."

My sister bursts into laughter, and my face turns bright red. I feel like an asshole, with my father hooking me up.

"Yeah," Maggie says, her face a little flushed. "Maybe we could."

"Can I get another glass of wine?" my mother asks.

"And another scotch," my father says.

Maggie smiles at me. "Sure," she says, then winks. "I'll be right back with those and to take your orders."

I flick ash into the tray again.

"You know, I was serious about what I said," my father tells me after downing what's left of his drink.

What? About kicking it with the waitress?

"No, Travis." My father goes, "I'm serious when I say you need to get your shit together."

He says, "Just because you're back, around all your friends again, doesn't mean you can keep fucking around. I didn't raise a loser."

I nod. Take a sip of my whiskey drink.

And my father continues, "I don't know what happened

last semester, and at this point I don't care. But something will have to change." He leans forward, waving a finger at me. "Please don't try me, son."

I nod again.

Maggie comes back.

My father's still staring at me.

What?

"Do you understand me?" he snaps.

Yes.

Raising his voice, he goes, "Are we clear?"

Yeah, Dad. Crystal.

"Good," he smiles, swinging his eyes from me to Maggie. "I think we're ready to order now."

After we're through eating, I ride with my parents and my sister back to the house in my father's brand-new Lincoln Navigator. My mother drives because she's not as drunk as my father, who doesn't want to risk being pulled over and at least charged with another DUI.

The house is in the Dove Hills, which means we have to drive through the financial district, go around Harper Square, cut through the Little Minneapolis neighborhood, and roll past the old township housing additions, up to the hills where the house sits, nestled within a huge mass of trees and ridges.

For most of the ride, I don't say a word. No one really does except my sister, who's been on her phone since we left the restaurant. And at one point, while we're sitting at a busy red light across from a downtown Macy's store, she says, "God, Amy. You can be such a little bitch sometimes," then ends her call.

I watch my mother and father look quickly at each other, and then I catch my mother looking at me in the rearview mirror. "Are you feeling all right, Travis?" she asks.

But instead of answering her, I close my eyes and lean my head against the window and pretend I'm sleeping. Pretending until my own cell phone starts ringing.

I pull it out of my pocket. Look at the caller ID. Michael. Hello.

"What the hell, brah?"

What?

"You came back to the city and you didn't even call me. Dick."

Sorry.

"You should be, man. Totally."

I know.

"So what the hell's crackin'? What are you doing right now?"

I'm going home. Why? What's up?

"Kyle just came by and dropped off a gram of the white bitch for me and I'm about ready to roll to this rehearsal space and jam."

You're in a band? Since when?

"I'm drumming. You woulda known, too, if you'd actually answered your phone or called me back, ever."

Yeah, sorry about that.

"Whatever, man. Fuck it."

What's your band's name?

"Lamborghini Dreams."

Cool name, man.

"I just wrote a new song called 'Pound Puppy Cemetery' and we're gonna work on it tonight."

Sweet.

"You should drop into the studio, man. Check it out."

I'm too tired. I just wanna sleep.

"Fuck sleep, dude."

I need to, man. Trust me. I really need to sleep.

"That's cool. But hey," he says, "there's a huge fucking blast going on tomorrow night at this pad on Livermore and Twenty-second. Get ahold of me. We'll get smashed."

Sounds good.

"So you're gonna call me, right?"

Yeah.

"Because I've called you like ten fucking times since I saw you in December and you never called me back once."

I know.

"You bailed for Hawaii and no one's heard from you until today."

I don't say anything.

"So call me."

I will.

"Don't be a fuckin' pie grinder, man."

Right.

I hang up just as we're pulling into the long driveway

that leads up to the house, and my sister goes, "Who was that?"

Michael.

"My friends think he's so hot," she says.

What about you?

She smiles. "He's okay."

I put my phone away and stare at my parents' two-story house with its huge basement—its twelve bedrooms, five bathrooms, and five-car garage, and its hot tub and swimming pool in the ten-acre backyard that's been fenced in.

It's just past eight. The sun is fading fast, although not quite as fast as I wish it would. My mother parks the Navigator in the garage and the three of them file into the house while I struggle with my things.

I finally get inside. The air conditioner is blasting. It's freezing.

Slowly, I move down the hallway that leads to the kitchen and notice that the family pictures that had been hanging along the wall when I was home at Christmas have been taken down and replaced by two odd-looking metallic pieces of art.

I try not to think about this and walk into the kitchen. Watch my father take a beer from the fridge, then walk into his work den and slam the door shut behind him.

Across the kitchen, through the large bay windows that surround the dining room table, I see my mother and sister standing by the pool, talking. I also notice the new portable bar and the new lawn furniture and the new top on the hot tub.

Swinging my eyes back through the kitchen, not a whole lot has really changed in this room since the last time I stood here.

The marble counters are still shining. The antique china cabinets my father had flown in from the Hamptons last summer still sit in the same spot.

Grabbing my things again, I walk through the living room and head upstairs to my bedroom and lock myself inside. Drop my things on the blue carpet floor. Sit down on the edge of my bed, black sheets still unmade from a Christmas visit. Light a cigarette.

Inhale. Exhale.

Laura. I think about her deep blue eyes, ocean waves. How soft her pink lips were as they slid down the skin of my chest, around the cusp of my ears. About the first time I saw her, fourteen years old, sitting on a faded green bench behind the peeling concession stand at school. The palm of her right hand pressing her blue skirt against the bench seat. Her black socks pulled to her knees. The thin veil of smoke, from the Virginia Slims cigarette she held between two fingers, that swirled loosely around her face, her sand brown hair. The pearl necklace that clung perfectly around the pale veins of her neck.

Laura. I think about the last time I saw her, Christmas night, the night before I left for Hawaii, when the two of us were here, in my room, and had just finished fucking for like the fifth time. And while I ran my fingers over the long, thin, red scar on the right side of her face—a sledding accident during the winter of fourth grade, she told me once—Laura told she me still couldn't understand why I'd left the city for college in the first place if I was so glad to be with her, and I said, Because that's what kids are supposed to do, Laura. They're supposed to finish high school and experience other things. Way better things. They're supposed to leave home and get away from it all.

"Well, I'm just glad we stayed together. It might have made us even stronger. It feels like we're past all that petty crap, baby."

She told me she was still happy and that she was going to visit me during her spring break and I told her that would be pretty awesome and that I was glad she was so happy.

I stand up and it still hurts.

Everything does.

I finish my cigarette and walk to the middle of my room and grab a small brown satchel from inside the bigger one of my suitcases.

Unzip it and rummage through it until I find the orange tinted plastic bottle that can make all of this go away for the rest of the night.

I open the bottle and dump its contents into a metal jar sitting on the roundish end table next to my bed, and run my fingers over all the Vicodins and Valiums and Xanax and find my last Percocet and swallow it with a glob of spit.

The way I figure, I have maybe twenty minutes before I won't be able to do shit, so I use this time to hang up the posters I brought back.

A shot of Vincent Gallo.

A promo for the movie *Badlands*.

And a Stooges one that Laura gave me after she got Ron Asheton to autograph it.

Once I've finished, I empty the trash bag of DVDs and CDs on the floor and fall to my knees and dig through them until I find what I want.

A knock at the door.

Who is it?

"It's me."

It's my mother.

What do you want?

"Will you open the door?" she asks. "I'd like to talk to you for a minute."

About what?

"Some things."

Like what?

"Please open your door, Travis. Don't make me talk to you through a piece of wood."

I push myself to my feet and get really dizzy.

Hold on.

Stepping over big piles of stuff, I make it across the room and open the door.

What, Mom?

My mother lifts a hand and dangles a set of keys from it. "A guy at the dealership owed your father a favor," she says. "There's an Eclipse out there. It's yours for the summer."

You two don't have to do this.

"Yes we do," my mother nods. "Take the keys."

I do.

"I know your father's upset with you, but he's still on your side, Travis."

That's pretty cool to know, Mom.

"I'm being serious, Travis. He's upset with what happened. We both are. But that doesn't mean we aren't rooting for you, because we are."

I know you are, Mom.

Our eyes lock together and neither of us flinches. I wonder if she can see through me.

I wonder why I can't see through her.

"Get some sleep," she says.

I will, Mom.

My mother disappears from the door and I push it shut.

The Percocet comes on strongly, like a black sword slicing through puffy pink clouds. And I get confused about which CD I wanted to play, but then I remember when I see this Stone Roses disc lying a few inches away from everything else.

I grab it. Pop it into the CD player and hit play. Crawl into bed. Smoke a cigarette. Then I take my phone out and scroll down to her name.

Laura.

I stare at it. My thumb on the call button. My heart speeding up. My cheeks turning red.

But I can't do it. Not yet.

I flip to my side and reach into the end table and pull

out a picture of Laura and me. It's a Polaroid, and in it Laura is sitting on my lap. She's wearing a gray wife beater and has an unlit cigarette hanging from her lips, both arms around my neck. I'm wearing a white V-neck T-shirt, left arm around her back, right arm across her stomach. We're also rocking these small party hats, these gold-colored cones that say "Happy Birthday" on them in big, crazy, blue lettering. It was Laura's eighteenth-birthday party. We were in the basement of this shitty Chinese restaurant that I'd rented out, and everyone was there. Tons of coke being passed around. Two kegs of Budweiser. Three strippers. Sitting on a table in front of us is the birthday cake I asked Michael to get her, lit with candles. The cake was decorated to look like Winnie the Pooh, except in this interpretation, this Pooh bear has two black eyes, tinged with purple. Lots of blood drips from this Pooh bear's nose. His left ear has been chopped off. A sharp vampire tooth has manifested itself out of the left corner of his mouth. And instead of the red shirt that has always read "Pooh" in crooked letters, this bear's red sweater says "Get Fat and Die." Or as Michael put it that night, "When the cartoon got canceled, Pooh did what every other child star does when the show they're on comes to an end: He turned into a gnarly drug addict, man."

Staring at this picture carves a big smile into my face as I remember how much fun everyone had that night as we screamed at the top of our lungs and yelled over each other and told each other the same stories over and over like they'd just happened and no one had heard them before, everything leading up to the very end, after all the drugs had been snorted and swallowed, the booze guzzled, and the strippers long gone with their residue-covered dollar bills, when I pulled out a gold-colored boom box, stuck in a cassette tape, jacked the volume, and we all sang along to Alice Cooper's "Eighteen."

Feeling my eyes beginning to water, I put the picture away and pick up my phone again and continue scrolling over the names of my past. I scroll past Claire and land on Cliff. This time I do make the call. It rings and rings and rings, and then Cliff's voice mail comes on, and before I've hung up, I've told Cliff that I'm back, and that he should call me, and that I'd like to see him real soon.

Click.

My headache fades away and my eyes begin to close and I laugh to myself a few times over, thinking about the joke the guy I was sitting next to on the airplane with this afternoon told me.

Guy: What has nine arms and sucks?

Me: What?

Guy: Def Leppard.

2

I WAKE UP AROUND ONE THE NEXT AFTERNOON AND WALK across my room and stand in front of the large mirror that hangs above my dresser. And although, sure, it is true that I may not look as good as I did my whole life (voted most attractive, best-looking, and best dressed by my high school graduating class), I'm not exactly ugly. My body is still fairly cut. My face still has a hint of that same boyish thing that drives girls nuts. And my dark brown hair is still kind of in order.

I feel better and decide to do some laps in the pool, and go downstairs. No one is home. In the kitchen there is a note for me on the dining room table. It's from my mother. She and my sister and my sister's friend Katie and Katie's mother all went out shopping for the day and won't be done until late. Next to the letter is two hundred dollars.

I leave it and walk outside. The air is blanket thick and brutal. My skin feels sore, almost blistered from the sun. Standing on the edge of the diving board, I watch the wind make small ripples in the water, wondering if my sister's friend Katie is the same Katie that got tag-teamed by Cliff and Michael in a bathroom during a party at Laura's parents' house last summer.

It probably is and I dive into the water, and even though it's very warm, it still feels good, and I start swimming laps and do almost fifty before I become too exhausted and have to quit.

Later that afternoon, while I watch this pretty good movie called *Me and You and Everyone We Know*, the front doorbell of my house rings.

It's Cliff, and he looks pretty wrecked. His shaggy black hair is all greasy. His stubble is thick but patchy. His white T-shirt is full of paint-drip stains. Black circles have devoured his droopy eyes.

Hey, Cliff.

Cliff flips his head back. "Hey, man," he says. Then he walks past me, into the house, a lit cigarette wedged between his chapped lips.

Out of all my friends, Cliff and I go back the farthest. We met in preschool and were pretty much best friends after that until I said I would be leaving the city to go to college. But Cliff was the kid I had a ton of firsts with. We did blow for the first time together. We both got laid for the first time by the same sixteen-year-old chick when we were thirteen, one right after the other, in the basement of an abandoned school just a few blocks from his parents' house.

Grabbing an ashtray from the coffee table, Cliff flicks some ashes into it and says, "You look like shit, Travis."

It's nice to see you too, Cliff.

"Don't fucking lie to me, man," he says. "Just 'cause

you're back doesn't mean you have to say nice things to me now."

What are you even talking about?

Pause.

"Never mind," he says.

When's the last time you slept? I ask him.

"I've been sleeping all fucking day," he snorts. "It's what I do now. Where the hell's the beer at?"

Where it's always been.

Cliff walks into the kitchen and grabs a bottle of Heineken from the fridge.

"You want one?" he asks.

No.

"I got some pot. You wanna smoke?"

Nope.

"Suit yourself, dude," he says, and opens the beer. Takes a long drink, almost half of it.

So what's new, dude?

"Not much, man. Still living with my dad. Working a few days a week at the American Apparel store on Kennedy Street."

How's that?

"What?"

Work?

"It's cool. Babes are hot. Cheap clothes."

I notice a couple of track marks on Cliff's left arm. Cliff slides that arm around his side when he sees me looking at it. He goes, "So, Arizona didn't work out. I told you it wouldn't."

It wasn't Arizona, Cliff.

"What was it then?"

My back stiffens.

I don't know what it was.

"I guess it doesn't even matter anyway. You'll never have to worry about your future. Not when your father owns half of the city."

I don't care about that.

"Since when, man?"

Since always, Cliff.

He makes this snorting noise and takes another drink. His cell phone starts to ring. He answers it and walks into the living room while I dig into the pocket of my jeans and pull my cigarettes out.

I walk out back and sit under a red table umbrella. Cliff walks out a minute later with a new beer and sits down next to me, lighting a Marlboro.

Who was that, Cliff?

Turning to me, grinning, he says, "Natalie Taylor."

Kyle told me you two were messing around.

"Something like that," he says. "She just moved into a trailer in Lowell Park."

That's . . . great, man.

"It's not that bad, Trav. It's cheap. The trailer was her aunt's."

It's still a trailer park.

"Don't start this bullshit critique stuff with me, man. Not all of us have what you have," Cliff snaps. "Fuck you for coming back home to live with your parents and talking shit on people."

Whoa, dude, I say, taking a drag. I wasn't trying to be a dick.

Cliff pushes a series of smoke rings from his mouth and says, "Bullshit." Poking and twisting a finger through the center of one of them, he goes, "You're always trying to be a dick."

I roll my eyes.

Yep. That's me. The big dick. The big asshole.

The corners of Cliff's lips arch. "See, even you can admit it, Travis."

Well, you didn't seem to think I was such a bad guy when you called me a few months ago and wanted me to lend you all that money.

"Shit, man. Like I've never helped you out before. Like I've never taken the fall for you during a pot bust or lied to Laura about being someplace with you while you were out nailing some sweaty meathog from the Diesel store. Nothing like that."

What's your point, Cliff? You trying to get at something?

"Nope. Not a thing." He looks down at his cell phone. "I have to get going. I have some errands to run."

I flick my smoke onto the cement and watch the wind push it back and forth until it rolls into the pool.

Pulling a joint out and handing it to me, Cliff says, "I know you said you didn't want any, but just take it as a sign of my new goodwill to you, Trav."

I take it from him and drop it into my cigarette pack.

Cliff gets to his feet. "Later, dude."

Later.

He disappears back into the house while I think back to March, when he called me and asked me if he could borrow some money.

How much? I went.

"Only three hundred dollars."

Only.

"Please, man. I'll fuckin' pay you back, I promise. I'm in a jam."

Fine, I told him.

"Really?"

Yeah, really. But I don't want you to pay me back and I do not want you to tell me what you need it for.

"You're the fuckin' best, Travis Wayne."

Yeah, man. The best.

3

MICHAEL CALLS ME AND TELLS ME THAT HE'S JUST LEFT his band rehearsal space and is on his way back to his parents' house to change and shower and wants me to meet him there, then hit the party.

I can do that.

"Cool, brah."

After I jack off to one of the Sydney Steele DVDs I brought home with me, I do fifty crunches on my bedroom floor, then shower and get dressed. Pair of jeans. Pair of Doc's. White V-neck T-shirt.

Then I'm off.

Michael's parents live in a huge house just past the financial district in the Snow Valley neighborhood.

The two of us have been friends forever, almost as long as me and Cliff. We were arrested for the first time together. It was in eighth grade and we were in the same gym class, and during one period, our coach left his car keys lying on a clipboard inside the locker room. Michael took them, and the two of us cruised around in our coach's ride for a couple of hours, listening to this rad Charles Manson tape we found in the guy's cab, but on our way back to the school, we got pulled over for not coming to a complete stop at a stop sign. We were arrested and held for the next eight hours and forced to complete fifty hours of community service. Fifty hours that consisted of painting a toolshed for some handicapped dude, and working four straight weekends at a nursing home doing things like wheeling old people outside for fresh air and cleaning bedpans.

I park the Eclipse at the top of the driveway and walk to the front door and Michael opens it, a red bandana tied around his forehead, the Pat Benetar lyrics "Love is a battlefield" tattooed across his stomach.

Michael's about six feet tall. His skin is more tan than I remember it being last summer. His brown hair is shaggy, unbrushed.

Hey, dude.

Michael tosses his arms around my neck and kisses me on the cheek.

It's nice to see you too, Michael.

"Isn't it," he says, smirking.

I follow him into the kitchen.

On one of the counters is the Replacements *Let It Be* vinyl with a pile of blow sitting on the cover. Michael hands me a Miller High Life forty and says, "I picked these up on my way here," then takes a pull from his.

Where are your parents?

"London. I think my old man's there on business and my mom went along for the ride."

Michael's father is a financial consultant for some big Midwest corporation.

Handing me a pen that's been hollowed out and cut in half, Michael goes, "Chop yourself a rail."

Nah, I'm good.

"Fuck you. You're not good. Do a fucking line, man."

Okay. I'll do a fucking line.

Pulling a bank card from my wallet, I make myself two rails. Do both of them. Hand the pen back to Michael.

Are you ever going to move out of your parents' house, man?

"I already have, you fucking pilgrim."

When?

"In March. I moved into a loft on Crystal Street, but shit got out of hand between me and one of the douche-wads who lived there, Siv."

What happened?

Leaning down and slamming two huge lines, Michael shoots back up and barks, "That dude showed up at the place one night wearing a moped helmet and a fucking cape, and started blasting this Dio album over and over, just loud as fuck, and I really like Dio, man. I loved him with Rainbow, but not twenty times back to back, ya know. So I knocked on his bedroom door and asked him if he would turn it down and he grabbed my hand and tried to bite it, so I broody slapped him as hard as I could in the grill, man."

Fuck yeah.

"Totally, dude," he says, reaching over the counter and laying me some skin. Cutting two more lines, Michael rips, "Anyway, like two nights later, he barges into my room and accuses me of stealing his socks."

What?

"Yeah, Trav. He was like, 'I used to have fifteen pairs of black socks and you used to have twelve, and now you have fifteen pairs and I have twelve.' And I was like, 'Get the fuck out of my room, man. If you ever come in here and count my socks again, I'm gonna light your fucking cape on fire.'"

You have to be tough sometimes.

I sniff, chocking down a huge drip.

"You're damn right," Michael says. He leans down and devours the other two lines. Popping back up, taking a huge breath, he goes, "So things calmed down for a few days until one day the dude jumps on the stair railing and tries to ride it like a surfboard and breaks the fucking thing."

Was he wasted? I ask, forcing a swallow of beer down my throat.

"No. He was dead sober, and I was like, 'Yo, dude. That shit might be cool on *Saved by the Bell* but not in real life.' And he was like, 'You're the reason why I hate everything in my life!' Then he tried to bite me again, so I had to bitch-slap him again, and after that I stayed with this total babe for a few days to let things cool off, and when I came back to the place, all my jeans were lying in the middle of my bedroom floor with the pockets cut out of them."

Awww. What a pie grinder.

"Yeah, man. That guy was a total troll humper," says Michael. "So I ended up moving back here the same night."

What about school?

Michael leans down and slams the other two lines he just cut. "I'm taking a year off," he grins, rubbing his nose real fast. "Gotta find myself, ya know."

I start laughing.

Fuck you.

And Michael carefully picks up the record. "Let's go down to the basement."

I follow him through the living room, then down some stairs, and Michael flips on the lights.

The first thing I see is the green sofa he and I jacked from the back of a pickup truck last summer after a Bad Wizard, Dead Meadow, High on Fire, and Year Future show at the Breaking Point.

Still got it.

"Obviously, man. Obviously."

On the walls are some posters. A *Lost Boys* one with Corey Haim and Kiefer Sutherland on it. A Kip Winger one with a vagina drawn on it. A Tom Petty and the Heartbreakers one. And a poster for the Vincent Gallo movie *The Brown Bunny*, with a shot of Chloë Sevigny about ready to suck Gallo's cock.

Across the room, someone's taken a black marker and sketched a gnarly fat girl with one tooth and spaghetti string hair, and underneath the sketch in red paint are the words "Grundle Pigs Stole My Undies."

I ask Michael who drew it.

"The bass player in my band, this guy Dave."

Who else is in your band?

"This guy Thomas. He sings. And this other dude named Rodney plays lead."

Michael sets the record down on a small table in front of the green sofa and turns on the stereo.

Wires on Fire start destroying and Michael goes into his bedroom to change.

Taking a seat on the sofa, I chop myself another rail and notice all these yellow Post-it notes that have been scribbled on. I pick a few up and read them, and realize that all of them are poems he's written. Poems that go:

the nature of the beast is how i define myself
lost and abortioned to these ancient days
the coffee of my spirit is what i'd call decaf
when i go outside it's like walking through a maze

Or:

the morning dew on the summer flowers is priceless
true beauty has always been my first command
all this time I've spent in here sitting
i coulda been like an indian and cultivated the land

I lean down and take the line and Michael walks out of his room wearing a Buddyhead T-shirt that says "Punk Is Dead" on it and a pair of girl's jeans, which he started buying like two years ago so he could get the tightest fit possible. He sits down next to me and goes, "What do you think?"

About what?

"My poetry, man."

It's pretty all right. When did you start writing?

"When I joined Lamborghini Dreams. But these . . . ," he says, scooping up a handful of the Post-it notes. "I wrote these toward the end of this four-day speed bender I went on last week, where I did nothing but sit in this basement and watch Van Halen videos and David Lee Roth interviews on YouTube. Shit totally inspired me, Trav." He cuts up another line and takes it. "It really did, man."

We stop by Kyle and Chris's pad a little past ten to score some more coke. My friend Claire is there with Kyle and his girlfriend, Emily, who's also one of Claire's really good friends from college.

When Claire sees me walk in, she runs over to me and jumps in my arms and kisses me on the lips. "Ohmigod! I just heard you were back in the city!" she shouts.

I set her down.

Yeah, I'm back.

"I know it," she shrieks.

Claire looks absolutely amazing tonight, but then again, she almost always looks this amazing.

Her blond hair is pulled back, pinned behind her ears. She's got on a white top that says Modern Lovers across the front of it. A black lace skirt with pink trim. A pair of bitch kickers. Black knee-high socks. And she's also added to her left arm a black and gray still frame of a man carrying a woman down the stairs from the movie *The Cabinet of Dr. Caligari*, to go along with the band of black and gray roses across the top of her breasts, and the Hank Williams lyrics "you win again" just above that.

Seated on a raggedy couch are Kyle and Emily, and sitting on the coffee table in front of the couch is a scale and a bunch of coke and stacks of small plastic baggies with red hearts on them. Most of the sacks have been filled with the coke, but a few haven't.

I walk toward Kyle and he stands up, bumps my fist, and says, "This is Emily."

Emily is very cute. She's got black, shoulder-length hair with bangs that have been cut straight across her forehead, these intense green eyes, and a full sleeve on her right arm.

She shakes my hand.

I'm Travis.

"I've heard a ton about you, Travis," she says, straightening her white David Bowie top. She's also wearing a denim miniskirt, black tights underneath that, and a pair of knee-high black leather boots with zippers on the sides.

Really? You've heard about me?

"Of course she has," says Claire, wrapping her arms around my waist from behind me. "We always talk about you when you're not around."

Kyle fills another baggie and Claire pushes me onto the blue reclining chair and plops on my lap.

Kyle has been dealing since we were freshmen in high school. Back then, it was strictly weed and painkillers—Xanax, Vicodin, Valium—until late last summer when Michael introduced him to the brother of this Asian girl he was humping. Apparently this Asian girl's brother had a small operation but didn't have shit going inside the rock underground clubs and hipster scene around Kennedy Street, so Kyle and him struck a deal, and from that moment on Kyle's been doping up all those kids with coke.

Michael walks around the coffee table and wedges himself in between Kyle and Emily on the couch and drops sixty dollars on the glass tabletop. "Two grams at discount price, please," he tells Kyle. "Mr. Wayne is back in town."

Kyle takes the money and slides Michael two baggies, then Michael tosses one to me and says, "My treat, dude."

I slip the coke into the left front pocket of my shirt and ask Claire if she's going to the party on Livermore.

"Maybe later," Claire says. "We're gonna go to the Inferno for some drinks first."

"Fuck that place," Michael snaps, after he pops his baggie open and takes his key chain out. "That place is bullshit."

"Free drinks for me and my friends," Claire says. "I just started barbacking there."

"And," Kyle jumps in, sealing another gram, "I can probably make a grand there in about an hour and a half. It's Friday night. Payday."

Michael rolls his eyes. He dips a key into the baggie, scoops out a large bump, and snorts it. "I don't care what you guys got going there, the place sucks. It's like a fucking scenester prom for girls with fat asses and bad makeup and bros who dig eyeliner and think the Bravery are the truth."

Everyone starts laughing and Michael hands the keys and baggie to Emily.

"Regardless," Kyle grins, weighing out another gram, "it's a good money night. I'm still thirty bucks short on rent and I still owe Chris for those parking tickets he paid off for me in April."

Where is Chris? I ask.

"Yeah, what's that pig doing?" Michael snaps, digging into the twelve pack of PBRs sitting on the other side of Emily and tossing me one.

"He went to that Nine Inch Nails, Mars Volta show in Chicago with his girlfriend," Kyle answers.

Who's his girlfriend?

Claire twists her neck around to look at me. "April Brown," she says.

Wasn't she a couple of grades below us?

"Yep," Kyle says, then finishes weighing out his last gram. "He'll be back on Sunday."

Emily stands and hands the baggie and keys to Claire, who looks at Michael and tells him thanks.

Michael winks. "For you, Claire—anything."

I open the beer and watch Kyle count all the baggies before he stuffs them into a plastic bag, and the plastic bag down the sock on his right foot.

Claire scoops out a bump and takes it and I ask Kyle to

play some music. He hits the play button on the stereo remote in front of him and the Murder City Devils come on.

Claire grabs my hand and puts the coke and keys in it. "It's really good seeing you again," she whispers, running a hand down the side of my face. "It sucks that we lost touch, but it's so awesome that you're back in town." She kisses my cheek. Stands up and goes to the bathroom.

Leaning forward, I dig deep and hard into the baggie and load a bump, then hand the stuff to Kyle and ask if Cliff is shooting heroin.

"Yes," Michael says. "The guy is completely fucked up. I heard that he went to Iowa City all cranked up and had sex with some girl and talked her into letting him cut her in the side with a knife."

Don't make shit up, man.

"I'm serious," Michael says. "The dude is out of his mind. He's done some bad shit."

Who here hasn't done some totally bad stuff? I ask.

No one says a thing.

So let's not talk shit about him when he's not here to defend himself.

"Wow," Michael snaps. "A little edgy tonight, aren't we?"

No. It's just . . . ya know. It's just not fair, man.

Claire comes back into the room and grabs a beer from the twelve box.

"Come on, Trav," Michael says, rising to his feet. "Let's bail."

Right now?

"Right now, man. I'm loaded. And if we don't leave, we'll

probably end up at the Inferno with these guys or just sitting here blowing rails all night listening to the same songs and trying to talk over each other."

All right, man.

Kyle does a bump and gives Michael back his drugs and keys, and then Michael walks over to the far wall in the room and kisses the large Joan Jett poster hanging on it.

"Good luck," is all he says, and I follow him out of the front door after telling Claire that I definitely, for sure, promise to call her later.

"No matter what," she grins.

No matter what, Claire.

The party we go to is in a large duplex and there are a lot of people there. Michael and I walk down this very long and narrow hallway crammed full with kids and crappy art and cigarette smoke and make it into the living room, where it's even harder to move.

Michael stops briefly to talk to this girl with a skunk stripe going down the middle of her black hair and she points toward somewhere and Michael turns to me and goes, "The kegs are out back."

The two of us push ourselves past small groups of girls and boys, and I notice a few girls shooting Michael some really nasty looks, and also hear these two girls talking and one of them goes, "Isn't that Travis Wayne?" And her friend goes, "I think it is," and the girl goes, "He's not like drop-dead, Johnny Depp gorgeous anymore. He's more like Joaquin Phoenix cute now."

Once we've made it out of the living room, we enter this really small kitchen, then move to the back door and down some steps into this courtyard.

Right away, Michael runs into Dave, the bass player in Lamborghini Dreams. He introduces us, then goes, "Nice shirt," pointing at Dave, who's a wearing a white T-shirt with the words: "I killed your parents" written on it in red marker. He's also wearing a pair of black jeans rolled up to his mid-shins, and a black hat over his thick, curly black hair.

"Thanks," says Dave. He goes, "This party sorta sucks. I say we get some people together and roll down to the studio."

"No way. Not yet," Michael shoots back. "We just got here."

I look across the courtyard and see the kegs and walk over to them. Pay for two cups and listen to this guy with a handlebar mustache and black blazer tell this girl in a black dress, with black hair cut crooked across her forehead, that he heard Jack White is going to be playing a solo acoustic show somewhere in the city this summer. And the girl goes, "We have to go. If I miss that, I will totally die. I just will."

I walk back over to Michael and hand him a cup and light a cigarette.

"Sweet," he says, taking a sip.

I'm superhigh and really paranoid, feeling like everyone at this party is staring at me and knows I'm tweaking, so I decide that I need to start getting really drunk, and I stay where I am when Dave and Michael walk to the side alley to do key bumps.

Finishing one beer, I fill my cup again, then take a swig from a pint bottle of Royal Gate Vodka that some guy, who swears he knows me, hands me.

He goes, "Here, Todd," handing me the pint.

I say thanks and finish another beer and this is when I see her.

Laura.

Standing in a small circle of people by the stairs, holding hands with some guy I've never seen before with shaggy black hair, a thin chinstrap of hair around his face, wearing a plain brown vintage-style suit.

My first thought is to run away. To fade.

I'm embarrassed. I'm by myself. I'm fucking alone.

This wasn't the way I wanted to see her for the first time again.

Making a quick move to my left, I try to blend in with a group of kids next to me, but I don't do it soon enough and I hear Laura shout my name. "Travis!" Her voice momentarily freezing my heart in midbeat.

Shit.

I look back at her and all of the people she's with are looking at me.

Damn.

"Travis," she says again. "What are you doing?"

My face feels like it's on fire.

"Travis, come here."

I can't do it at first. I cannot make myself walk to where she's standing, wearing pink lipstick. Fixing her hair. Looking at me with her blue eyes. Adjusting her black minidress.

But I do it because I can't help it anymore. I move closer to her.

"What are you doing?" she asks again.

Not much. Just hanging out.

"When did you get back?"

Yesterday.

"When did you decide to come back, Travis?"

A few days ago.

The guy that Laura is with extends his hand to me. "I don't believe we've met," he snorts.

I do not shake his hand. I just leave it hanging there and say, No we haven't.

Laura, whose face looks flushed, jumps in, saying, "Bryan . . . Travis. . . . Travis . . . Bryan."

"That's Bryan with a *y*," he says.

With a *y*. Right.

I look at Laura and she looks at me and I want to tell her how sorry I am for the way everything turned out. And how we should be working all this shit out. And that she's pretty much all I've known and had for the past five years and that I need to get back to that so I can have something again.

But I can't say any of this. My lips will not open.

"So how do you two know each other?" Bryan asks.

"We went to West together," Laura quickly snaps.

"Oh, so you're one of her old high school pals," Bryan starts. "I've met a few of you since we started dating."

Good for you, man.

I look back at Laura and I have that anxious, butterfly feeling, and I don't like it and wish it would stop.

"How long are you back for?" Laura asks.

I'm not sure. Maybe for good.

"Where are you back from?" Bryan with a fucking *y* wants to know.

I don't know.

"You don't know," Bryan laughs. "That's really weird, man. Sounds, ya know . . . interesting."

It's really not. Definitely not as interesting as your choice of facial hair.

"Travis, don't," Laura snorts. "Don't."

Bryan puts his arm around Laura's shoulders and kisses her cheek. My heart is in my throat, practically choking me.

I'm sorry about that.

"What?" both Laura and Bryan spit out at the same time.

Sorry.

"What?" they both ask again.

I'll see you around, Laura.

"Will you?" she asks.

Looking right into her eyes, I say, I hope I do. I really mean that.

Turning around, I walk up the stairs and cut past a bunch of kids waiting in line to use one of the bathrooms, kicking out these two girls who are in there fixing their makeup. . . .

It's not helping anyway, I think I say before splashing water on my face. Over and over and over again. Then I grab the baggie of coke from my pocket and my keys and start scooping out bump after bump until someone starts pounding on the door.

I'm busy in here, you fucking asshole!

"Open up," I hear Michael say. "It's me and Dave."

I close the baggie and open the door.

The two of them walk in.

"We saw you talking to Laura then head up here," Michael tells me, rubbing his nose.

Fuck her and fuck that guy she's with.

"Dude," Michael snaps. "Don't start getting all emo about this shit. You guys are done. You've been done since you went to Hawaii."

I don't say anything.

"Besides," Michael continues. "That dude she's with is a real turd burglar. He thinks he's like king of the hipsters and shit, but he's lame. He's like twenty-five, he doesn't work, his band sucks, and he's way too into the Strokes."

I light a cigarette and Dave pulls out his cell phone. He goes, "Here, man. I gotta number in my phone that will make you feel a million times better."

Whose number is it?

"James Spader's."

Really?

"Yeah, brah, we got James Spader's phone number," Michael says. "Dave's cousin was partying with him in LA one night and got it. You should totally call him and leave a message. For some reason it makes you feel better. Like really good. It's like . . ."

Pause.

Michael looks at the ceiling in deliberation, then looks at me again and goes, "Have you ever seen that video on YouTube of those retards just completely losing their shit to that transgender sludgecore band at the disabled home?"

No, I laugh.

"It's like that, man, but better. Completely mind-blowing, dude."

"Here," Dave says, shaking the phone in my face. "It's ringing right now."

Taking the phone from him, I put it up to my ear and hear "This is James, leave a message."

Sweat the donkey, I say for some reason, then hand the phone back to Dave, whose eyes are wide open, and he goes, "What the fuck does that mean, man?" And I go, I'm not even sure myself, dude.

Someone else starts pounding on the door and Dave pounds on it back. "We're giving each other hand jobs, okay. Five minutes!" he shouts, putting his phone away.

I take a deep breath.

I think I'm gonna go home, guys.

"Don't be stupid," says Michael. "Let's go to the bar."

"99 Bottles," Dave says. "I know a ton of people who are going there tonight."

But I feel like going home.

"Fuck that," Michael snaps. "Don't let that cunt ruin your night."

She's not a cunt, Michael. Please don't call her that in front of me.

"Whatever."

I'm serious.

"Cunt," he says again, mockingly.

Fuck you, Michael.

Michael rolls his eyes and I slide past both of them, walking out of the bathroom, back through the living room, down the hallway, out the front of the duplex, stopping at the street corner to wait for a cab.

"Trav," I hear Michael yell from behind me. "Come on, man, let's go to the bar."

I turn around and Dave and he are coming toward me.

"We can walk to 99 Bottles from here. It's like three blocks up," Dave says.

I know where it's at.

"Come on then," Michael says. "Let's keep the night going. It's only eleven thirty."

Pause.

"Come on," Michael pleads once again.

Fine, man. Whatever.

So we turn back up and head for the bar, and on our way we duck into an alley to piss.

With Michael on my left, and Dave on the other side of Michael talking about making a smiley face on the garage door we're all peeing on, I tell Michael that I'm sorry if I was being an asshole back there.

It's not that I'm mad at you or anything, it's that I'm dealing with a ton of shit. Internally. I'm totally strifed, man.

"It's cool," Michael says, tucking his dick back into his pants. "I don't care or anything. It's just that I've never seen you care about anything in your entire life."

I zip my fly.

And Michael goes, "I mean, I've watched you spend your whole life not feeling bad about anything you've ever done."

I say nothing and we continue to the bar.

4

THE WHOLE BIG TRIP TO HAWAII HAD COME ABOUT WHEN my cousin Seth, who lived in New York but was about to graduate from college in Paris, called me in November and asked me to go to Maui to celebrate with him. And I was so fucking into it.

Beaches.

Booze.

Blow.

I talked to my father about it and told him how badly I wanted to go and that he should get the ticket for me because I'd done well in school and stayed out of trouble. And he agreed. My father bought me my plane ticket as a Christmas present, but two weeks before the trip, my cousin got busted trying to bring mescaline back into the States with him, and he was forced to cancel on me.

At first I was going to cancel my ticket also, but then I thought, Fuck that! Earlier that semester I'd read a book called On the Road, and then I'd read Fear and Loathing in Las Vegas, and I figured maybe I needed my first great adventure, so I decided to do it by myself after talking my mother and father into letting me, and arrived on the island of Maui on the morning of December twenty-six.

Travis Wayne

5.

I WAKE UP IN THE MORNING, GASPING FOR AIR. IT'S like I'm suffocating. Drenched in my own sweat. I'm still freaked out from the dream I had—the exact same one I've been having since I came back from Hawaii.

Peeling my eyelids apart, the first thing I see is Michael sitting across from me, blowing his nose. When he's done pushing his bloodied snot out, he crumples the Kleenex into a ball and tosses it on the coffee table in between us with the other like fifty bloodied Kleenex balls, and goes, "My nose is so fucking raw."

I sit up and wipe the sweat from my face with my shirt and rip my tongue from the roof of my mouth and look around the room.

I'm at Kyle and Chris's pad.

"You all right, Trav?" Michael asks. "You look a little freaked out."

What happened last night?

"Dude, you got kicked out of the bar for taking a piss on the dance floor, man, and when we walked to Whiskey Red's to meet Kyle and Emily, you told the bouncer that you'd been doing coke with James Brown all night and then showed him your baggie, and he was like, 'Get your fucking friend home now,' so the three of us brought you here."

Patting myself down, hoping to find one last cigarette, I go, Thanks. I guess. That woulda sucked to have been arrested. I don't think my dad woulda liked that too much.

Kyle and Emily walk into the living room. They wanna go eat, so the four of us bail and head to Taco Bell, and while we're there, Kyle asks Michael, who's been scratching at his balls since we left Kyle's crib, "What the hell's wrong with you?"

"What do you mean?" Michael asks back.

"Why do you keep scratching at your dick?"

"'Cause it itches," says Michael. "What the hell do you want me to do?"

"Get checked," Kyle laughs. "You probably caught something from one of those nasty meatpits you slayed a few weekends ago."

I start laughing, and Emily goes, "God, Kyle, you don't have to be so fucking gross about it. I'm eating."

"I'm just joking, baby," Kyle grins, then kisses her, and Michael looks at me, and goes, "Maybe I should get tested."

Maybe, brah.

Back at Kyle's an hour later, we pass a bowl around and watch a *Saved by the Bell* rerun, the one where Zack Morris gets wasted and smashes Lisa Turtle's mom's car against a pole.

"That's so rad," Michael says. "But Screech is such a little bitch."

"Dude, don't forget about AC Slater," Kyle says.

"Remember that episode when he put on that spandex leotard and danced like a ballerina across the classroom?"

"Yeah, what a faggot," Michael smirks.

"'Fraid so," says Kyle.

Two episodes later, I finally get Michael to drop me off at my house again.

6

THE NEXT NIGHT I CAN'T SLEEP AT ALL. IT'S AFTER THREE in the morning and I call Laura and am so surprised when she answers her phone that I almost hang up.

But I don't.

"Hello," she says.

Um. Hey.

"What do you want, Travis? You're not like really high and strung out right now are you?"

No.

"Good," she says. "What do you want?"

To talk.

"Okay, what should we talk about? Oh, I got it. How about we talk about you blowing me off for three months and fucking me over."

Hey, I'm not the one who ended it. You're the one who called me in March and left a fucking message on my phone telling me it was over, Laura.

"Don't turn this on me," she says. "It was over a long time before I made that call."

You're right. I'm sorry. It was. But I still thought I had

you. I was going through some crazy shit and I didn't think I could talk to anyone. I was scared.

"What happened?"

Pause.

"Are you still fucking there, Travis?" she asks.

Yeah.

"I don't understand any of this. Why are you calling me?"

I had to.

"What does that mean, Travis?"

I don't know how to explain it.

She sighs into the phone. "You really embarrassed me at the party, ya know that, don't you?"

Who cares? Fuck that guy. You're way better than that trend hopper.

"Travis, you don't even know what you're talking about. This is complete bullshit. You can't just come back and wave a wand and try to make everything the way it was."

But I have to. I want to fix things.

"Well, you can't. Too much has happened. You had everything and you disappeared. I loved you and you destroyed my fucking heart, Travis Wayne."

Can we at least meet face-to-face and talk?

"No."

Why?

Pause.

"I don't think it's a good idea. That's why."

Because you know you'll feel something for me again.

"Travis, don't—"

But I cut her off.

I thought you told me that nothing was going to change. That you were happy.

"But *everything* has fucking changed!" she yells. "Big time!"

Then Laura hangs up the phone.

7

CLAIRE AND I MEET AT BOTTOMS UP BAR FOR HAPPY
hour a couple of days later.

Already there when I arrive, Claire's seated at the bar in
a Wires on Fire T-shirt and a pair of shredded jeans, with a
navy bandana wrapped around her right wrist, holding a lit
cigarette in one hand and a can of beer in the other.

Yo, yo, I smile, walking up to her, and she slides off the
stool and goes, "Fuck yeah," and hugs me and kisses my
cheek.

"How are you?" she asks.

I'm good. Better now that I'm here.

"Cool. Want a beer?"

Yes.

Claire slams both her hands against the bar and goes,
"Two more PBRs."

The bartender smiles and sets two in front of her. "Let's
get a table," she says, handing me one of the beers.

We take a seat at a small table next to the jukebox.

"So, thanks for calling me when you were at the party
the other night," she says.

That was almost a week ago, Claire.

"Still," she says. "We should be hanging out all the time."

I know.

Claire takes a big drink of her beer, finishing the one she was working on when I walked in. Then she opens her new one.

So how are things with you, Claire? How was your semester?

"It went well," she says. "I even made the dean's list."

Nice.

Claire is an anthropology major at Grant College.

"How was yours?" she asks.

It didn't go so well. I definitely didn't make the dean's list.

"That's okay," she says. "What are your plans now?"

Inhale. Exhale.

I don't know. My father wants me to go to USC way bad, his alma mater and all. But I was thinking about maybe State or Harrison. I don't know. My mind's all jammed up.

Claire reaches across the table. Grabs my hands. "I'm sure you'll figure it out."

You think?

She smiles. "Of course you will."

We should play some tunes on the box.

"Go for it."

You pick 'em out.

I hand her a dollar.

"Fine," she pouts and walks to the jukebox.

I finish my beer and go to the bar and grab two more PBRs. Back at the table, with Guns N' Roses ripping "Sweet

Child O' Mine," I ask Claire if her and Laura still talk.

Claire scrunches her face. "No. Not really. Not anymore."

Why not?

"She's a bitch. That's why. That's all I can really say."

I take a drink. Light another cigarette. Claire does the exact same thing.

She says, "Maybe it's cause we went to different schools and lost some ground, but every time I see her out she's fucking cold to me."

Pause.

"Have you talked to her since you got back?"

Twice. I saw her boyfriend and met him.

"His band fucking sucks," Claire says.

That's what Michael said.

Claire starts laughing and goes, "So how's it been to see everyone else?"

It's been, ya know, it's like . . .

I don't finish.

"Are you okay, Travis?"

Pause.

"Travis."

I don't know.

"What's wrong?" Claire asks as Guns N' Roses slam into the Nirvana song "About a Girl."

It's just that some shit went down while I was in . . .

Pause.

I look at Claire, at her beautiful face, her big brown eyes, and I feel so gnarly, so fucked up.

"While you were where?" she asks.

I don't know.

My hands shake.

Can I ask you something, Claire?

"Anything," she says.

If something happens, but you don't remember exactly how it did, or remember it happening at the time, altogether. Then . . .

Pause.

My heart is pumping fast.

"Then what?" Claire asks.

Are you responsible?

"Travis, what are you talking about?"

I don't say anything.

Claire says, "You know you can tell me anything, right?"

Can I?

"Yes," she says as Nirvana fades into the Tool's, "Pushit."

Claire goes, "Is this about you and Laura?"

No.

"Good," she tells me. "Maybe you shouldn't think about her so much."

I can't help it.

"Have you tried?"

Yes.

"I don't believe that at all. But you do have a different presence now. It's like you've dropped your attitude and checked your ego at the door. I noticed it the other night at Kyle's. There's a different aura to you."

I'm trying to fix some stuff and make things right. I think it'll help me figure some shit out.

"I like that," she smiles. Downing the rest of her beer, she looks at her cell phone. "Shit," she says. "I have to get to work."

Fine, I pout.

"But I get off around eleven if you wanna hang. We can talk some more or rent some movies or something. You have to come over and check out my place."

Where are you living now?

"At this killer space on Kennedy and Morgan. Right above that awesome Vietnamese dive."

Sweet.

"It's a huge spot. I live there with my friend, Skylar."

Sounds all right. I'll give you a call later.

"Cool."

I slam the rest of my beer and the two of us start heading for the exit, but on our way Claire goes, "You don't look so hot," and I say, I'm fine. I think. Maybe I should go home and lay down or something.

"Maybe you should," she says.

So I hug Claire and tell her good-bye, and then I run to my car.

I do not go home and lay down though. Instead I try to get ahold of Cliff. I call him and call him, but he doesn't answer. I want to talk to him. I need to ask him if what Michael told me was true and about the track marks on his arm.

I call him again and he doesn't pick up, so I drive to his dad's house.

It's almost seven.

His stepmother, Marcy, answers the door. She's wearing a bathrobe with a red nighty underneath it and is holding a cocktail in one hand and still looks like Susan Lucci.

"Hi, Travis," she slurs, wasted.

Is Cliff here?

"Cliff," she sneers. "I haven't seen him in a few days. Why?"

I need to talk to him.

"Is he in trouble again?"

Not that I know of.

My eyes momentarily slip down to Cliff's stepmom's cleavage. When I pull them back up, she grins at me, then nods her head, then pulls her bathrobe shut, and I wonder if Cliff is still fucking her like he was junior year and in the middle of last summer.

"I thought you left," Marcy says.

I did. I'm back.

"No shit," she smiles.

No shit, Mrs. Miles.

"Would you like to come in?"

No.

She looks behind her, then steps next to me on the porch and closes the door. "Do you have a cigarette?" she asks.

I slide a pack of Parliament Lights from my jeans and hand her one.

"How about a light?"

Here.

I hold my lighter out.

"Be a gentleman, Travis. Light it for me."

I do.

"Thank you."

Uh-huh.

The two of us stand in complete silence for like the next minute until this really nice Beamer cruises by, bumping some good hip-hop beats.

Well, if you do see Cliff, tell him to call me.

"I won't see him," she says.

Well, if you do.

"I'm telling you I won't," she snaps.

Are you mad about that?

Marcy slams the rest of her drink. "I'm fucking mad about everything," she sneers, then flicks her smoke all the way to the sidewalk and goes back inside the house.

I split. I pop in the new Entrance CD and drive to the American Apparel store on Kennedy Street where Cliff supposedly works, but this cute girl at the register tells me that he's called in his last two shifts and is off the schedule for the rest of the week.

Cliff was pretty right though, there are a lot of hot girls in the store, and I end up buying a couple of V-neck T-shirts and some short-sleeve ringer Ts and some pocket Ts and some underwear, and the cute girl at the register even gives me a 50 percent discount.

From the store, I drop by Chris and Kyle's. I walk up to their crappy one-story, smeared the color yellow, and knock on their red front door and wait and wipe some sweat from my face with the back of my hand. This girl finally opens up wearing a shredded Joy Division top, a cutoff denim miniskirt, a couple of leather wristbands, and a pair of red cowboy boots. Her light blond hair is parted to the left and pulled up tightly in the back.

"Hey, you," she grins. "I heard you were back in the city."

I know you from somewhere, don't I?

"It's me, April Brown."

That's right.

"I'm fucking Chris now," she says.

That's pretty cool.

I walk in the house.

Chris is lying on the nasty brown couch with a tall can of Bud in his hand watching a DVD of Big Black live shows.

"Travis," he says. "Good to see ya."

You too, Chris.

We bump fists and I sit down in the wheelchair that's sitting next to the couch, which wasn't there the other night.

April plops into the blue chair.

Mounting a wheelie, I ask Chris what the wheelchair's for.

"I don't even know anymore," he says. "Michael and Kyle bought it from some medical supply outlet in Little Mexico a couple of months ago. They were planning something big with it but I'm pretty sure it never happened."

I swing my eyes over to April. She's flipping through a photo album.

How was that concert?

"It destroyed," Chris says.

"Yeah it did," adds April, grinning.

Where's Kyle?

"With his lady," Chris says. "What the hell are you doing?"

Looking for Cliff.

Chris twists his head at me. "Really?"

Uh-huh.

"But the guy is gone, dude."

Where is he?

"I don't know," Chris says. "He's just gone."

The way Chris says this sends a chill down my spine.

I'm also trying to get Laura to see me face-to-face.

"Dude," Chris snaps. "You shouldn't do that. It's not worth it."

Shut up.

"I'm serious, Trav. You should leave her alone."

Why?

"Never mind why," Chris says. "You'll just be better off."

I light a cigarette.

Whatever, man. Fuck.

"Oh, here's one," April shrieks, pulling one of the pictures out.

"One what?" Chris asks.

"Here's a cute one of you and Travis."

Let me see.

April hands me the picture. It's one of Chris and me in probably like sixth grade with our faces painted like a couple of the dudes from Kiss.

Chris: Gene Simmons.

Me: Ace Frehley.

I remember that.

"Let me see it," Chris says, sitting up.

I hand it to him.

"Yeah, real fucking cute," he groans, then grabs the remote and shuts the TV off and says that he's going to bed.

It's like nine, man.

"And I gotta be at work by five," he snaps. "Some of us have to do that, ya know. Work."

Where do you work?

"I'm laying cement for the new minimall that's going up over on Linney Street." He hands the picture back to me. "You staying here tonight, April?"

"Probably," she says. "My mom and dad still won't talk to me."

"That's real nice," Chris says, then finishes his beer and goes, "Call me this weekend, Trav," before disappearing down the hallway toward his bedroom.

I hand the picture back to April.

She smiles and puts it back. "Do you still have a six-pack, Travis?"

Of beer?

"No. Your stomach. Is it still a six-pack."

No.

"In high school, my friends and I used to watch you swim in gym class and thought you were so hot."

And now?

"I don't know," she says. "You're still good-looking and you seem a lot nicer. I don't think you've ever actually had a conversation with me before. You used to blow me off."

Sorry about that.

"No worries," she smiles. "That was then and this is now." She stands up. "I'm gonna go fuck my boyfriend now."

Right.

I get to my feet and April walks by me, brushing her fingers against my stomach.

"It's still kinda there," she says, smiling. "Lock the door on your way out, pretty please."

I leave and drive around and listen to an Ugly Casanova CD. I end up across the city in the Hoffman Addition, parked in front of Laura's parents' house.

Taking one deep breath after another, I smoke two cigarettes and dry the sweat off my hands before stepping out of the car and walking up their winding driveway silhouetted on each side by a row of small trees and lights.

Nailed above the peephole on their front door is a marble plaque with the name Kennedy engraved into it. I grab the bronze knocker and slam it against the door and Laura's father, Marc, opens up in a brown sweater vest, looking pretty drunk.

"Travis," he exclaims, propping himself steady against

the side of the door. "It's really awesome to see you. Come in.
I insist."

Laura's father is a corporate attorney and is very successful, and the only time he's ever drunk is when he's home, and
the only time he's ever home he's always drunk.

I force a smile and step inside, and right when her father
closes the door, Belle, their huge Dalmatian, jumps on me,
catching the side of my face with her tongue.

Jesus Christ.

And Laura's father yells, "Yield, Belle! Belle, yield! Yield,
Belle!"

Belle squats in front of me with her tongue hanging
down. "She must miss you," Marc says.

I wipe my face off and try to smile.

"I think Laura's upstairs," he slurs. "Have you two talked
much lately?"

No.

Her father rubs his forehead and goes, "I just wish she'd
listen to me and her mother. I wish she'd go to medical
school like she always wanted to. I really tried to make that
happen for her, Travis. And out of the blue, she decided to
refuse my help."

Jump back to Laura and I coming to her house one afternoon during our senior year, and finding her father and his
twentysomething secretary fucking on the living room floor.

Laura made me promise never to tell anyone about it,
and as far as I knew she hadn't said a word to anyone else
either. But she really hated him for it, which was probably

why she backed out of the whole med school deal, to piss off her pediatrician mother.

Jump back to Laura's father.

He asks me about school and I tell him a little bit about Arizona, and then I follow him into the kitchen where Laura's mother and older sister are. They're scrapbooking at the table and Laura's father yells, "Laura!"

A very loud "What?!" comes from upstairs.

"You have a visitor!"

Marc smiles, and Kasey and Laura's mother nod and say hi and simply go back to scrapbooking as if I really didn't matter. Then Laura emerges from the doorway in a denim skirt and red tube top.

"Oh," she grunts when she sees it's me standing next to her father. "Hi."

Hey.

Laura turns quickly to the side and Bryan walks in behind her. She whispers something into Bryan's ear and he nods, staring at me, while her entire family, even the fucking dog, watches intently.

Placing her eyes back on me, Laura goes, "Come with me."

Where to?

"Just follow me, Travis," she presses, practically racing out of the kitchen, back through the living room.

She opens the front door. "Out here," she says.

I follow her out and she slams the door shut.

"Fucker!" She pounds her hands against my chest. "Fuck you! You have no business coming here!"

Just stop it, Laura.

I rip her hands off of me.

I have some things I wanna say that can't be said over the phone.

She takes a step back. "What do you want from me, Travis?"

I want you to listen.

"So start saying something. Tell me what you want."

You, Laura. I want you back. I need you back.

"You can't have that."

Why not?

"Why not?" she snorts. "How about the fact that you left for Hawaii the day after Christmas, right after we screwed, and I didn't hear another word from you until that bullshit front job you pulled at the party last weekend."

I pinch my forehead.

Laura, I'm sorry about that. I fucked up. But you did too. You still called me and told me it was over without even giving me a reason.

"Oh my god, Travis. Is that what this is about? Your own need of a justification for me ending whatever the hell was even left between us?"

No.

"I mean is that all you want . . . a fucking reason?"

I take a step toward her, stopping like an inch from her face.

I want you, Laura. I came back for this.

"Why are you trying so hard for this now? We were

together for five years and not once did you ever care this much about being with me."

Pause.

"I don't fucking get it," she says.

Don't you think you can right your wrongs, Laura? That you can make things better by trying to get back to everything you lost?

"How many chances do you want, Travis?"

One more.

I try to pull her into me and kiss her, but she holds me off.

"I can't kiss you, Travis. Bryan's right inside."

Fuck him.

"No, fuck you. Just leave," she tells me. "Please fucking leave."

She storms back into her house and I turn around, facing the city. From where I am, I can see all the way past downtown, up into the hills where I live.

But staring at all of this, especially the downtown area with my father's fingerprints all over it, makes me feel completely on edge, and I squeeze my eyes shut, closing out the neon glow of the city, and I just stand there and listen to the faint sounds of the honking horns and the helicopters. And when I open my eyes again, I walk back to my car and drive home and smoke the joint that Cliff gave me and fall asleep watching *Stand by Me*.

I'M STANDING ON THE EDGE OF A DIVING BOARD,
overlooking an empty swimming pool, and there's nothing else around me except for a few pieces of trash and chairs.

How I came to be here, I have no idea, as I stare into the skyline, this sort of half night of nothing, and I can hear this song.

Where it's coming from, I don't know. But this song is so faint that I can't really make it out—it's just this soft, sad, tune that has me really nervous.

And then I hear my name and turn around.

There, at the other end of this board, stands this girl, but I can't see her face at all as the song becomes louder—

Quickly.

And the sky becomes darker—

Quickly.

And then this girl, she begins to move along the board, coming straight at me, but I can't do anything. I can't move. I'm so scared. There's pee running down my legs.

And then this girl stops in front of me and the music goes dead.

A hand reaches for me and cuffs my wrist—

I'm in a bathtub, soaking in blood, and I can't see anything because of these bright lights shining right in my eyes, but I can hear these two voices whispering.

A door shuts. There're footsteps. The voices stop. And then a hand starts pushing my head underneath the blood, and I can't stop it.

My arms are tied together.

My feet are tied together.

And I can't stop it—

I'm back on the diving board again and I can see this girl's face now. The blood.

It's running from her eyes, her nose, her mouth, and this girl, she's crying blood, and she reaches for me again, and she says, "Jump," then pushes me off the board.

And then I'm falling. . . .

And this is when I wake up, shaking, sweating, sometimes even covered in piss, always thinking about the girl in the dream, Autumn Hayes, and the night I met her in Hawaii, the only time I would ever know her, except for now, in these strange dead mornings.

This is my dream.

Travis Wayne

9

I MEET MY FATHER FOR LUNCH AT A SMALL ITALIAN restaurant near his office building. Two and a half weeks have gone by since I've been back, and this is only the third time I've seen him.

Wearing a white Ralph Lauren suit and a dark blue tie, my father fingers his silverware while I look around the restaurant. I notice this cute girl with blond hair and braids, sitting across from this blond guy I think I used to go to grade school with. She's staring at me and I look away quickly because I know she's the girl that got trained by like twenty dudes at some house party I was at like two summers ago.

Looking back at my father, his black hair parted firmly to the right, he sets his knife down, folds his hands together, and says, "So, what would you do if you were me, Travis?"

What are you talking about?

"I'm talking about your complete lack of motivation. Your seemingly complete and utter disregard for your mother's and my wishes, and your complete unwillingness to do things the right way."

You mean your way?

"Well, look at me," he says. "I would say I've led a pretty damn successful life up to this point."

Pause.

"Except for the fact that my son doesn't seem willing to even try to do anything important."

I look away from my father and down at my sweaty hands.

My father continues. "I mean, I don't know where it all went wrong. You've embarrassed the shit out of me with your failure in Arizona, something that seems to be common knowledge to a whole lot of people. And since you've been home, what have you turned around? What have you done besides get trashed with your loser friends?"

They're not losers.

My father grunts. "Let's be real, Travis."

Not all of them, Dad.

"Well, regardless, son," he says, picking up his glass of ice water. "My point is you haven't done anything. I paid for your trip to Hawaii and you got back and flunked out of school. You dropped from a 3.0 to a nothing—to a big black X mark."

I just need some time.

"Time," he sneers, practically spitting out the drink he just took. "For chrissakes, you've had nothing but time your whole life."

I know. I know.

I look up from my hands.

I just need some more. I promise I'll figure something out.

"What about USC?" he asks.

What about it?

"Have you given it any more thought?"

No.

"Because I can pull some strings and get you in there with no problems. You'd be third generation."

I know.

Pause.

I lower my head so our eyes can't meet, and I tell him that I don't think I want to go there. I tell him that I didn't like it when we visited.

"Probably not enough losers going there for your taste."

Dad.

"Well, regardless," he says. "If you don't wanna go to USC . . . fine with me. But you will be in school, and you will be productive with your life, son, and you will *not* embarrass me anymore. Got it?"

I nod.

My father looks at his watch and shakes his head. "I canceled a very important meeting today because I wanted to give you the benefit of the doubt."

How do you mean?

"I mean this lunch has already turned out to be a complete waste of my—"

My father gets interrupted by his own cell phone. He stops talking and digs the phone from the inside pocket of his suit jacket and answers it.

This is your life, I mumble under my breath.

But my father doesn't hear this because he's still on his phone rescheduling the meeting he canceled.

Around two in the afternoon, I go to the Victoria Theater, this movie theater that's been around since the thirties. They're showing the David Lynch movie *Wild at Heart* on the big screen.

When the movie's over, and I'm walking back into the glaring sun and thick, sticky air, this older lady with gray hair hands me a yellow flyer that says "Help Save the Victoria Theater from Being Destroyed."

According to the little piece of paper in my hands, the city council is considering selling the building along with a handful of other sort of landmark buildings and parks across the city to make some money and help slow their bleeding budget.

I light a cigarette, and as soon as I turn the corner, I crumple the flyer into a ball and toss it into the first trash can I see and decide to make a surprise visit to Claire's.

Pulling up on Morgan Street, the Blood on the Walls CD *Awesomer* absolutely blaring, I slip into a parking spot near the corner of Kennedy Street and walk up to where the Vietnamese restaurant is and ring the buzzer.

A female voice answers.

Is Claire in?

"Who wants to fucking know?"

Um, Travis Wayne.

"Holy shit! It's me, dude—Claire! Fuck yeah! Come up!"

I get buzzed in and jog up a set of wooden stairs. The only door at the top is ajar. I push it open even farther and then Claire jumps out of nowhere, startling the hell out of me. She's holding a cap gun in her hand, wearing a pink bikini top, a pair of pink and white underwear, and has a leather holster strapped around her waist.

"Freeze, sucka," she smiles, pointing the red tip of the plastic weapon at me.

I throw my hands above my head playfully.

"Gotcha, man," she says, then shoves the gun into her holster and hugs me. "You finally made it over. You didn't flake. Twice in a row you didn't flake. Who is this guy?"

Who is this guy? The words slam around my head for an uncomfortably long time.

"Well, get your ass in here and check my shit out now." Claire pulls me into her place.

There are three other girls inside. Two of them are wearing the same style of underwear and top as Claire, and the other one, this black girl with a purple mohawk, is wearing a beater top and a pair of black running shorts.

"So this is it," Claire says, spreading her arms.

It's a huge space with high ceilings and hardwood floors. A bunch of paintings and framed photos align the walls and a ton of old *VICE* and *Mojo* magazines lie scattered around the living room floor and furniture. There are like two bedrooms and a spare room and a bathroom and kitchen.

I like it, Claire.

"I'm glad," she says. Then, "Hey, Skylar."

The black girl looks up from the chair she's sitting on. "What's up?"

"This is Travis," Claire says. "He's my friend who's back from Arizona."

"Oh, cool," Skylar grins, standing up. We shake hands, and she says, "It's nice to meet you."

Nice to meet you too. You're the roommate?

"Yeah," says Skylar.

Claire points to the other two girls. "This is Tara," she says, waving a finger at the blond one with two half sleeves. "And this is Brianne." Claire points to the other girl, who has dark brown hair and no visible tattoos.

Claire says, "We're modeling for Skylar right now."

What for?

"She's a clothing designer and her online store is getting launched in like two months and she wants us to try every-thing on to make sure the shit looks right."

It looks great.

"Thanks," Skylar says.

One of the other girls, Brianne, walks over to the CD player sitting on top of the entertainment center and slides some new CDs into it and hits play.

The newest Cage album starts bumping though the speakers and Claire hooks an arm through mine and pulls me into the kitchen.

On the large oak table, there are all these photo spreads of Claire. Claire in lingerie. Claire in ripped stockings and stilettos. Claire in a bathing suit with two studded belts crisscrossing one another around her thighs.

What are all these for?

"Just some preliminary shots for Sklyar's website," she says.

At the far end of the table sits the Guns N' Roses complete photographic history book with lines of coke already cut, sitting on the book's cover.

You blowing rails already?

"I haven't yet," Claire smiles, walking to the other side of the table. "But I'm working at the Inferno in like an hour and was gonna hit a couple before I spilt."

Pause.

"You're welcome to help yourself, dude."

Nah.

"I'm really glad you dropped by," she says.

Me too.

"You just feel better to be around now."

I light a smoke and decide not to ask her what that means.

Are you gonna go to the Pretty Vicious show tomorrow night at the Breaking Point?

"Oh fuck," Claire says. "That's tomorrow night? I forgot all about it. I'm working at the Silver Fox restaurant tomorrow night."

You still work there?

"I have to. The money is way too good to pass up. This place isn't cheap."

Get out of your shift.

"I can't. I traded with a girl who needs to be off tomorrow, and she took one of mine."

That sucks.

"I know it," Claire snaps. "I love that damn band." She walks to the G N' R book and grabs the straw lying next to it and snorts a line. "This is the only way I can deal with the assholes that hang at the bar these days," she smiles, holding her head back.

I would need a lot more than that.

"Tell me about it. There's only one good night at that bar anymore: their punk-as-fuck night on Saturdays." Claire leans down again and does another one, and about five minutes later I tell her I'm going to split and she hugs me again and kisses me on the lips, then does it again using her tongue this time.

I get a boner, and Claire smacks my ass and goes, "I'm so fucking high," then starts giggling as she shows me out of her place.

The next night is the Pretty Vicious show at the Breaking Point, which is a way chill place to catch shows. It's kinda small and there's no stage, so the bands have to play on the floor, and there's a Black Sabbath pinball machine next to the bar.

Michael, Kyle, Dave, and I get there and order beers and shots and we watch the first band play and then it's Pretty Vicious. They start destroying and halfway through their set,

Cliff wanders in and doesn't say much except, "The girl singing is cute."

When Pretty Vicious is done with their set, it's just after eleven, and while the next band is setting up, Kyle asks me if I wanna do a key bump and I say, Sure, why not, and he says follow me, and I do, and so do Michael and Dave and Cliff.

We follow him into an empty bathroom.

Dave jams his foot against the bottom of the door to try to keep anyone from coming in and then Kyle pulls out his keys and a baggie of coke from the stash he keeps for himself when he's out dealing.

"We should get the fuck outta here after this," says Cliff, who's putting out his cigarette in the sink, running two fingers though his hair.

Where to? I ask.

Cliff turns from the mirror. "There's this blast on Langley Drive, kinda close to City College."

"Screw that," Michael snorts, taking the blow from Kyle's hands. "I know that house and those parties always suck. Unless hanging out with white kids with backpacks who carry markers around and write on garbage cans is your thing."

"Whatever, dude," Cliff snaps back. "You hate everything."

"No, I just have good taste," Michael shoots back.

Someone outside the bathroom pushes on the door, almost knocking Dave over. Dave pushes back, then pries it open just a crack and says, "We'll be out in a minute, fuckin' chill."

Michael takes a bump and hands the coke to me, then says to Cliff, "Go there and have a bad time. We're heading down to the Hill and then to Kennedy Street to hand out our flyers."

The Hill is this small strip of bars in between the Grant and Harrison College campuses.

"Flyers for what?" Cliff sneers.

I scoop out a bump and do it.

"Our fucking show, man," Michael snorts.

Then I scoop out another one for my other nostril.

Cliff says, "What are you talking about?"

"My band, Lamborghini Dreams. We're playing a show the night of the Freedom Festival at the Renegade Studio with this other band, Patrick Bateman, and this San Francisco band, Von Iva."

Once again, someone outside the door tries to shove it open, and this time Dave slams it shut, and then Michael cuts in front of me and yanks the metal handle off the paper towel dispenser and slides it through the door handle as a lock.

"It's easier than hooking up with a dickpig at a Korn show," Michael says, and Cliff goes, "Let me see a flyer."

"They're in the car," Dave tells him. "I ran out of the ones I brought into the bar." Taking the coke from Cliff, he goes, "It's our antifreedom show."

"That sounds really stupid," Cliff says. "It doesn't even make any sense."

Michael lights a cigarette. "Yeah it does, assbag. It makes

sense 'cause we wanna run shit. We want everyone to listen to what we say and do what we tell them to do."

Slamming the rest of his Heineken, Kyle says, "You guys should wear turbans and fake beards when you play."

"Hey, that's not a bad idea," Dave grins, handing Kyle his drugs back.

Grunting loudly, Cliff says, "What the hell would you two cokeheads tell people to do or even do your fucking selves if you were in charge of anything?"

Michael: "Totally legalize crack cocaine."

Dave: "Kill Sammy Hagar."

Michael: "And anyone who listens to the Dave Matthews Band."

Dave: "And Flogging Molly."

Michael: And torture anyone who doesn't think *Appetite for Destruction* is the best album ever.

Dave: Or anyone who disses Mike Patton.

Kyle's laughing, and Cliff goes, "You guys are just so fucking cool," then knocks the dispenser handle away and walks out.

Three angry dudes walk in and start talking shit about having to wait, and Michael starts in, but it all turns into nothing and we all end up back at the bar, smoking cigarettes.

"I still think we should go to the party," Cliff moans, slamming a Jäger shot.

"So go, biooootchhhhhh," Michael rips.

"What about you, Trav?"

What about me?

"You wanna roll with me?"

Probably not.

"Oh, come on," Cliff whines. "I've barely hung out with you since you've been back. Besides," he tells me, "I got something to give you."

What?

"It's a fucking surprise, dude. But you'll dig it. Just come with me."

Pause.

"Please, man. Let's catch up."

Fine, I say, and Cliff says, "What about you, Kyle?"

"Fuck you two," Kyle says, tugging at the collar of his T-shirt. "I got a shitload of customers on Kennedy Street just waiting for me to get out of this show and meet them. They can't wait for me to leave this bar."

Cliff flips him off and then the two of us leave in my ride, and on our way to Langley Street, Cliff tells me to stop by his dad's house.

Down in the basement, while Cliff fumbles through a stack of CDs, I ask him if he's still banging his stepmom.

"Every once in awhile," he answers, without looking at me.

And my mind flashes back to this one time when I showed up at his house sometime late in our junior year—it may have even been early that summer. Cliff had wanted me to swing by and drop off this Guns N' Roses shirt that I'd gotten Steven Adler to sign for him after I'd seen Adler on a sidewalk while visiting New York with my father.

I knocked on the front door and rang the doorbell but no one answered. I knew Cliff was home, though, 'cause his car was parked in the driveway, so I walked around the side of the house to knock on his bedroom window after I noticed the light was on in his room. But as I stepped in front of the smeared glass panel, I was thrown by what I was seeing.

Cliff's stepmother, buck naked, perched on her knees, giving Cliff a blow job. Cliff had his hand cemented to the back of her dark brown hair, controlling her head's every movement, bobbing it back and forth like a bobblehead doll. It was intense. I stuck around. I watched Cliff pull his stepmother's head back and spit in her mouth. Then I watched him nail her from behind, her hands braced against the yellow wall, clawing at the bottom of a Jane's Addiction poster. And when it was over, after he came on her back, spatters of white clumps sliming down the crease of her back, I walked back to my car and drove away and let my sister sell the T-shirt on eBay, much to Cliff's protest. . . . I owed her two hundred dollars, I told him, which he didn't buy at all, and only dropped it a week later when I told him what had really happened. "Did you enjoy the show at least?" he asked me, wearing that sly grin on his face.

Yeah, Cliff, I told him. It was great.

Back to the basement.

I say, That's fucking crazy, man. What if your dad finds out?

Cliff laughs. Takes a deep breath. He goes, "Yeah, right.

My old man's too dumb." He says, "And even if he did, what's he gonna do? It's not like I don't know about him and the whore down the street. Plus, I kinda like the idea of being close to the people I'm stabbing in the back. Makes me feel good for some reason. Like I'm better than them or something."

So where's Natalie been? I ask.

Cliff stops fumbling and shoots me a nasty look. "What's that supposed to mean?"

What?

"Why do you care where she's at? You thinking about her? Thinking about banging her again?"

Whoa, dude. I'm not even thinking about that.

"That's good," he says. "'Cause she thinks you're a real asshole, man."

Are you shooting heroin, Cliff? I ask, switching gears quickly because I'm not liking where that's heading.

Cliff looks at his arm. "I've tried it. Why?"

It's a nasty drug, man. Makes you do some crazy shit.

Cliff begins flipping through the CDs again. "If you wanna know nasty, bro, I know a girl who got hepatitis in her nose from sharing dollar bills."

I don't say anything.

And Cliff says, "Now that's some gross shit."

I light a cigarette and start rubbing my nose.

"Here it is," Cliff snaps, holding up the new Husbands CD. "You heard this shit yet?"

A little.

"Well, here's a little bit more," he says, putting it on. He jumps to his feet. "I'll be right back." He runs up the stairs.

Taking a seat on the white leather sofa in the middle of the room, I pick up the new issue of *VICE* and begin flipping through it, slowing down in the Do's and Don't's section.

I stop on a Don't picture of this fat kid who looks about my age, wearing eye shadow and a bulletproof vest, posing next to a cardboard cutout of that fat dude who sings for that band, My Chemical Romance, and I start laughing.

Cliff walks back down wearing a new shirt—a pink one that says "I Shot Up the Brett Michaels Tour Bus and All I Got Was This Lousy Shirt" on it, and he tosses me an envelope with my name written on it in red ink.

What is this?

"Just open it," Cliff says.

Did you just make this envelope?

"Just open it," he says again, lighting a cigarette.

So I pull it open. There's thirty-seven dollars inside, along with a free lap dance token for the Wild Stallion strip club, and a baggie with about enough blow in it for five lines, maybe.

What the hell is this?

"It's my thank-you for lending me that money."

I reach into the envelope and pull out the money, most of which is wrinkled, and I say:

This is my thank you?

Cliff's shoulders arch. "I guess."

I don't want this. I told you not to pay me back and that I didn't want to know what the money was for.

And the whole thing about not wanting to know what Cliff needed the money for is that it's Cliff. Even though we've been tight since we were kids, most of the time it's just better to not know what he's mixed up in because it's always bad. So you just give him what he wants because he's still your friend and he'd never screw you over that bad.

"Just take it," he says.

No.

"Why the hell not?"

Because this—I shake the money in the air—this is something that fucking Michael would give me back, okay. Plus, I know you just went upstairs right now and took money out of your wallet and grabbed the dance token and stuffed it into the first envelope you could find.

"So?"

I stuff the money back into the envelope and set it on the small end table next to the couch.

Don't fucking worry about it.

"Whatever," Cliff groans, and takes the envelope back. "Do you at least wanna do the blow?"

If you want to.

Cliff dumps the rest of it onto the *VICE* cover and makes six lines, and while we're doing them, I ask him if he ever sees Laura.

"Not so much anymore. Why?"

Just curious.

"Why would you be curious about that? Did you hear something?"

No, I've been trying to work things out with her. I need to work things out with her.

"Whoa," Cliff barks. "What's that?"

You heard me.

I snort up a long rail.

Cliff lights a cigarette and walks to the other side of the room. "You should forget about her, man, and move on."

Why do you and Chris keep saying that shit?

"Just because, dude. She's trouble."

What does that mean, Cliff? Is there something I should know about?

"No," he grins. "It just doesn't seem genuine."

What doesn't?

"This whole stand-up, nice-guy routine you're putting on for everyone. Like you give a shit about people all of the sudden. It's not fooling anyone, dude. We all know you want things the way they were before you left just so you can have your king-shit, big-time status back."

Bunching my face, I go, Fuck you, man. What the fuck did I do to you?

Pause.

Seriously, Cliff.

Pause.

"I'm sorry about that," he finally says. "That was totally uncalled for. I'm high. The devil's dandruff can make you bark some silly things."

I guess so.

Cliff's cell phone starts ringing and he answers it, and when he hangs up, he goes, "Let's go," so we finish the lines and leave for the party.

On our way into the house where the party's at, Cliff stops and talks with a couple of black dudes, one with cornrows and the other with a shaved head. "Yo, Trav," Cliff says. "I'll catch up with you in a minute."

Whatever.

I walk in, already wishing I'd stayed with Michael or maybe tried to do something else with the rest of my night.

Tried to read a book.

Tried to paint a picture.

Maybe tried to write some shit down.

Pushing myself through the living room, past like ninety kids dancing to some weak hip-hop shit, I make it into the kitchen, which is just as packed.

There seem to be a lot of high school kids around the place.

I notice an empty slot of space in a corner next to these two girls and I go stand in it and light a cigarette and take my cell phone out.

No missed calls.

One of the girls next to me is telling her friend that Jack White is definitely playing an acoustic solo show at either the Glass Castle or Whiskey Red's in August.

Her friend goes, "How do you know?"

"It's all over MySpace," the girl answers. "It's going to be so awesome. I'm going to throw myself at him. I don't care if he's married now."

And her friend goes, "You're so bad, Kat," then burps and goes, "Let's go home and check the Internet to see if there are any more details yet."

They leave.

I scroll through my phone and I call Laura. I can't help it. But this time she doesn't answer. I get her voice mail—a verse from Patsy Cline's "Crazy"—and I say, Hey, Laura, this is Travis. I just wanted to say hi and that I'm sorry about showing up like that at your parents' house the other night.

Then I stop.

Pause.

I start again.

Actually, I'm not sorry. I want to see you as much as I can and I want to talk to you, really talk to you, face-to-face, so until you meet me halfway on this, expect more of the same. Bye.

I put my phone away and look around the kitchen, not really liking anything I see. Cranking my head all the way to the left, though, I notice this pretty okay-looking girl—big tits, blond hair, tight jeans, black tube top—staring at me while she talks to her even better-looking friend wearing a pink shirt with black kittens on it. And the girl staring at me seems vaguely familiar and she whispers something into her friend's ear, then walks up to me.

"What's up, Travis?" she asks.

I have no idea who you are. What's going on?

"Not much. Drinking, hanging out. Talking shit."

That's cool.

"It's been a while."

It has.

"How've you been?"

I'm hanging in there. What about, um, you? You doing all right since the last time I saw you at the ... um. ... Where was it?

"Fuck you," she snaps. "You have no idea who I am."

Who are you?

"You fucked my ass in a bathroom at the Speedwagon Warehouse during that Lightning Bolt and 400 Blows show last summer."

Christina?

"Lila," she snorts. "You piece of shit. You choked me and slammed my head against the wall and came on my face, then gave me a fake phone number."

Ya know, I'm sorry about that, I say.

"No you're not," she says. "You're too dumb to be sorry about that." Leaning into me, Lila goes, "I hope you rot in hell one day, man," then she swings her arm around and smacks me across the face.

And instead of reacting in a horrible and regrettable way, I tell this girl, Good hit, darling, and slide past her, into this hallway, then into this bathroom, where these two kids wearing baseball caps turned sideways, with their knuckles covered in tattoos, with backpacks strapped to them, drinking forties stuffed into brown paper bags, are writing their tag names on the mirror with markers, and one of them goes, "What the fuck are you looking at?"

A couple of virgins, I laugh.

"What's that?" the guy's friend says.

Come on, dudes, nothing says virginity quite like bringing a marker to a party and tagging a bathroom mirror.

I keep laughing, stepping back into the hallway.

This is when I hear, "Travis! Omigod!"

Spinning around, I see my sister running at me all swagged out in a pair of way-tight Levi's and a white halter top, with a navy bandana wrapped around her forehead.

By her side are two other girls, and all of them have bottles of Boone's Farm wine in their hands.

"Travis!" my sister shrieks again. "No way you're here!"

Well—

But she interrupts me.

She says, "You remember my friends, Amy and Katie."

Katie is definitely not the girl I saw get tag-teamed by Michael and Cliff. She is pretty cute, though. She's small, with long brown hair and high cheekbones.

Amy is hot. She looks like Paris Hilton with a few more curves.

My sister lights a cigarette and asks me if I can think of anyone, anyone at all that can hook her and her friends up with some X.

Nope.

"Come on, Travis. Be a good brother," she whines.

Hook yourself up.

"But I don't know anyone," she groans. "Please, pretty please."

"We'd be so grateful," says Katie, who has this sort of wannabe hipster look going on, with big round shades and the odd color scheme of her outfit. "At least I know I would be."

I'll tell ya what.

I look away from Katie, over to my sister.

Cliff's around somewhere, I say. I guarantee you he knows where to find it. If he gives you any shit, you can tell him I said it's all right.

"Thank you so much," my sister grins.

"You're pretty awesome," Katie adds, pinching my waist. Looking over her shoulder at my sister, she says, "He's still cute, Vanessa. He doesn't look as bad as you told me he did."

"Oh right," Vanessa grins. "I'm sure I was just *a little* overexaggerating. Give a girl a break, darling. Travis, you don't look *that* bad," she says.

In the basement of this house there are four red leather sofas pushed against the stone walls, which are covered with fake strands of ivy. I'm double fisting cups of beer, sitting on one of the sofas, staring toward the middle of the room at Chris's girlfriend, April, who's dancing with a few other girls.

Tonight April's got on a white off-the-shoulder shirt with a stencil of Terri Nunn of Berlin on it, a red leather skirt, black fishnets, and an old vintage pair of bitch kickers.

Chris, he isn't at the party, and when the OutKast that was just playing gets spun into an old Biggie Smalls jam, April struts over to me. She straddles my lap and begins dancing, squeezing her thighs around my hips.

It feels nice.

She smells nice.

Her skin is moist.

My knuckles are white.

But after the song is through, I gather myself and gently push her off of me like, Whoa.

My dick is really hard.

I walk up the stairs, then find the back door and go outside. April follows me, though. She locks her arms around me, trapping me against the side of the house. Then she tells me that she wants me to take her home.

I don't think that would be such a good idea.

She pouts her lips. "Why not?"

'Cause you're with Chris.

"And?"

That would be fucked up. Chris is my friend.

"I didn't think you had real friends."

What does that mean?

"You think you're a god, Travis. And gods don't have friends."

You're wrong. Chris is my friend.

"On what given day?" she snorts just as Cliff is walking around the corner.

Smirking from ear to ear, he stops when he sees the two of us so close to each other. "Well, what do we have here?" he snorts.

April's face gets bright red. "You had your fucking chance," she whispers.

Damn, that's too bad.

"Asshole," she says, then walks away without even looking at Cliff, who's still standing there grinning.

What, Cliff?

"I'm sorry, dude. I really didn't mean to fuck that up for you."

I wasn't gonna do shit with her.

Cliff winks and nods his way in front of me. "Sure," he says. "Nothing."

Fuck you, man. I'm not like that.

Cliff pulls a smoke from his pack. "Well, you should be," he says. "Because you just missed out on some good ass."

You're telling me you fucked April?

Cliff nods.

Really?

He shrugs. "What do you think?"

I don't know.

Cliff gets in my face. "Do you think I'm capable of fucking one of my friend's girlfriends?"

I don't know. Get outta my face.

Cliff grabs my throat. "How fucked up do you think I am, Travis?"

I knock his hands away and go, Dude, you're fucking crazy, okay? You're a fucking asshole.

Cliff starts laughing. He says, "I didn't nail her, but I would in a second. Fuck Chris."

Pause.

"I ran into your sister," Cliff says.

So what?

"I hooked her and her friends up with some OCs.

I thought they wanted X.

"They did," he says. "But the dudes I talked to about it only had OCs on them."

Whatever.

"Your sister's a smokestack," Cliff tells me. "And her friend, Katie. I'm totally getting her number, man."

I don't say anything.

I look past him, across the alley to the backyard of another house, where another, smaller party is happening.

The yard everyone at that party is standing in is intensely lit with bright porch lights.

Pointing in that direction, Cliff says, "You see those two guys with the shaved heads talking in front of the garage."

What about them?

"Last December, they double-teamed some transvestite who'd apparently had her dick surgically removed, and when they found out that the girl had really been a boy once, they fuckin' killed her."

Seriously?

"Yep. And when they went to trial, they got off because their attorneys got the jury to believe that because the tranny wasn't up-front with them about being a guy, their reaction was understandable."

Huh, is the only thing I can say.

And Cliff goes, "It just makes you wonder."

About what?

"About what we could get away with if we wanted to."

My throat tightens.

Cliff says, "Probably all kinds of stuff."

I feel nauseous.

Smiling, Cliff says, "Probably anything."

10

IT'S AFTER FOUR IN THE MORNING WHEN I STUMBLE into my parents' house. My sister and Amy are sitting on a couch in the living room watching the second season of the *OC* on DVD, bottles of Boone's plastered on the floor around them, and they really don't even acknowledge my existence until I plop myself in between them, asking them if they're feeling all right.

"I feel *so* good," my sister moans, petting her arm with a pink feather. "Cliff is like totally the raddest."

"Yeah he is. And he's supercute," Amy smiles. "But I'm kinda scared."

"Why, darling?" my sister asks slowly.

"Because I think I might like this a little too much," Amy tells her, craning her neck toward the ceiling.

I sit up and tell them I'm going to bed, and my sister starts laughing. She says, "Have fun up there," and then Amy starts laughing.

Climbing the stairs, the only thing I can think about is Laura.

Laura, fucking that dickdrool Bryan.

Laura, kicking me out of her parents' house.

Laura, refusing to leave my mind.

It's really starting to get to me and I'm not sure how to handle it because I can't remember ever letting anything get to me before. I can't remember ever feeling this fucking vulnerable.

Opening the door to my bedroom, I find Katie lying on my bed in her underwear, smoking a cigarette, watching videos on MTV2.

She sits up. "You finally made it."

You shouldn't be in here.

"Don't be silly," she says, stubbing her smoke out. "I want you inside of me like now." She undoes her bra, and gets to her knees and crawls to the edge of my bed, her tiny tits firmly perking up.

I stare at her.

"Come over here," she smiles, motioning me to her. "What are you waiting for? You can do whatever you want to me. Anything."

And for a second, all of the things that I could do to her, things I've done to girls in the past, it all slams through my skull and makes me feel gross and sick. So instead of standing there any longer, I turn around and go to one of the guest rooms and end up passing out to some shitty Maroon 5 DVD that my sister gave me for Christmas.

Even though she knows how much I really don't like that band.

KYLE CALLS ME A COUPLE OF DAYS LATER AND ASKS ME if I can pick him up from Emily's pad on Eighteenth and take him to Michael's band rehearsal space to drop off a package for Michael and Dave. Kyle tells me that his car is being worked on and that he'll make it worth my while if I'd like, and I tell him that it doesn't matter, and Kyle tells me, Oh. Huh. Okay.

Jumping into my Eclipse about twenty minutes later, Kyle bumps my fist and I ask him where exactly Michael's space is.

"It's right there on Redding and Taylor, jammed in between some of those abandoned buildings."

Sweet.

Kyle pulls out a blunt. "For your troubles," he tells me, then drops it into the glove compartment.

You don't have to do that, man. You don't have to pay me off for my help.

"Right," he nods, squinting at me. "Wait. You're serious, aren't you?"

Yeah, dude.

"Shit . . . well just keep it anyway."

Isn't it sorta early to be making a delivery? I ask him.

"Dude, those two have been going at it since last night. They bought like three grams from me and went to the studio, and I guess the whole band's there for practice now, so they need to keep it going."

How much coke are you selling them?

"I'm not selling them any coke. They asked me for two grams of glass, which I normally don't do, but Michael knew I'd picked some up on the side 'cause a few of my regulars have turned into hardcore tweakers."

Part of me sometimes wonders how it's so easy for Kyle to take all that money from his friends and keep them just fucked up enough to take more money. But then again, I guess if the demand wasn't there, then he wouldn't be doing what he was doing. And it wasn't as though he was being secretive about any aspect of how he made his money. Everything was always up-front. Here's the price. Here's the deal:

—I won't spot anyone anything.

—I'll only shave the price for close friends.

—I won't do the deal if you actually mention the words "blow," "coke," or "gram" on the phone.

—And if I don't answer my phone after four in the morning, then don't call again, otherwise you're cut off.

I slow the car to a stop at a red light and Kyle's cell starts to ring.

"Hey, baby," he says, answering it.

I turn my head to the left and look out the window toward the developing skyline of the city. At the high-rise buildings, one huge panel of glass after another, and listen to Kyle talk, saying, "Yeah, Travis just picked me up from your place. . . . No, I'm going home to shower and change after we're done. . . . For sure. . . . Really. . . . I'm totally into that. . . . Well swing by when you get off and we'll pick some stuff out together and I'll shut my phone off. . . . Okay, you too. . . . Bye baby."

He shoves his phone back into one of his jean pockets.

Emily? I ask.

"Yeah."

How long have you two been together?

"Since New Year's Eve, when Claire introduced us."

I swing my eyes to Kyle.

You're fucking glowing, man. I've never seen you like this.

"It's 'cause I've never felt this way about anyone before. I fucking love that girl."

Up to that point, I don't think Kyle had ever used the word "love" to talk about a girl. In fact I don't know if I'd really ever heard him say anything nice about a girl.

Here are a few other things about Kyle:

His mother bailed on him and his father when he was eight. His father got remarried, and two years after that Kyle's stepmother filed for divorce and won everything in the settlement, including their house, which forced Kyle and his father into a very small apartment where his father still lives.

And Kyle says, "It's like when I'm with her, all the shit

from my past doesn't even matter. Nothing does. I don't think about anything but her."

Whoa.

"And she's so fucking cool, Travis. I'll be up all night dealing with assholes and she doesn't go crazy about it, ya know. She'll be like, 'I'm gonna go home, call me later,' and she leaves."

Behind us, a car starts honking and I look at the traffic light and notice it's turned to green. I hit the gas and tell Kyle that I'm stoked for him.

"It's nice to feel happy," he says. "There's nothing else like it."

Graffiti covers the entire building where the Lamborghini Dreams and about twenty other bands practice. I follow Kyle up a flight of stairs, the sounds of deluded drumbeats and guitar riffs coming from the different studio rooms, and into the space where Michael's band is.

They're in the middle of a jam but stop when Kyle and I walk in.

"Thank god," Michael says, rising from his drum set. "I was about ready to pass out."

The room is pretty dark, and equipment cases and empty forty bottles and food wrappers cover most of the floor.

Kyle says what's up to the two guys in the band I haven't met, so Michael introduces me to Thomas, the lead singer. He's a heavyset dude with a beard and a Melvins T-shirt on.

He's older, almost twenty-seven Michael tells me. And then Michael introduces me to Rodney, their lead guitarist. He's like twenty-four and black and is wearing a short-sleeve plaid button-up shirt, tucked into a pair of brown slacks.

"And you already know Dave," Michael says.

Dave plays a note on his bass and nods at me.

"You ready to do this?" Kyle asks Michael.

"More than ready," Michael snorts, pulling out a handful of twenties.

Kyle holds up two baggies of crystal meth.

The two trade and then Michael grabs a set of keys lying on one of the chairs and goes around to each of his band mates and gives them a bump up each nostril, then does two himself, before offering me some, but I'm like, No way, dude, and he's like, "Suit yourself, brah."

"You guys gonna stay for a jam?" Thomas asks.

We can do that.

"Awesome," says Michael, who looks absolutely strung out and beat-up. "Let's play 'Electric Vampire.'"

The other three sorta nod along, and then Michael takes his seat and counts off and they start playing. And to my surprise, they don't sound that bad. They actually sound pretty damn good.

Like Helmet meets the Melvins meets High on Fire meets Vaz.

And the lyrics, at least to this song, are pretty awesome:

"Electric Vampire, you are my new best friend. . . . Electric Vampire, I do not intend to hurt you. . . . Electric

Vampire, your teeth aren't so sharp. . . . Electric Vampire, you've stolen my heart again. . . ."

When the song's over, Michael goes, "What'd you think, Trav?"

Fuckin' destroyed, man.

"Right on," he says.

Then Kyle turns to me and goes, "I need to split. I need to meet Emily."

Let's stay for another jam.

"No, dude. Let's go. I really wanna see my girl."

That bad.

"That bad, man."

12.

THE THREE MOST POPULAR THINGS TO DO DURING
the Freedom Festival are:
1. Get loaded.
2. Get really loaded.
3. Wave a flag.

It's the day of the city's third annual Freedom Festival,
which is supposed to be like the Fourth of July, except it's
like a week before the fourth and it's in June.

My father walks out back holding two bottles of Corona
and hands one to me, then sits down on the piece of patio
furniture beside mine.

Already drunk, the first thing my father tells me is that
he's just closed a huge business deal on the eighteenth
green. He slurs, "Let this be a lesson to you, son. The only
thing I had to do was miss a two-foot putt. That's how this
world works. To get a lot, you have to at least give a little. You
have to make a concentrated effort to let it be known that
you'll do whatever it takes to get ahead."

Pause.

My father takes a drink from his beer while I stare
at him.

Smirking, continuing, he says, "Once you accept this fact of life, you'll be able to do whatever you want to do and have anything you want to have."

I close my eyes and tilt my head back.

"I expect big things from you," he snaps, and my eyes pop open.

Pulling a business card from his wallet, my father goes, "I think you should talk to this guy. He's a friend of mine. I think he might be able to help you."

Help me with what?

"Getting motivated, Travis. Getting organized. He is a *very* good friend of mine."

I take the card from my father and pretend to look at it before attempting to hand it back to him.

"What are you doing?" he laughs.

I don't want this.

"What?"

I don't need to talk to any of your friends. I don't need that kind of help, Dad.

"The hell you don't. I think that's exactly the kind of help you need."

But it's not. If I can just get everything back the way it was before I left, then . . .

"Then what?"

Everything else will follow.

My father stands up, planting himself in front of me. He goes, "That's impossible, son. What are you even saying?"

That I don't need your help.

"You don't need my help, huh?"

I didn't mean it like—

But my father cuts me off. He snags the card from my hand and goes, "You ungrateful piece of shit!" Then he pulls a fancy, gold-plated Zippo from his pants pocket and sets the card on fire.

You didn't have to do that, Dad.

"You shut your mouth!"

"Lance!"

My mother storms out of the house. "Quit talking to your son like that."

"Don't tell me what to do. This is my house. I built it. This is *my* city. I built it!"

My mother grabs him by the arm and tries to calm him down, but he shakes her loose and whips his Corona bottle to the pavement, sending shards of glass and beer everywhere.

"You have some nerve, young man," he snaps at me before charging into the house.

My mother stands there, her hands on her hips, shaking her head. "Do you always have to push his buttons like that?" she asks.

I wasn't trying to, Mom.

"Then what are you doing?" she asks.

I'm, ya know, I'm just sitting here, doing nothing.

My mother sighs and goes back inside the house.

I smoke a cigarette and finish my beer and walk to the utility closet and grab a broom and begin to sweep the glass until my sister walks outside holding the telephone.

"Here," she says, extending her arm. "It's for you. It's Laura."

Don't lie to me, Vanessa.

"I'm not. Take the phone."

I grab it from her.

"But don't take too long," she grunts. "I'm expecting a call on that line."

I wait for my sister to leave me alone before putting the phone to my ear.

Hello?

"Hi."

Pause.

I take a deep breath.

"What are you doing?" she asks.

Sweeping glass.

"Wait. You're working?"

Kind of.

Pause.

So what's up?

"I've been thinking about what you told me the night you showed up at my house, about why you deserved another chance."

I take another deep breath and then another and then I rub my face.

And?

"I don't know, Travis."

So you called me to tell me that you don't know what to think about me asking you for one more chance.

Pause.

Quit playing games with me.

"Don't yell at me, Travis."

I'm sorry.

"You should be. You show up at my parents' house out of the fucking blue and then you call me and leave me a message about how you're going to keep doing that kind of shit."

It's just hard for me. Knowing you're with someone else and wanting you back. You were my girl, Laura.

"Until you fucked it up."

I don't say anything.

"Travis," she says.

It may not have always been the best between us. But it was better than it is now.

Laura sighs into the phone. "I just don't know," she tells me. "I don't know if I can go through it again. So much has happened. So much is different."

We could fix everything.

"Do you really believe that?"

We could try.

This time there's a very long pause.

And Laura goes, "I have to go."

Don't.

"Don't what, Travis?"

Don't go.

"I have to," she says. "Bye."

□ □ □

Around eight, I drive to Claire's to meet her. The plan is to slam some drinks and then go to the Lamborghini Dreams show.

Walking into her loft, the first thing I hear is the newest Depeche Mode CD, and the first thing I see is Claire, dancing around by herself with a cocktail in one hand, wearing a black halter top and a very short white skirt with black polka dots on it.

When Claire sees me standing there, she slides over, grabs my hand, and goes, "Come dance with me."

I shake my head.

No way.

"Don't be afraid," she shrieks. "I'm the only one who can see you. I'm the only one here!"

I'm not a dancer, Claire.

"You are if you want to be. Come on! Please!"

I still don't want to at all but there's no way to resist her.

It's fucking Claire.

So I dance.

And when the song ends, Claire turns the volume down, and asks me what I'd like to drink.

What are you drinking?

"Vodka cran."

Then a vodka cran I'll have.

"Just one moment, sir." She pecks me on the cheek and walks into the kitchen, returning moments later with my drink.

I take it from her hand.

Cheers.

"Cheers," she says, clanking her glass against mine, sitting down next to me on the couch.

"I'm already kinda wasted," she grins.

Don't get too drunk too early.

"Okay, Dad," she laughs. "Come on, dude, how long have we been getting fucked up together?"

A long time.

"I can probably outdrink you now."

You probably can.

"I know I can, actually," she says. "So don't worry about me. I'll be fine."

I open a new pack of cigarettes and slide two out and hand one to Claire.

I light it for her, then mine, and then I tell her about Laura calling me earlier.

"Do you really want to get back with her that bad, Travis?"

I need to get something back.

Pause.

"What the fuck happened to you while you were away?"

I don't know what happened.

"Where?" she asks, leaning into me.

I don't know, Claire.

"Travis," she moans. "Whatever's eating at you, whatever's hurting you so bad that you completely disappeared from everybody's life for five months . . . whatever that is, you're going to have to talk about it eventually."

I stand up.

Don't push it, Claire. Please.

"I won't. All I'm saying is that I'm here for you if that day ever comes."

Thank you. I appreciate that.

"I'm serious," she says, getting to her feet.

I know you are.

"Do you really?" she grins, wrapping her arms around me, burrowing her head into my chest.

Of course I do. You've always been a good friend to me. Even if I never told you that, I've always loved the fact that you've been awesome to me.

"Awww," she says, tilting her head back. "Did we just have a moment?"

I think we did.

"Nice."

Probably like two hundred people are already crammed into the Renegade Studio warehouse basement by the time Claire and I roll in. Our names are on Michael's guest list so we don't have to pay the eight-dollar cover.

The basement is dimly lit and hot. A small stage is at the far end of the room and to the left of that is a bar.

Lamborghini Dreams is the first band up.

They're already onstage tuning up, and they're not wearing turbans or beards. In fact, there's nothing at all, not one thing anywhere mentioning anything about this being the antifreedom show.

After Lamborghini Dreams, that band Patrick Bateman is up, followed by the touring band from San Francisco, Von Iva.

Claire and I grab some beers from the keg behind the bar, then work our way to the front of the crowd just in time for Michael's band to start.

From the stage, Thomas goes, "I'm fucking wasted already and that dude with the Scott Ian beard keeps giving me shit." He's pointing at some guy with a shaved head and a beardsicle hanging from his chin. "But whatever, man. Keep talking. It's like David Lee Roth said once: I want my cake, I want it frosted pink, I want it prepaid and precut and delivered right now. So let's fucking rock 'n' roll."

Michael starts tapping his symbols.

And Thomas goes, "This first song is called 'The Ricky Rockette Nightmare' and it's dedicated to Mike Patton. Let's go!"

And they just start destroying shit, just completely annihilating the crowd, and it's fucking amazing, fucking awesome, and about halfway through their set, I look around and see Kyle and Emily. I see Chris.

Everyone is here except Cliff.

When the Dreams are finished playing like thirty minutes later, everyone dripping with beer and sweat, Claire and I slide our way to the side of the stage where all those guys are standing.

Claire and Emily give each other these huge hugs and huge kisses and then Chris pulls me aside and tells me he's sorry if he's been edgy with me since I've been back. "It's not anything you've done," he says. "I've just been dealing with a ton of April and her mom and dad's shit lately. But everything's cool, man. I'm glad you're back. I'll even buy you a shot."

I'm not sure what he means, but I take him up on it.

We go to the bar and both do a shot of Jameson, and when I spin around, I see this superhot Asian girl Jasmine, who I went out with a couple of times during my senior year and had amazing sex with when Laura and I were taking some time apart.

Strutting to me in this white see-through minidress with long slits cut in the bottom of it, a pair of black leather boots that end where her knees begin, and a pair of black leather gloves that run to her elbows, she throws her arms into the air and yells, "Yay! Travis. It's so good to see you again!"

Hey, you too, I say with a smile.

Jasmine wraps her arms around me and says, "Do you have any coke?"

Not on me.

"That's too bad," she says.

Is it?

"Not really," she tells me.

I inch closer to her.

You look good. You're a stone fox.

"Stop it," she says sarcastically, tapping my arm. "You're embarrassing me."

No one can hear me but you.

"I know, dude. I was just trying to be modest. I know I look fucking great." She looks over my shoulder, then looks away.

I swing my head to the left.

Laura.

She's fucking here. Standing near the basement entrance with her arms folded, looking directly at me, her boyfriend, Bryan, right by her side.

I wait for Bryan to look at me before I wave at Laura. Like five of his boys roll up behind him. He points me out to his friends, who all pretty much look the same as he does—bandanas around the neck, scruffy facial hair, incredibly tight jeans, black hair cut superbad—so I wave at all of them, then turn back to Jasmine and put a hand on her waist. I know Laura is still watching and I know she hates Jasmine and I know that this, if anything, will get to her. 'Cause maybe this is the only language she'll understand.

So I lean into Jasmine and kiss the corner of her mouth and say, It's really great to see you again.

Then I cut back up to the stage just as that band Patrick Bateman starts playing, and they're fucking heavy.

Think early Sabbath.

But the vocals are very sweet sounding and melodic.

Think late Sonic Youth.

It works really well together. They destroy. And not halfway through the first song, a huge pit breaks out in front of the stage and their lead singer, this totally hot girl, jumps into it and slams herself around until the song is over.

Killer.

But like two songs later, the pit grows and people start slamming around everywhere and it gets superhot, and for a moment I get really dizzy, so I step back from everyone and cut over to the entrance, where a small breeze has filtered in from upstairs.

I light another cigarette.

And that's when Laura shows up.

Not saying a word, she grabs my hand and pulls me into the girls' bathroom and we start making out.

Stopping to catch my breath, I go, What the hell was that?

And she goes, "That was me apologizing for hanging up on you earlier."

You also hung up on me a few weeks ago.

Laura slams her mouth against mine again, and I push her against the wall, our tongues pressed firmly together until we stop to catch our breath again.

Staring at me, Laura goes, "I'm not through with you yet, Travis Wayne."

What about Bryan?

"What about that bitch, Jasmine?"

Just reacquainting myself.

"Right."

But what about Bryan?

"What about him?"

He's here.

"I don't care about that right now," she snorts, lunging

forward again and pressing her lips against mine. And this back-and-forth goes on until Patrick Bateman finishes their set and a shitload of girls start filing into the bathroom.

Let's leave together.

"Not tonight," she says, then walks out of the bathroom.

I get my shit together, then follow her out, running right into Bryan and his boys.

Shit.

Bryan gets right in my face. He says, "That's fuckin' it, asshole. I've had enough of your bullshit."

Whatever, dude.

I try to get around him, but a couple of his friends cut me off.

"I don't understand someone like you," Bryan keeps at it. "Laura's told you to stay away from her countless times but you just won't listen."

He backs me into a wall.

Laura comes running over.

My fists are clenched.

"Bryan, quit it," Laura snaps. "Don't touch him."

"Keep your fucking mouth shut," Bryan snaps back.

Don't talk like that to her.

"Fuck you," Bryan says.

He pushes me, and my head smacks against the wall, and then out of nowhere Kyle's fist flies into the side of Bryan's skull and that's when pretty much all hell breaks loose.

Chris and Michael and Rodney and Dave come charging

over and the small circle that was surrounding me grows into a puzzling mass of arms and fists flying all around, sometimes landing solid blows, but most of the time hitting only the air.

At one point I pin one of Bryan's friends against the wall with Kyle, and we take turns pounding him as hard as we can in the gut, but then someone nails me in the back of my neck and I lose my balance and fall to the ground, and then these two tree-trunk-size arms wrap around me and drag me from the crowd.

It's one of the security dudes, and he hands me over to another one of the security dudes, who holds me against this metal pole while I watch Claire jump into the middle of the brawl. She pulls one of Bryan's friends to the ground by his shirt and kicks him in the ribs, and then I see Dave put some kid into a headlock and give him a really hard noogie.

Michael starts laughing when he sees that, but then gets a kidney shot from Bryan. Then Rodney, the guitar player for Lamborghini Dreams, he smashes Bryan square in the nose and blood starts gushing everywhere as he gets pulled away by the same security guy who got ahold of me.

Chris is nowhere to be seen anymore, which means he's probably under the huge pileup on the cement, and when Claire tries to pull this guy off of Kyle's back, someone rolls against the back of her legs and she falls on top of the pile, and when she tries to get off of it, her legs flap open, giving everyone a really great crotch shot.

Coming from the invisible speakers aligned somewhere, I hear the remains of a Chinese Stars jam before they
slam into the Bronx.

And when I see this fucking guy elbow Claire in the
back, I try to push the bouncer away from me to go after
him, but it doesn't work at all.

Instead I get put into a choke hold and taken outside.
The bouncer lets go of me. I try to run back in but he pushes
me to the ground and tells me that if I don't leave right now,
he's calling the police.

My friends are still inside, asshole.

"We'll deal with them soon enough, but you need to
leave."

Fuck you.

The bouncer grabs my shirt. "Don't push me, punk. I
will beat your ass right here if you don't leave, and call the
cops later."

I roll my eyes.

"You understand?" he snorts, tightening his grip on my
shirt.

Yeah.

"Good." He lets go.

I go to dig for my cell phone, but then remember that I
left it in my car. Great.

I have no other choice than to walk away, so I wheel
around and start moving, and hail the cab that's turning
down the alley.

□ □ □

Once I get to my car, I grab my cell and see that I have thirteen missed calls and seven new voice mails.

One from Kyle: "Fuck yeah, man. We brought the thunder."

Three from Michael: "Axl's still a fag!" "I wanna punch
Meg White!" "We're partying with Von Iva at Rodney's
house for after-hours!"

One from Laura: "What the hell was that?"

Two from Claire: "Travis, where are you?" "Answer your
phone. I'm worried about you."

I erase all of them.

It's just past midnight.

In the closet of my bedroom, there's a PUMA shoe box full
of pictures from high school. I pull it out and open it up on
my bed. Most of the pictures are from senior year.

Flipping through them, one Kodak memory at a time, I
pass over the frozen images of all of us. Michael doing lines.
Kyle licking a blunt. Claire flashing the camera. Chris walking around naked in my backyard with a beer in his hands
during a party. Laura and Claire making out.

Images that could ruin someone's life someday.

Images that could be used as blackmail.

This must be the way the paparazzi get their start, I'm
thinking when someone begins pounding on the door to my
bedroom.

I toss the pictures in my hand back into the shoe box, then
toss the shoe box into the closet, before opening my door.

It's Laura.

Blowing past me with her purse swinging in the air, she zigzags to the other side of the room and leans against my dresser.

What are you doing here?

"I came to see you," she says. "I wanted to see you again."

How'd you get in?

"Your sister let me in."

I shut the door.

Laura holds her arms out and goes, "Come here."

I walk to where she is and put my arms around her waist.

"That's nice," Laura snaps, then—BAM—she punches me square in the gut so hard that my ears start ringing.

I buckle over in pain.

What the hell was that for?

And Laura steps at me—SMACK—and nails me across the face.

Fuck, Laura.

I cringe and stumble to a wall, falling against it.

What's your fucking problem?

"The gut shot was for you being an asshole after you left in December and the face shot was for tonight."

Are you serious?

"Obviously," she snorts, falling down on my bed.

Pressing my arms against my stomach, I slither down the wall to the floor.

The last time Laura hit me like she just did was during our junior year of high school. She was out getting loaded one night with this girl Ashley Morgan, and I was getting shitfaced with Cliff, when my cell started blowing up with calls from Laura. At first I ignored them, sending each one straight to my voice mail, but after like the tenth one in five minutes, I finally answered it, and Laura was on the other end screaming, "What the fuck, Travis? I've been trying to call you."

So.

"So I wrecked my car on this level-B road outside of the city and we need you to come pick us up."

No way, babe. I'm annihilated.

"I don't care, Travis!"

I don't wanna get in trouble, Laura.

"You had better get your ass here soon, dude, or we're so over."

I started laughing, and Laura went, "Please, baby. I need your help. I'll give you money, anything you fucking want. I promise I'll make it up to you. Just come pick us up."

Fine, I finally said, and left right after she told me exactly where they were stranded.

But the thing is, I was probably a lot more wasted than I thought, 'cause when I saw the two of them standing on the side of the dirt road next to the car, which was stuck in the ditch, I accidentally hit the gas pedal instead of the brake and started fishtailing and lost control of my ride, smashing it into Laura's car.

My eyes drifted shut.

And when they opened again, Laura was on top of me in

the middle of the road punching me. Screaming, "You stupid idiot! You dumb fucking retard! You're such a fuckup!"

And the two of us ended up getting cited by the police for some bullshit minor offense after my father talked to a couple of the officers on the scene.

Laura lights a cigarette and I ask her where Bryan is.

"I don't know. He told me to stay away from him after the fight was over."

I take a deep breath.

It wasn't my fault.

She runs her other hand through her hair. "It's never your fault, Travis."

My face scrunches and I slowly get to my feet and walk over to the bed and sit down beside her.

Why'd you come here?

"I couldn't think of anywhere else to go."

Home.

"Do you want me to leave?" she asks.

I don't say anything.

The side of my face is still burning from her hitting me.

Laura takes another drag of her smoke then hands it to me. "Will you ash that out?"

I twist it out in the ashtray on my end table.

I say, Maybe I shouldn't have thrown all of this on you when I came back, but I felt like I had to. I feel like I need you back. You know everything about me. I mean, I know we had some huge fucking problems and all, but shit, we made it almost five years.

"Then why did you quit talking to me after you went to Hawaii if that's how you feel?"

I don't know.

"What does that mean, you don't know? You do know. You just won't tell me."

Calm down, Laura. Would you? My parents are sleeping.

Laura leans into me. She whispers, "Travis, I want to do this. I want to so bad, but things have happened."

I don't care about any of that. I don't want to know about what happened while we weren't together. I just want to get back what I lost. I want to feel like I did before I ever left the city.

Inching even closer, Laura says, "I'm too drunk to really know what that means, dude." She kisses my cheek then jumps back. "Shit."

What?

"Your bottom lip's bleeding."

I stand up and walk over to the large mirror on my dresser and watch a tiny line of blood trickle from my lip.

"Do you think that's from me?" Laura asks.

I wipe the blood away.

Yeah. You hit me on the same side of the face.

"I'm sorry. I didn't mean to make you bleed. I just wanted to hurt you without yelling."

Pause.

I'll be right back.

"Where are you going?"

To the bathroom.

I leave and walk down the dark hallway past my sister's and parents' bedrooms and into the bathroom.

I splash water on my face and clean the blood off, and then I walk back to my room and Laura is lying underneath the blankets of my bed, listening to an Elliott Smith CD.

I take off my shirt and jeans and crawl next to her, and she rests her head against my neck and cuddles against my body.

"Thanks," she whispers into my ear.

For what?

"For coming back."

13.

WHEN LAURA AND I WAKE UP THE NEXT DAY, WE GO FOR
a late breakfast at Dee's, this twenty-four-hour diner on
Hammond Street.

After the two of us order, Laura checks her voice mail
and tells me she's got seven messages from Bryan and in all
of them he apologized. "I really need to talk to him," she
says, sipping a glass of ice water.

What are you going to say?

Laura sighs. "I don't know. What should I tell him?"

That your boyfriend's back.

"Oh, god," she blushes. "Do you remember when we cut
school on the same day and seriously watched that movie
and *Fast Times at Ridgemont High* like three times?"

Yep. Sophomore year.

I light a cigarette and look out the large, dirty window
we're sitting next to. There's an empty parking lot adjacent
to an elementary school that's been closed. There are lots of
construction machines where the playground used to be,
and there's no hint of life. The waitress arrives with our
food.

"Can we get some more coffee, too?" Laura asks her.

The waitress nods and says, "Sure," and then disappears into the kitchen.

Lifting my fork, I start picking at my hash browns and eggs.

So I was thinking that maybe we could go out sometime.

"Like on a date?" Laura asks, taking a bite of bacon.

Like to a movie or out to eat or something.

"I'd like that," she smiles as our waitress refills both of our coffee cups. "When?"

How about tonight?

"I can't tonight. I'm working."

Where do you work?

"At the Waterfront Grill."

Still.

"Yeah still. Why?"

I don't know.

I dump more cream and sugar into my coffee.

I thought you hated it there.

"I've never said that, Travis. I love it there."

Huh.

I sip my coffee and add some more sugar to it, and then I take a bite of my eggs and watch Laura text someone on her phone.

When she's through, she stuffs her phone back into her purse and I ask her who she just texted.

"Bryan," she answers, spooning up a mouthful of biscuits and gravy.

Oh.

"Is that okay?"

I guess so.

"Good," she says, then reaches across the table and pets my forearm. "You have nothing to worry about."

Later that afternoon I find a note stuck to my bedroom door that says Cliff stopped by twice while I was out, and that I need to get ahold of him as soon as I can.

Standing next to a window on the far side of my bedroom, I dial his cell phone number and wait for him to answer, staring at the heat that I can see rising from the black pavement of the road leading up to my house.

"Travis," Cliff says, his voice strained. "I've been waiting."

Why didn't you call my cell phone?

"'Cause you never answer it."

Yes I do.

"No you don't."

Yes I do.

"No you don't."

Whatever, man. What's going on?

"My dad kicked me out of his house this morning. He gave me till the end of the day to leave."

Why?

Pause.

Is it because he found out you've been slaying your stepmom?

"No, no. Fuck that. Fuck her. It's because he found out that I never went to a single class last year. That I paid my enrollment with the check he gave me, then dropped all of my classes at the end of my first week and spent the refund money the school gave me."

You did that?

"Yeah," Cliff barks. "And my shitty whore of a stepmom just sat there nodding her slut head while my old man told me he was cutting me off."

That sucks, I tell Cliff, because I really don't know what else to say, and he says, "So I wanted to know if you could help me move my shit."

Where to? Your mom's?

"Hell no, Trav. You know I don't talk to her anymore. I'm going to stay with Natalie."

Here we go.

"What?"

You really think moving into a trailer park with a girl you're screwing around with is a good idea?

"Where else am I gonna go?" Cliff snaps. "Who's gonna let me crash at their place with my shit?"

Pause.

"Are you?"

You know I can't.

"Then quit talking shit. I don't have a lot of options or time."

All right.

And Cliff says, "We gotta hurry up, man, 'cause if I'm in this house for much longer, I'm going to fucking murder both of them."

Cliff doesn't sound like he's even close to joking, so I tell him I'll be right over.

"Awesome," he says. Then: "There's something else, too."

What?

"I know you've been helping me out of all these jams lately and I appreciate it, I really do, but . . ." His voice trails off.

But what Cliff?

"I was wondering if you could spot me the dough to rent a U-Haul and hire a couple of those Mexican dudes who hang out in front of the rental spot."

This is the real reason Cliff called me. The real reason he ever seems to call me anymore. It's always about cash, and since I've never been able to really say no to the guy, I say, Sure, and, No problem. *For sure I'll spot you the loot because you got kicked out of your parents' house for ripping them off. Really, it's no problem.*

I pick up Cliff and drive him straight to the only rental store that has a truck left to rent, which is all the way on the south side of the city, a side that has long become a homeless camp haven, with its low-income housing, boarded-up store-fronts, and illegal immigrants.

On the way, I tell Cliff how I was with Laura for most of the day and that I spent the night with her and he lights a cigarette, and says, "Don't get back together with her."

Why not?

"Because you might learn some things you don't want to."

Like what?

Cliff says nothing. He looks out the window and takes a drag.

Cliff. Like what?

"What are you trying to do, Trav?" he asks. "Why are you trying to come back and make things like they were—when you were king shit of everything and Laura was your girl?"

Turing down the Queens of the Stone Age CD that's jamming, I ask Cliff if that's how he thought about me all these years.

I say, Did you think I was trying to put myself on a pedestal above everyone else?

"You didn't try, man. You did. And you know you did."

Fuck you. I'm helping you out. I helped you out back in March and I'm doing it again.

"You're not a god. Your family isn't royalty, man. Just because you want shit to happen and people to change doesn't mean they will."

Shut up.

"That's all I'm saying."

Shut the hell up.

"Laura sucks."

I turn and jack him in the side of his arm.

Douche bag.

"Asshole."

I light a cigarette. Spin the Queens back up, and roll the window down a crack. Thinking how sometimes I'd really like to fuck Cliff up, then never talk to the guy again. But at the same time, I feel sorry for him. I feel obliged to him. For as big an asshole as Cliff can be, he'd taken the rap for me numerous times growing up, even this one time during our sophomore year when I was caught with a bag of pot in my car.

Turning into the store parking lot, I drive through a crowd of about two hundred Hispanic dudes who cram around my car and beg for work.

"I think I got my two picked out already," Cliff tells me after I've parked.

I'll take care of the truck while you grab them.

"My fuckin' servants," he says with a smirk, but I pretend not to hear that, and walk inside and rent a truck with my emergency credit card.

Back outside, Cliff meets me by my car with two Mexican boys at his side. One looks about eighteen, with a tiny moustache and long braided hair that runs all the way past his shoulder blades. And the other looks about twenty-five, with a shaved head and goatee.

"I'll take these guys in your car," Cliff says. "So meet me at my place when you're through with the truck checkout."

Fine. Just be careful with my shit.

"I will," Cliff says.

I light a cigarette, my eyes glued on the guy with the shaved head. I'm fuckin' serious. Do not let anything happen to the car. It's not mine and I love my CDs.

It only ends up taking like an hour to get all of Cliff's shit loaded into the U-Haul. I don't even lift a finger. I actually

spend almost the entire time smoking cigarettes on the front
steps of the house, watching Cliff order the two Mexican
kids around with his stuff.

After the last item—an entertainment center—gets
loaded, Cliff sits down beside me on the top step and lights
a cigarette and asks the two other guys if they wanna smoke.
Both of them suddenly look really confused, almost scared,
and shake their heads, and Cliff starts laughing and says, "I
bet I could've said anything right there."

Probably.

Pause.

Cliff shakes his head. He runs a hand over his eyes. Says,
"Damn, this is weird. It's been a long time coming and all,
but still, I'm out. I'm fucking broke. And I'm about to be living in a trailer."

I thought it wasn't that bad, living in a trailer.

"It probably won't be," he says. "Natalie's cool. I mean, I
guess I like her okay. She's better than most of the girls I get
with."

Is she the one who got you shooting dope?

"It's not that bad, Trav. You don't know. You've never tried
it. It's not like it's an everyday thing. I got it under control."

Did you cut some girl with a knife in Iowa City a while
back?

Cliff rolls his eyes. "Don't ever ask me anything like that
again," he snaps, and gets up. "I'll take the two dudes in the
U-Haul. Follow us in your car."

Fine.

But just as Cliff and I have started for our rides, Marcy emerges from the house again and tells Cliff to wait.

Spinning around, Cliff's like, "What the hell do you want?"

Marcy runs a hand through Cliff's greasy hair. "I'm sorry it came to this."

"No you're not."

"I am. Call me if you need anything." She grabs one of Cliff's hands. "Anything."

Cliff yanks his hand away. "You're just as bad as my dad." He looks at me. "Fuck her. Let's go."

Natalie Taylor is standing in a patch of grass, the one right in front of the three small stairs that lead to the only door of her trailer home.

She's wearing a pair of black jeans with both knees blown out, tucked into a pair of black cowboy boots, and a gray wife-beater.

She's still hot, too.

Her hair is a wild mix of black and brown and blond and it hangs down to her shoulder blades.

She actually looks better than I remember her looking the last time I saw her toward the end of my senior year—when she, Michael, and I went to Chicago for a night to catch the Dillinger Escape Plan, 400 Blows, and Wires on Fire show at the Fireside Bowl. One of the best shows I've ever seen.

It was later that night, in the motel swimming pool, when Natalie and I finally had sex. She was a year older and a grade up from us, but throughout high school we had always messed around here and there—when Laura and I were taking a break or fighting real bad—and it finally happened that night, and I hadn't seen her since the day after, when the three of us drove back to the city.

I stop my car behind the truck and wait for Cliff to open the trailer door and get the Mexicans started before stepping outside.

The sun is already setting and the sky has turned into a huge picture of orange flames and ocean-blue waves.

I light a cigarette and walk around my car to where Cliff and Natalie are standing, and the first thing Natalie says, is, "Well look who it is."

It's nice to see you too, Natalie.

I swat a gnat off the back of my neck.

"You got any beer?" Cliff asks her.

"There's some in the fridge, darling," she says, putting her hands on the side of his face. They start making out and I can hear the slurpy, sloppy sounds of their saliva and lips smacking together.

When their little show is finally over, Cliff walks into the trailer, a forty-by-eight-foot tan slab of nothing, right after the Mexican dudes walk out joking and laughing with each other about something—most likely the three of us.

And Natalie goes, "I heard you were back, but then again"—she grins, leaning forward and grabbing the inside of my left arm—"I don't ever remember you leaving."

I shake my arm loose.

It's a nice life you're making for yourself these days, Natalie.

"Fuck you," she snaps. "What's so good about your life, Travis Wayne? You dropped out of school and you live with your parents."

I know that.

"What's so great about it?"

There's nothing great about it.

"Then keep your mouth shut about mine."

Cliff walks back out with three cans of Busch Light. "So what do you think, Trav? Honestly?" he asks.

I open the can he gives me and take a long drink.

It is, ya know, what it is, Cliff.

I'm staring straight at Natalie.

Cliff and I drop the truck and the Mexicans off about an hour and a half later. On our way back to the trailer with beer and pizza, Cliff tells me that my sister's friend Katie and him have been fucking around the past couple of nights.

"But don't even mention her name to Natalie, okay?"

I won't.

"Do you promise?"

I promise.

"On your mother's life?"

On my mother's life, Cliff.

Once we're back, the three of us eat and drink and play cards and listen to the new PJ Harvey CD that Natalie picked up while we were gone. Then these two black guys show up, the same ones I remember Cliff stopping to talk to outside of the house party we were at last week.

Natalie takes the one with the shaved head by the hand and leads him to the other end of the trailer, into another room, and closes the door behind her.

I'm glaring at Cliff.

What's going on? I ask him.

I stand up, but the guy with the cornrows pulls a .22 out of his waistband, and goes, "Is there a problem?"

"Travis, sit down," Cliff says.

The guy moves his gun closer to me. "I said, is there a problem, man?"

No.

I look at Cliff. He's just sitting there staring at his hands.

I guess not.

"Good," the guy says. "So sit the fuck down."

I do.

He pulls out the chair across the table from us and sits in it, setting his gun in front of him.

I don't get it, but Cliff doesn't seem fazed at all. He actually looks intrigued.

The guy with the cornrows stares at me and grins.

"Where could I get a gun like that?" Cliff asks, shattering the silence.

"You serious?" the guy snaps.

"Yeah."

"What the hell does a rich white kid need a gun for? You got the pigs?"

"Fuck that," Cliff smiles. "You think I'm rich? We're sitting in a trailer. I just moved to a fucking trailer park today."

"By choice. You live here by choice."

"Screw that."

I swallow like three huge wads of spit down my throat. Light a cigarette.

The black dude starts laughing. "I like you," he says. "At least you ain't scared." He looks back at me and rolls his upper lip back. "If you're really serious about a gun, you know how to get ahold of me."

"Sweet," says Cliff.

The door to the room Natalie is in swings open. She walks out with the shaved head guy and he goes, "Let's roll," and the guy with cornrows gets up and the two of them leave.

Natalie sits back down at the table and drops a small baggie of brown powder onto it.

She looks at me, her lipstick a bit smeared around the edges of her lips. She wipes her eyes.

Cliff slides an arm over her shoulders. "Are we square with them?" he asks.

"Yes," she says.

"Thank you, baby," he tells her.

Natalie looks at me again before walking to the sink. She yanks one of the counter drawers entirely out.

At the table I watch Cliff slide the heroin toward him, the tip of his tongue hanging between his lips.

A series of still photos of Natalie behind that door just

now smash through my head. I feel like throwing up and leaving, but for some reason I don't.

Reaching into the empty space where the drawer had been, Natalie pulls out a plastic bag and comes back to the table.

Inside the bag are four things: a syringe, a spoon, a needle, and a bright pink lighter.

And Natalie says to Cliff, "I think you should go first, baby."

Me, I say, Well I'm not going to do any at all.

Neither of them pay any attention to that as the PJ Harvey disc slams into the Smiths album *Louder than Bombs*.

Cliff wraps a leather belt around his left arm and Natalie turns the dark powder into liquid in the rim of the spoon with the lighter.

I light another cigarette.

Setting the lighter down and picking the needle up, Natalie draws the heroin into the syringe while Cliff finds a vein.

"Got it," he says, smiling.

Natalie sets the spoon down and grabs his arm. "You ready?" she whispers, as the Smiths sing . . .

"Call me morbid, call me pale. . . . I spent six years on your trail. . . ."

"Yes," he says.

She sticks the needle into his vein and the syringe fills up with Cliff's blood while his eyes close and his body falls gently against the chair.

"That's my boy," she whispers, pulling the needle out.

She leans over and kisses Cliff's forehead. "You're so perfect . . . just beautiful," she tells him before setting the needle back down, picking the spoon back up, and dumping more heroin into it. . . .

"And if you have five seconds to spare, then I'll tell you the story of my life. . . ."

14

MY FIRST COUPLA DAYS IN HAWAII WERE ACTUALLY pretty mellow. I spent most of my time on the beach, lying around, getting fucked up, listening to good shit like Big Business and Spacemen 3 and Cage on my iPod. I took some surf lessons, but I didn't really enjoy them—I couldn't get into it, it wasn't my fucking thing, so I gave up and went back to lying around.

A few times I hung with these dudes from New York who I'd met in the lobby of the hotel I was staying at, and we took some sightseeing tours around the island and drank some beers in their room one night, listening to some great music, and they were totally cool, and one of them showed me all these photos in his cell phone of him and Steven Adler after an Adler's Appetite show, and they even hooked me up with a number to score some coke from.

I spent one afternoon shopping for things that my sister or my mom or my dad might like, but I couldn't really decide on anything for them. I did find some things for Laura, and ended up buying her this amazing seashell necklace, this grass hula skirt, this framed painting of a young boy and girl holding hands on the beach during sunset, and a postcard of the ocean, which I used for this note:

Laura, it was so great to be with you again even if it was only for a few days. I miss you and can't wait for you to come visit me in Arizona. It will be amazing to be able to make love to you again. Hope you're doing well and I'll talk to you as soon as I get back to Arizona.
Love, Travis

I packed this, along with everything else, into a box, and even wrote her address on it, then set it next to my suitcase in the hotel room with plans to send it to her the morning of my flight to Arizona, which is something that never happened.

Not even fucking close.

Travis Wayne

15.

MY MOTHER CALLS ME FROM HER CELL THE NEXT afternoon, right after I've just done some laps. She asks if I want to meet her and my sister for lunch in an hour. Apparently the two of them have been out shopping since this morning, hitting boutique after boutique after boutique.

Where do you want to meet?

"Bailey's."

In an hour?

"Yes."

Pause.

Mom.

"What is it, Travis?"

Pause.

My grip on the phone tightens.

"Travis?"

It's nothing.

Arriving at the upscale bar and grill fifteen minutes late, I already feel like I should've declined my mother's offer.

This place has always bothered me.

It was decorated to look like some vintage, common man's dive with its purposely beat-up wood paneling and its dirty neon glow, but in reality, it's hardly that.

Not with twenty-dollar burger plates, fifty-dollar steak dishes, and eight-dollar draws of Bud.

Seated at the bar, sipping drinks, are my mother and sister.

"Well look who decides to show up," I hear my sister groan as I'm approaching them.

My mother, who's smoking a clove cigarette, turns her head in my direction, then pulls down her Gucci shades. "There he is."

I take a seat next to her.

Sorry I'm late.

"It's okay," she says between sips of her white wine. "Would you like something to drink?"

"Oh, get one of these," my sister blurts out, holding up a half-full glass of bright blue liquid.

What is that?

I pull out my cigarettes.

"Liquid cocaine," she smiles.

"It's surprisingly good," my mother nods, ashing out the rest of her cigarette.

I know. I've had one before, only it was in a shot glass.

"*So?*" my mother asks.

I light a cigarette.

I'll just have water when we order.

A few minutes later we get seated.

Looking through the menu, nothing really jumps out at me. Not the thirty-dollar seafood meals or the forty-dollar pasta plates.

I end up settling on the twenty-dollar quesadilla platter, and I set the menu down and take a sip of water.

Are you guys done for the day? I ask.

"Not quite," my mother tells me.

"Yeah, we still have to go down to Kennedy Street, and for sure to the new Diesel store they just opened on top of Blaine Tower," says my sister, who's wearing a pair of white jeans and a black lace top.

"Don't forget about the doctor's, too," my mother smiles after finishing another glass of wine.

What are you going to the doctor's for?

"Your sister needs a refill on her birth control, and I need a few different refills myself."

Huh.

My sister jabs her tongue at me, then tells my mother and me that she's going to use the bathroom and that we should order the chicken salad with Caesar dressing for her.

My mother removes the sunglasses from the top of her head. "How have you been, Travis?" she asks.

All right. Why?

"No reason," she yawns. "I just haven't seen you around much. What have you been doing?"

Hanging out . . . the usual stuff.

She seems to force the grin on her face before lighting another clove. "Well, you're looking a little better. You have some color now. You were actually walking with your back straight when you came in."

Was I?

"Yes." My mother coughs. "But your father is still very frustrated with you, Travis. He wants to know what your plans are."

My plans for what?

"For next year. He really thinks you should give USC a try and I'm starting to think that maybe it wouldn't be such a bad idea."

No. I do not want to go there.

My mother sighs. "What's going on with you?" she asks. "Did something happen to you in Arizona?"

Inhale. Exhale.

No.

"Then how did you go from a 3.0 to flunking completely out?"

Pause.

She leans forward and whispers, "Did you get addicted to meth? Your father heard it's the big thing these days."

I almost laugh, but don't. Instead I take a drink of water, and tell her that I'm trying to figure things out.

I'm trying to do what's right.

My mother leans back. "That sounds good, Travis. It really does. But actions speak a lot louder than words, especially to someone like your father. And you need to understand how unhappy he is with you."

Pause.

"I mean, I can only keep making excuses for you for so long," she tells me.

Fine.

"You know, your father really—"

But she gets interrupted by our waiter, Mark, who asks if we're ready to order.

We are.

And by the time we're finished, and he's brought my mother another glass of wine, my sister has rejoined us and looks completely out of it.

"Your chicken salad is on the way," my mother tells her.

"My what?" my sister asks back.

Your food. We ordered it for you, I say, lighting another cigarette.

"What did I get?" she asks, lighting her own cigarette.

My mother tilts her head to the side and leans closer to my sister. "Chicken salad with Caesar dressing," she says. "What's wrong with you?"

Pause.

"What's that white stuff on the top of your lip?"

My sister freezes for a moment, then quickly regains her composure. "Oh, it's this herbal stuff that Katie's been using as an energy supplement." She wipes the residue, which I'm sure is OxyContin, off and says, "When you break it down, sometimes it gets a little chalky."

I take another drag.

My mother scoots back. Takes a sip of wine. "Huh. I've been looking for a new energy supplement."

My sister and I are staring at each other.

"Maybe I'll ask the doctor about it today," she finishes.

And hardly another word is spoken the rest of the time we're there.

After I leave the restaurant, I drive downtown to Defiant Records and pick up this new Lightning Bolt CD and this DMBQ DVD of their last United States tour, and when I'm leaving the store, I run into Kyle and Emily on the sidewalk. They're holding hands and look all super fucking happy, standing in front of me, completely smiley faced.

"What are you doing tonight?" Kyle asks me.

I don't know, man.

"You should come out with us," Emily says. "We're celebrating. I just got this killer design job at the Johannson fashion studio."

Awesome. Congratulations.

"Thanks," she smiles. "It's gonna be so fucking rad. I've been working to get a break like this for the last three years. This is like the best fucking day. It's finally happening!" she shrieks.

Her and Kyle kiss.

Where are you guys going?

"We're starting at Bottoms Up around five for happy hour," Kyle says. "Claire's gonna be there."

Maybe I will.

"You really should," Emily says. "It'll be amazing."

But when I get back to the house, Laura calls me and

tells me that the Victorian Theater is showing *Buffalo '66* at ten. "And I was thinking that if you still wanted to . . . well, this could be like our date, Travis."

Pause.

"I mean, if you were serious about what you said the other day at breakfast."

Pause.

"Were you?" she asks. "'Cause if you weren't, I'm gonna feel like a fucking asshole."

My heart pounds hard against my chest. I'm blushing.

"So were you?" she asks again.

I totally was, Laura.

"Awesome. Why don't you pick me up at the Waterfront around nine when my shift is over," she says.

I pull up to the Waterfront restaurant a little bit after nine wearing a light blue V-neck T, a pair of Levi's, and a pair of ankle high black boots.

Laura is standing out front, smoking a cigarette, talking to this dude who looks like he's trying to look like one of those guys from the band AFI.

Think long black hair purposely styled to look messy. Big, black earplugs. A rushed sleeve of ink on his right arm. A black Cinderella T-shirt. Tight black denims. And a hint of black eye shadow underneath both his eyes.

When Laura sees my car pulling up, she dumps her smoke on the ground, then hugs the guy before jumping into my car.

"Hey," she smiles, kissing my cheek.

Hey.

"I'm so excited," she says. "I've always wanted to see this movie in a theater. Remember how we used to watch it all the time, like almost every night we spent together."

Yeah.

"Plus"—she smirks—"I made a ton in tips tonight, so it's my treat."

I turn down the Year Future CD that I put in on my way over and ask her who that guy was.

"Who?"

The guy you just hugged.

"Oh . . . Jared. He's a bartender at the restaurant."

Pause.

"Why?"

No reason.

Laura leans over and kisses my cheek again and again and again. "This already feels nice," she says. "Just like I thought it would."

After the movie is over, Laura and I stop and get some ice cream, and when we're walking out, we run into April and Chris.

April has some dark bruising underneath her left eye and I ask her what happened.

Chris puts an arm around her.

"I . . . I ran into a wall when I was drunk," she stutters.

I look at Chris and Chris looks at me, and then I look

at Laura, who looks at April, and goes, "Funny how that happens."

"I saw Cliff earlier today," Chris says. "He was talking about you, Laura."

Laura covers her mouth and tenses up. And Chris goes, "We have to get going," then pulls April past Laura and me without saying bye.

That was weird, I say.

"Chris is such a prick," Laura snaps.

How so?

"Come on, Travis," she says as we cross an almost empty parking lot, battered orange from the glow of the street lamps. "She didn't run into a wall."

So what are you saying?

"I'm saying that Chris is a prick."

Pause.

"You can figure out the rest."

I don't say anything.

I just unlock my car and take her to my parents' house.

In the kitchen, while I'm making the two of us margaritas, I ask Laura what the whole deal with her and Bryan is.

"We're done," she tells me.

Really? Are you two really done, Laura?

"Yes," she presses. "He fucking hates me now."

Oh, that's too bad.

"Don't start shit, Travis."

I slide her drink across the counter.

"He was good to me," she says. "We had a lot of fun. For

my birthday, he got us tickets to three straight nights of Björk shows at some really small club in Chicago. He even got us backstage. He took awesome care of me," she finishes.

I can respect that, I guess. But if he was so good, why are you with me now?

Laura sighs. "Because, Travis. In the end . . ." She stops and takes a drink. "In the end he's not you, baby."

I smile and take a drink, and I say, So I was thinking that maybe we could drive up to the lake and stay at my parents' cabin for the fourth.

"You would really want to do that?" Laura asks.

Yeah. I think it would be good to get out of the city, just the two of us.

"I would love to," she says.

I'll run it by my mom. I'm sure it won't be a problem.

My sister walks in from the garage. She's completely wasted. Stumbling. "Laura!" she screams, sliding her way down the hall, against a chair. She jumps onto Laura's lap, almost knocking the two of them off of the stool Laura's sitting on.

Cut it out, I tell her.

"Fuck you," my sister hisses, then gropes Laura's neck. "You look awesome, Laura."

"Thanks," Laura says back.

Get off her lap, I say.

"It's all right, Travis," Laura smiles.

"Ha!" My sister snorts. "Don't be so uptight all the time, dude." Flopping toward the edge of the counter, bracing herself against it with her left arm, my sister goes, "You always think you're the boss of everyone." Waving a finger at me, she says, "But you're not the boss of me."

Laura starts laughing.

And my sister goes, "That was a close call today at lunch, huh, bro?"

What did Mom say at the doctor's?

"Nothing, duh," my sister blabs. "Did you see how many glasses of fucking wine she drank? She didn't remember a thing. She was hammered and flirting with all the guys in the shops downtown."

Don't say that.

"She waaaaassssss," my sister slurs. "Man, you don't even know. While you were gone, pissing your life away, all's Mom did was watch *Sex and the City* DVDs."

I slam the rest of my drink and my sister tilts back against Laura's body. "Laura," she says. "You shouldn't waste your time with my brother. He's not worth it. You're way too good for him. He used to treat you like shit."

Just shut up already.

"Hey, dude, I'm just helping another girl out," my sister giggles. She scoots right up to Laura's face. Says, "He's probably screwed like ten other girls since you two started talking again."

This time I lunge across the countertop and snag my sister's arm, and when she tries to yank herself loose, she slips off Laura's lap, thumping hard against the floor.

"Travis, what are you doing?" Laura barks.

I walk around the edge of the counter.

She's fine, Laura.

My sister props herself up with her arms. "You're an asshole!" she yells before her hands slide out from underneath her.

Laura jumps off the stool. "Help me," she says.

The two of us get my sister to her feet.

Where were you? I ask her.

"With Katie. We got loaded on some booze and pills Cliff gave us—"

But my sister doesn't finish. Instead her mouth blows wide open, her head drops, and she starts spewing this yellow and brown shit onto the floor, and Laura and I almost drop her while we try to avoid getting splashed.

We need to get her upstairs, Laura. I don't want my parents to come down and see her like this.

So Laura and I each hook one of my sister's arms over our shoulders and carry her to her room and lay her down on her chest so she can't choke on her vomit. Then we leave my sister's room and go back down to the kitchen, and while I'm mopping up the large puddle of puke, Laura goes, "Did your sister mean Cliff as in Cliff Miles?"

I'm sure she did.

Laura holds her face in her hands. "Doesn't that bother you?" What?

"That Cliff got your sister wasted like that."

No, not really. He wouldn't do anything bad to her. He wouldn't fuck with me like that.

Laura takes a deep breath. "How do you know?" she asks. "Have you been hanging out with him a lot?"

Not a lot.

"I don't think you should be talking to him at all."

Why not?

"Because you're way better than him, Travis. Clifford Miles is a fucking asshole and he's only gonna drag you down with him."

Don't talk shit, Laura.

"I'm being serious," she says.

So now you're gonna tell me who I should and shouldn't hang out with. Is that it?

Laura sighs and grabs my hands. "I'm not telling you, Travis. All I'm saying is that I think you'd be better off not hanging around him."

I yank my hands away.

But he's my best friend, Laura. I can't just quit talking to him. I did that to everyone when I left after Christmas and I ended up losing my fucking head. I won't do it again.

A long pause.

"I understand," she pouts.

Do you?

"Yeah," she whispers. "I do."

After I've washed up from cleaning, Laura and I go up to my room to hang out and it doesn't take us long to start fucking around. She pulls me on top of her and we make out like two junior high kids under the bleachers—heavy breathing, tongues in each other's ears, bottom lips being bitten—it feels super nice. I have a huge boner. But when I start pushing my hand down the front of Laura's jeans, she stops me and tells me that she's on her period.

She's fucking ragging.

Of all the nights.

Kissing her lips again, I roll off of her, onto my back, eyes pointing to the ceiling, and I say, We could use the bathtub. It would be cleaner. At least you wouldn't bleed all over my room.

Laura shoots straight up. "No, Travis. That is not an option. It's been six months since we had sex, and I am not going to start back up with you like that."

But I've got a mega boner, Laura.

She leans over and kisses me and goes, "Deal with it. Jack off."

You could help me out, I suggest after sitting up.

"I could, but I won't. I want everything we do for the first time again to be special . . . all right, Travis?"

Yeah. That's fine.

Laura stands up and looks at her cell phone. "I have to go. Will you call me a cab?"

Just stay the night.

"I can't. I have to go home and let my dog out. My parents are out of town tonight."

I groan, Are you ever going to move out of their house, Laura?

"Someday," she answers.

When?

"When I've finished breaking my father's fucking heart," she says.

Ya know, you could just tell your mom about his affair, Laura.

"No I can't," she says. "I can't tell my mom anything. And besides, even if I did, it wouldn't make one bit of difference. My mom is a weak person. She wouldn't even think about getting a divorce so the only thing it would lead to is a bunch of fighting and tension all the time."

Maybe you should tell your father that you know about it.

"No, Travis," Laura snaps. "Telling either of them anything is stupid. You don't confront people about things that are out of your control. You bury it inside and you move the fuck on. That's how you deal with shit. It makes you stronger. That's why I'm not weak like my mother."

Laura.

"What?"

We're all fucking weak.

And she goes, "Just call me a cab. Please."

16

KYLE SAYS, "HERE, DUDE, PUT THIS IN," AND HANDS ME the new Dead Meadow CD, so I slide the disc into the CD player of his revamped Camry and kick up the volume.

The two of us are headed to the cop shop on Paradise Street to pick up Michael, who spent the night in one of their holding cells after he was arrested outside of the Lost Soul bar.

Apparently Jordan Knight, one of the guys who used to be in that group New Kids on the Block, was doing a solo show at the Lost Soul, and Michael and Dave bought tickets so they could heckle him while he was performing, but things got a little out of control.

Think bottles getting smashed onstage.

A backup singer receiving an atomic wedgie.

Think a poster of Jordan's brother, Jonathan, going up in flames.

Coming to a stop at a red light, Kyle turns to me and says, "I'm moving in with Emily next week. I can't live with Chris anymore. Not after he punched April in the face. Fuck that, man."

So that's what happened to her.

"You saw her too?" Kyle says.

The other night, when Laura and I were out.

Kyle shakes his head. "I don't respect that motherfucker. I can't live with anyone who would do that to a girl."

Have you told him you're moving?

"I haven't seen him to tell him yet. I only know about it 'cause I saw April when we were celebrating Emily's new gig."

Why'd he hit her?

"He heard that she banged some kid from State and she didn't deny it."

Oh. Damn.

Kyle squints, craning his neck away from me, and I look out the fingerprint covered window, and my eyes land on the car stopped next to us.

Crammed inside of it are five younger-looking, fifteen-, sixteen-year-old boys, and one girl who looks exactly like my sister's friend Amy, but I just can't tell if it's her or not. Whoever it is, though, she looks at me looking at her, then sticks what appears to be a crank pipe against her lips and takes a hit, and then I slide my eyes over to the driver, who's wearing a cowboy hat and an Avenged Sevenfold T-shirt, and this kid makes a growling face at me, then flips me off.

The light turns green and I think I hear Kyle mutter something, but when I ask him what he said, he bunches his nose and goes, "Not a fucking thing," and then guns his ride around two slower cars and takes the avenue's exit all the way to the police station.

Michael's standing outside the front entrance smoking a ciggie when we pull into the parking lot. Jumping right in, he goes, "Kyle, you got anything on you?"

Kyle starts laughing as he pulls onto the street, and Michael says, "I'm fuckin' serious, man. I need drugs like bad."

I look at Michael and ask him where Dave is.

"Dave didn't get arrested. He scrammed when the pigs showed up. He's smart like that."

"What'd they charge you with?" Kyle asks, jumping back onto the freeway to cut to the other side of the city.

"Public intoxication and lewd conduct. Nothing serious. Just some fines. I would've been out last night but I couldn't get ahold of my parents to post the thousand-dollar bail they stuck me with."

Where are they?

"I don't know. Either LA or Boston," Michael snorts, jamming another smoke between his lips.

Did you at least come close to punching Jordan Knight?

"Nope."

Sucks.

"The whole thing does, dude. That totally wasn't worth it. I could've done way more awesomer things than that last night. I mean, that dude got paid and I got arrested. It wasn't nearly as fun as I thought it was gonna be when I was blowing rails and talking about it a coupla nights ago."

At least you're honest, man.

"Shut the fuck up," Michael says back. "Yo, Kyle, I need a half."

"Just wait till I drop you off," Kyle sneers.

Michael pulls his wallet from his jeans and opens it. There's only one dollar in it and he looks at me. "Hey, Kyle," he says. "Do you think you could spot it to me."

"No," Kyle answers, whipping a sharp left toward the downtown parking lot where Michael says his car's at.

"What about you, Trav?"

What about me?

"Spot me twenty for the half, man. I'll get you back."

Are you serious?

"I need it for practice. I'm driving straight to the studio."

I look at Kyle, then back at Michael, and say, Fine, whatever, and hand him a twenty out of my wallet, and Michael goes, "That's why you're cooler than everyone else I know."

Sure, I nod. Cooler.

Later on I call Laura to tell her that if she's still into it and not that mad at me, I got the cabin for the third and fourth.

"That's wonderful," she says. Then: "I'm sorry I got bitchy with you the other night. Are you mad?"

No.

"Okay," she sighs. "I can't wait to go to the cabin. It'll be like old times. Remember how much fun we had the last time we were there?"

The last time we were there: First night, Laura puking on me right as I'm undressing her so we can have sex. Getting so stoned the next afternoon that I passed out. Waking up and watching Laura talk to this tall, blond, muscular guy from a cabin window, and how much it looked like she wanted to fuck him. Going to dinner, getting really loaded on Singapore slings, and laughing later that night when Laura told me to "Put it up my butt." An ugly sunrise. Two beautiful grams of blow. Chris and Michael crashing the place with a case of Two-Buck Chuck. The cops showing up. A minor possession-of-alcohol ticket. And Laura telling me to straighten up, after lighting a cigarette and finishing a bottle of champagne, because she either missed her period altogether or is "really, really late."

Yeah, I say. I remember.

17

THE CALL COMES JUST BEFORE SIX A.M., AND THE ONLY reason I answer the phone is because I'm still awake watching *Pirates of the Caribbean* in the living room.

On the other end of the line is Chris, who sounds all jacked up, and the first thing that smashes through my head while he's asking, "Dude, have you seen Kyle? Have you seen him at all?" is, *Lay off the blow.*

But instead of saying that, I say, No, I haven't seen him in a couple of days.

"You sure? Are you sure you haven't seen him anywhere?"

Yeah, why? Is this about him moving out?

"Moving out? No. He didn't move out, but the fuckin' cops—"

What, Chris?

"The cops were just here looking for him."

What? I ask again.

"The fuckin' cops just came to the house looking for him, dude."

What for?

"They wouldn't tell me shit, but I overheard one of them talking about a car accident . . . a hit and run."

Are you serious or is this a prank? Are you high right now, Chris? Huh?

"Yes, but this isn't a prank, you dick. This is for real."

There's another long pause.

Then Chris says, "Dude, what should we do?"

What can we do, Chris? I mean if the cops are looking for him and can't find him then he's probably hiding, man.

I hear him make this moaning sound, and then he says, "I'm gonna have to call you back."

Click.

I walk upstairs to my bedroom and open up a window and try to breathe but it doesn't help.

Then I remember that I have some pot stashed in my sock drawer and roll a joint.

It's still raining outside.

18.

IN OUR TOP STORY THIS NOON HOUR, POLICE NOW SAY they have in custody the driver of the motor vehicle that crashed into a house at the corner of Eighteenth and Walnut Streets early this morning, leaving two children, ages eight and six, dead, as well as the lone passenger of the car, a twenty-one-year-old female whose name has not been released.

Police say they apprehended the driver, Kyle Joshua Rhodes, just over an hour ago after they received an anonymous call informing officers of a bloodied individual trying to climb a tree on a residential property in the Richmond District.

While police aren't confirming anything at this point, alcohol and some illegal substances are believed to have been involved.

Again . . . to repeat our top story this noon hour, Kyle Rhodes, age nineteen, has been taken into police custody at this hour and is believed to have been the driver of the automobile that crashed into the side of a house at approximately four thirty this morning, leaving two young children dead, and also the passenger of the vehicle, a young female who has yet to be identified.

As soon as more details come in, you can be sure that we here at Channel 7, the city's leading news source, will pass as much information along as we can.

19.

LAURA CALLS ME AND SAYS THAT SHE'S NOT FEELING well and please, pretty please, will I come over to her house and be with her tonight, and I tell her I will and in a whisper, she says, "Okay," and hangs up.

I stop at this Chinese restaurant on my way to Laura's and pick up some soup for her and some kung pao chicken for me, and when I'm walking back to my car, my cell starts ringing.

It's Claire. She's crying hysterically and tells me that Emily was the girl in the car with Kyle and that they've just charged Kyle with vehicular homicide, DUI, fleeing the scene, reckless endangerment, failing to maintain, and a few drug possession things.

"That fucking asshole!" she screams. "He killed my best friend!"

Calm down, Claire.

"No!" she yells. "I hate him!"

Claire, don't say that.

"Fuck you, Travis. You couldn't give a shit less. Screw you."

Click.

I try calling her back but she doesn't pick up, and when

I try again, her phone doesn't even ring. It goes straight to her voice mail, and I drive to Laura's.

Lying on a couch when I walk in, a mimosa by her side, Laura tells me that she's the only one home, then scoots over so I can sit next to her.

I brought you some soup.

Laura sits up. She kisses me and squeezes her arms tightly around me. "How are you handling things?" she asks.

As best as I can, Laura.

"I saw Kyle's mug shot on the news," Laura sighs. "It didn't even look like him—not the Kyle I remember."

Pulling her arms from my neck, I say, I don't think I can talk about this right now. I'm sorry.

"That's okay," she says. "Here. Look what I found in my room the other day." She reaches to the floor and opens this black leather journal, pulling out a piece of paper.

What is that?

"This," she smiles, holding it in front of my face. "This is the first thing you ever wrote for me."

Let me see it.

I snag it from her hands and read it. It goes:

Even in this crowded room, we are the only ones truly here,
The only ones who matter,
All the way across this packed hall, this dirty floor,
Through all of these people,
Your lips are the only thing that matter to me,
Pink,

Smiling,
Wet,
When you turned at me, then turned quickly the other way,
I saw your truth and I wanted you to stay,
And for the first time ever, I found comfort

Blushing, I'm like, Oh, wow, that's not very good, and Laura goes, "Don't be embarrassed. It's beautiful. You were fifteen. Everything's lame when you're fifteen, baby. I think it's great."

You really do?

"I love it," she says, taking the paper from me and sticking it back into the journal. "I also think we should still go to the cabin."

I don't know about that, Laura. I don't know if it's a good idea, considering what just happened.

"That's why we should go, baby." She kisses my lips. "It'll be good to get away from all this for a night or two. None of us can really do anything at this point, ya know."

I guess you're right.

Laura slides up against me. The soft skin of her face rubs against mine, and she goes, "Come on, what do you say?"

I'm into it.

"Awesome, baby."

emily.

THERE'S A MODEST MOUSE SONG THAT USED TO ALWAYS get stuck in my head. It went:

It's hard to remember we're alive for the first time.... It's hard to remember we're alive for the last time.... It's hard to remember to live before you die.... It's hard to remember that our lives are such a short time.... It's hard to remember when it takes such a long time.... It's hard to remember....

Kyle told me he was okay to drive. He went, "You're more wasted than me. Plus I wouldn't want you to get in trouble."

The decisions that we make.

I mean, I was really wasted too. It was so surreal. We're on the road and a split second later—*BAM*—we jump a median—*BAM*—we jump a curb.

And then there was this house.

And these sounds.

Splintered glass.

Broken bones.

Severed veins.

And that's all I know.

The decisions that we make.

20.

THE NEXT MORNING I WAKE UP AROUND SIX. LAURA'S still asleep, and I don't feel like waking her, so I write her this note that says:

I went home to pack and shower.
Call me when you get up.
I love you.
Travis

But then I decide I cannot say that last part. Not yet. So I crumple the note and leave her a different one.

I stop by the accident scene.

Kyle's Camry has been removed and there is police tape all around the sight. Almost an entire side of the house has been completely annihilated and I can see into the bedroom where the vehicle went in.

There are all these stuffed animals lying around. A bunk bed is completely smashed up, wedged into what remains of a wall on the far side of the room, and it looks less than half the size of a single mattress now. There's a strip of border still left with bears and rainbows on it, and bouquets of flowers have already been placed everywhere.

I feel totally sick staring at this, but I can't turn my eyes away.

I shut my headlights off and I lean back. Close my eyes. Try to put myself there.

I wonder if anyone even screamed. I wonder what flashed through the minds of the two children before they were nailed. The news at ten said that they died instantly, as did the girl—Emily—who flew through the windshield and ended up underneath the car, skull crushed, neck and spine shattered.

Kyle, they said, was saved, if you can really call it that, by the airbag, and only had minor injuries, and was able and coherent as he fled the scene in what police think was less than a minute after the crash.

I wonder how big the eyes of the children got when they turned their heads the split second before they were killed.

Their names were Brandon and Adam, and apparently they liked to play with their toy cars and two dogs.

Also, someone who was at the scene said the smell of the burning flesh from the fire that had broken out, leaving the boys' bodies charred, was making officers on the scene sick.

I take a one-hitter from my stash, flip the headlights back on, and a few moments later, while I'm still trying to get away from it all, Tool comes on the radio:

I will work to elevate you just enough to bring you down....

21

LAURA AND I GET TO MY PARENTS' CABIN, WHICH SITS right on the edge of the state's biggest lake, at like four that afternoon. Halfway through the four-hour drive it began to rain, and since that very moment Laura's been all super-bummed about it and also because I wouldn't let her put in the Shins CD while I was playing Ugly Casanova.

She went, "The only reason why you don't like them now is because everyone else does."

No. That's only kind of true, Laura.

"It's completely true, Travis. After we watched *Garden State*, I saw you give all your Shins CDs to your sister."

That movie sucked.

"I liked it."

Of course you did. You and every other hipster who thinks that kind of odd, offbeat romance is all super warm and fuzzy.

"And what makes you such an expert?"

I took a film theory class my first semester of college.

Laura rolled her eyes and smiled. She went, "You always gotta be the chillest dude in the room."

And I went, That doesn't make much sense, considering how good of friends I am with Michael.

Then I gave her two Xanax and told her to relax, and she swallowed both of them at the same time with her spit.

After we take our things inside the cabin, I mention that we should probably drive into town and pick up some things like food and booze and smokes before the stores close, but Laura heads straight for the master bedroom and flops on the bed, moaning, "You go, baby."

Fine, I groan.

And she says, "You can take some money from my purse and use it on whatever."

Awesome. I get free rein on your purse.

"Just take what you need, Travis."

Yeah, sure. Do you want anything in particular?

"Just get whatever sounds good," she yawns, and I shut the door to the bedroom and leave.

The town my parents' cabin is in is very small and quiet and doesn't even have a stoplight or anything. Even in the downpour, the kids here run around as if they have no worries at all in the world, and deep down, I feel a little jealous.

Pushing the grocery cart through one store aisle after another, I toss frozen pizzas and bread and lunch meat and way too much alcohol into it. The girl who is working the register is young and cute and smiles at me and she asks me where I'm from, and when I tell her, she tells me that everyone she meets from the city usually seems impatient and preoccupied when they come into the store.

I pull out my fake ID and cash.

What about me?

"What about you?" she asks.

How do I seem?

"Distant."

Distant?

The girl nods. "You don't seem like you're really here," she says, handing me my change. And for a moment I don't move. I don't say a fucking word. I just stare at this girl and think about what I could do to her if she ever came home with me.

"Hey," she says, snapping me out of my trance.

I blink.

What?

"You're holding up the line," she points out, and I rub my eyes, then tell the girl thanks and drive back to the cabin holding on to the steering wheel as tightly as I can.

Laura's asleep in bed when I get back. I try waking her. I shake her arm and say that I got us some food and drinks, and she says, "Give me another hour, dude. Please?"

I walk out to the kitchen and open a bottle of champagne and a jug of orange juice and make a mimosa.

Although my parents have had this cabin for almost fifteen years, I can only remember two times that the four of us—my mother, father, sister, and me—ever came here together, all at once. And even those memories seem hazy. Both times were before I was ten, and neither of them really stands out much. Most of my visits here have come during the past four or five years: me with my friends, me with Laura, me with my father and a few of his college buddies, and once with my sister and two of her friends when I was sixteen and she was twelve.

On that trip, the first afternoon there, I was out jet skiing by myself, and when I came back to the cabin, I found the three of them snorting lines of coke off a CD case in the living room. When I asked my sister, What are you doing? she began laughing in my face and went, "Fuck, Travis. I've been stealing the shit from you since last summer," then chopped off another rail.

The cabin itself is very subtle and casual in the same way Brad Pitt's subtle with a fifty-thousand-dollar-a-night hotel room on some Caribbean hideaway.

Laid out and spread into seven rooms, including three bedrooms, the cabin has been constantly upgraded over the years and is now equipped with a big-screen television, leather sofas, overpriced pieces of art on the walls, marble countertops, black and white tiling in both bathrooms and the kitchen, and a hot tub that sits right outside the tinted sliding glass door on the other side of the living room.

I walk over to that same door and sip my drink and look out onto the lake. It's completely lifeless. No one's out at all. In fact the sky is so dark that the only sign of anyone else here is the faded glow coming from the other cabins.

This makes me feel uneasy, and I turn away and move to the couch and try to watch TV, but the clouds and storm are blocking the satellite signal so nothing comes up except a black, empty screen.

Thoughts of Kyle sitting in jail smash through my head. Almost make me sick. And I spend the next hour or so, back in the kitchen, playing solitaire, opening a new bottle of champagne, listening to a Cat Power CD, filling an ashtray.

22

LAURA EMERGES FROM THE BEDROOM IN A PAIR OF ripped jeans and a wife-beater with a silhouette of a girl blowing her head off.

I've just finished off my fourth bottle of champagne and am shitfaced, watching as she looks at the empty bottles, the full ashtray. "Looks like someone's been having a good time," she says.

I roll my eyes.

Really? Who? Who's having a good fucking time?

"Oh god, Travis," she groans. "I'm just trying to be funny."

Right.

I open another pack of cigarettes.

Funny.

Laura slides behind my chair and rubs my shoulders and asks me what I want to do.

I don't know. It's still raining.

She sits down on my lap. "We could watch TV."

I haven't been able to get a signal all night.

"Huh." She kisses me. "We could play some cards."

I've been playing cards since we fucking got here. I'm kinda over it. I don't wanna play cards anymore.

Laura stands up and slides behind my chair, running a hand across the back of my neck. Then she moves to the fridge, pulls out a can of club soda, then grabs the bottle of Johnny Walker Black Label I picked up and makes herself a drink.

"I brought the first season of *Arrested Development* on DVD with me," she tells me.

Let's watch that, I say.

"I also brought a gram of blow with me."

I swing my arm back.

Awesome.

So Laura goes into the bedroom to get the DVD and the coke and I walk into the bathroom to piss. Leaning over the toilet, I wrap my piece in my hands and stare at my reflection in the mirror—the dark bags under my eyes, the stubble on my face, the way my hair is all bunched up from continuously running my hands through it.

Laura's cell phone rings. It's sitting on the sink top next to me, so I pinch off the rest of my pee and look at the caller ID.

It's Cliff.

What's up, dude? I answer.

He doesn't say anything.

Yo, Cliff. Are you there?

"Who is this?" he asks. "You're not Laura, why do you have Laura's phone?"

It's Travis, man. Laura and I are at the cabin.

"What? No. Don't fucking lie to me."

Cliff. What the hell's wrong with you? You sound weird.

"No!" he screams. "You're the one who's weird. Why do you have Laura's phone?"

Are listening to me, Cliff? We're at my parents' cabin.

Pause.

From the other end, I hear a lighter click and the sound of him inhaling something.

Cliff, I bark once more, and he says, "Fuck off, man, whoever this is. Laura didn't go to any cabin with anyone."

He hangs up.

I zip my pants and walk back out to the kitchen and Laura goes, "Did my phone just ring?"

Yeah. It was Cliff.

"Oh," she says very slowly. "What did he want?"

I have no idea. He was wasted and got mad at me for answering your phone.

"Weird," Laura blushes.

I wonder why he called you.

"I have absolutely no idea why he would. . . . It's pretty weird."

I don't know about him right now.

"Then you should forget about him."

I can't. He's really messed up right now. He's fucked himself on heroin. I don't even think he knows what he's doing sometimes.

Laura reaches around my waist and pulls me into her. "Which means you shouldn't believe anything he does or says. Ever."

I really don't.

"Good."

She kisses my cheek and leads me into the living room and I put in the first disc of the first season and sometime into the third episode, and after we've finished the entire gram, Laura goes, "I hung out with David Cross and Janeane Garofalo at a party back in April when I was in Chicago."

How was that? Pretty cool?

"I guess so. They weren't like famous people, ya know? They were real. Not all conceited and stuck-up."

You've been around, haven't you?

"What the fuck is that supposed to mean?" she snaps.

I light a cigarette.

Dating Bryan with a *y*, the so-called King of the Hipsters, and hanging out with David Cross and Janeane. Kicking it backstage at Björk shows. You're like a little social butterfly. A little Paris Hilton.

Laura jumps up from the sofa we're sitting on and goes, "You can be such a dick sometimes, Travis."

Oh, calm down. I'm kidding.

"No, that's bullshit. You're not joking. You said that because you wanted to rip me. You wanted to hurt me."

So what?

Laura chucks her arms into the air, above her head. "So what?"

I was joking again. You're coked out of your mind. Sit down.

She flips her right hand around and gives me the finger.

Yeah, that's real nice.

"Asshole," she snaps, and stomps into the bedroom, slamming the door behind her.

After Laura and I have apologized to each other some hours later and popped some Xanax, we discuss it and we decide that we should fuck, being how it's been since Christmas and all and the fact that she isn't on her period anymore.

It begins next to the dresser and moves quickly to the bed, Laura in a pair of light blue underwear and me in a pair of black sweatpants. The lights are off and the only light we have to guide us is the small sliver of moonlight that's laid itself out nearly perfectly across the room and bed, despite the thunderstorm.

We strip each other down and she bites my neck and bites my chest and I lean over her sweaty body, and slide myself inside of her. She's superwet and moans loudly while I maneuver her arms underneath mine.

"I'm still in love with you," she whispers, digging her nails into my back. "I always have been."

I cover her mouth.

Let's not talk now.

"Okay," she says, closing her eyes. "Whatever you want."

I wrap my hands around her neck.

23.

I GET OUT OF BED THE NEXT MORNING AND STAND IN front of the large mirror attached to the big red oak dresser across the room, thinking about this girl Erin I occasionally hooked up with in Arizona, who asked me this one time, while I was staring at myself in a mirror behind this bar we were at, "Why do you always look at yourself in mirrors? Are you that self-absorbed?"

And I turned to her and went, "I just want to make sure that I'm still here. That's all."

She smiled and kissed me and we never went out again.

I slip on a pair of jeans and white T and walk out to the living room.

This is where Laura is.

She's sitting on the couch, rolling a joint, watching a *Saved by the Bell* rerun, the one where Zach and Screech find an old radio station in the basement of Bayside High and talk Mr. Belding into letting their entire gang broadcast their own shows. Only it turns out that AC Slater isn't much of a radio guy. He's really awful and quits when he finds out that the rest of his so-called friends think so as well. But when the radio station gets pushed to its limits due to a lack of funding, Slater makes one more bold and courageous move and single-handedly saves the Bayside radio station by energizing the dedicated people still listening at one in the morning.

Laura pulls her eyes off of the joint and says, "There's no way Slater could be that good all of the sudden. I mean, he sounded so fucking stupid and bad at the beginning of the show that I almost turned the channel because I was so embarrassed for him."

I sit down next to her.

The whole show really isn't that realistic, sweetie, so to them it makes perfect sense.

"You're probably right," she smiles, handing me the joint along with a pink lighter. "Do the honors," she says.

I light up.

Inhale. Exhale.

I hand her back the joint and ask her what she wants to do.

"I think we should go down to the beach. It's not raining anymore."

Then the beach it is, I say, leaning over and kissing the corner of her mouth.

So Laura and I spend the entire afternoon at the beach, lying around, her in a red and white two-piece suit and me in my black trunks. We drink all the beers from the cooler we packed and eat the sandwiches she made and smoke the other two joints she rolled. A few times, we go into the dark blue water, but even though the sun is out, the water feels too cold to both of us and we stay on the beach after that. We listen to some old tapes I find in the back shed behind the cabin—tapes from years ago:

Guns N' Roses *Lies*
Faith No More *Angel Dust*
Nirvana *Bleach*
Dr. Dre *The Chronic*

The stereo we brought down is very old, though, and the batteries run out, and neither of us wants to walk back to the cabin to grab more, so we let the wind and water and faraway screams and laughter of kids with their families be the soundtrack for the rest of our day.

At some point, when I can't see anyone even remotely near us, I roll over and grab Laura. I run my hands along her sandy thighs. I kiss her. We make love.

An hour later we make love again.

An hour after that we make love once more.

We do this under an extra beach towel. Our warm, dry bodies pressed together. The scent of fresh water, of stale beer on our breath, of suntan lotion flooding our nostrils.

We do this until the clouds roll in, and we end when Laura, who's just finished sliding her bottoms up, checks her cell phone and says, "It's almost five, baby. We need to get moving if we're gonna make it to the restaurant by seven."

Okay. But, Laura.

"What's up?"

I love you.

"I knew it! I love you too. So much. I'm so glad we're back together."

Me too.

This is how the two of us spend the afternoon of the Fourth of July.

24

WHILE LAURA AND I ARE WAITING FOR THE DRINKS WE just ordered with our fake IDs, Laura starts pressing her neck, wincing every time her fingers jab against it.

I light a cigarette and ask her what's wrong. "I think you fucked up my neck while we were having sex earlier," she tells me.

I didn't mean to be so rough. I'm sorry.

"Don't apologize, Travis. It's okay. It was good. I enjoyed it immensely."

Inhale. Exhale.

Laura says, "It's always good to get it a little rough, ya know. That's how you like to screw me. You always have."

I try to smile.

Then Laura goes, "You look a little tense."

I'm just thinking about Kyle. I'm superbummed about it.

I take another drag.

Plus Claire called me the day after it happened and lost it on me and I feel bad about that. Emily and her were pretty close.

"I tried calling her," Laura says. "But she didn't pick up. I don't think she likes me anymore."

Our waitress returns with our drinks—two Bloody Marys—and when she splits, I ask Laura what happened between her and Claire.

Laura lights a cigarette. "Nothing specific," she says. "All of a sudden she was like too cool for me. She started chillin' with new people and not returning calls. We drifted apart. It was bound to happen, I guess."

That sucks.

Laura shrugs. "Whatever."

Our waitress returns again to take our orders, and while we're waiting for our food, starting in our second round of cocktails, these two guys—a little older looking, wearing long Khaki shorts, sandals, and polo shirts—walk over to our table and say hi to Laura.

"Oh," she says, darting her eyes at me, then back to them, then back to me, then back to them. "Hi, Bruce. Hi, Greg."

The Bruce guy leans over. He gives Laura a hug. "Fancy seeing you up here," he says.

Both dudes look at me and Laura goes, "I'm up here with my friend, Travis. We're here for the holiday."

Both of them nod at me and Bruce says, "Hey there, buddy, I mean Travis. Nice to meet you. I've not heard one good thing about you."

His friend starts to laugh. I say, To be completely honest with you, man, there's really not a whole lot of good shit to say about me.

"You're probably right," he snaps back.

"Bruce, don't start," Laura says.

No, no. Don't stop him, Laura. It's fine. Let him keep talking. I don't mind at all. He's pretty funny.

"Shit," Bruce says, looking at his friend. "I told you I was funny."

"This guy doesn't know shit," his friend says, pointing at me.

Laura squeezes her forehead. "Come on, guys."

"What?" asks Greg.

But Bruce goes, "No, you're right, Laura. We'll leave you two alone now." He turns to me. "Nice meeting you, Travis."

Pleasure was all mine, boys.

Bruce hugs Laura again. He says, "We'll see you back in the city."

"Okay," she whispers. "Bye."

They walk out a side door that says EXIT above it.

I slam the rest of my drink, and stand up.

I'll be right back.

"Where are you going?" Laura asks.

To the bathroom.

"I'm sorry about that," she says, reaching for me as I walk past her.

I knock her hand away.

Don't be.

In the bathroom, I splash water on my face repeatedly. My body shakes. It feels like I just got punched in the gut, but I'm not as mad as much as I am scared.

I need Laura. I need this to happen.

Inhale. Exhale.

I dry my face off and walk back to the table and sit down.

"Travis," Laura says, "nothing ever happened between me and those two guys. I know them from work. They come in—"

Laura.

I cut her off.

I'm not mad. I don't care about them. I just need this to be real. I need something I can hold on to right now. I don't care about anything else.

"Okay," she says.

I trust you.

"You do?"

Yes.

Laura leans forward and her mouth opens like she's about ready to say something but nothing comes out. She just nods and smiles instead, her lips pressed together hard.

And from the restaurant, Laura and I drive to the town's park and watch the fireworks display from the infield of a small baseball diamond. We split a pint of Jim Beam and we make out. And when the red, white, and blue explosions in the sky have finally concluded, we walk to my car, hand in hand, and drive back to the cabin with the windows rolled down, listening to an old Beehive and the Barracudas CD.

"Do you remember when we drove to Minneapolis and saw them play?" she asks me.

Of course I do.

"That was one of the best nights of my life, Travis. I'm serious. I've had the best times with you. I missed you so much while you were gone," she says before throwing her arms around me and letting out this little high-pitched scream. Biting my neck, she says, "Goddamn, I missed you."

Back at the cabin, Laura rolls a joint and I make mimosas, and when I hand her one of the glasses, she looks at the joint, then looks back at the drink, and goes, "The mimosa, now this is a real gateway drug."

We smoke and we drink and we watch the rest of the *Arrested Development* episodes.

And after almost all the booze I picked up the night before has been drunk or accidentally knocked over and spilt, the two of us are back in the bedroom, fucking and clawing and choking each other. And when I've finished coming all over Laura's stomach and chest, and when she's through cleaning herself up—shower, mouthwash, that sorta thing—the two of us lie in bed and listen to the Vincent Gallo CD *When*.

It feels nice to have her body pressed up against mine the way it is. To feel her breath blowing gently against my neck. To hear the light breeze outside blowing and the sound of Gallo singing. . . .

"Let's find a place, a happy place . . ."

And for a moment it feels about perfect, and then Laura digs her elbow deep into the mattress, propping her face against the palm of her hand, and she asks me if people who mess up, like fuck up really big-time, she asks me, "Do you think people like that deserve a second chance?"

I roll onto my back and I think about this.

Yes.

"Even if it's something terrible? Something that could really hurt another person?"

I rub my eyes and sit up.

Everyone deserves a second chance, Laura, no matter what they may or may not have done.

Pause.

Why?

"No reason," she moans, dropping her arm, falling back on the pillows underneath her. "It was just a question."

Bullshit.

I flip on my side.

Nobody asks something like that for no reason. Especially no one that I know.

Laura lets out this huge sigh. She pushes herself to her knees. "I wish . . . I just wish . . ." She stops and rubs her forehead.

You wish what, Laura?

Crawling on top of me, she snorts, "I fucking wish I would've known what the hell you were thinking, what you were fucking doing during those months we didn't talk at all. That's what I fucking wish, because maybe then if I'd known what I'd done to drive you away . . ." She stops, covers her face with her hands.

Then what, Laura?

Her hands part. "I would've made better decisions and things wouldn't be the way they've been," she snaps, pounding her hands into my chest.

She jumps out of bed and I sit up and I ask her, What sort of bad decisions did you make?

Slipping on a pair of shorts and a white Pound Puppies T-shirt, Laura goes, "I did some stupid things—things I wouldn't have done if I'd known what was going on between the two of us."

Like fucking other people? Those kind of things?

Laura sighs. "All kinds of things, Travis. Because I just didn't know anything. You left me in the dark, baby. I didn't know." Laura covers her face and she begins to cry. "Why did you leave me?" she sobs. "Why couldn't you have told me what I did wrong so I could've fixed it?"

I lie back down and stare at the ceiling. I'm at a loss for words at the moment. I'm surprised by Laura's sudden outburst. And this is when it all hits me. Everything. Hitting me like a big sack of shit. I need to tell Laura everything, right here and now.

I need to tell her about Hawaii and what happened and how scared I got and how I didn't know what to do because I wasn't sure I'd even done anything wrong.

So I grab her hand and I go, I need to tell you something.

"Travis, you don't have—"

No. You need to hear this.

"Fine," she says, done crying. "What is it you have to tell me?"

After Christmas, when I was in—

But I get cut off abruptly by that eighties band the Bangles.

It's Laura's cell phone and it's blowing up, and she has one of those ring tones that's the tune of a song. And the song she's assigned to whoever's calling her is the Bangles song "Walk Like an Egyptian."

"If they move too quick ... (oh-way-oh) ... they're falling down like a domino. ..."

Laura pulls her hand away and walks over to her purse and pulls her phone out. "I have to take this," she tells me.

You do?

"Yes."

And like a second later, Laura's freaking out, going, "No fucking way! You bad girl! I cannot believe you did that! You dirty little slut! Ohmigod!"

So much for my big, bold moment of anything.

I reach down to the floor and grab the *VICE* I brought with us and fall back on the bed and start flipping through the pages, landing on a CD review of this Oakland band, the Lovemakers, who have this totally hot girl for a singer.

Laura hangs up the phone.

She knocks the magazine out of my hands and goes, "Holy shit. I need a cigarette after hearing that."

Annoyed, I ask her, What? What's so big of a deal?

Lighting a smoke, then bumming me one, Laura says, "Do you remember Michelle Thomas from high school? She was in our grade. She's Puerto Rican."

What about her? I didn't know you guys ever hung out.

"We didn't," Laura snorts, "until she started working at the Waterfront a few months ago with me."

I take a drag.

So what, you're like best friends now or something?

"Not exactly. But we've been hanging out some," Laura answers, flicking some ashes into an empty Heineken bottle. "Actually we've been hanging out quite a bit. We went and saw the Yeah Yeah Yeahs in Minneapolis back in May and we also saw Cat Power play at Gabe's in Iowa City."

So what's the big deal, Laura?

Laura takes a drag. "She slept with one of our old teachers from high school tonight."

Which one?

Hysterically, Laura's like, "Mr. Hodge."

What did Mr. Hodge teach?

"American History, Travis. Like Paul Revere and the fucking Indians," she snaps, obviously annoyed.

Is he old?

"He's gotta be in his late forties," she shrieks. "Ohmigod!"

I take another drag and I shake my head but I'm really not that surprised.

And Laura says, "I can't believe this," right as I'm trying to get a visual of Michelle taking it from Mr. Hodge, but it doesn't work because I can't remember what Mr. Hodge looks like.

"And you wanna know the funniest thing?" Laura asks.

What's the funniest thing, Laura?

"The funniest thing about it is that Michelle told me it was in the backseat of her Volkswagen, which was parked behind Bottoms Up bar. That little slut," she smiles.

And I take a huge drag, wondering what exactly Mrs. Hodge may have done, but this thought ends abruptly when Laura wraps a hand around my arm and says, "Oh, I'm sorry. You were about to tell me something before Michelle called."

A big lump forms in my throat.

It wasn't important.

"Are you sure?"

I'm sure. It was nothing—especially compared to Michelle Thomas sleeping with one of our old high school teachers.

Laura smiles.

Totally not important.

Let's find a place, a happy place . . .

25

ON THE SECOND-TO-LAST NIGHT OF MY TRIP, BORED OUT of my fucking mind, I decided to call the number of the connect that the New York dudes had given me.

I met the guy outside of this record store and scored two grams of coke, then went back to my hotel room. My plan was to do one gram that night and go out and hit some bars and save the second gram for my last night, but of course that didn't happen. Things never go the way you plan them when you're on cocaine. That's not the way this shit works.

What ended up happening is that I got back to my room and cut up four huge fucking croc lines and blasted them one right after the other—BAM—BAM—BAM—fucking BAM—and got so tweaked out of my mind that I couldn't possibly leave my room. I was way too paranoid, and when you're that paranoid and blazed only on blow, you end up trying to act normal, which makes it that much more fucking obvious to the people around you that you're fucked out of your brain. And I ended up staying in my room instead and did both grams and listened to the first 400 Blows album sixteen times in a row (it was that good) and made phone calls to people I hadn't talked to in years. There were even a few hours where I flipped through the pages of the escort listings. I made calls. Asked for prices. Said I would call back.

But I never did. What I did do was stand in front of a mirror next to my bed and got undressed and jacked off, imagining the gnarliest scenarios possible, scenarios full of young chicks and ropes and bruises and crying.

A couple of times I picked up a notebook and wrote down these plans for my life. What I'm really gonna do. What I'm really into. Plans like these seem so righteous and amazing at the time 'cause you're so fucked up, only to realize later, during those boring, sober moments, that none of it is an option and there isn't any sort of way that shit will happen.

So I closed my notebook and restarted the Blows album and cut some more lines and ended up downing like five Xanax to pass out so I wouldn't have to see the sun come up.

Travis Wayne

26.

AFTER I DROP LAURA OFF AT HER PARENTS' HOUSE THE next afternoon, I drive to see Claire. I park my car near her pad and start walking and it's hot. I'm having a hard time breathing.

The front gate to her stairs has been left unlocked and I push it open and walk up and knock on the door.

Her roommate, Skylar, opens up wearing a black skirt, a black blouse, and black heels. "How'd you get up here?" she asks.

The gate was wide open.

She looks past me, down the stairs. "Shit."

I probably should've rung the buzzer anyway.

"Don't worry about it," she says. "You here to see Claire?"

I nod.

"Come in," she says, stepping back and letting me in. "She's in her room. She might be sleeping. We just got back from Emily's funeral."

Oh. How was it?

Skylar stops dead in her tracks. "It was a funeral, dude. That's how it was."

I'm sorry.

"Don't worry about it."

I follow Skylar down a small hallway to Claire's bedroom. The door is closed, so Skylar knocks and Claire goes, "What is it?"

"You have a visitor, sweetheart."

"Who?"

Skylar turns to me. "What's your name?"

Travis.

"Travis," she yells.

"Just a minute," Claire says. A minute comes, a minute goes.

"She's had a long day," Skylar tells me. "Claire!" she shouts, much louder this time.

"Okay, you can come in," she groans back.

I tell Skylar thanks and open the door and slide into Claire's bedroom, the sound of the Jesus and Mary Chain coming faintly from a CD player somewhere.

Huge piles of clothes sit everywhere. A fucking mountain of shoes, mostly heels, has transplanted itself smack-dab in the middle of the hardwood floor. Like seven pounds of accessories litter the areas around her bed not already littered by books and *VICE* magazines and drawings.

"Sorry about the mess. It's not always like this," says Claire, who's laid out across her bed with a glass of wine in her hands, still somewhat stuffed into a black dress. Smiling, she scooches herself up the headboard. "You look warm, Travis."

I sit down next to her.

So do you.

"I'm fucking hot," she says, running her fingers down the side of my arm. "It was like a hundred degrees during the funeral. I felt so bad. Two old women fainted during it and one of them had to be taken away in an ambulance."

Jesus.

"It was awful," Claire stresses.

How are you feeling?

She takes a sip of wine. "I'm doing better now. Emily's little brother Jake gave me a couple of Xanax at the reception afterward. He told me he gets them from this old guy in Waterloo who sells his prescription drugs to pay his bills."

Whatever you have to do, right?

Claire nods, half-smiling. "Right." She reaches across my body to the edge of her Kleenex-covered nightstand and grabs a pack of cigarettes and an ashtray. "You want one?" she asks, opening the top of her pack.

Sure.

"You want a glass of wine also?"

I shake my head.

Claire lights a cig then hands it to me, then lights her own. She goes, "Did you go somewhere a few days ago?"

I went to the cabin with Laura.

Claire rolls her eyes. "Oh."

She said she tried calling you but you never returned her call.

"A lot of people tried calling me."

I take a drag.

Have you thought about Kyle at all?

"Dude," Claire shrieks. "Don't start with that shit. I'm not in the mood. I just saw the person he fucking killed get buried this morning."

I roll my eyes.

"If you really want to help me, just lie with me and listen to music with me." She drops her smoke to the bottom of the glass then picks up a remote for her stereo and changes the Jesus Mary and Chain to Blonde Redhead.

Patting the pillow next to her, she says, "Lie," then scoots over so I can snuggle in next to her.

Claire wraps an arm around me and buries her face into my chest. Like two songs later, she flips her eyes at me and goes, "Do you think I'm a good person, Travis?"

I think you're fucking rad, Claire. Maybe the best person I know.

"But why do you think that?"

Because you give a shit. Your dad bails on you and your mom when you're like three. Then your mom gets arrested a bunch of times for shoplifting and you end up bailing her out of jail every single time with your own money from working. You've had a fucking job since you were thirteen. I mean, shit, you just made the dean's list. . . . You're Claire, ya know, that's all anyone has to say.

She squeezes me. "Thank you for that," she says.

I light another cigarette from her pack and then she yawns and says, "Tell me a funny story, Travis. I wanna hear something funny."

You're gonna put me on the spot like that, huh?

"Yep." She burrows her face deeper into me.

I look up at the ceiling and notice all these tiny white stars sticking to it that probably glow in the dark.

"Anything," Claire yawns. "Just as long as it's amazing and funny."

I think hard. So many stories start pounding through my skull. I could tell her a million but I want it to be right. I want to take her mind off of Emily. It's the fucking least I could do.

So I say:

When I was fifteen, I went to visit my cousin Eric out in San Francisco for a long weekend. He had apartment on Haight Street, and one night while we were hanging out, this guy he knew from some odd job, maybe even community service, stopped by to pick up some CDs that he'd loaned my cousin.

The guy's name was Buttrock Steve, and he had long, gross red hair and was wearing these really tight stone-washed Bugle Boy jeans, and a Nelson T-shirt, and he was like twenty-nine and had a way bad lisp. Anyway, he stayed and chatted for a while and my cousin mentioned that he was trying to put a band together but that his amp was shot, and Buttrock Steve was like, "Dude, I have two really good amps at my mom's house up north in Happy Camp. If you wanna ride up there with me and pick them up, they're yours for a hundred each." And my cousin was like, "If you're serious, we'll ride up there with you right now. Tonight." And Buttrock Steve was serious. So the three of us left in his minivan. It took us like six hours to get there and his van broke down once. His mom lived in a shack out in the middle of the sticks and we rolled in there at like four in the morning and Buttrock's mom was sitting in a chair in front of the television, sleeping, and Steve was like, "That's my mom, and that's my cat and that's where my room is." My cousin and I spent the night in the van, and the next day we loaded up the amps, but before we left town, Buttrock stopped at his friend Eugene's house. Eugene was out back with some friends, sitting around a fire pit boozin', and we ended up sticking around there for way too long and had to spend the night again because we were wasted. Some girls came over to Eugene's later that night and they were all fucking haggard, and at one point, while I was pissing, I saw Buttrock Steve making out with this really chubby blonde with glasses, wearing black leotard bottoms and a purple shirt with a unicorn on it.

After he pulled his lips away, he was like, "If you're not busy sometime, maybe we could get together and hang out and rent some Kevin Costner movies. Maybe *Waterworld*, *The Upside of Anger*, maybe even *The Postman*. We'll get some popcorn and some Junior Mints and maybe some Diet Coke. It'll be really fun."

And the chubby girl got really stoked and smiled and she was like, "*The Bodyguard* is my favorite," and Buttrock was like, "Yeah, it's one of mine, too." And then they started kissing again and he cupped her left breast and kept trying to go up her shirt with his other hand, but she kept stopping him because she wasn't ready to go there with him yet.

And the next day, on the way back to San Francisco, I called him out on it and he tried to deny it at first, but ended up admitting it, and then he was like, "I slept with a tranny on Polk Street once, too." Then he started crying and talking about driving the van off the road into a ditch, so my cousin gave him two hundred dollars cash, right out of his wallet, so he wouldn't do it. And then he dropped us back off at Eric's pad and Eric let him crash there, and the next day Buttrock took a shower, and when he was through, he knocked on my cousin's room door and was like, "Do you have a hair dryer?" And my cousin was like, "No." And Buttrock went, "Really?" And Eric went, "You need to leave, Steve."

And he did.

Claire is laughing hysterically. "That's so awesome," she cries, wiping her eyes with the back of her hand. "Thank you so much for that."

You're welcome, I tell her, petting the soft skin of her arm as gently as I can, and not five minutes later she's asleep and I smoke a few more cigarettes and listen to a few more songs before bailing from her pad.

27

I'M SITTING AT A METAL TABLE THAT'S BEEN BOLTED TO the white tiled floor watching Kyle as he emerges from a small doorway, stuffed into an orange jumpsuit.

I close my eyes and breathe in deeply, but the smell of ammonia and peroxide blaze the walls of my nostrils and make me nauseous. I exhale quickly and pull my eyelids apart.

It hurts.

The hard fluorescent lights stab my pupils. I blink wildly. Everything slowly falls back into place. My eyes are back on Kyle. Glued to him as he shuffles toward me with his head bowed and his arms hanging loose and apart, put back together where his hands meet, one palm pressed tightly against the other.

My heart slams against my ribs. A cool tingle runs down my back. My mouth gets dry.

Kyle pulls the chair out from the other side of the table and drops himself into it.

I squeeze my own hands together as tightly as I can.

Hi.

"Hi." Kyle cocks one eye at me. "I was wondering if you were ever going to show up."

Well, I've, um, been—

I cut myself off though. It wouldn't be fair at all to start lying. Considering the circumstances, the two of us should be well beyond that.

I say sorry instead.

"Sorry is the last thing anyone should feel for me." He snaps his head back and runs his scraped and scratched hands over his scraped and scratched face, through whatever's left of his hair. Pushing an enormous breath out, he flips his head at me and asks me if I'm nervous.

Yes.

"Me too."

Pause.

He drops his hands against the tabletop and squares his body perfectly in front of mine. "Every day," Kyle says, "I wake up and I feel nothing but guilt and nerves. I'm really scared, Travis."

Along with the two of us, there are exactly sixteen other people in the visiting room. Six of them are other inmates, all of them in the same jumpsuit, sitting with the same pose, but all of them are at least twice the age of Kyle.

So what's the situation?

Kyle shakes his head slowly. "I have another court date next week. It's just some proceeding. It doesn't even matter. There's nothing I can do at this point anyway."

You could go to trial.

"For what, Trav? I did it. I killed my girlfriend. I killed two kids. My fucking car was in the side of the house. I deserve this shit."

Don't say that. You could go to trial and tell them—

Again, I cut myself off. Kyle is glaring at me.

I'm sorry, man.

"Don't be," he groans. "You're not the first person that's come to visit and tried to tell me how I could get out of this—how if I just do this and that then this whole thing will go away." He runs a finger across the purple and blue bridge of his nose. "I always hated that shit when we were growing up."

What shit?

"You know, like when we'd be at some party in high school and the cops would bust it and all those kids would be sucking on pennies because someone told them how their older brother said that copper neutralizes the alcohol on a breathalyzer."

Pause.

I shrug.

And Kyle goes, "Or when someone would get a ticket and another kid would tell them that he had a friend who had the exact same thing happen to them, but got out of it because they decided to fight it, and found some strange loophole in the law that no one's ever found before."

I know what you're saying, man. Everyone's got a friend who's got a friend who's done something gnarlier than you, more fucked up than you, and beat the rap.

Kyle nods, scrunches his lips together, says, "And the thing is, the only person I know who has ever gotten off of anything because of a technicality is Michael."

Michael?

"Yeah," he snorts. "Don't you remember senior year? When he got picked up leaving Bottoms Up bar?"

I'm not sure I do.

"The cops pulled him over like a block after he started driving, and during the first sobriety test, I guess he gave up and went, 'Okay, you got me,' so they took him in and booked him. But while he was being released the next morning, they gave him the ticket to sign and instead of signing his name, he signed it 'I'm in jail' and no one even noticed until his lawyer brought it up and that's how he got out of it."

Huh? Maybe I remember.

Pause.

A little bit.

Kyle exhales. "I guess I'm the last person who should be talking lightly about driving around all loaded."

I lean back in my chair and crane my neck around a few times over.

"Are you all right, Trav?"

I'm cool.

Leaning forward, digging my arms against the table, I stare at Kyle, this kid I've known since second grade.

"What?" he asks.

This is probably gonna sound all sick and stuff, but I wouldn't ask if I didn't wanna know.

"Ask what?"

Huge beads of sweat form along my hairline and I wipe them away.

What was the accident like?

Kyle buries his face into the palm of his left hand.

Seconds pass.

I can actually see his chest thumping up and down.

You don't have to tell me, Kyle. It won't make a difference anyway. Sometimes not telling people anything is a good thing.

Kyle slowly lifts his head. His face is full of tears.

I say, If no one else knows what happened, at least you have a chance to get past it.

"But I don't really know what happened," he says.

Really?

"No," he sniffs. "Me and Emily had been out partying all fucking day. Bloody Marys that morning at Casanova's. Doing bumps. We scooped up a pair of Bronx tickets and went out for more drinks."

Kyle stops. He presses his lips together and looks into the light above us.

Me, I almost say, *Hey man, I thought we were all supposed to go to the Bronx show together.*

But I don't.

Thank fucking god I don't.

I catch myself and run my hands through my hair and lean back again.

What's the last thing you remember?

"We were at this weird party one of my customers was at. Steve Albini was supposedly there or supposed to be coming and I guess some of the dudes from the Shins were already there, or on their way there. Anyway, I was on the roof selling to this chick and she was telling me how she'd once walked in on her older brother fucking a blow-up doll, trying to get off as fast as he could because he'd punctured a hole in it and the doll was deflating."

Kyle stops and jams his fingers into his forehead.

That's it?

"No," he says. "Then I was running. It was daylight. And blood was gushing from my forehead. I had no idea what was going on."

Pause.

"So I just kept running."

Damn.

I choke down the huge lump in my throat.

"Then," Kyle blurts, sucking back the saliva rolling out of his mouth. "Then they told me about Emily." He turns his head to the side. His whole body starts to shake. "They told me what happened to her. How I took her life, and one of the detectives even showed me a picture of her dead body all tangled up in the frame."

Kyle chokes back more tears and more spit. The veins in his neck bulge.

He says, "Then they started in about the two kids I ran over inside the house."

Pause.

"Oh fuck, man," he sobs. "And the next day in court, they charged me with all kinds of shit, and now . . ." His voice drifts away for a moment. He wipes his face with his arm.

"And now the only thing left for me to do is plead guilty and that's it. That's my life. Gone."

A moving picture of Kyle jumping some stairs on his skateboard for the first time smashes through my head.

And I hate this. I hate being here. I hate sitting in a jail. I hate myself for coming to a jail.

For everything I've done.

Listen, Kyle, I blurt out. I have to go. I have to meet some people.

Kyle shakes his head and looks back down at the table.

I forgot, I tell him.

"It's fine," he snaps.

I really did forget, Kyle. I have things to do.

Kyle swings his eyes on me again. "It's okay, Trav. Don't be sorry. I know you. I know how you are. You don't have to explain anything. You've always been like this."

I say nothing and Kyle stands up. He turns and walks back through the door he'd just walked out of.

I leave the jail shaking. I'm standing in the parking lot under the blazing sun and it's like I'm covered in this thick blanket with no air. I bend over and I start heaving. Nothing comes out but black colored spit. My armpits are soaked.

Crawling into my car, I crank it on and blast the air conditioner and light a cigarette.

I don't know what to do. I'm absolutely hopeless. I need someone to be with me but I don't want to be around anyone.

I call Laura.

"I'm going into work, Travis. What do you want?"

I need to see you. When can I see you?

"I'm closing. I'll call you when I'm done."

Tell them you're sick and you have to go home.

"No. I can't do that. I need the money."

No you don't.

"Yes I do."

I'll fucking pay you.

"Travis, stop. We can talk later tonight."

She hangs up.

I have nowhere else to go but home.

This is how I felt at the end in Arizona.

No one is home when I get there. I need to do something with myself. Fuck someone or work out.

I try jacking off to this gnarly Nicole Sheridan porno but I have trouble getting hard. My mind is too busy. I'm sitting in front of a computer screen with my pants around my knees, pounding my limp dick. My face is bright red.

Nothing is working.

I look down at my lap and get depressed. My dick looks like some burnt red hot dog that fell out of its bun as it lies idly against the top of my thigh.

I sigh and take a break. Walk into the basement bathroom and find a bottle of Vaseline and walk back to the computer and try something else.

I go for a celebrity. I type in the name Evan Rachel Wood on a Google search and this page pops up with a whole shitload of her photos on it. I double click on one of her in a pair of garter panties, a bikini top, and a pair of black leather boots that run all the way up to her thighs.

The photo triples in size and I squeeze a ton of lotion straight onto my penis and start going at it again.

I jerk harder and harder and harder but I cannot get a boner. Nasty thoughts begin to pound through my skull and I have to stop because it's so gross. Really fucking gross. Chucky Manson gross.

Fuck this!

I put the lotion back and wash my hands and change into a pair of shorts and run outside and do a hundred crunches and fifty push-ups, and then I start doing laps. Somewhere after seventy, I lose count, and when I can barely lift my arms above the water, I drag myself out and lie down on the gray cement with my eyes closed.

I listen to the world and I don't hear anything. No birds chirping. No wind. Nothing like that.

I open my eyes.

My body is dry from the heat.

The sun is dropping fast.

I feel much better and go inside the house, and see my sister. She's sitting at the dining room table, her head between her hands.

What's wrong, Vanessa?

I must scare her because she jumps. "Huh?" she goes.

My sister looks sick. She looks thinner than she did a week ago and has these intense, dark colored patches under her eyes and brownish scratches on her neck.

Are you okay, Vanessa?

She grins. "I'm fine, dude. I've just had a rough couple of nights."

Maybe you should lay off the partying for awhile.

"Maybe you should stay the fuck out of my life, man."

I'm just saying, is all.

"Well don't," my sister snaps. She jumps to her feet and blows past me, outside, then pulls her cell phone from her jeans and lights a cigarette.

I could try to do something but I don't even know what to do with myself. I go upstairs. Take a long shower. And listen to every live Modest Mouse CD they ever put out, listening until Laura comes over.

She lies with me in my room and I tell her about visiting Kyle and she listens to everything without saying a word. And when I'm through, she undresses for me and tells me everything will be all right, and then we make love, but even though it feels awesome to be back with her, to have her next to me silhouetted by the stars, there is still a certain emptiness here, and something still feels a little bit off.

28

MY FATHER CALLS ME AT THE HOUSE WHILE I'M WATCHING this old videotape full of Guns N' Roses live footage and music videos that I stole from my coke dealer in Arizona. He tells me to meet him for lunch at the Golden Buddha, this Chinese restaurant not far from Harper's Square.

Fine.

"Be there."

I will.

"You better."

I will.

A half hour later I'm driving to the restaurant blasting the Coachwhips album *Bangers vs. Fuckers*.

Circling endlessly around one downtown block after another, I can't find a single goddamn parking spot. I end up flipping a nut in front of some tour bus crammed with old people and park in the garage I passed two blocks ago.

Five minutes later, I'm being seated across from my father, who is wearing a light blue buttoned Versace top with a white collar and white wrist cuffs, and a pair of dark blue Versace slacks.

I sit down and watch my father look at his watch instead of me. "You're twenty minutes late," he says.

That's how long it took me to find parking.

He turns his eyes at me. "Why didn't you park at the office and walk down?"

I don't know.

"It would've saved us both some time."

I didn't think about it.

"Obviously," my father rips, picking up his glass of scotch. He takes a huge swig from it. "Do you even think about what you say anymore before you say it?"

Sometimes I do, Dad.

I pick up the menu sitting in front of me, and our waitress, a very pretty Asian girl who looks about my age, comes over and asks me if I want anything to drink.

I'll have a Budweiser.

My father shakes the ice around his otherwise empty glass. "I'll have another scotch."

The waitress smiles and tells us she'll be back and I set the menu down after deciding on the sweet-and-sour chicken.

My father loosens his tie. "I must say, Travis, you are looking better," he tells me.

How's that?

"Well, you're not nearly as pale as you were when you first came back. Your face looks healthier, and it looks like you've put on some good weight."

Pause.

My father saying these things makes me very uncomfortable. Maybe it's the fact that I never knew he was paying that much attention to me, or maybe it's the fact that he is paying that much attention to me. Either way, I don't know how to respond. I don't know what to say. So I say nothing.

He grabs his empty glass again and twists his body in the direction the waitress walked and I slide a pack of Parliament Lights from the front pocket of my faded Levi's and light one up.

Twisting back around about halfway through my smoke, my father asks me something that I don't understand at first. It almost sounds like he's asking me about a crack pipe.

What?

"Your friend," he says. "What's his name? You know, the one who slammed his car into a house and killed all those people."

Kyle.

"What?" my father snorts.

His name is Kyle, Dad.

He's slept over at our house at least fifteen times. He's gone out to eat with us at least twenty times. You've dropped him off at his dad's at least ten times. You've told him how good of a kid he is at least thirty times.

None of this I say to my father.

I flick some ashes and take another drag.

"Well," my father nods. "What's the word?"

Word?

"Yeah," he says. "The word. The latest update?"

I set my elbows on the edge of the table and glare as hard as I can at my father because I know he doesn't care.

He's fucked, man.

"Jesus, Travis."

What? You asked.

"Well use some fucking tact next time," my father snaps, dropping the knife he'd been fingering back onto the table.

I take another drag.

Sorry.

Our waitress comes back with our drinks. "Here you two are," she grins. My father and I both say thanks and then she takes down our orders and disappears.

"She's a fox," I think I hear my father say under his breath. Then: "So, Kyle?"

What about him?

"It's a shame, Travis. Don't you think?" he suggests, putting the scotch to his lips.

Probably more of a waste, dude.

"Dude?" My father's eyebrows rise.

Dad.

My father takes another pull. "Well I'm just glad that you weren't—"

Dad.

"Huh?"

I stub my smoke out.

I don't want to talk about this with you.

My father shifts nervously in his seat. "What would you like to talk about?" he snaps.

Nothing.

"Nothing?"

Nothing.

I take a drink of beer.

I'm not into it.

"I see," he says, rolling his eyes, shaking his head. "What exactly are you into, Travis?" he asks.

But I don't get a chance to even answer him because his cell phone starts ringing, and after he checks the caller ID, he glances at me and says, "I have to take this."

He tells me that it's important.

My father says that this call, this very one, "is the only thing I want to think about right now."

That's pretty cool, Dad.

I finish my beer and have another smoke and then our food gets served along with two more drinks, and about halfway through my dish, my father gets off the phone and says, "Sorry about that."

It's fine.

I look across the room and watch this family of three— two parents and their daughter—being seated by the same man who seated me. The daughter is wearing this pink layered skirt from Miss Sixty. She has a Dior bag clutched between her hands. And she looks exactly like the girl I saw in the last restaurant I met my father at for lunch. My hands start shaking and I close my eyes, and when I open them again, the only thing I see is my father taking a drink from his scotch.

"So anyway," he starts, "there were a couple of things I wanted to go over with you."

What did you say?

"Are you listening to me, son?"

Yes.

"You look pale now."

I'm fine.

My father quickly checks his watch. He says, "At the end of the month I'm going to be honored at an international business conference right here in the city."

Awesome.

"Yeah, son. Awesome. Thanks," he snorts, lifting a forkful of kung pao chicken to his mouth. Still chewing and talking, he continues, "Anyway, I need you to be there. It's a black-tie event, so you're going to have to get fitted for a tux."

I take a huge bite of chicken and feel a line of sweet-and-sour sauce dribble down my chin.

All right.

I reach for my napkin but it's all crumpled up into a small ball with brown stuff all over it, so I wipe my face with my hand, then my hand against my jeans.

"Nice, son," my father says.

I take a drink of beer.

"I also need you to make sure your sister is going to be on her best behavior."

What do you mean?

"Come on, Travis. I don't know what she's mixed up in, but she looks like shit. Your mother told me that her mood swings are out of control."

So do something.

"No. My daughter's better than this. Her pride and genes will eventually kick in and she'll straighten up and get her shit together."

Pause.

"Same as you."

I eat another piece of chicken.

And my father goes, "On that note, school."

What about it?

His shoulders bunch up. "Have you been giving it any thought?"

Here and there.

"For Christ's sake, Travis. School is not optional. If you want to be anything in life, you're going to have to finish college and work at it."

I don't say anything.

"I've talked with the USC people. All you have to do is apply and you're in. You'll have a fresh start. You'll be third generation, son."

I don't want to go there.

"What the hell is wrong with you? Where did my son go?"

I'm right here.

"No," he snaps. "I don't think you are. I don't think you get it yet." He slams the rest of his drink and leans across the table. He says, "You're gonna take a little ride with me when we're finished."

But—

"No fucking 'but's', son. You need to get some things straight in your head."

□ □ □

I have no idea where my father is about to take me as he balls out of his parking spot with all the windows rolled down on his Mercedes.

The things I do know are that one, I do not want to go with him; two, he's totally drunk; and three, he told the host dude in the front lobby to eat his ass.

Slamming his car through one alley and then another, my father goes, "Travis, take the CD case in the glove compartment out."

I open the compartment and pull it out.

"Find Phil Collins's greatest hits and put it in," he orders as we shoot out of the second alley.

I find it. Slide it in. And my father slams on the brakes for a red light.

"Look at all of this," he grunts, over the blare of the song "Another Day in Paradise." He points at the windshield, toward a block of sprawling metallic sculptures sprouting from fake green lawns in the front of glass cased buildings. "Just take a good look at what you are now a part of, Travis. What people are doing with their lives now. Look at the opportunities people have because of a few select visions."

My father hangs a left two blocks later and puts on a pair of shades. "This is it, son. The future of this state. Your future, if you just do what I ask of you and listen to me and quit fighting me."

I roll my eyes. It all seems so fixed.

I'm not fighting you, Dad. I'm fighting myself.

My father does not hear me say this. To be honest, though, I'm not even sure if I said it out loud.

My father holds his arms out. "Look at the masterpiece I've created. I've given people a purpose. This is what counts, Travis. Making other people happy so that you can be happy. All of this," he says, flipping his shades down, "is a reminder that you have to take things seriously to get anything done in life." He nudges me with his elbow. "This is what I see when I drive through this part of the city." My father flips his shades back up. He cranks the stereo volume and bolts through the traffic, jumping onto an exit that takes us out of the city.

Where are we going?

"You'll see," he smirks as we blaze by bright green fields caged in by barbwire fences.

A few miles later we're turning off the highway and onto this gravel road that we follow until it spills into a huge pasture, pierced in the middle with a large billboardesque sign that says WAYNE REALTY on it.

My father brings the car to a stop and steps out holding a brown sack in his hands. "Come on," he says.

I get out and follow him.

"This is why I asked you to lunch today, Travis."

What is this?

"The new superheadquarters for Wayne Realty," he grins. "Fifteen wide-open acres of whatever-the-fuck-I-want-to-do-with-it property, all tax free, approved by the same friends I got elected to the city council." He turns to me. "What do you think?"

It's pretty nice.

I light my second-to-last cigarette.

"That's it?" my father snorts. "Nice?"

I like the sign, Dad.

"Jesus, Travis! Have you listened to a word I've said to you today? This is all yours if you just do what I tell you to do. You'll never have to do shit work like I had to."

But—

"But nothing," my father snorts. He charges at me, stopping a couple of inches in front of my face. "Here's what I think."

What?

My father grabs the collar of my shirt and balls it into a fist. "I think you're going to get your shit together starting right now, right here, today." His jaw clenches tight. "I don't know what happened to you in Arizona or Hawaii and at this point I don't give a shit."

Crap. My cigarette falls from between my fingers.

Inching so close to me that I can see the food stuck in his teeth and smell the scotch and chicken on his breath, my father goes, "You will be in school in August. If you don't want to go to USC, fine! But you will have at least applied to three schools by the end of next week, and if you haven't, then shit is going to start disappearing from you. The car. Money. Your CDs. Your DVDs. Anything I think might be important to you. Are we clear?" he asks, eight lines of his spit nailing my face, some even hitting my lips.

Yes.

"And just so you know that I mean business," he says, reaching into the sack, "watch this." My father pulls all five of my Nirvana CDs out of the sack.

What are you doing?

"Motivating you, son," he barks, then snaps each CD in half, dropping them on the ground.

You didn't have to do that, Dad. Shit.

"You didn't leave me any choice, Travis." Wiping some sweat off his face, my father says, "I have a meeting in Vanguard, which is that way." My father points away from the city. "And I'm already running late because you don't know how to park a fucking car."

You're not taking me back to my car? I ask.

"*My* car," he says. "And no, I'm not."

So what am I supposed to do?

"Improvise. Make it happen for yourself," my father laughs. Then he jumps into his car and tears back down the gravel road and leaves me wiping the dust out of my eyes.

Pilgrim dick.

I stand there, squinting into the sun, waiting for something. Maybe he's just joking and he'll come back and take me home.

Maybe, maybe, maybe not.

I dig into my pockets and pull my cell phone out and scroll down to Laura's name. The sun is torching my skin. I hit the call button and it starts ringing and it rings until Laura's voice mail comes on. I don't even bother to leave a message. I hang up and then I call Michael and Michael picks up like right away.

"Baby, what's going on?" He sounds a little loaded.

I need you to pick me up.

"From where?"

I'm stranded on a gravel road a few miles outside of the city.

"Awesome."

I'm not joking, man. My dad brought me out here to show me some land he bought and then he bailed.

Michael starts laughing. He goes, "Your old man ditched you, brah. That's fucking righteous. That's fucking rock 'n' roll."

Whatever, dude. Come pick me up.

"I don't know."

I'll fucking pay you, man. Please.

"All right," he says. "But you have to hang out with me for the rest of the day."

Fine, dude.

"And you can't bitch about it."

Okay.

"Promise?"

Promise.

"Tell me where you're at."

Michael shows up an hour later driving a brown van the size of one of those short yellow buses, with yellow and orange flames painted on the sides of it.

Sticking his head out of the window, he goes, "Get in, you fucking loser," and I walk around to the other side and jump in.

Thanks for picking me up.

"Pleasure's all mine, baby." Michael makes a U-turn.

Whose van is this?

"My lead singer's. He bought it a couple of days ago. It's gonna be our touring van."

I light my last cigarette and look behind me at the four other seats, the huge bed in the back, and the track lighting along each side of the roof.

Shouldn't you guys play more shows before you start thinking about a tour?

"We're playing this Karen O look-alike contest at the Glass Castle the first weekend of August."

Karen O. The chick from the Yeah Yeah Yeahs. Awesome.

"Not really," says Michael, who's stuffed in a Skid Row wife-beater and white jeans. "It's sorta lame, but it's a gig." He turns onto the highway. "I'm sure there's going to be a ton of dickpig scenester babes just ready to be slayed."

Inhale. Exhale.

Michael reaches for the tape deck and hits the eject button. He flips over the tape he's just ejected.

The song "Under the Milky Way" by the Church starts playing and Michael lights a cigarette. He goes, "We're going to cover this for the show."

Really? You want to?

"I don't, but Dave and Thomas want to."

I flick some ashes out of the window.

Where are we going?

"We're making a delivery to Cliff at his trailer."

You're selling heroin now?

"Fuck no," Michael snorts, sliding on some black shades. "I got speed for him. I took over Kyle's business."

You what?

"I took Kyle's shit over. I went to the jail and talked to him about it and we made a deal."

I toss my smoke.

What was the deal?

"That I could go to his house and take whatever he still had, plus all of his customers just as long as I gave half of the profits I made off of that stash to his old man."

Have you?

"Not yet. I haven't sold all of it. I just went over there like two days ago." Michael blows some smoke rings. "And when I went to pick the shit up, Chris tried stepping at me. He told me that I was an asshole for even thinking about dealing the rest of Kyle's shit."

What'd you do?

"Laughed in his face. Chris is fat and dumb and pretty much a piece of trash." Michael tosses his ciggie. "The dude barely graduated high school. He works a construction job, dates a high school chick, slaps her around, has a really horrible tribal tattoo on his arm, and drinks like a twelve pack of Old Milwaukee every night."

I start laughing.

Come on, man. You shouldn't say that shit about him.

"Fuck you, Trav. He didn't have the nicest things to say about you."

What'd he say?

"He told me he thinks you're an asshole for putting Laura ahead of Kyle when you went to the cabin with her instead of his arraignment. He thinks you only care about yourself, and that even if it's bad news, you don't like it when other people have the spotlight."

He said that?

Michael nods.

Fuck him. What a turd burglar. It's not like Kyle isn't one of my best fucking friends. I just went to see him the other day.

"Hey, don't kill the messenger," Michael smiles. "I'm just telling you what he told me."

That dick.

Michael steers the van onto an off-ramp, then reaches over and shuts the tape off. "What'd you think when you went and visited Kyle?" he asks.

It was depressing, man. Way too intense.

Michael comes to a stop at the top of the exit and rubs his nose. "Tell me about it," he says. "When I was there, after we talked business, Kyle really pissed me off."

How?

Michael makes a left and says, "Because he's already given up. He's already committed himself to going down."

Lighting another cigarette and bumming me one, he snorts, "While I was there I told him everything he needed to know."

About what?

"About how to beat the rap, Trav. All he has to do is listen to me and he's a free man."

I take a drag and can't help but laugh again as we reenter the city and melt in with the rush-hour traffic.

29

I FEEL LIKE AN ASSHOLE AS MICHAEL SLOWLY MANEUVERS
the van around the small, winding road of the trailer park
that Cliff calls home.

This is creepy, I tell him, looking out of the window at
young children who stand there and stare at us.

"What is?"

This fucking van. This is the exact same type of van they
use to abduct kids in TV movies.

"So what?"

I'm just saying.

"Hey, dude, you're in the Mobile Rape Unit now. Live
with it."

The what?

Michael lowers his shades. "The Mobile Rape Unit.
When you got in, did you see the letters MRU branded along
the side?"

Yeah.

"MRU," Michael smiles, stopping in front of Cliff's trailer.
"Mobile Rape Unit."

That's fucked up.

"Quit being a pussy, man."

I open the door and step outside. The sun is still pressing. I'm sweating all over again, and I can hear the faint sound of the Velvet Underground coming from Cliff's home.

I follow Michael up to the trailer door and he knocks on it hard.

"Goddamn," he snorts, smacking a gnat off his shoulder. "This place sucks." He takes a deep breath and holds it in. "Do you smell what I'm smelling, Trav?"

Yeah. It smells like shit.

"It smells like a rotting corpse covered in dog feces."

Michael lights a cigarette and knocks again and Cliff opens the door this time, wearing nothing but a pair of jeans torn up so bad that Kurt Cobain would've been jealous.

"Hi, Michael. Hi, Travis," he says, rubbing his left arm, which is all bruised up. "Come in."

Michael and I squeeze in between Cliff and the wood paneling of the doorframe, then Cliff closes the door behind us. "What took you so long?" he asks Michael.

"I had to pick up Travis. His old man stranded his ass."

"Where at?" Cliff asks me.

Nowhere, Cliff.

I ask Michael for a cigarette and he bums me another one and I light it and look at Cliff. I barely even recognize him. His face is pale. Sunk in. Scabbed. His teeth are rotting yellow. His fingernails are brown. There are dirty, black colored Band-Aids on his neck and on the lobe of his left ear.

Cliff's eyes dart the other way when he sees me staring at

him. "It's all right that you're late," he tells Michael after walking over to the CD player and turning the volume down. "You guys wanna see something cool?"

"What is it?" Michael asks.

Cliff walks to the sink and opens the cupboards underneath it. He pulls out a brown paper bag and walks to the trailer table.

Inhale. Exhale.

"What is that, a fuckin' sandwich?" Michael jokes, lighting another cigarette.

Cliff opens the bag and pulls a gun from it. A silver .22 with a black and brown handle.

"Sweet," Michael nods. "Let me see it."

Cliff hands it to him and then looks at me and I don't have to ask because I already know where he got it.

"Is it loaded?" Michael asks.

"No way, man. I'm not stupid."

Michael wraps both his hands around the gun points it in the direction of the door. "How much did it cost?"

"One fifty."

"I like it."

"I can get you the guy's info and set up a meeting."

"Let me think about it."

I don't even know Cliff anymore.

Michael hands the gun back to him.

"You wanna hold it, Trav?" he asks.

I'm cool.

Cliff and Michael smile at each other and then Cliff puts

the gun away. I see the bedroom door in the back move.

Emerging from the shadows is my sister's friend Katie. She's barefoot, wearing a white halter top with a red rose print all over it and a dirty mesh skirt. Fingertip bruises cover her entire neck.

"What up, Katie?" Michael grins.

"Hey," she says, looking down at the ground.

Hi, Katie.

"Hi, Travis," she whispers without looking at me.

I run my eyes up her body and stop when I notice this huge cut on the right side of her stomach. It's purplish and healing and I want to say something but don't.

"So," Cliff starts. "You wanna do this, Michael?"

"Cool." Michael pulls out two small baggies of glass. "Forty," he says.

Cliff cracks a smile and digs through his pockets like four times each before producing a balled up twenty-dollar bill. "This is all I got right now."

"Fuck you," Michael snaps, putting the baggies away.

"No, no, just wait. Can't we work something out?" Cliff flips his head at Katie. "What do you think?"

My chest feels like it might explode.

"Not this time," Michael says. "I told you on the phone I wasn't going to make an exception this time. I mean, fuck, Cliff, I'm already cutting twenty bucks off what I would charge anyone else."

"I know it," Cliff whines, picking some dry skin off his bottom lip. "And I appreciate it."

"No you don't," Michael snorts. "You're a fucking junkie and junkies don't appreciate shit."

"So what the hell do you want me to do, Michael?"

"Give me another twenty."

"Are you sure we can't do a little trade-off?" Cliff presses.

Katie's shoulders tense up.

She looks broken.

"No. That was a one-time thing," Michael rips.

Cliff turns to Katie. "Do you have anything on you?"

She shakes her head.

Cliff shakes his head. "Just go sit in the fuckin' room, Katie. Christ."

She nods and walks back down the short hallway and disappears into the room and closes the door.

Where's Natalie? I ask.

Cliff looks at me. "In Chicago with some dude she met. And ya know what?"

What?

"I don't even care," he laughs.

And Michael goes, "So what am I doing, Cliff?"

Cliff turns to me again and stares.

What, Cliff?

"Could you spot me?" he asks.

Come on, man. I'm not your fucking piggy bank.

"Please, Trav," he begs. "I need this. I'm about to lose it. I'll never ask you again."

I look at Michael and Michael looks at Cliff and then at me.

"Please," he whispers. "I need this."

Fine. Whatever.

I pull my wallet out and hand him a twenty.

"Thanks man. You're so rad. This is why we go back so far."

I roll my eyes.

No, Cliff. We go back so far because we go back so far and that's it. There's no other reason.

"Exactly," he nods and hands Michael the money in exchange for the crystal. "You guys wanna stick around for a minute and do some?"

No.

"No."

"All right," he says. "Then you should both leave. Okay?"

I roll my eyes and push the door open and walk outside. I ask Michael for another smoke.

"Here." He hands me a whole new pack from a pocket in his jeans.

Do you want money too?

He shakes his head. "No." He climbs into the van and I light a cigarette. Cliff walks out.

"Travis," he calls.

What, Cliff?

"I'm sorry."

For what?

"For being me."

What does that mean?

"It means I'm sorry. Don't forget, okay? I'm sorry."

Whatever.

I open the door and jump in and Michael starts driving.

He turns out of the trailer park and goes, "Let's go to Kennedy Street. I gotta run some errands."

That's cool.

"Don't think about Cliff, dude. I'm sure he's done worse shit than that."

I'm not thinking about him, Michael. That's what's strange. I don't care.

"You've never cared," he says. "Who are you trying to fool?"

On Kennedy Street, the two of us duck in and out of stores. Michael buys a few things—pair of Lucky's, pair of BKs, new shades, white T-shirts.

At the Lower Playground store, Michael grabs the annual *VICE* photo issue and tells me that him and Dave are moving into this righteous pad just up the block at the end of the month.

"Shit's gonna destroy all, brah. It's huge, it's cheap, and it's right across from Bottoms Up."

Nice.

On our way out of the store I notice this green poster on the storefront window that says:

Peaches & Death present the first annual
Karen O look-alike contest August 7th with musical guests:
The Shoelaces, The Jill Kelly Experience,
Lamborghini Dreams,
and Modern Romance (A Yeah Yeah Yeahs cover band)

Michael. Check it out.

Michael looks over. "Fuck yeah," he smiles. "Shit looks good. Our names getting out there, man. We might be the best band in the city right now."

That's a pretty big statement.

"Not really. Our stuff is that good," he says. "Let's move."

So we continue down the sidewalk, fanning ourselves with our shirts, cigarettes between our lips.

"Let's walk down to the Brown Jug and grab a beer," Michael says. "Outdoor seating and shit."

Sweet.

We stop at a crosswalk.

Thanks for picking me up again.

"No worries."

I called Laura before I called you but she didn't answer.

"Does that surprise you?" Michael asks, staring at this blonde walking by with two ink sleeves, a red satin miniskirt, fishnets, and a Lovemakers shirt.

A little bit. We're pretty much back together.

Michael takes his shades off and rubs the sweat off the bridge of his nose. "What's so special about Laura, anyway?" he asks. "Why do you want to be with her again? You're Travis Wayne, dude. You can have a lot of other chicks who don't suck nearly as bad as her."

She doesn't suck, okay, Michael? We were together for a long time.

"That means nothing."

Yes it does.

The light turns green and we cross the intersection. I flick my smoke at the side of a building.

"You guys used to cheat on each other all the time," Michael says. "You fought constantly. She tried punching your lights out a few times. What was so fucking great about that?"

Because there were times when we were alone and not all messed up on drugs. We'd go on drives during the afternoon and lie around and say the stupidest things to each other. But they were things that seemed so important at the time.

Michael drops his smoke on the ground.

And there were other times when no one was around and she took care of me and listened to what I had to say. When my cousin Alex was shot and killed, she was with me every night. She came to Chicago with my family for the funeral. She stayed up with me while I told her things I've never told anyone, and she never said a word. She just listened. That's the shit you guys never saw.

"So what, Trav? I still don't get why you think you need to be with her now. You're the one who quit talking to her. Where were all those rosy fucking times you just told me about then?"

I stop walking.

I need her back, Michael.

"No you don't."

Yes I do. I need to have something again.

"You already have everything, Travis. What more could you want?"

I want to go back.

"Why?"

Because it's the only thing I know.

30

MY LAST NIGHT IN HAWAII I GOT REALLY WASTED ON BOOZE and tried calling the coke dealer again, but he wasn't picking up, so I decided to go out and ended up playing an AC/DC pinball machine at one of the bars I'd hopped to and that's when I saw her.

She walked across the bar in this green hula skirt and white lace top. She was beautiful and had long black hair that was tied in the back and matched the milky dark color of her skin.

Walking by me as she left the bar, she smiled and I smiled back, but I didn't give it another thought until I was out of quarters. Instead of going back for another drink, I felt like getting some fresh air and stumbled the thirty feet down to the shoreline, and heard someone say hi.

I turned around.

Behind me was the same girl from the bar. She looked amazing, standing under the bright stars of the Pacific sky, and I was so drunk, so ready for anything.

"Didn't I just see you losing a game of pinball?" she asked.

You did, I slurred.

"Bummer," she went.

This whole night has been kind of a bummer.

"Mine too." Pause. "I have a thought," she said.

What's that?

"*Maybe we could turn it all around. I have a lot of fun things in my room.*"

I smiled.

Really?

"*Of course. I wouldn't lie about something like that. Some things . . .*"

Are too sacred, I finished.

"*Exactly,*" *she said.* "*So, what do you think?*"

I don't have to. You had me at "fun" and then again at "room."

The girl grabbed my hands. She led me all the way across the beach to this motel in the middle of nowhere and went, "*So what's your name?*"

Travis. What's yours?

"*My name is Autumn,*" *she said.* "*Autumn Hayes.*"

                                             Travis Wayne

31

LAURA AND I GO OUT TO EAT AT THIS ITALIAN RESTAURANT
downtown a couple of nights later. When we're finished, she
hooks an arm through mine and says, "Let's not go to a bar
for drinks."

What do you want to do instead?

"Let's go somewhere more personal."

Your house?

"No," she smiles. "Let's get a bottle and go to Rawson Park."

Shit, I haven't thought about that place for a few years.

"Let's go, then," she begs. "We can sit at the tables and
drink like we used to before we got fakes."

So the two of us get a bottle of Beam and a bottle of Coke
from the liquor store across the street and drive.

Rawson Park is very small and very modest compared to
most of the other parks in the city, especially some of the
"mega" ones that have been built recently by some of the
downtown businesses. It has a small patch of cement for a
basketball court, a tennis court with no net, a small brick
building used for bathrooms, a swing set with only two
actual swings, and a fairly large rectangular sandbox fully
equipped with a lopsided merry-go-round, and the tornado

slide where I took Laura's virginity on her fifteenth birthday.

We get to the park a little after ten. No one else is there. Posted near the small road entrance of the park is a large sign that says AS OF 9/01/06, THIS LAND WILL BECOME THE PROPERTY OF WAYNE REALTY.

"When the hell did your dad buy this?" Laura snaps, letting go of my hand.

I don't know. I didn't even know he had.

"What do you think he's going to do with it, Travis?"

He's probably going to tear it up and build some condos or something.

"Well, you can't let him. This place is special to me. It has history."

What do you want me to do about it?

"Talk to him."

I start laughing.

Laura, my father drove me to the middle of nowhere last week, during one of the hottest days ever, and left me stranded there. I mean, do you really think he's going to listen to me right now?

She pulls a cigarette from her purse and lights it. "You won't even try."

No, I won't. Did you even hear me? My father doesn't give a shit about sentimentality unless it's me being third generation at USC and following his every move.

Laura blows a cloud of smoke out. She looks annoyed. "You're being a fucking jerk," she says. "You're acting just like your father."

And you're acting like Winnie Cooper during that episode of *The Wonder Years* when their neighborhood park is about to be destroyed.

"So?" Laura says, holding her arms wide. "What's wrong with that? This is sad."

Do you wanna split? We can go somewhere else.

"No," she says. "If the park is going to be destroyed we should hang out here tonight."

Laura tosses her smoke and grabs my hand again. The two of us walk down the narrow, weed-filled sidewalk, and stop at the lone picnic table.

It's hard to see. There's only a sliver's worth of moonlight, so I walk to the light pole and open the circuit box and pull the generator lever down.

Very slowly, the yellowish glow of the bulb begins to flicker more and more and more until it flickers all the way on.

Laura claps her hands and cheers, and even though it feels completely cheesy, it makes me smile. It feels good to smile from something other than one of Michael's stories or jokes. I haven't smiled and really meant it in a long time and being with Laura at the park means everything right now.

I walk back to the table and sit down with her on the tabletop. She passes me the Beam and Coke and I take a few drinks and hand them back to her.

"Do you remember the last time we were here?" she asks, lighting another smoke.

I don't.

"Me neither," she says. "It has to have been, what, like almost four years ago by now."

At least.

She takes a few drinks and passes me the bottle again.

"But I do remember the first time we were here together," she says. "The summer before we started high school."

I choke down a pull of Beam.

So do I. We ran into each other downtown during the Fourth of July, where all the carnival rides were at. You were spending the night at Amanda Doyer's house and I was staying at Chris's parents' with Cliff and Kyle.

Laura smirks. She's like, "I had the biggest crush on you, ever since you saw me sneaking that cigarette during study hall. That was also the night we started talking and you told me that you were going to sneak out of Chris's and walk over to Amanda's to help me sneak out."

I take another drink. Pass the bottle back to Laura, and take a drag of my cigarette and lay my chin against her shoulder.

I say, And I did it, too. You snuck out with me and we walked here and that was the night we decided to go steady.

I point at the basketball hoop.

We kissed for the first time right over there.

Laura turns to me. "And the second time we ever came to the park . . ." She grins wildly.

I start laughing.

The tornado slide night. That was your idea.

"No it wasn't."

Yes it was.

"No it wasn't, Travis. I wanted to go into the bathroom to screw but you said they smelled too bad and that the only place with enough cover was at the top of the slide."

Okay. Fine. You're right. Maybe it was my idea.

"I'm positive I'm right."

We begin kissing and my body gets warm.

Laura pulls away. "This is nice."

I know it.

She takes a pull from the bottle. "Do you know what you're going to do in the fall?"

Not yet. But things are becoming more clear to me. I feel like I've got my feet under things again.

"You're staying in the city though, right?"

Yeah, I have to. Leaving again would be a bad idea. I don't even know why I left in the first place.

"To experience other things. That's what you told me. You said you could only go so far living here. That kids are supposed to leave home and go to college."

I know that's what I said. But I don't know.

I take the bottles from Laura and drink.

It was bullshit. I lost everything when I left.

"What did you lose?"

I take another drink.

Everything.

Laura puts her hands on my face and turns it so our eyes are even with each other.

"Do you love me?" she asks.

Yes.

"Do you promise?"

I promise.

She smiles. "Let's go then."

Where?

"Let's climb to the top of the slide and fuck."

Laura jumps off the table and runs for the slide. I do the same.

She gets there first and starts climbing the ladder while I stand at the bottom and take more drinks. Once she's at the top, she looks down at me and goes, "Come on, baby. Hurry up."

I start climbing, and when I get to the top, Laura grabs me and we kiss again. She grabs onto the bottom of my T-shirt and pulls it over my head and off, then pushes me onto my back after taking the Beam from my hand.

She straddles me.

I slip her navy blue top off and squeeze her breasts.

"They're a lot bigger than they were when we were fifteen." She laughs, then takes a huge pull from the bottle and leans down and starts kissing me. Jim Beam runs everywhere—down my chin. Over the sides of my face. All over my chest—and right before I close my mouth, Laura spits some more booze into it and I swallow it.

"I want you inside of me," she moans. "Get inside of me, Travis."

I sit up and put my hands on the sides of her waist and roll her over, pinning her back against the cool surface of the slide. Then I unbutton my jeans and push them down.

Laura does the same with hers. Then she wraps her hand around my dick and begins massaging it.

I lean closer to her, planting my hands above her shoulders, and we rub the tips of our tongues together.

"Spit in my mouth," she says.

I draw a glob of saliva to the front of my mouth and drop it into hers.

"Awesome," she swallows. "Now fuck me."

I push her legs farther apart and rub the tip of my penis around her vagina until she grabs the back of my neck, pulling me closer.

"Go ahead, Travis."

I slide myself inside of her and start thrusting her as hard as I can. Our skin going *smack, smack, smack.*

Digging her nails into my back, Laura goes, "I want you to stay inside of me. Do not pull out."

Okay.

We fuck for like a half an hour, until I can't hold it anymore, and I come inside of her.

Laura removes her claws from my skin. "That was really good," she pants. "That was fucking amazing."

I roll off of her body.

Thanks.

She wiggles her jeans back up. Puts her shirt back on. Grabs her purse and digs through it, pulling a tube of lipstick out.

"Watch me," she smiles as I button my jeans and reach for my shirt.

What are you doing?

"This," she says, then draws a big heart on the plastic top covering the slide.

What's that supposed to mean?

Laura looks at me, grins, then turns back to the heart and writes "Laura + Travis" in the middle of it.

"There," she says, sticking the cap over the lipstick. "We didn't do this last time. We never wrote our names on anything."

32

THE DAY I TURNED SIXTEEN I WAS IN LA WITH MY PARENTS and my sister. We'd all flown out a few days earlier so my father could be honored during some alumni banquet at USC. It was one of his "proudest moments," he told a packed audience of his peers as he accepted his big achievement award.

After the whole jack-off and pat-myself-on-the-back ceremony was over that afternoon, my father took me around the central campus with one of his old college buddies, who also sat on the board of trustees. The two of them took turns telling me how wonderful it was to go to school there. They told me story after story about their "glory days" as "Trojan men" and when the tour was over, my father's friend looked me square in the eye and said, "Come here when you're done with high school. You won't be disappointed."

Two days later it was my birthday.

My mother wanted to do a nice lunch with just the four of us, but my father had other things planned. An investment partner of his was having a barbecue at his house in the Hollywood Hills. "We have to go," my father told my mother. "We were invited and we all have to go."

So we all did.

We went to my father's investment partner's house and were there the entire day, which meant I spent all of my birthday that year watching my father getting wasted, hitting on young blond girls in bikinis, while my mother just sat there, giving cigarettes to my sister, pretending not to notice.

These are the things that smash through my head as I apply to USC, the last school I apply to after City College, State, and Harrison, on the very last day that my father gave me to *get my shit together*.

When I'm finished, I send an e-mail to my father telling him what I've just done and then I walk upstairs from the basement.

I hear my mother talking with another lady in the kitchen. My mother must hear me also because she yells for me to come to the kitchen.

She's sitting at the table across from this very pretty and much younger girl.

"Travis," my mother says slowly, holding a cigarette between her fingers, "this is Rachael. She works for Gucci and is doing all of our outfit measurements for your father's ceremony dinner."

"Nice to meet you," Rachael says, turning around in her chair.

You too.

My mother takes a sip of red wine. She stares at me and I feel embarrassed because I'm not wearing a shirt, only sweatpants, and this Rachael girl, this complete stranger, is watching my mother stare at her shirtless son.

"Let's get started," Rachael blurts, reaching into a small bag sitting on the floor next to her chair. She pulls a piece of measuring tape, a pad of paper, and pencil from it.

I go and stand by the table and watch my mother pour herself another glass of wine and light her cigarette.

Rachael gets to her feet and walks around me.

"Hold your arms out," she says. "Thank you."

My mother is still staring.

What, Mom?

"I hate your tattoos, Travis. I despise them," she says.

I know you do.

Rachael wraps the tape around my chest, under my outstretched arms. "Okay," she says, letting the tape go. "You can put your arms down."

I drop them.

That was one of the perks of getting them done, Mom. Pissing you and Dad off.

"Well done," my mother smirks. "Add that to a list of many other things."

Rachael loops the tape around my neck, then jots some more numbers down on her pad.

Did I do something to make you mad at me, Mom?

She stands up. "No."

Then what's with this crap?

My mother shakes her head and looks off in the distance. "I don't know, Travis. I . . . I . . ." But she doesn't finish. She downs the rest of her wine and smudges her cigarette out.

I spread my legs and let Rachael take my inseam measurements.

"Your sister tells me that you and Laura are back together again," my mother snorts, changing the subject.

I say, We are.

Rachael jots my inseam numbers down.

"How is she doing?" my mother asks.

She's good. She's still at Grant College going for advertising.

"And her parents?"

I don't know.

Rachael asks me what my shoe size is.

Twelve.

"Thanks."

My mother taps her fingers hard against the kitchen counter. "You can invite her to the awards ceremony if you want."

No.

My mother sighs. "So I take it you getting back together with her again means that you've decided about next year."

Nope.

My mother sighs again. "One-word answers. This is what I get after all these years."

Here we go, Mom. You're starting to sound like Dad.

"And you sound exactly like your sister, Travis. All she does is ignore me too. She doesn't want to talk, and when I do see her, all she does is give me one-word fucking answers, then locks herself in her room."

I look at Rachael and she looks really uncomfortable as she puts her things into her bag.

Mom, we have a guest.

"I know we do! I invited her!"

Rachael's face is red. She picks the bag up and looks at my mother. "Do you want me to wait for you somewhere else, Mrs. Wayne?"

"That would be great, dear," my mother answers.

Rachael walks outside through the back door and gets on her cell phone.

"Christ," my mother quivers, her hands shaking as she briefly covers her mouth. "I didn't mean to do that in front of her. I have to spend the rest of the day with her and now I'm embarrassed."

Don't be. Shit like that happens.

My mother drops one hand to the bottom of her chin. "I'm drunk," she says.

I know you are.

"I'm worried about your sister, Travis. We had another fight this morning. I think she's doing drugs. Hard drugs."

Have you asked her?

"No."

Maybe you should.

My mother's mouth pops open. "Maybe you could, Travis. Maybe you could talk to her. She'll at least listen to you."

No she won't, Mom. She's not going to listen to a word I tell her.

"Well, do you know anything at all? Can you tell me anything, Travis?"

I stare at my mother, who at times has been as strong as any person I've ever seen, and at other times as weak as any person I've ever seen.

"Anything," she says.

A very long pause.

No I can't.

My mother rubs her eyes. "I'm tired," she yawns. "I'm so tired, Travis."

Maybe you should go back to bed then.

"Maybe I should, but I have so much to do. It feels like I just woke up."

Well.

Pause.

Maybe you shouldn't have.

I drive to Chris's the next afternoon. I want to talk to him, to try to square away some of the bullshit between us.

On the way there, I get a call on my cell from Claire. She wants to know if I want to go to Chicago with her. Apparently some models from suicidegirls.com—Snow—Reagen—Posh—are doing some sort of promo shoot and burlesque show for the launch of this new fashion and political magazine called *Bette's Closet*, along with some other girls—Catra, Kate, and Erin—all of whom used to be on the Suicide Girls site but aren't anymore because they're on this new website, godsgirls.com.

When are you going? I ask her.

"Tonight," Claire says. "We'll have to leave in like an hour."

No way. I can't. Not tonight.

"Please, please, please with a fucking cherry on top," she begs. "It's free for us. Skylar is doing some of the photo and design work for the show and she gave me two passes."

I really can't tonight, Claire. I'm sorry.

"What the hell in your life is so pressing that you can't come with me to watch hot naked bitches dancing around?"

I have to talk to Chris. There are some things that I need to talk to him about.

"That's lame, Travis. Chris is an asshole who hits girls."

But I still need to talk to him.

"That bad?"

Yes.

"Fine," Claire grumbles. "Have fun with Chris."

I'm sorry.

"Don't be sorry, dude. I guess you're doing what you think you need to be doing."

I am.

My heart skips a beat.

Hopefully.

"Well, hit me up soon," Claire snorts. "I miss you tons. We need to be hanging out way more than we are."

I know it.

"Later," she says.

I park across the street from Chris's and step out of the

car, staring at these two gnarly trash cans sitting near the front door of his bright yellow home. Both of them are surrounded by huge piles of wasting garbage that have spilt over their sides. A ton of large flies loom above it all.

It smells fucking horrible, like a bunch of spoiled shit that's been melted by the sunlight.

I open the door to the house and walk in and see Chris sitting in the wheelchair dumping an entire gram of coke onto a mirror.

Chris, you need to do something about that trash, I tell him.

He looks up from the mirror. "Do you know that I saw you walking up to the house through the window?" He points to the window. "I saw you through the glass."

That's good, Chris.

"What are you doing here?" he asks, the bags under his eyes the shade of a jet-black nighttime sky.

I came to see you.

"Well, shit. I feel important now."

I step over more piles of trash.

Food wrappers. Empty cigarette cartons. Drained bottles of booze. Piles of socks and underwear.

The air in the house is muggy and musty and stale. I sit down on the sofa across from him and watch as he runs a blade across the blow.

How long have you been up, Chris?

"Long enough to know that it's probably been too long."

Which means?

"I've been up since two days ago when April came over here after work and told me she was pregnant, but that she wasn't exactly sure who the father was." Chris jams a red straw up his nose. He leans down to the mirror and snorts two lines. He holds the mirror out. "Do you want some?" he asks, voice strained and cracked from exhaustion.

I shake my head, pull my cigarettes out and light one.

What'd you do when she told you? I ask him.

Chris doesn't answer this. He takes the mirror and sets it on the small end table next to him and covers his eyes with his hands.

Hey, Chris.

The tension is high. I know what he did.

Chris.

"What?" he snaps, tearing his hands off his face. "What do you want from me, Trav?"

Inhale. Exhale.

I want you to tell me what you did when your girlfriend told you she was pregnant but didn't know who the father was.

"I hate you," Chris says.

Tell me, Chris.

"I slapped her face and she fell down, okay? And when she got up"—Chris stops and twists his neck all the way around—"she tried to punch me back, so I grabbed her arm and yanked her across the room and threw her out of the house."

You're a fucking asshole.

"Fuck you, Travis."

You beat the shit out of a seventeen-year-old girl.

"Fuck you!" Chris flies out of the wheelchair, stepping over the coffee table, getting right in front of me. "Do you know what you are, Travis?" he snaps, veins bulging from his neck.

Yes.

Chris bends down so that we're at eye level. "What are you, Travis Wayne?"

I'm an asshole too.

I take another drag.

"Yes you are. I remember you and Cliff taking turns nailing that freshman girl who was passed out at Michael's house sophomore year. So don't come over here, to my fucking house, and act righteous and act like you're some-how better than me now, 'cause you're not."

I know I'm not, Chris.

"Good." A tiny line of snot drops from the bottom of his right nostril. Chris snorts it back up but it quickly drops out again. "I look at the way you acted after Kyle's accident and it makes me hate you, Travis."

How'd I act?

"Like a pussy. One of your buddies was sitting in a jail cell and you went on vacation with a fucking slut."

Watch it, man.

"What are you gonna do, Trav?"

Just watch it.

"You chose to hang out with a whore instead of support your friend."

I lean closer to Chris so that our faces are only inches apart.

I'm only going to tell you one more time, man. Do not call Laura names. She's not a slut or a whore.

More snot falls from Chris's nose. This time he wipes his hand across his face.

"No, Travis," he says. "You're wrong. She is a fucking whore. Your girlfriend is a whore!"

I shove Chris against the coffee table behind him and he falls onto it. I jump to my feet and stand above him with my fists bunched tight.

"What are you gonna do?" Chris screams.

All I want to do is hurt him. I want to pound on him and tie him down and call April so that she can come over and pound on him like he did to her.

"What are you gonna do?" he screams again.

Nothing, Chris.

He rolls over to the other side of the table and pushes himself up.

You're pathetic, man.

"I'm a good friend, Travis."

No you're not. Kyle was gonna move out because he thought you were a dick.

Wiping more snot away, Chris goes, "What are you talking about?"

He told me the night before his accident that he was going to move in with Emily because he couldn't live with someone who would beat up a girl.

"You're lying."

No I'm not. He hated you. He wanted nothing to do with you so.

"Get out of here," Chris snaps. "Get the fuck out of my house."

Gladly.

I kick over an old stack of *Thrasher* magazines and keep kicking through piles of shit until I get to the door.

Then I turn back to Chris.

Chris in his dirty clothes.

Chris with his face covered in thick stubble.

Chris with eyes as red as blood.

"What are looking at?" he asks.

Someone I don't know.

"What's that mean?"

You've changed, man.

"We've all changed."

No. You're a scumbag. You spent almost your entire life hating your old man and trying not to be like him or your older brothers, but that's exactly who you are.

"Well, ya know what, Trav," Chris sneers, the words seething through his clenched teeth.

I wrap my hand around the door handle.

What, Chris?

"Why don't you take your self-righteous bullshit and go ask Laura what that three hundred dollars you gave Cliff in March was for."

My hand slips off the handle.

How do you know about that?

"Because he came to me for the money first, but I wouldn't give it to him after he told me what he needed it for. I'm a good friend."

Why would Laura know what it was for?

Chris starts laughing. "Man," he says. "You really got fucked. You really aren't that bright."

What are you talking about, Chris? What are you even talking about?

He continues laughing harder and louder.

I say, I'm not listening to this anymore. You've been up for days. You don't know what's going on.

Chris steps over the same picture book April was flipping through at the beginning of the summer and stops in front of me. He quits laughing on a dime. His face goes straight. "You're right," he snorts, his voice sounding almost rejuvenated. "I have been up for days. I am fucking exhausted. But I do know about the money you gave Cliff and I do know what it paid for. So ask Laura about that. Ask her why Cliff needed the money so bad and why a week later she called your ass in Arizona and told you it was over. Ask her."

My entire body goes numb for a second.

My eyes slam shut.

And Chris says, "Then come back here and tell me she's not a whore."

BAM.

BAM.

BAM.

Everything I tried to put back together. Everything I tried to build back up. All of it begins to break apart.

Just like that.

It cracks and it falls and it shreds into a million fucking pieces and when I open my eyes, it's just me and it's just Chris.

In this room.

In this house.

It's just me and it's just Chris and we both have blood on our hands and we're both horrible people and we both know exactly what he's talking about.

I have to go, Chris.

"So go," he says.

I walk back to my car, the sun and the smell fighting me every step of the way, and when I open my car door, my stomach turns and my mouth opens and this green and yellow matter falls out of it in big, thick chunks, and it falls out of it in long, skinny strings.

I look over my shoulder, back at Chris's house.

There is nothing.

I wipe my face.

Dry my lips with my shirt. Then I climb into my car and blast the air conditioner.

Think.

I almost call Laura but I know she's working.

Think, Travis.

I should've gone with Claire and watched hot naked

girls like Snow and Kate dance around. At least I would've seen something beautiful.

Think, Travis Wayne.

I turn the steering wheel toward Cliff and the trailer, and I start to drive.

33.

I GET TO THE TRAILER AND WASTE NO TIME. I SLAM THROUGH the door and scare the shit out of Cliff, who jumps from the chair at the kitchen table to his feet.

"What are you doing?" he blurts out.

Getting answers! I scream.

Grabbing Cliff by his collar, I slam him so hard against the fake wood paneling of the wall that it comes unglued.

"What are you doing?" he stutters again, his beady eyes squinted halfway shut.

I'm only going to ask you this once, so don't lie.

"Ask me what?"

Did you fuck Laura while I was still with her, knock her up, then borrow the money for the abortion from me?

Cliff closes his eyes. He turns his head to the side and doesn't say anything.

Answer me, Cliff. You're not getting out of this.

I push harder against his chest.

Cliff swings his head back around. "Yes."

You fucker!

I ball my hand into a fist and swing it into his face, my

knuckles cracking against his jaw, sending his head slamming against the wall.

Fuck!

I punch him again, this time square in the nose, and
blood immediately starts running from it.

Why? I yell, letting go of him and stepping back. Why
would you do that to me?

And Cliff goes, "She said you didn't love her anymore.
She told me it was over."

Grabbing him again and slamming him back against the
wall, I take another swing, but this time I don't hit him.

I shove my face right into his.

Ya know what, Cliff?

"What?"

You're not even worth this.

I step back again.

Fuck you, man. Fuck both of you.

I wipe my face with my shirt and leave the trailer. Drive
to the Waterfront. Inside I ask the hostess where Laura's section is.

"She's off."

I thought she was closing.

"She switched with someone."

Fuck.

I turn to leave.

"She's still here though," the hostess girl says. "She's at
the bar drinking with some people."

Bursting through these two chandelier-lit dining rooms

and into this other room where the bar is, I spot Laura right away. She's seated at the bar with like six guys and one other girl.

I begin to make my way to where she is and she sees me and hops off her barstool and goes, "Hey!" Then she runs around the corner of the bar and tries to give me a hug, but I hold her off.

"What's wrong, baby?"

You! Fuck! You stupid fuck!

I yank a glass off the bar and whip it to the ground, sending pieces everywhere.

"Travis!"

I hate you!

"What?"

How did it feel to have Cliff's abortion? I scream at the top of my lungs before grabbing another glass and throwing it to the ground.

Laura covers her mouth and runs to where the bathrooms are. Everyone in the entire place is watching me, watching this, watching this whole thing unravel.

I have nothing.

Fuck you, Laura Kennedy! I yell as I turn around to leave. And then I pull fifty dollars from my wallet and toss it at the bartender.

For the glasses, I tell him, then run to my car.

34.

JUST OUTSIDE OF THE CITY, NEXT TO AN ABANDONED
motel called the Last Chance, on a road that had once been
the city's main point of entry before most of the big housing
additions and the super interstate had been built, there is a
sign that says EXIT HERE.

An arrow points down.

I pull my car to the shoulder of the road and shut it off.
Step outside.

It's nighttime and the air feels so much better out here.
It feels better than it does in the city. I think about lighting
the joint I found in my glove compartment but decide not
to, and I actually throw it into the ditch, then look back at
the sign.

EXIT HERE.

My eyes follow the arrow down the sign's legs and I see
the dried remains of a flower bouquet still loosely attached
to the sign by a metal band. It blows in the light breeze.

There must've been an accident here.

I wonder what happened, how many people died. I
wonder what the articles said and if anyone was called a
monster and a killer and a murderer.

I close my eyes and inhale deeply.

I begin thinking that maybe going to USC is the right thing to do. Maybe if I leave again, I can forget that anything bad has happened to anyone.

Maybe if I leave again, I'll be able to forget about everything.

35

ALL MORNING I LIE IN BED, SMOKING CIGARETTES,
drinking ater, watching over and over the part in the Vincent
Gallo movie *The Brown Bunny* where Gallo gets head from
Chloë Sevigny.

All afternoon I try to get ahold of Claire, screening
phone calls, listening to the messages Laura leaves on my
voice mail. Messages that are all basically the same thing:
She needs to talk to me right away; it's important that I call
her back; she needs to explain a few things to me; she really
does love me. . . .

I erase them all.

I stalk around my room. I take out this notebook and
start writing things down.

Things like:

When I see her, I see need,
I see a black gift wrapped in pink paper,
I see a skeleton draped in red velvet,
I see a frown hiding in a smile,
I see filth and dirt, covered by a rose garden

I crib:

What the fuck is love anyway?
Is it a phone call the next morning?
Is it picking up a hundred-dollar-meal tab?
Is it flowers on the fifth date?
Or is it sleeping on the wet spot?

With my notebook in my lap, my left hand draped against the side of my face, I slam:

You are wrong to think I have no feelings,
You are wrong to think I would not care,
You are not sorry so don't tell me that you are,
You are nothing to me, just some distant black star

I scribble:

July eighteenth.
Three forty-five in the afternoon.
A Team Sleep CD spinning around the player.
I have no one else but myself to blame.
This is all my fault.
It hurts.
It will always hurt.
I will never forget.
I could try, and I will try, but I will never forget.

It will burn in my memory forever.
Just like everything else.
I will not be able to put this away.

I write and I write and I write and even though it's all
horrible, it makes me feel better. It helps me calm down. So
I keep going. I keep writing until Claire finally calls me back
around seven. She's back in town.

Will you meet me tonight? Like soon. Like at eight, Claire.

"Where do you want to meet?" she asks.

The Drunken Whale.

"At eight?"

Yes.

"Okay."

Pause.

"Is there something wrong, Travis? You sound bad."

No. I'm fine. Everything is great. Everything is perfect. I
am fucking wonderful.

"You're lying."

How do you know?

"'Cause nobody in the world has ever felt that good,
dude. Not even James Brown on grade-A coke has ever felt
that fucking good."

I laugh for the first time in days.

"I'll see you in an hour," she says.

I beat Claire to the bar and order a PBR and a shot of Jäger, and while
I wait, this 311 song starts playing. It's horrible. It hurts my ears.

I turn around in my seat.

Standing next to the jukebox is this kid with short spiked hair dyed blond. He's wearing an American Eagle-type button-up shirt and baggie shorts with flip-flops on his feet. I watch him make another selection. Then he walks over to the pool table and starts talking with these three other guys who look just like him, who are probably his bros, who all probably have Bob Marley posters hanging above their beds, right in between the Dave Matthews and Jason Mraz ones.

When the bartender sets my drinks down, I ask him when the hell they added bad shit like 311 to their box.

You guys used to have one of the best jukeboxes in the city, I tell him.

"We didn't add it," he says, taking the five bucks I hand him. "We got one of those new Internet boxes a couple of weeks ago and now you can look up any band online from the bar."

That sucks.

I slam the shot.

"Tell me about it," he grimaces. "At least you don't have to work here five nights a week."

I take a drink of beer, make my way over to the box and pull out a five-dollar bill and slide it in.

According to the screen, I get ten picks.

This is what they are:

Van Halen, "Jump"
Scorpions, "Wind of Change"
Faith No More, "Epic"

Alice Cooper, "Eighteen"
Digital Underground, "Humpty Dance"
Kiss, "God of Thunder"
Alice in Chains, "Down in a Hole"
L.A. Guns, "The Ballad of Jayne"
Aerosmith, "Dream On"
Dio, "Rainbow in the Dark"

I go back to the bar and down the rest of my beer and light a cigarette.

Like a fucking rock star, Claire bursts into the joint strapped perfectly into this short pink dress with black lace trim all around the bottom and top of it. There's a black skull and crossbones stitched near the bottom of the dress, on her upper thigh. Her forearms are draped with white fishnet sleeves, and she's wearing a pair of black midcalf boots.

I slide around the stool to meet her and she throws her arms around my neck. "Muthafucka," she says, stretching both words out.

Squeezing her back, the dry skin of my face pressed firmly against the soft, sweet, moist skin of hers, I tell Claire how glad, how really fucking glad, I am that she's here with me right now.

You have no idea, I tell her.

"Awwwww," she smiles. She kisses the corner of my mouth. "That's so sweet."

I let go of her and she plops down on the stool next to

me. Turns to the bartender. "I'll have a gin and tonic," she says, showing him her fake.

The bartender winks and goes to work on it.

I ask Claire about the show in Chicago, right as the superlame Linkin Park song that douche bag picked to follow 311 turns into some awesome Van Halen.

"It was a blast," she says, opening her purse, pulling out her Parliaments. "I had just gotten back to my place when you called again. But I'm so glad you did."

The bartender sets Claire's drink in front of her. "The first one is on the house, on me," he grins.

"Awesome." Claire winks, sliding three bucks over to the guy, who stuffs them into his tip jar.

My eyes flip back to Claire. Her legs are cocked wide. She lights a cigarette.

I say, You seem to be holding up well.

"I am," she says. "Some days are better than others, obviously. I mean, Emily and I had become so close." She stops for a moment, staring at the bar. "It's like my right foot was chopped off, replaced with this completely useless left one."

Pause.

"If that makes any sense."

Van Halen flips into the Scorpions.

I guess it does.

Claire and I both take sips of our drinks.

"How are you doing?" she asks, arching her back, shaking her neck loose.

Pretty well until yesterday.

"What happened yesterday?"

I found out that Cliff fucked Laura while I was still with her.

"I fucking knew it!" Claire snorts.

What?

"Well, I didn't—"

I cut her off.

You knew, Claire. And you didn't tell me. What the hell?

"Travis, I didn't *know* know."

I choke down a mouthful of beer.

What does that mean?

"I didn't know for sure or anything like that," she says.

I roll my eyes.

"Just listen," she pleads, putting a hand on my thigh. "A few months ago I saw Laura at the Glass Castle talking to Cliff. She looked superupset. So I asked her about him later that night, if they were sleeping with each other, and she freaked out on me. She started screaming that I was a horrible fucking person. Then she stormed out of the bar." Claire stops to take another sip of her drink. "And after that I figured they'd at least done something, but I wasn't sure, ya know, so I didn't want to say anything to you."

That's not even all they did.

The Scorpions flip into Faith No More.

Chomping at the bit, Claire asks, "What else happened?"

I finish my beer and light a cigarette. I go, Laura got pregnant and had Cliff's abortion.

"What?" Claire snaps, practically falling off the stool. "Are you fucking serious?"

Yep.

And Claire says, "Oh-my-fucking-god! I cannot believe that."

Pause.

She flips her eyes toward the ceiling. "Well, I guess I sorta can."

Pause.

She looks back at me. "But I'm so sorry for you," she frowns. "I am." She slams the rest of her gin and tonic. "I really feel horrible about it," she swallows.

And that's not all.

Claire's jaw drops.

They got the money to pay for the abortion from me.

Claire yells, "What?" And all the other heads in the bar turn at us. "You're not serious are you, Travis?"

I'm completely serious, Claire.

"How could you be the one to pay for it?"

Faith No More slams into Alice Cooper.

Claire and I both light cigarettes.

Cliff called me in March begging me, absolutely begging me, for three hundred dollars.

"And you gave it to him?" Claire snorts, jiggling her empty glass to get the bartender's attention. "You gave Clifford Miles three hundred dollars."

Pause.

"Dude."

Pause.

"Why?"

My shoulders drop.

Because I thought he was in a lot of trouble, Claire. Because he was a friend.

The bartender walks over and Claire orders us both double whiskey sours.

"That's good that you were trying to help him," Claire snorts. "And I've always felt bad for him, knowing some of the shit his father put him through growing up. But still, it's Cliff. You had to have known the money was for something shady."

I did, Claire. I just didn't care. I wanted to help him out.

"Damn," she says. "You tried to do a good thing and ended up subsidizing your own girlfriend's abortion."

I squeeze my lips tightly together, and watch my hands start to shake.

And Claire goes, "Come here." She gives me a hug. "I am so sorry for you. That sucks so fucking bad." She lets go. "Fuck those two."

You're right. But it goes deeper than that, deeper than "fuck those two."

The bartender brings our drinks over and I pay him as Alice Cooper bumps into Digital Underground.

"Cheers," Claire smiles, tipping her glass against mine.

Cheers.

She swallows a drink. "How did you find out about it?"

Chris told me some things.

I take a drink, smudge my smoke out.

Then I confronted Cliff and he told me it was true.

"Have you talked with Laura?"

Oh yeah. She knows.

Claire rubs her forehead. "This is some heavy shit, Travis. We should probably do some heavy-duty partying."

The corners of my lips arch. I pound half the drink down my throat.

Should I call Michael?

Claire grins. "No need to, man. I dropped into his new place on my way here and picked up a gram."

I thought he was moving at the end of the month.

"That was the plan, but the landlord called and said that him and Dave could get in there earlier, free of charge if they wanted. So they were moving their things in today."

Splitting her legs again, Claire presses her dress against the stool with an open hand, then leans into me and whispers, "Let's go to the bathroom and do some River Phoenixes."

Some what?

"River Phoenixes. It's the nickname Skylar, Emily, and I came up with for doing bumps in the bathroom of the Viper Room while we were partying in LA in April."

Let's do it.

Digital Underground changes to Kiss.

Claire hops off the stool. "Girls' or guys'?" she asks.

You pick.

"Girls'," she says, shaking her entire body out. "But I gotta pee first. Meet me there in like two minutes." Claire downs the rest of her drink and heads for the bathroom. I watch her walk until she disappears around the corner. I finish my own drink and smoke another cigarette and walk to the ladies' room.

Inside, Claire is standing in front of a mirror running a tube of gloss over her lips. "You ready?" she asks without peeling her eyes off of herself.

Yes, Claire.

"Awesome," she says, dropping the gloss into her purse. She gestures me with her right hand. "Follow me."

Claire leads me into a stall. I shut the door and lock it.

She says, "I haven't been in a bathroom stall with you since me, Cliff, Michael, and you went to Omaha to see Jack White play bass with the Stooges." Claire lifts a baggie of coke and a small, shiny knife from her purse.

I ask Claire if she's heard anything about Jack White playing a solo show in the city.

Claire hands me the knife and baggie. "Yeah. From a bunch of overactive, overimaginative retards who think he's the new Lou Reed."

I pop the baggie open and dig out a large bump with the tip of the knife and move it toward my nose.

"But I doubt it's true," she says. "I doubt Mr. White is going to come to any dive bar and play a solo set in this fucking city."

Tell me when I'm good, Claire.

"You're good," she giggles, pushing herself off of the stall. "Snort now, Travis."

I shove the knife up to my left nostril, snap my head back, and sniff hard with everything I have.

Damn.

Claire takes the knife and drugs from my hands. She dips into it and scoops out a big bump. "Tell me when I'm good," she says.

You're good.

She inhales the pile. Hands the knife and baggie back to me, and starts telling me about this girl she met last fall during her first semester of college. "Her name was Brenda," she says. "She lived on the same dorm floor as me. We had this American History class together and sat next to each other."

I dig into the bag.

Claire continues. "She was from this wealthy suburb of Chicago. Her parents were absolutely loaded. They would put five hundred dollars a week into her checking account, which she used on blow. And this chick would do two fucking eight balls a week. Easily. She was always loaded."

I lift the knife from the bag.

"You're good," Claire tells me. I snort the bump.

"So anyway, about halfway through the semester, we're in the history class, and right in the middle of lecture Brenda sneezed. And there was this superloud, superintense popping noise, like *BANG*, like a fucking champagne cork being squeezed out."

Claire stops.

What?

"Do another bump," she grins.

I do one.

And Claire goes, "When Brenda sneezed, she blew her

fucking septum out, and this stream of blood started pouring from whatever was left of her nose, all over the classroom."

Pause.

"And I never saw her again."

I almost drop the coke on the floor.

What the fuck was that?

She takes the coke and knife back from me. "What, Travis?"

Why would you tell someone that kind of a story while they were doing blow? It's pretty fucked up.

"But"—she giggles, stabbing the knife into the baggie—"does it make you want to stop what you're doing?"

I don't say anything.

"Does it?" she presses.

I guess not, Claire.

"A story like that, does it make you want to never do drugs again?"

No.

"Do you think anyone's stopped driving around drunk since Kyle's accident?"

I doubt it.

And Claire shrieks, "Exactly." She says, "Because until it's your septum, or your fucking spinal cord that gets destroyed, and as long as this shit still makes you feel good, better than it does to be sober, there is absolutely no reason to stop doing any of it."

Claire stops. She knifes up two more bumps, one up

each nostril. Then she closes the baggie, folds the knife away, and drops both of them back into her purse.

I am superhigh and I ask Claire if she has a marker or a pen on her.

"No. Why?"

I want to write something on here.

I point to the wall of the stall.

Claire looks toward the ceiling as if she's in deep thought. Her mouth pops open. "I know," she says. She digs through her purse and pulls out a stick of black eyeliner. "Here." She hands it to me.

I twist the cap off and press my hand against the wall on my left, right next to this spot where someone's written "COBAIN IS GOD." But nothing comes out. I cannot think of anything to write.

"I'll go first," Claire says, running one hand down the part in her hair.

All right.

I'm embarrassed. It was my idea and I couldn't think of anything.

Claire takes the eyeliner. She scans all the walls before flipping the toilet seat down and straddling it. She writes "Fuck you, Jordan Catalano, and your so-called life. Fuck you for being that hot. Fuck you for being that cool. Fuck you for breaking the hearts of millions of girls around the world. You bastard!"

"There," Claire smiles, standing up. "Now you try again."

I take the eyeliner back, but still nothing comes out. My

head is completely jammed. So once again Claire takes the eyeliner away from me. "Let me write something for you," she says.

Go ahead, Claire.

Claire inches up to me and drags her fingers down the side of my face. "I got it." She turns around and writes "Fuck you, Clifford Miles and Laura Kennedy. Fuck you for doing what you did. Fuck you for going behind people's backs and lying for all these months. What do yo—"

I grab on to Claire's forearm.

I think you made your point.

"Did I?"

I think you did.

"Okay," she whispers. "Here." Claire puts her hands over mine. "Like this." She sets my hands on her waist. "How does that feel, Travis?"

It feels pretty okay.

"Just pretty okay?" she presses, leaning into my neck.

It feels amazing.

Claire pushes her crotch against my pelvis. She bites the lobe of my ear.

Aerosmith changes to Dio and Claire sings, *"There's no sign of the morning coming, you've been left on your own, like a rainbow in the dark, just like a rainbow in the dark."* Then she bites my ear again.

What are you doing, Claire?

"Nothing." She pushes me away from her. "I'm just glad you called me tonight," she grins. "Really fucking glad."

□ □ □

Fast forward two hours.

Claire and I are at this bar the Jungle Gym, two blocks over from the Drunken Whale.

There are two good things about the Jungle Gym—two good things only. One: They have a nickel-pitcher night every Thursday. Two: They have a pre-'91 G N' R pinball machine. And I have been dying to play the machine since we got here, but I haven't been able to because this guy with long and gross blond hair, wearing jean shorts and a NASCAR tank top will not get off of it. He wouldn't even take the twenty bucks I offered him, telling me, "I'll be done when I'm done, stud."

I sit on a bar stool and stare angrily until Claire stumbles out of the ladies' room and falls all the way across the room to me.

She jumps onto my lap after handing me her like tenth vodka tonic, then she bites my ear again.

What's up with that, Claire?

"I don't know," she smiles, begins rubbing my crotch.

Is that what you want?

"I want another motherfuckin' drink! Will you buy me another drink?"

What do you want?

"Vodka tonic."

I turn to the bartender, order two. Claire buries her head in my shoulder and goes, "Can I tell you something, Travis?"

Anything.

She tilts back so that our eyes are dead on. "My mother has no idea, absolutely none whatsoever, who my real father is," she slurs.

I thought your dad took off on you when you were little.

"Yeah," Claire slurs. "Probably like five minutes after he nutted inside of my mom."

The bartender brings us our drinks and I pay him.

"Wanna know something else?" Claire asks.

What else?

"I was born in the back of a used station wagon . . . on some dirt road outside of Dysart, Iowa."

Nudging her to the edge of my knees, I say, That's some pretty weird stuff.

"I know it," she whimpers. "I've never told anyone that before. But I wanted to tell you, Travis." Claire smothers her hands over her face.

I won't tell anyone.

Pause.

Are you going to cry, Claire?

"Maybe."

But I don't think you have to. You've made it this far without anyone knowing.

She parts her hands to the sides. Looks at me. "I'm really sorry," she says.

Don't be.

"But I feel terrible now. That was like fucking heavy and shit."

So what?

Claire leans back into me. She bites my ear again. Sticks her tongue inside it, sending this awesome chill down my back. Every strand of hair on my neck stands up.

"Can we go now?" she asks.

You wanna leave?

"I do. I want you to take me home. I want you to fuck me, Travis Wayne."

"Wanna know something, Travis?" Claire asks in between a series of yawns, me trying my absolute hardest to navigate my car through the city streets without sideswiping pedestrians or running over people on bikes.

What's that?

"I've always had a crush on you. I've always wanted to hook up with you."

You're drunk, Claire.

"And you're fucking hot, Travis. I wanna fuck you!" She bites my ear again.

Chills attack my spine, and while I'm shaking my back out, Claire falls against the door and says, "Will you promise me something?"

What?

"Will you promise me you'll stay in the city? That you won't leave again?"

Claire, I—

"Just please, Travis. Promise me. I love you. So do this for me. Promise me you won't leave again."

Okay.

"Okay what?" Claire snaps.

I promise I won't leave again.

"Thank you," she says, trying to control another yawn.

I pat my legs down to feel for cigarettes but I'm out so I ask Claire if she has any.

"I'm out too," she says.

Awesome.

"Stop and get some," she says. "There's a mini-mart right up the street here." Claire points to the windshield.

Cool.

"Sweet," she smiles, yawns again, and at the next block, I turn into the empty parking lot of this really small gas station.

"Hurry up," Claire sighs, patting her mouth over and over with her hand.

I walk into the station and grab two packs of Parliament Lights. Pay and leave.

While I'm standing on the sidewalk in front of the gas station, I hear glass breaking to my left and spin in that direction, a gust of wind blowing past me, almost knocking me over.

My eyes latch on to a thin streak of shadow as it darts across the darkened edge of the parking lot, and as I regain my balance, Cliff steps out of the deep shadows, shedding his framed outline, becoming real to me.

"Travis."

I feel relief—then I feel complete anger.

Are you following me, Cliff?

He takes another couple of steps closer to me.

"No way. I'm not following you. I don't follow people," he informs me while crossing his arms and scratching the tops of both of them with his fingers.

What are you doing out here? I ask him.

"I'm just," he starts, stops. Looks around. "I'm just lurking around I guess. Did you hear about my dad?"

No.

I start packing one of the boxes of smokes.

Cliff leans down and scratches the bottoms of his legs left uncovered from the cutoff jeans he's wearing. He says, "My old man found out that I've been screwing Marcy and he got into a fight with her. She tried hitting him with a pan, but missed, and then my dad smacked her across the face and knocked her clean cold, and when she came to, she called 911 and my dad got put in jail for the night." Cliff stiffens his back and looks at me. "Isn't that funny, Trav? My dad in jail for a night."

I don't say anything. Open my cigarettes.

"Who's in your car?" Cliff asks, moving even closer.

Claire.

"She drunk?"

Yeah, Cliff.

I light a cigarette.

And I have to get going.

I start for my car.

"Hey, man," Cliff says.

I stop but don't face him.

What?

"Can I use your cell phone real quick?"

It's dead, Cliff.

I push forward.

"Travis."

This time I flip back around.

What do you want, Cliff? I fucking hate you! What do you want?

"Can I have some change for the pay phone?"

Are you serious?

Cliff nods. "Please, man. It's important."

And it's now when my eyes drop and I notice the two big gashes on his right arm that are still kinda bleeding and the fact that he's barefoot.

"Please, man," he whispers this time.

Fine.

I reach into my pockets and scoop out a handful of change.

Here. Come and get it.

He takes the money.

"Thank you," he says.

Fuck off, Cliff.

But as I'm turning away from him, he grabs my arm and goes, "Do you remember that girl me and you lost our virginity to? The one we tag-teamed in the abandoned school basement."

Ripping my arm away, I say, Yeah, what about her?

"She was sixteen and she was hot," Cliff says. "And we were only thirteen."

So what, Cliff? What are you even talking about?

"Do you remember what happened when it was over? You came first and then I came and while we were getting dressed again, I made that really bad joke."

Pause.

I sigh.

I remember you saying something. So what?

"Do you remember the joke?"

I don't.

"Because I do, Travis. And after I said it, both of you looked at me like I was a complete retard. Like I was this big pie grinder. And you rolled your eyes and told that slut not to pay attention to me and she laughed and said that she'd take your advice."

So what, Cliff? It was a stupid fucking joke.

"So you do remember it."

Yeah, I do. You went, "Why did Travis cross the road?" And the girl asked you why, and you said, "'Cause his dick was stuck in the chicken." It was so fucking stupid, man. And you made both of us look like complete jackasses when you said it.

Cliff rolls his head back and flips his chin to the sky. "Oh, I'm sorry," he quips. "I made the great Travis Wayne, the guy everyone's supposed to love and be cool with, look human. What's the world coming to?"

What'd you want me to do after you said that, Cliff? Laugh? It wasn't funny.

Cliff slides away and throws the change I just gave him across the parking lot.

You're not getting any more, I tell him.

"I hated you after you laughed at me that day," he snaps. "I never forgot about that shit." Cliff thrusts forward, making me step back.

I'm sorry I laughed, Cliff. What do you want me to do about it now?

And he says, "Nothing. I just wanted to make sure that you still remembered."

I never forgot, asshole.

"Good," he says, then walks away from me, disappearing into the same shadow.

Me, I continue to my car and climb back inside of it. Claire is sleeping. She's passed out in her seat, her head against the window, one of her hands stuffed under her face.

Dropping the cigarettes in between us, I push my hands through my hair and lean back and close my eyes.

But the thought that Cliff's still watching me, standing all alone, just staring at me, makes me uneasy, so I start my car and drive Claire back to her apartment.

Only once we're there, she will not wake up. I shake her and say her name and even try tickling her stomach but none of it works. So I step out of the car and walk around to her door and pull her outside and stand her up. I dig through Claire's purse until I find her keys. Then I hoist her off her feet, draping and folding her over my shoulder very carefully, like a towel made of diamonds, and carry her up to her room.

And when I lay Claire gently onto her bed, her eyes open briefly, and she smiles, and she says, "I love you, Travis."

I know you do.

Claire scoots a pillow under her head. "You promised me," she says.

What's that?

"You promised you wouldn't leave again."

I know I did.

Claire's smile fades as her eyes drift shut again, and once I'm through covering her with a sheet, I kill the lights and walk out to the living room.

I drop to the couch and turn on the TV and pass out at some point while watching *License to Drive* on the USA network.

36

I LEAVE CLAIRE'S THE NEXT MORNING WHILE SHE'S STILL
asleep and drive home, and when I turn into my parents' driveway, I about run *smack* into Laura's car, which is pulling out of it.

I give her the finger and race to the top of the driveway
and bring my car to a stop and step outside.

Laura does that same thing. She steps out of her
seventeenth-birthday present, saying, "Travis, do not go
inside. I need to talk to you. I have to explain to you what
happened."

Jesus Christ, Laura. I know what happened. You
screwed my best friend and I paid for your abortion.

I turn my back to her and continue for the front door.

"Travis!" she screams at the top of her lungs.

I stop. My ears are ringing.

"Please hear me out," Laura begs. "Please listen to what I
have to say."

I don't want to at all. I do not want to listen to anyone
anymore. But I turn back around to face Laura, who folds
her arms across her body and walks toward me, shaking.

Go ahead, Laura. Talk.

Laura stops at the bottom of the front steps and takes

off her sunglasses. Her eyes are red. "Nothing," she starts. "Nothing I could say to you right now would even begin to let you understand how I, me, Laura, your fucking girl-friend, was feeling when Cliff and I did what we did."

Did what you did.

My face is bright red.

You two fucked, okay. Just say it! You guys fucked while we were still together.

"I didn't know that, Travis. I didn't know we were still a couple."

Bullshit.

Laura grabs her hair. She fakes like she's pulling it out. "Baby, if I'd actually thought that you and I were still going out, or that you weren't doing the exact same thing to me, then I would've never let Cliff near me."

No, fuck that! That makes no sense, Laura, because if you were really thinking that way, then why would you call me in Arizona and break up with me?

Laura presses her fingers into her forehead. "Because I wanted you to know that for once I wasn't going to wait for you to tell me everything was all right. That you and I were still cool," she snorts.

That's a bullshit answer, Laura.

"It's the truth," she sneers.

The truth.

I wipe the sweat from my face with my shirt.

The truth is so beyond you at this point. The truth is something you obviously can't get a handle on.

"And you can?" she asks.

No. I don't think any of us can.

A long moment of silence. The two of us stare at each other.

You broke my heart, Laura.

"And you broke mine," she says. "I was your girlfriend, Travis. Do you understand how bad it hurt when you quit talking to me? You didn't even tell me what was going on. I had no idea what you were thinking."

Because I didn't either.

"Why couldn't you have just called me back?" She starts to cry. "I was so happy and then you made me hate myself. I hated myself, Travis!"

Don't try to pin that crap on me. I am not the one who made you feel that way, Laura. You've hated yourself since before we were ever together.

I turn around again and reach for the front door handle and Laura grabs on to me.

"Don't leave me," she pleads.

I swing around.

Get your fucking hands off of me.

"Don't be like this," she screeches.

I knock her hands down, grab her arms and start shaking her.

Don't you get it, Laura? You mean nothing to me anymore.

"I do too."

You're dead to me.

I press down on her arms even harder.

You are nothing, Laura.

"Travis, quit it. You're hurting me."

Nothing we had means anything anymore.

I'm shaking Laura so hard that her entire body pounds back and forth, carving the humid block of air around us into soft pieces of breeze.

"Let go of me, Travis."

Not until you tell me that you are nothing.

"Travis, let go."

Tell me, Laura.

"Travis." Laura throws her arms into the air, destroying my grip. But her momentum carries her backward. She loses her balance and tumbles down the stairs.

You are dead to me.

Laura lies there weeping.

I hate you.

"I'm sorry."

I hate you.

"I didn't mean for this to happen."

I push the door open.

"Travis."

You are an ugly fucking person.

I step into the house.

"Well, fine then!" she screams, as I face her one last time. "Be that way, you small-dick faggot! See if I care. Cliff was much more of a man than you'll ever be."

I slam the door shut as hard as I can. Picture frames rattle. I light a cigarette.

Inhale.

Exhale.

37

I WAKE UP FROM A NAP LATER THAT AFTERNOON, shivering and sweating and breathing so heavily that my chest hurts.

I'm scared.

My bad dreams are back.

I lift the sheet that's covering me and look at my jeans and they are soaking wet from me pissing myself.

I slide the jeans off and get out of bed and walk to my closet and my stomach turns violently. My bowels start to move. Sprinting out of my room, I blaze down the hall and duck into the bathroom, slamming onto the toilet.

My asshole opens and shit starts falling out of it so hard that the toilet water splashes against my butt.

There's a knock at the door.

I'm busy.

"Travis." It's my sister. "I need to talk to you."

I'm busy.

"I have to talk to you now," my sister says, then opens the unlocked door and walks in wearing a blue shirt with an image of Gwen Stefani on the front of it.

I cover myself as best I can.

Get out of here.

"No." She storms across the room, stopping like five feet from me. "Did you tell Mom that I've been doing drugs?"

No. Now get out.

"Bullshit," my sister snaps, fanning the air in front of her face. "Don't lie to me."

I'm not.

I fart loudly and more shit falls and more water splashes. Now get out.

"You're lying. Mom told me she talked to you about what I've been doing and then she asked me if I've been abusing drugs."

She's worried about you, that's all. Now leave.

"So you did tell her."

No, I told her I didn't know shit and that she needed to ask you.

More shit comes out and I feel clumps of it sliding and falling off the lower parts of my butt.

Exhaling loudly, my sister sneers, "You stupid fucking asshole. Why didn't you just tell her I wasn't doing anything at all. Now Mom and Dad are saying they may not let me get my license when I turn sixteen next month because I might be using."

I'm sorry.

"I hate you."

I thought you already did.

"You are so pathetic. Look at yourself."

I'm going to the bathroom.

"No," my sister snorts. "Look at your life. You dropped out of school. You don't have a job. You live at home. And your girlfriend of five years had your best friend's abortion."

My shoulders tense.

How did you find out about that?

"Katie told me. She was half asleep in the back room of the trailer when you went over there. She heard everything and now everyone knows!"

I want to stand up and shove my sister out of the room but I can't.

"You big loser. Your life sucks so bad."

I rip a huge fart and more poop tumbles out.

Just leave me alone.

"Gladly," my sister says, smiling, fanning the air again.

I take a deep breath.

She exits the bathroom.

And I want to start crying, but I can't figure out how to.

And then more shit falls out.

38.

"DUDE, IT COULD BE WORSE. YOU COULD'VE BEEN ONE of the chicks that had to kiss Corky Thatcher in an episode of *Life Goes On*," Michael snorts from the other end of the phone. "You could've been the other kid at summer camp who got molested with Wesley in that really awkward episode of *Mr. Belvedere*, brah."

Fuck you, Michael.

And Michael says, "Hold up."

He goes, "Dave says you could've been one of those guys who 'pretended' they were all into Natalie from *The Facts of Life* just so they could get superclose to Blair."

I start laughing, which is the whole point of this conversation. Them cheering me up. Because according to Michael, things could be a lot fucking worse. According to Michael, I could be the dude who played Boner on *Growing Pains*, twenty years later. He says, "Not being able to get another acting gig. Falling completely off the face of the earth. Becoming so irrelevant, not even jokes about you make much sense."

It could be a whole lot worse for me, according to Dave, because instead of finding out that I paid for my girlfriend to have my best friend's abortion, I could've found out that my mom had been a groupie on the tour that Joey Lawrence did to promote his very first CD, *Soulmates*, and this, according to Dave, through Michael, would be much, much worse.

I'm laughing so hard, my body hurts.

That's awesome.

"Of course it is," says Michael.

And I say, But I'm still mad. I'm still pissed off.

"Dude," Michael snorts. "What did you really expect? I mean, if Laura's naive enough to spend three straight nights going to Björk shows in Chicago with her ironically hipster boyfriend, then she's obviously naive enough to bang Cliff without any protection."

But Cliff was my friend, Michael.

"So. He was my friend too. But that still doesn't change the fact that he's a fucking bastard. Don't you remember like two summers ago when his old man got trashed and burnt him with a cigar before the three of us went to a party?"

I remember.

"And at the party, you remember what Cliff did?"

Pause.

Yeah.

"He put that chick's cat into a microwave and cooked it."

I said I remember, Michael.

"Cliff's a scumbag."

I don't say anything.

And Michael says, "What are you doing tonight?"

I wanna party. I wanna try to forget about all of this for a few hours.

"Righteous. That's what Dave and I are doing right now. We're partying. Trying to forget about shit. You should drop into the new pad and kick it with us."

Cool. I'll be right over.

I show up at Michael and Dave's crib around ten, wearing a pair of dark blue Levi's and a plain white T-shirt.

Dave answers the door in a pink T-shirt that says "I Heart Izzy Stradlin" on it. He smiles and gives me a hug and says, "I hope you feel better now."

Yeah, man. Thanks.

I follow Dave down this long hallway plastered with posters then into this huge living room aligned with three bay windows that overlook Kennedy Street.

The Bronx are blasting from the computer sitting on the desk to my left, and Michael is sitting on a bright red couch in the middle of the room, talking to a couple of kids I've never seen before, who look young—like fifteen, sixteen young—and who are seated on the sofa to his left.

"What up, what up," Michael shouts, turning his head.

I like it, man.

Michael looks back at the kids on the couch. He gives them some coke. They give him some money. Then they get up and leave.

I sit down on the couch to his right after bumping fists with him, and Michael says, "Those two kids have been up partying since last night. I was in the bathroom doing bumps at this girl's house in Little Minneapolis and they walked in and wanted to buy some coke. And the one who was wearing the shirt that said "Fuck You, Mom," he was like, 'I've never done it before—what's it like?' and I thought about it for a minute, then said, 'Imagine having to say something so bad, worse than at any other moment in your entire life, and then imagine finally getting the chance to say it to everyone, only no one is listening because they're saying the most important thing of their lives at the same time. It's kinda like that.'"

I start laughing.

That's awesome, dude.

And Michael goes, "Anyway. Welcome to the new palace, Mr. Wayne."

Dave sits down across from me, right next to the huge television and entertainment system.

I say, This is the dream, man. This is what everyone wants.

"This, and a threesome with those gnar babes in t.A.T.u.," Michael smirks, leaning forward in his charcoal colored jeans and black Hüsker Dü shirt. He grabs a can of Budweiser from the case sitting on the floor and hands me one.

I open it and take a drink, and pull my wallet out and grab two hundred dollars out of the three hundred I pulled from the ATM on my way over, and set it down on the coffee table in between the three sofas.

Let's do this, boys.

Michael and Dave smile at each other. Michael tosses five baggies of coke at me.

Putting three of them into my wallet, I take the other two and dump them into one big pile on this pretty big mirror. Then I pick up one of the three razor blades lying at the top of the mirror and begin cutting.

"Do you wanna go to this party tonight on Baltimore and Twenty-eighth?" Michael asks. He picks up a flyer from the coffee table and hands it to me. "My presence has been requested."

By who?

"Every coke head in this fucking city," he snaps.

I look at the flyer. There's a picture of a girl in a bra and underwear. She's wearing a crown on her head and underneath the picture it says:

Delila—Katie—and Page
present the first annual
It's Getting Hot In Here,
So Take Off All Your Clothes Party

Then:

Fuck The Heat! It's Our Treat!
Free Kegs—Jungle Juice—And Wet The Bed While It Lasts!

Cool.

Then I slide a line from the pile and ask them how long they've been blowing rails today.

"Since we were at the studio trying to practice," Dave snorts.

I chop another line from the pile.

Trying?

And Michael goes, "We didn't get shit done. Thomas and Rodney showed up straight from an all-nighter, and two songs into practice, I look up from my drum set and Thomas is sitting in a chair passed out."

From being up all night?

I slide another line from the pile.

"No. From being fat. He's fat and he ran out of oxygen while he was singing and passed out for almost ten minutes, and by the time we revived him and went around the room sharing our own special experiences about what had just happened, none of us felt like playing anymore so we started doing drugs," Michael says, answering his cell phone.

I make a third line and put the mirror on the table.

And Dave says, "Travis, you know what you need to do now?"

What's that?

"You need to fuck one of Laura's friends, take some photos of yourself while you're doing it, and MySpace them to her."

I take a drink of beer.

I probably won't do that.

Grabbing this black straw with Michael's name engraved into it, I do a line and the tension falls from my body immediately.

Michael sets his phone down. "Holy shit," he sneers. "That was April. Chris got his ass kicked by April's dad and is in the hospital with some broken ribs and a concussion."

What'd he kick Chris's ass for?

"She said it was because he found out it was Chris who knocked her up, so he went over to Chris's house and beat up on him." Michael picks up the mirror and does a rail.

I say, So Chris is the father.

"Duh, Trav. That's what I just said. Were you listening to me at all or were you thinking about Laura."

Shut up, man.

Pause.

Should we go to the hospital?

"Fuck no," Michael smirks. "Fuck that piece of shit."

Dude, I say.

Michael turns to me. "Don't, *dude* me, Travis. Fuck that. Besides the fact that he ripped on you every time you weren't around, he came over here to score some shit the other day and snapped on me while we were passing a baggie around."

For what?

"I told him that he and April should name their kid Cheese Sandwich and he completely freaked out on me. He put me in a choke hold and pinned me against the wall."

I rub my eyes, trying not to laugh, but the image of Michael saying that to Chris is making it supertough not to. Cheese Sandwich.

And Michael goes, "If you wanna go to the hospital, fine. But I can guarantee you Chris would not do the same for you."

Dave takes the mirror and sets it on the table, and I look over my shoulder and stare at this wall-size poster of Kool Keith pinned next to the desk where the computer is.

A knock on the door.

"It's open!" Michael yells.

Dave does the line.

And in walks this dude with full ink sleeves on both arms. Long black hair. Wearing a blue T-shirt, a pair of tight jeans, holding hands with this Latina girl in a white dress, black fishnets, a blond streak running down the middle of her black hair.

Michael and Dave seem really stoked to see the guy. Dave sets the straw on the mirror, then hands the mirror to me, and I set it down next to me on the couch.

"Trav, this is Tommy Hart and his babe, Heather," Michael tells me, pointing at the both of them.

I tell them hi, and Tommy and Heather squeeze next to Dave, and from what I'm understanding, Tommy Hart plays lead guitar and sings for the Jill Kelly Experience, the band playing the Karen O look-alike contest with Lamborghini Dreams. Tommy and Heather know Michael from that, and also through Kyle, who was Heather's coke dealer.

Michael hands both of them beers and Tommy asks him if he's gone to court for the Jordan Knight thing yet.

Michael nods. "Yeah. I plead guilty and paid a few fines."

"That's it?" Tommy snorts as the Bronx turn into Blood on the Walls. "No celebrity scandal bullshit? No exclusive interviews with *Entertainment Tonight*?"

"No way, man," Dave sneers. "No one gives a shit about that guy anymore except for a few middle-aged queers with acne."

Everyone starts laughing and Heather goes, "I told all the girls I dance with about it and they all thought it was hilarious."

You're a stripper? I ask.

Heather nods. "I dance at the 540 House on Friday and Saturday nights. You should come by sometime."

I pick up the mirror and divvy out ten more lines and Dave goes, "What did the stripper do to her asshole before she went to work?"

"What?" Heather snaps, like she's all irritated and heard one too many stripper jokes.

Dave giggles and wipes his nose and says, "She dropped him off at band practice."

"Nice," Tommy says, reaching over and bumping fists with Dave.

I hand the mirror across the table to Tommy and tell him to go first.

"Hey cool, man," Tommy says. "I like you. What was your name again?"

Travis.

"I like you, Travis," he says, and Heather winks at me. She grins real sexy like. And Michael asks Tommy if he has a lot of Jill Kelly porn.

Tommy sets the mirror on his lap. "Every single one she ever made," he grins, then slams both lines.

"So does Travis," Michael tells him. "Travis has the entire Jill Kelly and Sydney Steele and Nicole Sheridan collections."

I look at Heather and she looks at Dave and Dave is looking at the ceiling, rubbing his nose really fast. He looks at his hand, then wipes off whatever is on it.

Tommy holds the mirror in front of Heather. She picks the straw up and does both lines, then Tommy puts the mirror back on the table and gives Michael a hundred dollars. Michael gives him two grams and tells them about the party we're going to.

"Maybe we'll meet up with you guys later," Tommy says with a sniff. He wipes his nose. "We're meeting some friends at the Glass Castle. Maybe we'll see you guys for after-hours."

"Awesome, man. Call me," Michael says.

Tommy and Heather leave. And then Michael, Dave, and I finish the coke on the mirror. Pouring another gram onto the mirror, Michael goes, "Hey, Trav, I might know something that can cheer you up."

I'm not calling James Spader again, I tell him.

"I don't want you to," Michael says. "I was gonna show this fan video on YouTube for the Shellac song 'Prayer to God,' but if you're gonna be a dick about it, then I won't."

I'm not being a dick, man. Let's see the video.

All three of us walk to the computer and Michael pulls the video up. It starts playing, and the words to the song, which is about this guy who wants his ex-girlfriend and her new lover destroyed, are making me feel really good. . . .

"*To the one true god above, here is my prayer . . . there are two people here, and I want you to kill them. . . .*"

When the video has ended, I'm like, That's fucking awesome. I wish the fan boy who made that video was my friend.

"I already like him better than I like you." Michael points to me. "And you," he says, pointing to Dave next.

The three of us do another round of lines and Michael goes, "Check this live Sonic Youth video out for 'Making the Nature Scene.'"

That video pops on and Michael spins around in the computer chair and goes, "Are you watching Lee Renaldo play guitar, Dave? You see how he's moving around the stage and *putting* on a show along with the music." Michael says, "That's what you and Rodney should be doing more of. You two need to be more active onstage. I don't wanna play a show with statues, man. No one goes to a show to see a bunch of statues standing on a stage."

Dave takes another line. "Calm the fuck the down," he says. "We've only played one show."

"I'm just giving you some friendly advice, man. We're not the fucking Strokes."

"I know," Dave says. "We're better than that."

"Exactly."

We finish the rest of the coke on the mirror and call a cab and split for the party.

There are a lot of people at the party on Baltimore and Twenty-eighth. The music is loud, mostly hip-hop, and although most of the girls and guys are fully dressed, a few of them aren't, dancing and running around in their underwear and some with nothing on at all. The whole place smells like sweat and beer and vomit.

When we step into this room right next to the kitchen, this girl with purple and pink hair runs up to Michael and freaks out. She grabs his arm and screams, "Isn't this the best party ever!"

And Michael says, "Only if you were completely naked."

But the girl must not hear him or understand what he says, because the next thing she yells is, "I met Gwen Stefani last week in Minneapolis! It was my dream come true. I could die now and everything in the world would be right."

Michael starts laughing in her face. He yanks his arm out of her hands and goes, "Listen. I only want to talk to you if you have money and can buy the shit that I'm selling. I'm not giving out free bumps. I'm not giving you any free shit. You can either pay or you can get on your knees and suck me and my friends off."

The girl scrunches her face. Her cheeks get red and she runs past us and disappears into the crowd.

"Fucking coke whore," Michael snaps, his eyes darting back and forth.

I rub my eyes and wipe the sweat from my forehead. I follow Dave and Michael and like ten other people into this bedroom with blue velvet sheets and large oil paintings of naked black girls hanging from the walls, the Liars blasting from the stereo.

The door slams shut and Michael pulls his coke out and starts selling to these girls. Baggies getting passed around. Everyone yelling over everyone else. Some dude in a blazer telling me a joke:

Dude: What do Pink Floyd and Dale Earnhardt have in common?

Me: The wall was their last hit.

Dude: That's right. You've heard it before, huh?

Me: You just told me that same joke ten minutes ago.

Dude: Right.

It's all pretty chill until Dave turns to this guy Roger, who has a bandana around his neck, and goes, "Hey, man, what are you? Some kind of flute player?"

And Roger choke-slams Dave against the wall, and when he lets go, Dave says, "Why the fuck would you do that to me, Roger?"

And Roger starts breaking down and crying about his mother and growing up in Ohio, and this chubby kid, Denny, who beat him up in fourth grade, and when Michael sees this happening, he points at Roger and starts laughing, and I leave the room when I realize that one of the girls standing near me is the same one that sucked me off in her boyfriend's bedroom two summers ago while her boyfriend was passed out on the floor beside the bed.

I keep moving and pushing through the party. I get to this table that's been set up in a corner and I give the girl in the red nighty standing behind it ten dollars, and grab a cup and fill it with jungle juice, and when the girl asks me how much change I want back, I go, "Change?" and pound what's left of my cup, then fill it up again, and keep moving.

I light a cigarette and realize how coked out I am. I walk to the other side of the room and lean against a wall. The new Bloc Party single starts blasting and I smudge my smoke out and light another one.

"Got one of those for me?" I hear, and snap my head to the left.

Natalie Taylor is standing beside me wearing a navy blue halter top and a pair of crotch tight Miss Sixty jeans that are tucked into a pair of black mid-calf boots, and she has new tattoos on both her arms.

I hand her a smoke and light it for her.

"Thanks." She takes a drag. "I'm a bit surprised to see you here, Travis."

I don't even know why I'm here, to be honest with you, but I am. I'm just here.

Arching her eyebrows, Natalie goes, "I heard about what happened between you and Cliff."

Who told you?

"Claire," she says. "I saw her last night at Bottoms Up. She told me all about it. She also told me that you two almost hooked up."

I take a drag.

Almost.

Natalie steps into me. "I think she really likes you, Travis. You should try to make something work with her."

No. No. I don't think so. Claire is too awesome and sweet and beautiful.

"And what are you?"

I'm not that. You of all people should know that. You should know that I would only destroy those good things about her.

"Or maybe you're just scared," she says.

Fuck you.

I take a drink.

What are you doing that's so special?

"I'm moving to San Francisco at the end of August. I'm selling the trailer, packing my shit, and leaving this stupid city."

Where's Cliff gonna go?

Natalie takes the last drag and blows the smoke in my face and tells me she doesn't care. She tells me, "I kicked him out a couple of days ago. I don't know where he's at." She drops the smoke to the ground and smears it out with her boot, then she pulls her shirt up just past her belly button. "You see that?"

What am I looking for?

Natalie points just above her belly button at this brownish scar. "Cliff did that to me while we were all fucked up. He cut me right before he was ready to come on me."

I don't say anything.

"I thought about pressing charges, but what would be the point? I'm moving, ya know. He'll get what he deserves some day." Leaning even closer to me, Natalie whispers, "We all fucking will." Then she kisses the side of my face and walks away, her cell phone to her ear.

I need to do more drugs. So I walk upstairs and look for a bathroom and find one that's empty.

Standing in front of the mirror, I look at myself. I stare at my dry lips, the dry skin peeling away just below my nose. I pull another gram from my wallet and set it down on the faucet and try to break as many of the clumps down to powder with the butt of my lighter as I can. Once I feel like it's good enough, I hold the baggie in front of me and flick it quickly, back and forth, back and forth, until all the coke sits in one big block. Then I pop the baggie open and start keying out some bumps.

I do four, five. I do a sixth one. And right after I've put everything back and wiped my nose clean and checked my nostrils in the mirror, the door bursts open and in walks these two girls, fourteen, maybe fifteen years old, very skinny and tan. Wasted. Giggling uncontrollably.

"Do you have any drugs?" the one in the purple and black underwear asks.

Nope.

"Then what are you doing in here?" she screams. "Were you jacking off and watching yourself in the mirror?"

I was doing the rest of my drugs and now they're gone.

"Liar," her friend, the one in the orange underwear, snaps.

I roll my eyes and begin to exit when the girl in the purple goes, "No, wait. I know you. I know your sister. Are you Travis Wayne?"

I spin around.

I might be.

The girl in purple goes, "I . . . I mean we . . . we go to school with your little sister, Vanessa. We know Vanessa Wayne," she slurs.

"I loved her, she was like, the coolest, raddest chick in our whole grade," the orange girl stutters. "Until we saw her the other night."

"Shut up," the other girl snorts. "You're talking about his sister."

I shut the door.

What was the other night? I ask.

"Nothing. My friend doesn't know what she's talking about."

"Bullshit," her friend barks back. "She got fucked by this dude for some OCs at a party."

My face gets red.

I don't believe you. You're full of shit.

"It's true, dude," the girl in the purple tells me. "I saw it too. He had her handcuffed to a bed and was taking turns with one of his friends."

Who—I come at them with my fingers flying in the air— who was doing that to her?

Both of them shrug. "Just some guy she wanted some shit from," the purple and black girl says. "I don't know his name or his friend's name. We were both surprised. A lot of people were. Your sister used to be fucking gorgeous, but now . . ." The girl shakes her head. "She's totally not. She looks worse than you."

I dig the rest of that baggie back out of my wallet and hold it in front of them.

"You do have drugs," they both say.

I did.

Popping the baggie open, I flip it upside down, and dump it on the floor.

"What the hell?!" the girl in the purple and black screams.

And I leave the bathroom and run right into this girl wearing a pair of emerald green underwear and a matching bra. She's crying, telling this guy in a pink button-up shirt and sunglasses how she just threw up in someone's bedroom and feels super, super horrible about it and the guy in the pink shirt puts his arm around her and goes, "It's okay. Don't feel bad. Puking is cool. Everyone's doing it." Then he shoves his index finger down his throat and makes himself throw up, but some of it spews onto the girl, on her chest and on her legs, and she starts screaming and smacks the guy across the face, and runs into the bathroom I was just in.

Me, I shrug at the guy when he looks at me. Then I go back downstairs to look for Michael or Dave, but I can't find either one of them. So I go back to the table and chug three more cups of jungle juice, and the girl in the red nighty is like, "Dude, is everything okay with you?"

You don't need to ask me that. You don't care. You don't give a shit that my sister might've fucked some dudes for some OCs and that my girlfriend fucked my former best friend, who is now into cutting chicks open while he's fucking them.

The girl stands there, staring, her mouth wide open. She goes, "Are you Travis Wayne?"

This Cage song starts bumping.

No.

I flip around, knocking a cup to the ground, and think I see Dave standing near the kitchen, talking with a black girl.

I push these two girls standing in front of me, who have no business wearing garter panties in public, out of the way, and I slide to where I think Dave is, but it's not Dave at all. This guy has blond hair and the black girl he's talking to is really a white dude with long hair.

I'm exhausted. I wipe more sweat from my face. I try to call Michael but it goes straight to his voice mail and I don't leave a message.

Craning my neck around, my eyes land on that Bryan with a *y* kid. He's standing in between these two other hipstered-out kids with his shirt off, pointing straight at me, talking into the ear of the guy on his right, his bad tattoos exposed.

And when the kid he's talking to starts laughing, I move right at them yelling, What?

What do you have to say?

What do you have to give?

Then this other guy pops out of nowhere and steps in between me and Bryan.

I'll kick your ass right now, I say.

And Bryan squirrels up behind the guy holding me back. "Fuck you and your whore," he says.

I jab my finger at Bryan, just missing his face.

Let's do it. Me and you. I'll fucking destroy you.

Laughing, Bryan goes, "You can't do shit to me."

Around us, a small crowd has formed. I push hard against the only person standing between me and this pie grinder, this pilgrim dick, and I yell:

What do you got to give?

"Fuck you, man!" Bryan screams. He slaps the side of my face.

I swing back but I miss and then another guy comes up behind me and puts me in a headlock. "You're outta here, faggot," he rips. Then he drags me across the living room and past the front porch, and shoves me through the porch door.

Once I catch my balance, I charge at him, but stop when I realize it's like six guys, all bigger than me, blocking my way back into the house.

You can't kick me out and not him.

The guy who dragged me out laughs. "Yes I can. See, we know Bryan and we like Bryan and we don't know you and we obviously don't like you."

Everyone watching starts laughing.

Screw you then. You fucking steakhead.

"Oh, yeah?" he says.

Yeah, because I'm better than you. I fucking own you. All of you.

I step closer.

I own this fucking city!

If only my father could hear me. He would be so proud.

And the guy goes, "Do yourself a favor and go home." He walks back into the party with his friends and I'm left standing there all by myself.

I light a cigarette and cut down to the sidewalk in front of the house. Take my phone out. I scroll through the names. I call Claire but she doesn't answer. I call my sister and it's the same thing. I take a drag and then I call Laura.

"Travis," she answers.

Why did you do that to me, Laura?

"Travis, I'm sorry."

No you're not!

"I am too. I love you!"

What the fuck does that mean, you love me? What is that supposed to even mean?

"I don't know. I want to see you. Where are you?"

I don't know where I am. I'm not here.

"Where are you?"

I don't know, Laura. You're dead to me! You're dead to me! You stabbed me in the back and you mean nothing!

I hang up and lean over, groping my knees with my hands. My heart is racing so fast that it feels like it might break through my chest.

Someone yells my name and I look up.

Crossing the street in a shredded Billy Idol top and a white lace skirt, with a red bandana tied backward around her head, brown-bagging a pint of something, is this very cute girl. She looks very familiar, but I'm not sure where I've seen her before.

"How are you?" she asks, lighting her own cigarette.

I'm sorry, I don't—

"The Red Tie," she blurts out. "I was your waitress at the Red Tie a couple of months back when you ate there with your family."

Oh yeah. It's Maggie, right?

She nods. "Good memory."

It's like a thing with me.

Maggie shakes her head. "What is?"

What?

"What's a thing with you?" she asks.

I don't forget the names of pretty girls.

"God," she grins. "How high are you?"

I'm, ya know, I'm pretty fucking high.

Maggie hands me the brown bag. "Take a drink of this."

I take a huge drink. It's Jim Beam. I take another one.

Thanks.

She takes the bottle back. "What are you doing right now?"

I got kicked out of that party right there.

I point at the house.

What are you doing? I ask.

"Well, I was at this party a few blocks over but had to leave 'cause this creepy guy wouldn't leave me alone. He was like, 'My parents are gone for the weekend, so if you wanted to go all the way, I really think tonight would be the night,' so

I left and I'm walking to my house. It's just down the block. You wanna come over?"

I'd love to come over, Maggie.

Maggie's place is pretty rad. It's like a flat in the basement of this duplex, where you have to walk down these dark stairs, trapped between two stone walls, to get inside.

On the walk over, she told me she's a junior fine arts major at Grant and that her favorite movie is *Blue Velvet* and that her favorite band ever is the Replacements—Guns N' Roses a distant second—and I think, *Shit. Sweet. Not only is she hot, but she actually likes awesome shit.*

Maggie opens the door and lets me in. Tears for Fears is on the stereo. And she introduces me to two of her roommates, this guy Dirt and Jocelyn, and three of their friends, this chick Morgan, this dude Kenny, and this other girl, Haley, who are sitting around a table playing Texas Hold 'em.

Sprawled out on the sofa is this guy in a pink shirt and ripped jeans, with a blue scarf around his neck, wearing a visor that says "I Love the Killers," and someone's written "MySpace" across his chin in black marker.

"Everyone, this is Travis," Maggie says. "I met him at the restaurant back in June."

I sit down and pull out a gram, my last one, and toss it on the poker table.

If someone wants to cut that up we can all do some.

"The whole thing?" Dirt asks, eyes wide.

Of course. If you're not gonna do plenty, don't do any.

And Jocelyn's like, "I love you already, Travis."

Maggie comes back from the kitchen with two beers and hands one to me. Lifting her foot, she softly kicks the guy on the couch. "Is he all right?" she asks.

Everyone at the table kind of shrugs as the Tears for Fears fades into an Echo and the Bunnymen song, the one from the movie Donnie Darko that plays during the opening part, where Donnie wakes up on the edge of the woods and looks all confused before getting on his bike and riding home to his parents' house.

"Who is he?" Maggie asks.

And Dirt goes, "Chris and Mark brought him over here last night. I can't remember his name, though. He's been sleeping since before they left."

"God," Maggie groans, twisting the cap off her Miller Lite bottle. "Someone should really do something with him."

"We should drag him outside and strip his clothes off and leave him in an alley," Haley smiles. "Let the crackheads have at his body."

"We shouldn't do that," Jocelyn says.

"Well, alls I'm saying is that we need to do something else besides putting 'MySpace' on his fucking chin," Maggie snaps.

We could write Good Charlotte lyrics on his back and have someone come over and tattoo them into his skin.

"We could definitely do that," Jocelyn says.

"Or we could draw a picture of Richard Simmons on his chest and have someone tattoo that on him," Morgan laughs.

Kenny takes his cell out. "My buddy Eric has a gun and ink. I can call him right now. I guarantee he'd do it," he tells us.

"Call him," Maggie says.

Everyone in the room looks around at each other. No one says not to. So Kenny makes the call while Dirt starts chopping up the blow.

"I got his voice mail," Kenny says, setting his phone down. "He'll call back."

The front door opens suddenly and these two girls walk in, hammered and loud, falling all over the place. They sit down on the other sofa in the room. It seems that they're friends with Haley, or Morgan, or Jocelyn, or maybe they're friends with all three of them or none of them. But they ask if they can have some lines and I tell them it's fine, which it is, until the tan one with fake breasts and black hair starts shouting over everyone about how she knows this guy whose cousin knows this girl whose boyfriend used to roadie for the White Stripes and that if everything works like it could, if the stars are aligned just right, she might be able to get some sort of passes for the acoustic show Jack White's playing, if he indeed is playing one.

This pisses me off. I start grinding my teeth and walk into the kitchen and lean against the counter next to the fridge and light a cigarette.

Maggie walks in, swigging from her pint. "Are you feeling okay, dude?" she wants to know, handing the bottle to me.

Why does everyone always ask me that?

"I didn't know everyone always did."

I take a drink and choke it down my throat.

Is it not okay to be not okay?

Maggie slips the smoke from between my fingers. "I could give a shit less, Travis. It's just something to ask. It's like a conversation starter, an ice breaker," she says.

I swallow another pull and she takes the bottle from me. Tells me to open my lips. I do. Then Maggie slides the cigarette between them again and goes, "I haven't shown you the rest of the pad yet. My room is pretty rad." She smiles, taking my hand. "Would you like to see it?"

Uh-huh.

I trail Maggie into her room, the walls painted a dark shade of red. She closes the door behind us and goes straight for her bed, sprawling out across the top of it.

Taking a seat on the small sewing stool across from her, I make a comment about the Devo poster hanging from the wall above her bed and she mutters something about how she was supposed to go see them play in LA last year with her cousin, but a week before they were going to fly out to the coast, her cousin's stepmother put her cousin in rehab 'cause "she's a fucking queen bitch like that."

I chug my entire beer and Maggie picks up a remote for her CD player and turns it on, and this band the Knife starts playing.

There's a knock on the door.

Maggie tells whoever it is to come in. It's Dirt. He's holding a book with lines of coke on it and he says that we should go first since the coke is mine, and I'm thinking, *God, I've done a ton of blow tonight.*

Dirt sits down on the edge of Maggie's bed and hands the book to me.

Does anyone have a straw?

Maggie hands me one. I blow two rails and then Maggie does hers and then Dirt leaves and Maggie pats the mattress beside her. "Why don't you come over and sit next to me?" she says.

I get up, kick my boots off and crawl next to her, resting my back against the headboard.

"Is there any more coke?" she asks me.

There's always more fucking coke, but I don't have any more on me.

"That's probably for the best," she says, then asks me how old I am.

Like twenty-one.

"Really? The ID you used at the restaurant said you were twenty-three."

It did?

Maggie nods, setting the pint of beam on the nightstand beside her. "How old are you really?"

Nineteen.

She starts laughing. "Wow."

Should I leave?

"No," she says. "It's fine. You're cute. I want you to stay and get me off."

Maggie leans over and kisses me and I awkwardly put a

hand on her waist and push her on her back. We start undressing each other and everything seems to be fine until I slide my underwear off and notice how small and shriveled and soft my penis is.

Maggie looks at me. "Are you going to be able to get that up?"

With some help.

Sitting up, Maggie puts her mouth over my cock and gives me head for like twenty minutes, but nothing happens. I try jerking off. I spit on myself and she tries jerking it off. She gives me more head and I still can't get it up.

"Fucking great," she snaps.

An hour passes.

Nothing.

"Will you at least eat me out?" she asks.

Yeah. I can do that.

So I crawl in between her legs and stick my tongue on her pussy and start to give her head, but like five minutes into it, she shoves me away.

"What are you doing, Travis?"

What?

"That doesn't even feel good. You didn't touch my clit once."

I didn't?

Maggie groans loudly. "Are you a virgin?"

I shake my head.

"Well, you need to learn a few things. I'm serious." She reaches into her nightstand and pulls a dildo out and tells me to put my underwear and pants on.

I'm sorry, Maggie.

"Shhhh. Quit talking."

I lean against her headboard again.

"Do not say another word," she sneers. Then she squirts some lotion onto her dildo and starts fucking herself with it and I sit there and watch her. She gets off four times in like twenty minutes and when she's through, she throws the dildo on the ground, turns so that her back is facing me, and shuts her lamp off.

I feel like an asshole.

I don't even know what to do so I just sit there, my arms above my head, and like two hours later, Maggie flips over and goes, "Will you please leave?"

You want me to go?

"Yes. I don't know why you're still here. Just go."

That's pretty fair actually. I respect that.

I grab my things and walk out of the room and no one is up still. Even the dude on the sofa is gone. I look at the clock. It's almost six in the morning. I turn my phone back on and there are five messages from Michael wondering what happened to me.

I call him back.

"What do you want?" he snorts. "I'm kinda busy."

Doing what?

"Dave and I are showing this Delila chick those David Lee Roth videos on YouTube, and then we're gonna tag-team her and two of her friends."

So you're not up partying anymore?

"What are you even saying, Trav? Watching David Lee Roth and then fucking three girls with your roommate is a party. Quit being lame."

I don't say anything back.

Like thirty seconds of dead silence pass before Michael grunts, "Do you wanna come over and fuck them too? Is that what you're trying to ask? Because if you want to, then just come out and ask and maybe I'll say yes, and you can come over and finish them off."

Thoughts of my sister being fucked by two guys, one right after the other, smash through my head. And I tell Michael that I'm probably not going to come over and he goes, "What does that mean, though? You still might? You're either coming over or you're not."

I'm not.

"Fine," he snaps. Then: "Travis, sometimes you can be about as cool as an after-school special."

What the hell does that mean?

"Think about it," he groans, while some girl in the background giggles. "Just think about the way you're acting."

Click.

I put my phone away and walk outside.

The rising sun makes me cringe and groan. It makes me hate myself and makes me hate this world, and while I numbingly contemplate the best way to hail a cab back to my parents' house, I hear someone crying.

I look to my left and it's the kid who was passed out on the couch earlier.

He's sitting in this white plastic lawn chair that's missing half its back left leg, holding his face in his hands.

I walk closer to him and ask him if he's okay.

He lifts his face. His eyes are super red and puffy. "Who did this to me?" he sobs. "It hurts."

Did what?

"This!" he screams, standing up and ripping his shirt off, exposing the portrait of Richard Simmons giving a thumbs-up signal that's been tattooed onto his chest.

I take a step back.

And the kid says, "Do you know who did this to me?"

No, man. I'm sorry.

"It hurts," he cries, saliva falling from his bottom lip. "It hurts so bad."

Maybe you should go to the hospital.

The kid slams the palms of his hands against his skull. "I can't. I'm not even eighteen. Someone will call my parents and they'll find out I've been out doing drugs. My dad will kill me!"

I take a few more steps back, telling him that I'm sorry and that I don't know what he should do. The kid falls back into the chair. He stares vacantly in front of him, then looks back at me and says, "Why would someone do this to me? Why would someone tattoo Fred Durst onto my chest? I don't understand. I've never done anything to anyone. Why would someone hurt me like this?"

Fred Durst? I think that's Richard Simmons, man.

"Same fucking thing," the kid whines. "Why would any-one do this to me?"

I don't know.

I take a deep breath.

But maybe you shouldn't wear a visor that says you love the killers on it anymore. Maybe you should just be better than that.

And the kid goes, "What?"

I jump the front porch stairs and run all the way, like three blocks, up to Redmont Street.

I hail a cab and take it to my parents' house, staring at my dirty hands and my dirty fingernails, and tasting my shitty breath, the entire way there.

39

I WAKE UP AND IT'S DARK OUTSIDE AND I DON'T KNOW how long I've been sleeping or what day it is. My head is pounding. It's like there's an army of tiny men inside of it banging my skull with hammers, and my mouth is dry. My throat kills. It hurts to swallow. Very slowly, I peel my tongue from the roof of my mouth. It feels like my skin is being torn away and I want to cry but my body won't let me.

I'm cold and I'm hot.

I'm shivering.

Sweating.

I get out of bed and the nausea hits me right away. Whatever I have left inside of me is about to come up, so I run into the bathroom down the hall and drop to my knees and I wait.

I know it's coming, but I have to wait, and waiting is the worst.

Thoughts of Laura begin to play in my head. I think about how much I hate her. Then I think about how much I wish she was here.

My mouth pops open.

My body tightens.

My stomach starts pushing and thrusting.

Small chunks of my stomach lining fall into the toilet covered in this brownish colored liquid.

Same thing happens again.

It happens again and then again and then again but nothing comes out on the last heave. I have nothing left to give. Nothing at all. And I fall to the ground and wipe my eyes and wait for something even worse to happen, but nothing does.

I walk down to the kitchen later that night to get some ice water, and my sister and her friend Amy are sitting at the dining room table playing war, drinking Zimas with Jolly Rancher candy sitting in the bottom of the bottles, a Gwen Stefani DVD playing full-blast on the television in the living room.

"Mom and Dad wanted to talk to you earlier," my sister says. "But your car was gone, so they figured you were out."

Are they here now?

"No, they had dinner plans with some friends from out of town."

I grab a glass from the dishwasher.

Do you know what they wanted?

My sister shrugs. "No. But Dad was glowing about you actually applying to USC."

I fill the glass with water and look at my sister. For a moment I think about asking her if it's true what those girls told me in the bathroom at the party the night before, but then I decide not to because I'm sure it is true, in fact I never thought otherwise, and at this point I really don't care—not anymore.

Amy flips her last card over. "I won, bitch," she says. "Drink up."

My sister sticks her tongue out and starts chugging the rest of her Zima. When she's done, she slams the bottle down and burps really loud, then looks at me and goes, "Do you have any coke, Travis? I could really use a line to sober me up."

"Me too," Amy says.

I finish my glass of water.

Nope.

My sister scrunches her face. "Christ. What are you good for if you don't have any drugs?"

I fill the glass again.

If you want drugs so bad, why don't you call Katie? I'm sure her and Cliff are doing some right now.

"No one knows where she's at," my sister snaps. "Her parents are in Turkey and no one can find her or Cliff. Not since that bitch Natalie kicked Cliff out."

"That's not totally true, Vanessa," Amy blabs, lighting a cigarette. "Josh told me that some guy told him that his girl-friend's brother saw Cliff and Katie at some dealer's house in Sioux City."

"Who the fuck cares, Amy? That doesn't do us any good right now. Don't bring up irrelevant shit."

Amy blushes and looks down at the table.

And my sister goes, "There are ways to get drugs besides

my lame brother and Cliff. Cliff's a fucking loser anyway. I'll make calls if I have to." She looks at me. "I don't need your fucking help anymore, Travis."

I shrug.

That's good to know.

Then I finish what's in my glass, fill it up again, go back to my room, pop a Valium, and watch *Donnie Darko* for like the ninth time since I've been home.

40

I TAKE A CAB TO GET MY CAR FROM MICHAEL'S THE NEXT afternoon, and before leaving, I go up to his pad and knock on the door and this hot girl with short black hair, wearing a sleeveless hoodie and a pair of pink yoga pants, with the words "Man's Ruin" inked across her knuckles, answers and tells me that Michael and Dave are at band practice.

Who are you?

"Who are you?" she asks.

I don't know.

"You don't know who you are?" She looks confused.

My name's Travis.

"I'm Serenity. I tattoo at Dead Rick's parlor."

Pause.

"You wanna come in?"

No.

"What do you want, then?"

I'm not sure.

Pause.

Has anyone ever told you that you look like the actress Gina Gershon?

"No," she laughs, rubbing her tattoo covered arms. "But

when I was younger and lived in Madison, I was real frail and skinny and some boy told me I looked like an anorexic, female version of Nikki Sixx."

That's pretty cool.

"Pretty?" she shrieks. "Shit, I was stoked for like a month."

I smile. Ask, How do you know Michael?

"I fuck him sometimes."

Are you going to their next show? The one coming up.

"Maybe."

Well, maybe I'll see you there.

I turn to leave and Serenity yells, "Hey."

What's up?

"Are you on MySpace?" she asks.

No.

"Why not?"

I don't know.

She rolls her eyes. "Well, you should be," she says, and closes the door.

I walk back to my car. I feel like seeing a movie. I drive to both the big cineplexes but nothing good is playing at either of them, so I drive to the Victoria Theater to see what's playing but the ticket booth is closed. I try to yank the doors open but they're locked.

I step back and look at the building and I don't get why it's closed, but it is, so I start to walk away when I hear one of the doors creak open.

I spin back around.

Poking a head out of the door is an older, bald man with a round face and glasses. "Can I help you?" he asks.

Is the theater closed today?

"It's closed for good," he says.

For good? Since when?

"Since yesterday. It was our last operating day ever. The city sold the theater last month."

So that's it? No more Victoria?

"That's right. We tried to save it. All we needed was two thousand signatures on a petition to at least hold hearings in front of the city council, but we fell about five hundred short."

I swipe at the fly hovering in front of my face.

What are they gonna turn it into?

"They're gonna try to put a Wal-Mart in. They're trying to clear the whole block for a goddamn Wally World, if you can believe it."

I can believe anything.

The guy smiles and I start walking away, but turn around again.

Wait!

The guy pokes his head back through the door. "What now, kid?"

What was the last movie you showed?

"The greatest movie ever made."

Which is?

"*Chinatown*. You seen it?"

Yeah. It's a Polanski film.

"You bet it is. When it first came out in seventy-four, we showed it right here. This was the only theater for a two-hour radius that you could see *Chinatown*, starring the great Jack and Faye." The guy takes a deep breath. "But nothing lasts forever. This city is changing for the worse. Sure it's getting bigger and it looks nicer, but the novelties are disappearing. The culture is fading. This isn't progress, kid. It's neighborhood genocide. You think about that."

I nod.

And the guy slips back into the theater and shuts the door and locks it.

41

A FEW DAYS LATER, I GO TO THE HOSPITAL TO SEE CHRIS.
He's in a room all by himself, lying on a bed, draped in a
white hospital gown decorated with little violets, watching a
rerun of *The Simpsons*. A gnarly purple gash runs from the
top of his upper lip to the bottom of his nose.

"Hey, Travis," he says, a forced grin emerging on his face.

Hey.

Chris lifts his hand and we bump fists, then I sit down
on the chair beside his bed.

"So, what's going on?" he asks. "I didn't expect to see you
here."

I didn't expect to come, Chris, until I started thinking
about some things.

Chris stares at me but his eyes seem distracted, as if he's
not really here. "Like what?"

I wanted to say thank you for not giving Cliff the money
for Laura's abortion.

Chris flips his chin up. "You're welcome. I guess."

I appreciate it, man. And also you giving me the heads-
up about the whole thing.

Chris makes this grunting noise and pushes himself

forward. "It was gonna come out sooner or later." Wincing, he falls back against the pillows stacked underneath him. "Broken ribs suck," he groans. "It hurts to breathe."

What exactly happened? I only heard bits and pieces of it from Michael.

Chris takes a series of short breaths. His eyes close.

Are you okay, Chris?

He grimaces, slowly prying his eyelids apart. "I'll make it." He forces another grin. "April's dad can fucking fight. Dude used to be an amateur boxer I found out a couple of days ago."

Pause.

"He musta been pretty good, 'cause"—more short breaths—"I've never lost a fistfight before."

What are the police charging him with?

"Nothing. I told the cops I didn't want to press charges. Me and April and her parents and my parents made a deal."

What kind of a deal?

Chris turns very slowly, very precisely to his right, and reaches for a paper cup full of water.

I jump to my feet.

Relax, man.

I grab the water and hand it to him and he takes a sip.

"Thanks, Travis."

So tell me about the deal.

"The deal is"—he breathes—"April is going to have the kid and she's going to move in with me."

To yours and Kyle's house?

Shaking his head slowly, Chris goes, "No. My parents are making me move home once I get out of here and she's moving in with us."

He hands the water back to me and I set it down and walk back to the chair.

How did you come up with that?

"She wanted to have the kid," he snaps, holding his arms against his chest. "She said she had a dream about it and that she had to go through with it. So her parents told her if she wanted to have the baby, she was gonna have to live somewhere else. That's how we came to the deal."

I roll my eyes.

Is that what you want?

Chris closes his eyes. More short breaths. "No," he grunts. "But if she's going to go through with it, I'd rather be a part of it and try to make it work." He inhales carefully. Opens his eyes. "I just wish I hadn't hit her. Every time I look at her, I wish that. There's a lot of bad shit I've done that I wish I could take back, but that's the very first thing I would."

Does her dad know you hit her?

"I don't think so. My parents don't know either. I talked to her. She says she's past it. I don't know if I'll ever be, so I'm trying to make up for it."

Pause.

He exhales slowly, stammering, "Sitting in here for the past few days has got me thinking about everything, ya know. It's weird. I never knew how much I had to hate about myself until I had the time to think about it."

Pause.

"It's been ugly." Deep breath. "But it's been good."

When do you get to leave?

"Maybe next week. Around the third or fourth of August. The doctor says I'm recovering faster than she thought I would."

Has anyone else come to see you?

Chris shakes his head. "No," he says. "Why would they? I'm sure everyone thinks I'm a giant asshole, and they're right. I have been. The only people that show up are my parents and April. She's here all the time."

Is it nice?

"It's nice to know someone else outside of my family cares." He wipes his eyes. "Shit." He wipes them again. "I'm surprised to see you here."

I look down at my hands and they're shaking. I wish that I could take back the horrible things I've done to people. I wish I could go back in time and make things right, because even though I've been trying to, I might be making everything worse.

I do not know what to do.

And Chris says, "Have you been to see Kyle?"

I look up.

Only once.

"When you go again, will you make sure he knows why I haven't been there in a while?"

I can do that.

"Thanks, man."

I get back on my feet.

"Are you leaving?" Chris asks.

Yeah. I think so.

Chris holds his fist out. "Thanks for coming. I'll see you soon."

Right.

I bump his fist.

Soon.

From the hospital, I begin driving for Claire's, but like four blocks away from her place the traffic on the road comes to a complete standstill. Apparently someone's found some sort of mysterious bag, some sort of out-of-place backpack near a bus stop, so what the police have done is block off the surrounding eight blocks and send in the bomb squad.

I know all of this because some guy on the radio knows all of this.

But it all ends up being a whole lot of nothing: just a backpack full of schoolbooks that some kid left behind. And by the time the armed officers are waving the traffic through again, the sun is already setting and I realize, *Wow, I've been sitting here for almost two hours.* Sitting there waiting because of a bag of outdated physics and sociology books. And when I do get to Claire's, her roommate answers the door and tells me Claire got called into work and left about ten minutes ago.

42

TONIGHT IS THE NIGHT OF THE AWARDS CEREMONY
where my father is to be honored. It's being held downtown
at the Morton Convention Center, and the four of us—my
father and I swagged out in the Gucci tuxes we were fitted
for, my mother and sister strapped into black Gucci dresses—
arrive at the center in a limo after an entire ride of silence.

We spend the first hour being introduced around to all
of my father's business acquaintances and clients and close
friends of his we haven't met before. We're introduced to
city officials and their families. We pose for two family pictures. We split a bottle of champagne between the four of us
in the Jefferson Room of the center, a private room set up for
those being honored and the people speaking and present-
ing the honorees.

At one point, while my father is at the bar getting another
bottle of champagne, I look at my mother and she looks like
she's almost ready to cry, and when she looks at me looking at
her, she tries to smile but it's weak and vague and it doesn't
work and she looks away.

My sister is high. It's so fucking obvious. Her eyes are
jacked. Bright. Red. And she's having a hard time following

what little conversation there's been between any of us. When she does speak, her thoughts are incomplete, and even though I know that my parents realize what's going on, they just nod their heads like they understand because it's much easier than asking her to repeat herself.

After the second bottle of champagne is gone, my mother, sister, and I are seated at a round table in front of the stage, and my father takes his place behind the enormous table on the stage. A waiter comes by and asks us what we want to drink.

My mother: Manhattan, please.

My sister: vodka, um, yeah, and cranberry.

Me: double whiskey sour.

And by the time the ceremony has actually begun, the waiter has hit our table three times, and I'm getting pretty drunk and I want to do some coke, so I text-message Michael about making a possible delivery, but then I get a text message back that says "Fuck you, gnar pillager. I'm going to bed. Even Satan's gotta nap. Lamborghini Dreams on Saturday, biooooooooootch!"

I shut my phone off.

Then there's a short introduction by this very pretty, much younger woman, who, according to what she has to say, "works very closely with my father." The waitstaff brings around all these appetizers and salad plates but neither my mother, sister, nor I touch a thing.

I just wanna get loaded. That's it. Maybe fuck one of the hot waitresses or one of the hot wives or one of the hot daughters. I almost hit my sister up for drugs, but I don't, because fuck OC's. If I'm getting jacked, I want some fucking cocaine. And by the time the main course—prime rib, twice-baked potatoes, deviled eggs—comes around, I'm wasted. My skull feels heavy. My speech is pretty off. Then my father gets honored. One by one, men in tuxes, women in suits and dresses, march up to the podium and stand in front of the microphone and sing the praises of Lance Wayne. "An amazing businessman." "A revolutionary dream builder." "A loyal husband." "A loving father." "A great family man."

We all order another drink.

Then it's my father's turn. He stands proud and tall, godlike as he looks over the three hundred or so people gathered around him, listening as he talks about dreams and possibilities and the future: "As we forge forcefully into an age when everyone, no matter what walk of life they come from, will have the chance to flourish, and the world becomes a place where every goal can be obtained, and every aspiration realized." Then he thanks everyone, especially his marvelous family—my high sister, my uninterested mother, and me, drunk, the ungrateful son—and after the standing ovation is over, my father walks off the stage and sits down with us at the table, and by the time he's looked over each one of us, his huge smile has been wiped away, replaced by a blank expression.

So he gets up and walks around. He shakes hands with everyone, and then the reception starts. It's a ballroom-type dance party with a jazz orchestra, and about ten minutes after the music has begun, I slam my sixth whiskey drink and pull my father aside and tell him that I've made up my mind about the fall.

"What's it gonna be, son?"

I'll go to USC.

My father's face lights up.

But only if you do one thing for me, Dad.

"And what would that be?"

Rawson Park.

"What about it?"

You bought it, right? It's going to be your property in about a month?

"It will."

I'll only go to USC if you donate the park back to the city with a written agreement that it will never be developed into anything else and will always be open to the public.

My father stares me dead in the eye. He's waiting for me to blink or look away but I am not going to this time.

I am not going to back down from him.

That is the only way I go to school out there, Dad.

My father slides his jaw out. He bobs his head back and forth, back and forth, as if he's weighing it all out. "Done," he finally says.

Really?

"Yes. If that's what it takes for you to be at my alma mater, then I'll do it, son. I'll have one of the lawyers draw the papers up first thing tomorrow."

Thank you.

My father's smile returns and he pulls a cigar from the inside pocket of his jacket and lights it. "So here's what I'm thinking."

What's that?

"I have some business to do in LA on the twentieth."

Okay.

"So we'll drive out to LA. Just the two of us. We'll leave on the fifteenth, get there on the eighteenth, and that will give us two days to get you situated before I need to take care of my own needs." My father blows a ton of smoke into the air. "Sound good?"

Sounds great, Dad. Just as long as the park deal is done before we leave.

My father smacks me in the side of the arm. "It'll be done before the end of the week, son."

43.

CLAIRE AND I MAKE PLANS TO MEET FOR DINNER AT EIGHT at a small, upscale Korean restaurant near her apartment.

Wearing a navy blue dress with white trim and a black chiffon scarf wrapped tightly around her neck, Claire sits across the small table from me and tells me she saw the picture of me and my family at the awards ceremony on the front page of the paper yesterday. "You look good in a tux," she says.

That's good. I haven't seen it yet. But my sister was all over her phone blabbing about it.

Claire lifts her glass of ice water. "Is everything all right with your sister?" she asks. "I've heard some things."

So have I.

I light a cigarette.

But she's gonna do what she wants to do. No one in my family can really stop her. She is who she is, and she knows it.

"Kind of like you?"

I have no idea who I am anymore.

Claire lights a cigarette. "That's pretty dramatic, don't you think, Travis?"

No.

I blow a smoke ring.

Maybe.

I blow another one.

It's been a weird summer. Maybe that's it.

Claire fingers over the drink menu and goes, "It's been a pretty shitty one."

Nodding, I'm like, I got a friend in jail, a friend in the hospital, there's another girl dead—

Claire's eyes slam shut.

It's like some *Boyz n the Hood*, *Menace II Society* type bullshit.

The corners of Claire's mouth jump and she starts laughing to the point of tears.

I'm serious, Claire.

"I know you are."

Everything has fallen apart.

Claire stops laughing suddenly and takes a drag. She says, "Shit, Travis. Like anything was ever put together in the first place."

I smudge my cigarette out in the ashtray.

Good point.

Stepping up to our table, a small Korean woman in an apron skirt smiles and nods before asking us what we would like to eat.

Claire picks up the menu and points at it, ordering a vegetable and rice dish and an apple Martini.

The waitress turns to me.

What's the most unhealthy meat dish on the menu?

The woman looks confused by this question. She nods again, asking me what I would like.

The most unhealthy meat dish.

"Travis," Claire snaps, smudging her smoke out. "Quit being a dick." She picks up the menu and points at it again. "He'll have the pound plate of spiced pork."

Plus a side of green beans.

The lady nods again and says okay, and walks to the kitchen and places our order.

Claire takes another sip of water, glaring at me while she swallows it.

I only wanted to know, Claire. They were just questions.

"Sometimes you can be such a jerk about things though."

I bunch my face, light another cigarette.

"I'm serious," she says. "You're like a sweetheart most of the time until this dark side comes out in you."

I lean back, shaking my head.

What-the-fuck-ever, Claire. You don't seem to mind it much. You keep hanging out with me. So just drop the critique, all right?

"Fine." Claire lights another cigarette. "I want this to be a nice night. I want this night to build into something."

What does that mean, Claire? Build into something.

"I like you."

You like me?

"Yes."

Like how?

Claire's face gets a little flushed. "Like maybe we could start dating or something."

The Korean lady returns with Claire's martini and sets it on the table.

Claire, I—

But she cuts me off. "Just hear me out, Travis. Please."

Fine.

She takes a sip of her drink. "I know you're attracted to me physically—most people are."

You're right.

"But I think we have something else besides the physical thing," she says. "We're fucking rad when we're together. We know everything about each other. It's like everyone always thinks we're doing that couple bullshit anyway when we're hanging out. So I'm thinking, why not. I'm kinda sick of hooking up anyway."

Inhale. Exhale.

I run a hand through my hair and pinch the bridge of my nose.

"So there it is," she says, smiling.

Claire, I say. It's like—

She cuts me off again. "Don't give me a fucking speech, Travis. Just don't. I know you want this. Let it happen."

But I'm leaving again.

Claire's whole body jerks back. "What?"

I'm moving to LA. I'm going to go to school at USC. I'm gonna be third-generation.

Slamming a hand down on the table, she says, "You

fucking liar. You said you were staying. You told everyone you were back for good."

Things have changed, Claire.

"Fuck you."

Whoa, Claire.

"No. You knew you were leaving and you still let me say everything I just said. That's fucked up. Does your ego need to be padded that much?"

I grind my smoke out.

Just stop for a second, Claire.

"No, I won't. I'm so fucking embarrassed. You're such a prick. You lied!" she shouts. "You promised me that you wouldn't leave again!"

Well, ya know what, Claire?

"What?"

Life changes everything—even promises.

"Fuck you," she snorts, and stomps right out of the restaurant, just as the Korean lady brings our food out.

With a perplexed look on her face, she sets the food down and stares at me.

It was too unhealthy.

She keeps staring.

The meat dish. It was too fucking unhealthy, I say slowly, loudly, then pick up a fork and start munching on my green beans.

44

MORNING.

I lie in bed and think about jacking off for what seems like an extraordinary amount of time before I finally decide not to and slowly make my way down the stairs.

I see my mother. She's sitting on a couch watching an episode of *Sex and the City* and I try to sneak back upstairs but she hears me and says, "Please come back here, Travis."

Shit.

I turn around.

And my mother's like, "You don't have time to talk to me anymore. Is that it, Travis?"

Anymore? I'm thinking, but I say, I've been busy with some things. I had some tough things to decide.

My mother lifts the DVD remote and pauses the episode. "Your father and I are proud of you. You gutted it out. You have your whole future to look forward to now."

I yawn.

Did you take that from his speech the other night, Mom? Or was that your own little anecdote?

"You don't have to be at war with me, Travis. I only want for you what you think you want for yourself. Can't you and your sister see that? I'm not pushing you two away. I'm giving you two your space. There's a huge difference."

I know there is.

"So why the attitude? Why are you always so defensive around me, like I'm your enemy?"

I don't know.

"What's going on with you? You haven't been the same kid since you came back. You were more relaxed and much more pleasant to be around during Christmas."

So what, Mom? Things happen and people change. You can't be the same person all the time.

"Your father is."

I roll my eyes.

Well, maybe I'll be more like him after I become a Trojan man and turn into his prodigy, which is all he wants anyway. Someone who looks like him to take his life over when his own looks begin to fade.

"That's not true at all," my mother snaps.

I toss my arms up.

It's probably much closer to the truth than you'd like to admit.

I spin around and start for the stairs.

"Travis!"

I stop but don't turn around.

"Have you heard anything from your sister since yesterday?"

No. Why?

"Because she and Amy told me they were going to an

early movie last night and that they'd be back around ten, but they haven't come home yet."

I haven't heard anything. Maybe you should call Amy's parents.

I hear my mother sigh. Then the TV starts making noise again.

"I probably should," I hear her say as I head up to my room.

Afternoon.

I head down to Kennedy Street and stop by Canteen Records and pick up the new issue of *VICE*, as well as the new Fleshies CD and the new one by Everything Must Go.

When I step back outside, the change from the cool air of the store to the humid air is so intense that it feels like I've run into a wall and I almost fall down, catching myself on the door handle on my way to the cracked and burning pavement beneath me.

I quickly gather myself and keep moving down the street and run into Dave and Rodney, the guitar player for Lamborghini Dreams.

They're each carrying twelve packs of Budweiser, and Dave has these really horrible black marker drawings all over his arms—some dicks, some boobs, a blob that looks kind of like Kelly Osbourne, a bigger blob that looks a lot like Britney Spears.

I swing my eyes up to Dave's face.

Dude.

I point at him.

"What?" he smiles.

Have you looked in the mirror the past couple of hours?

"Probably not since last night. Why?"

I start to laugh.

You have so much cocaine on your grill right now.

"Nah-huh, shut up."

I'm serious. It's like someone put a facial mask of coke on you.

Dave turns to Rodney. "Do I?"

Rodney nods his head and starts laughing. "It's all over you, man. You even have some in your hair."

"Fuck, man." He hits Rodney in the chest. "Why didn't you tell me before we left, asshole."

"I didn't know, dude. I swear it," Rodney laughs.

And Dave goes, "Do you realize I saw like four people I know on the walk to the liquor store? I talked to one of my fucking coworkers."

"I know," Rodney answers.

"Fuck. Not cool at all."

I start busting up and Dave goes, "We need to get back to the pad, like now. You wanna come, Trav? Michael's up there."

No, I got stuff to do.

"Fine," Dave snorts. "But you're gonna be at our show on Saturday, right?"

I am.

"'Cause we're putting you on the list," he says. "And that's big-time, baby. Huge."

For sure I'll be there, man.

And Rodney's like, "See ya in a coupla days."

I watch them run across the street and eventually they just fade into everything else.

Evening.

At like nine I get home and the house is empty. On one of the kitchen counters I see a photocopy of the Rawson Park deed giving the property back to the city. I take it up to my room with me then change into my swimming trunks and walk out to the pool, switching the underwater lights on.

I dive in.

The water feels amazing against my skin, like a thousand years of scars and bruises and fractures and sprains are going away with each passing second. I take a huge breath and swim under the surface and hold everything in until I can't any longer. Then I pop up, gasping for air.

I do this over and over and over again, until I can't anymore, then I float over to the small ladder and climb out and begin drying off.

My mother walks outside with my father and they stare at me from across the water.

What's going on?

I walk around the edge of the pool.

"Your sister is what's going on," my mother says.

What happened?

"We just bailed her and Amy out of jail for shoplifting,"

my mother snaps. "They were caught stealing clothes from the Gap this afternoon."

My father punches the side of the house. He walks inside and lurks into his work den.

I cover my shoulders with a towel.

What's gonna happen to her?

My mother steps in closer to me. "Nothing will happen to her record. Your father took care of that. But we're checking her into rehab first thing tomorrow morning."

Is she here right now?

"No," my mother moans. "She's at the hospital getting a psyche evaluation. She'll be there overnight. Then she's off to rehab at the Tomlinson Clinic in Russdale."

Pause.

"How long have you know she's been abusing OCs?" my mother asks.

Since June.

"Travis!" My mother lunges at me, and for a moment I think she's going to hit me, but she stops just short of my face with the palm of her right hand. "Why would you keep that from us?"

You guys knew she was fucked up. Dad even told me that he assumed she was on something.

"You still should have told us."

No I shouldn't have. You guys told her she might not be able to get her license because she might be using.

"So?"

So you guys knew.

"We didn't know what she was on."

I whip the towel off of me and throw it to the side.

But you still knew, Mom. She's been messed up for a while. This whole family has known.

"What's that supposed to mean?"

I walk past her.

You know exactly what that means, Mom.

I open the door and slam it shut and walk up to my bedroom and watch that movie *Me and You and Everyone We Know* again.

45.

THE FIRST ANNUAL KAREN O LOOK-ALIKE CONTEST IS tonight at the Glass Castle. I park like three blocks away from the club and walk there, passing at least fifty girls who look like they're trying look like Karen O.

Think lots of black hair styled every which way.

Think lots of really big sunglasses.

Think lots of blue eye shadow streaked across both eyes.

Think also lots and lots and lots of shredded and V-neck and mismatched color tops and off-color pantyhose.

There're about a hundred people in line at the door and I hop into it, smoking a cigarette, listening to the couple in front of me. The girl is wearing a white shredded top with a big red heart on the chest, a red mesh scarf, indigo colored pantyhose, a pair of gold and white high-top Chuck Taylors. Her black hair is straight, except for the bangs, which hang crooked, just above her sunglass covered eyes.

The guy on the other hand is dressed like he wants to look like the guitarist for the Yeah Yeah Yeahs.

Think really big black hair puffed up high.

A white T-shirt with the sleeves cut off, dotted with random black paint drops.

A pair of tight black jeans, cuffed to his mid shins.

Think also black eye shadow, black coated fingernails, and a pair of knee-high black boots.

The two of them talk fast and rub their noses a lot and are going back and forth about how cool it would be if Karen O was actually here to judge the contest.

"I would just die," the girl says, and the guy goes, "No offense to you, babe, but if she is here, I'm going after her," and the girl goes, "Fine by me. You fucking her would only make you hotter to me," and then this other girl, who's standing in front of those two, turns around in her saggy red V-neck blouse, her black ruffled skirt, and her turquoise colored fishnets, with her eyes streaked blue, and she says, "Karen O's not even going to be here? What the fuck? If she doesn't need to be here then I don't need to be here." Then she walks off, disappearing into a sea of impersonators, and behind me these two girls start clapping, and one of them goes, "One less person to stand in the way of me winning this thing."

I finish my smoke in two long drags, then smear it out with my foot and hear someone scream my name.

I look toward the door and see Michael standing outside the front entrance smoking, wearing a pair of ass-tight black jeans, a Deep Purple shirt with no sleeves, and a red do-rag wrapped around his forehead, tied in the back.

"Yo, Trav, what the fuck are you doing back there?" he yells, waving me to him. "You're on the fucking list. Get your ass in here."

I walk to the door, past all these people in line, some pointing at me, maybe wondering if I know someone who knows someone who knows Karen O. Or maybe they're wondering, How is he going to show up here wearing what he's wearing?

Think a pair of white Levi's.

A light blue V-neck T.

A pair of low-top Adidas.

Think also no styled hair, no face makeup, no painted fingernails, and no visible do-rag.

"Yo, yo bioooooooootch!" Michael sniffs, rubbing his nose before hugging me. "You're Travis Wayne, brah. You never have to wait in line."

I shrug.

Maybe you're right.

Michael flicks his smoke and flips his head at some girls. "It's like a farmer's market of dickpigs in there," he snorts in my ear as the two of us walk inside the Glass Castle, packed full, wall-to-wall with kids, mostly girls—girls who look like they want to look like Karen O.

And *blah, blah, blah,* I'm thinking.

"Here," Michael says, handing me an orange bracelet. "Put this on. Free PBRs all night."

Thanks, man.

"Shit, I got you, dude." He rubs his nose. "Grab a beer and come backstage. It's where we're all at. We're partying hard. I'm like on my third straight day of being up."

Okay, Michael.

He turns, cutting and weaving through a ton of traffic, and I push my way to the bar, wedging myself between this guy with a black mullet and a pin-striped blazer, and this girl wearing two off-the-shoulder tops—a yellow one underneath a black one—a pair of black spandex, a black leather glove on her right hand, and black boots.

I order a shot of Jäger and a PBR and look at the girl, a martini in her gloveless hand, the Yeah Yeah Yeahs' song "Maps" blasting from the invisible speakers. She swings her eyes on me. "Do I look good?" she asks.

You look like every other girl in here except maybe those two.

I point across the bar at these two girls. One has bright red hair and pink sunglasses on. She's pretty chubby and is wearing a yellow top with a bear on the front of it.

The other has orange colored hair and no sunglasses on and she's wearing a zebra-striped turtleneck with half sleeves and long, dangly earrings.

"Those girls look like shit," the girl with the martini tells me.

They don't even look that much like girls.

Martini girl laughs, then turns away, and the bartender puts my drinks in front of me. I pay him for the shot, then slither and slide my way into the backstage area.

All the bands are in one big room.

The room has purple walls covered with graffiti, three leather sofas, a fridge, a CD player, and a long table with a glass top.

When I enter the room, Michael's like, "There he is, the man who will someday own everything." He introduces me to the girls and guys from the other bands, my eyes fixed on the girl from the Yeah Yeah Yeahs cover band, Modern Romance.

She really looks like she wants to look like Karen O. For a moment I even think it is Karen O in the flesh.

But it's not.

The girl's name is Rachael. And her band is from Chicago. And tonight Rachael is wearing a shiny red tank top with yellow Xs all over the front of it and leather gloves on both her hands, and her jet black hair is much shorter than most of the other girls I've seen tonight, hanging just below her ears. Rachael also has on a pair of black jeans and a red and yellow belt, and she has a purple streak running from one eye to the other.

I shake her hand and she says, "Michael was just telling us that your dad owns like sixty percent of the city."

I look at Michael, who's holding two grams of blow between his fingers, and he shrugs. Says, "It might be more like seventy-five percent."

None of that's important.

"Sure it is," Rachael says. "Someday you're gonna own this whole damn place."

I don't say anything.

And she's like, "Do you have a cigarette?"

I fish one out and light it for her.

Michael dumps both grams onto the glass tabletop and

goes, "*Scarface!*" Then he drops his face right into the pile and shoots back up. "You guys can cut the rest of that shit up and do whatever you want with it," he says.

I light my own smoke.

"Trav," Michael says. "Make sure you do some of my free drugs."

Nah, I'm good.

"What? No. Fuck you. Do my shit. Don't disrespect me by turning my goodwill down."

I'm just drinking tonight, Michael.

"Asshole!" he screams, wiping the coke residue off with his fingers. He rubs his fingers against his gums. The whole room gets really quiet. "You don't come back here and not do what I give you to do."

Fuck you, Michael.

"Fuck me?" he says. "No, fuck you. Get the hell out of here."

I smirk and look back at Rachael and take a swig of beer.

"I'm serious, big shot! Get out of this room. You're being an ungrateful piece of shit and ungrateful pieces of shit make me come down, so leave."

"Dude, chill out," Dave snaps. "He doesn't want your drugs."

Michael turns to Dave. "Stay out of this, Dave. He either wants my drugs or he wants to leave the room."

Pause.

He takes a huge pull from the bottle of Jack Daniel's in his hand and some of it runs down the sides of his face. "If you're gonna act like a faggot, Travis, I'm gonna treat you like one, so what's it gonna be?"

I'll leave.

I slam the rest of my beer. Whip the empty can against the wall and tell everyone else, Have a good show.

"Get out, fag," Michael says.

Fuck you, Michael. I'm moving to LA anyway.

I flick my smoke to the floor.

Fuck you, man.

"Faggot," he yells, then takes a swig and spits it at me, most of it missing, but some of it spraying against my skin.

I shake my head and flip him off and leave the bar.

Walking to my car, I run into Claire like a block away.

She's walking to the show with Skylar, and the two girls I saw her modeling Skylar's clothes with way back in June.

I try to avoid her by looking down at the sidewalk, pretending I don't hear her going, "Travis, hi. Dude. Travis."

But it doesn't work because she grabs me as I'm passing her. "Travis," she snaps.

I tilt my head up and look at her. I glare at Claire.

Claire with her blond hair done up in short pigtails.

Claire with a brand-new tattoo on her left arm of Dennis Hopper, holding an oxygen mask over his face from *Blue Velvet*.

Claire looking amazing, stuffed into a pink dress with white polka dots all over it, a pair of white and pink socks pulled to her knees, and a pair of black Chuck Taylors strapped to her feet.

"Where are you going, Travis?" she asks.

I'm going home. I'm over it already.

"What for? Didn't the doors just open?"

I knock her hand away and step back.

I don't know if they did. I don't know when the fucking doors opened.

"What's wrong with you, Travis?" She tries to grab me again.

Don't touch me, Claire.

I take another couple of steps back.

You don't have any business asking me why I'm leaving, not after the other night when you left me.

Claire turns to her friends. "I'll meet you guys by the front door, okay?"

The three of them walk away from the two of us.

Claire pulls two cigarettes from her black purse, handing me one and lighting hers. I light mine.

"I'm sorry I left you the other night," she tells me. "I totally am. But I was embarrassed as shit."

I don't care what you were. You bailed.

"I'm sorry."

Fuck your apologies, Claire. Fuck everyone's apologies. I'm sick of hearing them. No one is sorry about anything. None of us care that much to be sorry about anything.

Claire shakes her head. "You're wrong, Travis."

No I'm not.

Complete silence passes.

And Claire goes, "What happened inside? You looked really pissed walking away from the club."

I take a drag and look at the ground.

Michael and I got into it in the back room. I'm sure he was just trying to mess with me and I took it all seriously.

I look up at Claire again.

But who knows. I might be losing it. I'm completely on edge right now.

"I can see that." She reaches out and grabs me again and this time I let her because it feels too nice to stop her. "Do you wanna kick it with me tonight?" she asks.

I'm not going back in there.

"No, we can go back to my crib. I'll tell the girls—they won't care. Skylar drove, so I can ride with you."

Finishing my smoke, I tell Claire that I don't want to fuck her plans up.

You shouldn't have to bail on your friends because of me, I say.

"I'd rather hang with you, though. You're moving soon."

Pause.

She squeezes my wrist.

"Okay?"

Fine.

Claire tosses her smoke and tells me she'll be back in a sec, then bolts for the club, and I stand there all alone, looking around, feeling uneasy.

Thoughts of my sister in rehab pound through my skull.

I wonder what Cliff is doing.

I wonder where he is.

I wonder if Cliff is even alive.

A thought of him and Katie, sleeping in a car somewhere in the middle of nowhere, smashes through my head,
but disappears quickly when I hear this girl freaking out.

She's walking from the Glass Castle with a friend, crying
hysterically, and her friend has an arm around her and is
telling the crying girl that everything is going to be okay.

"No it's not," the crying girl sobs. "I spent ten hours getting ready for tonight."

"That guy judging the outfits didn't know what he was
talking about, sweetie," the friend says.

And the crying girl sobs, "He told me I looked like a PG
version of Ashlee Simpson. I'll never get over that for as long
as I live."

"Yes you will," her friend goes. "I think you look good.
You look more like Karen O than Karen O does."

And the crying girl says, "You really think?"

Pause.

"Um, of course I do," her friend says as they turn a corner.

Claire comes back. "You ready to go?" she asks me.

If you are.

"Let's do it," she says in a deep, manly tone. Then she
hooks an arm through one of mine and we walk to my car.

46.

HARDLY A WORD GETS SPOKEN DURING THE RIDE. WE fill the silence with a Sparklehorse CD, smoking cigarettes, rolling through the neon glow of the city, all the way to Claire's.

I follow her inside and she takes my hand and leads me into her room and shuts the door behind her.

A minute later it begins.

She takes my shirt off and kisses my chest and my stomach and then I push the dress straps off her shoulders, sliding the dress all the way down to her feet and she steps out of it, one foot at a time.

We kiss slowly and we don't look each other in the eye and then I grab the back of her thighs, her warm, soft skin squishing between my fingers. I lift her up. She wraps her legs around my waist, and I lay her gently onto the bed.

"Do you have protection?" she asks.

I close my mouth and nod. I unbutton my jeans and roll them off.

Claire grabs my shoulders. "I'm already wet. You can put yourself in anytime you want," she tells me, smiling.

Whatever you say, Claire.

I reach into my wallet and pull a condom out and slide it on and shake my shoulders out.

"Just relax, baby," she says. "Take your time."

Making fists with my hands, I drop them both into the pillow, right above her shoulders, and scoot close enough to rub the tip of myself against her.

This is when I look Claire in the eyes.

She smiles and she nods, and then I slide myself inside of her, and the two of us have amazing sex.

47.

AROUND ONE IN THE MORNING IT BEGINS TO RAIN, THE soft pitter-pattering sound of the raindrops caressing Claire's windows.

I lie in her bed, shirtless, smoking a cigarette, listening to the Team Sleep CD she put in before leaving to go to the bathroom.

Part of me thinks I should go home—that it can't get better than it has during the past four hours, but another part of me, the stronger part of me, thinks I should stay—that I need this and that being alone is not a good idea.

Claire pops back into the room in her pajamas. She climbs back into bed, setting a pillow on my lap. Burying her head in it, she goes, "I'm exhausted. Are you sleepy yet, Travis?"

I'm beat.

"Let's go to bed."

My throat tightens.

I don't wanna sleep anymore.

Claire pushes herself up. "But you're tired."

I know I am.

Her eyebrows rise. "I don't understand," she yawns, patting her mouth with an open hand. "Do you want to leave? Is that what you're saying?"

No. I wanna be here with you, Claire.

"Let's go to sleep then. Pleeeeease." She makes this pouty face.

I drop my cigarette into an empty wine bottle sitting on the floor next to the bed and rub my face.

I'm afraid to.

Claire moves the pillow to her side of the bed. "Afraid to do what?"

To sleep. I'm afraid that if I fall asleep, I'll lose this feeling. I'll start dreaming and everything good that's just happened will mean nothing.

Claire reaches into her nightstand and grabs a small sack of pot. "Do you want to smoke some of this? It'll help you relax."

I knock it away.

I don't want drugs right now, Claire. I don't know if I want drugs ever again.

She drops the pot on top of her nightstand and says, "What's wrong with you? Why are you afraid to sleep?"

'Cause I might dream.

"Why are you afraid to dream?"

Pause.

This huge chill runs down my back. My hair stands straight up and I start shaking.

Claire leans over and runs a hand through my hair. She kisses my shoulder. "Tell me what's wrong, Travis."

I inhale and hold my breath and when I exhale, I tell Claire, It's this dream I've been having.

"What about it?"

It started the night I left Hawaii and it's barely stopped since.

"How does it go?"

It's not important how it goes.

I pull a blanket over me.

It's what happened in Hawaii. That's what's important.

"Tell me, then," Claire says.

I pull the blanket back down and swing my legs over the side of the bed and lean forward. Drop my face into my hands.

"Travis."

It wasn't my fault, Claire.

"What wasn't?"

What happened to that girl.

"What girl?"

I flip around and face Claire, who looks startled, almost scared.

The girl I met in Hawaii. Autumn Hayes.

"What happened to the girl, Travis?"

I don't know for sure. I don't remember.

Claire leans over and kisses my forehead. "Tell me what you do remember," she says.

And this is when I finally let it out of me. I finally open up. I tell Claire the story as best as I can remember it.

I say:

It was my last night in Maui. I met this girl on the beach. She was really pretty. Her name was Autumn. Anyway, we started talking and she invited me to her motel room, which was in like some piece-of-crap economy building. On the way there, she told me that she'd been in Maui for almost a week and that the friends she'd come with had split two days earlier because one of them had gotten food poisoning or something and the other one missed her boyfriend. I don't really know.

What I do remember is that right when we got there, she started doing all sorts of crazy shit. She was taking coke hits, shooting speedballs, just mixing everything together. So I started getting into it with her. We started going at it, going all crazy, getting really aggressive, but then I couldn't get it up and she pushed me off of her and told me to take a break. I grabbed this bottle of lotion sitting next to her bags, and I started stroking myself while she shot another speedball.

I stop for a moment to catch my breath.

I feel like crying.

I look at Claire and she says, "Let it out, Travis."

So I do. I keep going:

That was when I kind of lost it. I like spaced out for a minute. It was weird. But when I came to, I was hard and ready to go, so I went back to the bed and crawled on top of her.

I hold my hands over my mouth and shake my head.

I go:

I could've sworn she was breathing, Claire. I mean, I heard her moaning while I was inside of her. I heard her! But when I finished, I rolled over and passed out, and when I woke up the next morning, she was still lying in the same spot and there was puke and blood on her chest and these gnarly hand marks all over her neck. Her eyes were closed, all normal, but her skin was cold. I tried everything to wake her up but she wouldn't move, and I got scared. I was still jacked. So I threw on my clothes and slipped out of the room and I left her there.

Claire is glaring at me. "Are you lying to me, Travis? Please tell me you're lying to me."

I can't tell you that. I'm not lying.

Claire pounds her mattress. "Did you kill that girl, Travis?"

No, Claire. I don't think so.

"How do you know you didn't?"

Because she might've ODed. She had to have.

"You don't know that, Travis. You could've killed her."

Maybe.

"And no one's looked for you at all?" she asks.

I don't think anyone saw me. I don't think anyone cares. I haven't heard anything about it in the news at all. Nothing.

Claire squints. "That's really weird."

I shrug.

Pause.

And that's why I don't want to sleep. Because I'll dream about the girl in Hawaii and I know I did something fucked up, but it wasn't my fault.

"Yes it was."

What?

"Travis," she shrieks. "You might've killed that girl. It is your fault." She covers her mouth. "Oh my god."

Claire.

I reach for her but she moves away from me.

Claire.

"Travis," she says, getting to her feet. "You have to leave. You can't be here. I don't want you here."

But I—

"Leave!" she screams. "I can't believe you did that!"

I don't know what I did.

"You left! You fucked that girl up and you left. Get out of here!"

I stand up, tears rolling down my face.

What are you going to do?

"I don't know," she says.

Are you going to tell anyone?

"I don't know. Just leave!"

Don't tell anyone, Claire. Please. Please don't tell anyone else.

"Travis, I—"

Please, Claire, I beg again.

She runs a hand over her face.

Please.

"Fine, Travis. I won't. But you need to leave my place right now. Go!"

Okay, Claire. I'm sorry.

"Apologies don't mean shit, Travis. That's what you just told me."

48.

IT'S JUST AFTER EIGHT IN THE MORNING AND I'M STILL awake, lying in my bed, listening to my mother crying about my sister in the next room.

I'm cold and I'm sweating and I use my T-shirt to dry my face off, and then I put my head back down and stare at the ceiling and try to relax.

Everything has gotten worse.

Inhale. Exhale.

My eyes find a spider.

It's a big black one and it's inching across the ceiling, trying to get back to its web, and it's actually doing pretty well, going really strong, until it gets too close to the air vent then—

WHOOSH.

It gets blown away, just like that.

All of that work and all of that time just for nothing, and maybe that's how things have to be sometimes.

And it's right now, at this exact moment, when I finally make a real choice, a real fucking decision.

I finally figure out what really needs to be done next.

SO I LEAVE MY HOUSE AND DRIVE TO THE NEAREST ATM and empty everything I have out of my checking and savings accounts, before doing the exact same thing with my credit cards. Then I figure out where the nearest airline ticket office is and I drive there and purchase a one-way airplane ticket that leaves for the island of Maui in four days.

THAT AFTERNOON, I GO TO VISIT KYLE.

He's sitting across the metal bolted-down table with a black eye and fat lip, and I ask him about it, but the only thing he can say is, "Altercation. Cigarettes."

For most of the visit we sit in silence. He tells me he already knows about Laura and Cliff from Michael. He tells me he already knows about Chris from Michael. He tells me that Emily's mother and father were here last week and told him that they'd never be able to find it in their hearts to forgive him. Then he tells me he heard I was moving to LA and I don't want to say anything about Hawaii, so I nod, and I tell him how stoked my father is about everything.

"I thought you hated your father," he says, sneering.

Maybe I do. But he's stoked.

We span more time, saying nothing, looking everywhere but at each other—spanning time until one of the security guards behind Kyle yells, "Visiting time is over, folks. Wrap it up now!"

Kyle nods his head slowly. "I have to go back to my cell," he says.

I know you do.

"Have fun in LA."

I don't say anything.

He stands up. "Write me sometime."

Okay, Kyle.

I hold my fist out.

"Bye, Travis."

Kyle turns around without touching my fist. He walks away from me instead and I watch him disappear into a small doorway with the much older, much bigger, much more violent prisoners.

51

LATER THAT NIGHT, MY PARENTS WANT ME TO MEET them at the Red Tie for dinner, but I do not want to go to the Red Tie because I do not want to run into that waitress Maggie ever, ever again.

I take a shower, rubbing my skin raw with hot water, thinking about how I'm going to get out of the dinner, thinking about how I don't think I can go through with it, thinking about popping a thousand-milligram Vicodin, or a twenty-milligram Valium, or maybe a handful of Xanax, and sleeping until I die.

I'm tired. I do not want to do anything anymore. And when I'm through with my shower, I call my father and ask him if he'll at least pick another restaurant.

Anyplace besides the Red Tie, I tell him.

"I won't."

Please, Dad.

"The Red Tie was your mother's idea. Tonight was your mother's idea. She thought it would be nice if the three of us spent some time together before you and I leave for LA."

But I—

"Travis Matthew Wayne," my father says, sternly, coldly,

"your mother is going through a tough time right now with your sister in rehab. So fucking humor me and get your ass to the restaurant."

Fine.

I arrive at the restaurant almost forty minutes late and walk through the tinted doors, telling the hostess I'm with the Wayne party. She tells me to follow her and leads me up the stairs to the VIP room.

A small sense of relief hits me as I approach the table my mother and father are seated at and don't see Maggie anywhere.

Maybe she's off tonight.

There are two empty chairs on the other side from them and I slide myself into the one across from my father, who tonight is dressed down in a white Gucci shirt, sleeves rolled to his mid-arms, unbuttoned at the top, tucked into a pair of beige slacks. He finishes off a glass of champagne and then grabs the bottle of Dom Pérignon sitting in front of him and refills his glass.

From somewhere above me is the sound of Frank Sinatra singing "The Best Is Yet to Come," and suddenly I'm eight years old again and it's winter, nighttime, and a small shower of snowflakes trickling down from the starlit sky outside.

I'm sitting at a table, illuminated by the wavy, orangish light coming from the candles floating on the water in the wineglasses at the center of the table, wearing a black tuxedo and a pair of shiny black shoes. My hair is combed and parted firmly to the left, and people keep coming up to me and grabbing my arm and telling me how much I look like my father.

Sitting next to me in a white dress with black laces strung around the waist of it is my little sister. Her snowy blond hair hangs past her shoulder blades and has been combed out extensively, and all of these people keep telling my mother and father and me that Vanessa is an absolute doll. A perfect-looking girl. As beautiful as they've ever seen. "You guys are gonna have to keep an eye on her when she grows up," they all wink and smile and nod.

The place we're at is called the Chateau Ballroom, and more than three hundred people have gathered here to celebrate the tenth wedding anniversary of Lance and Scarlett Wayne, who soon leave the table to dance.

About halfway through Frank Sinatra's "The Way You Look Tonight," my sister leans over to me, twirling an elastic hair bow between two fingers, and says, "Mommy and Daddy look really happy."

It's 'cause they are, Vanessa, I say.

And then my mother's aunt whispers, "I've never seen two people who look that in love. I only hope all of you stay this happy forever. I really do."

Jump back to right now.

My father sets his glass down after taking a drink, killing almost half of it. Looking at his wristwatch, he says, "You're really going to have to do some work on this punctuality thing, Travis."

My lips squeeze together tightly as my eyes dart from him to my mother, who has her elbows on the table, her face between her hands, and is staring idly at the empty chair across from her, the one beside me, the one my sister would normally be occupying. And I actually miss Vanessa right now and all of her snotty, bullshit looks. The condescending remarks. Watching her get loaded on liquor. Every single guy staring and gawking at her with their mouths wide open, lines of drool hanging from their chins.

These are the things I miss most about my sister.

But when my mother notices me watching her, she tries to force her lips into a smile, which doesn't really work well at all, and then she drops her hands and looks at my father, who's still talking about my tardiness.

Saying, "You're not going to get anywhere by showing up late."

Snapping, "Ninety percent of anything you do is simply showing up."

Snorting, "Your being late for everything is really turning into an epidemic."

"Christ, Lance," my mother cuts in. "Just stop it."

My father scrunches his face. "What?"

And my mother goes, "Just cut the shit, okay?"

And I'm thinking, *The Wayne Party.*

I'm thinking, *Some fucking party.*

My father grunts and downs the rest of his champagne.

Maggie walks over to our table with an order pad.

"Hi, Travis," she smiles. "How are you? Good, I hope."

I feel like an absolute ass. A fucking joke. Sitting here with Maggie standing over me, her face reminding me of all of my failure, like this huge poster, this giant list, this big mirror reflecting back to me everything I've never done right.

Her face is the word "innocent," the word I misspelled during the first round of a spelling bee competition in fifth grade with my parents in attendance.

It's the goldfish that died because I forgot to feed it when I was in seventh grade.

It's the night I forgot to pick up my sister from a friend's house when I was sixteen and she was mugged and beaten up while she walked around trying to find a cab.

Instead of it really being Maggie's face I'm staring at, it's the face of a dead girl in a Hawaii motel room.

"Would you like something to drink?" Maggie asks after my lack of response to her previous question.

How about a Bud?

A large grin cuts through her face. "A nonalchoholic Budweiser."

Don't start shit, I say. You won't win this.

"Hey, I'm just doing my job, Travis. I know you're under-age and me serving you a beer is against the law. It could get me into a lot of trouble."

Both my mother and father look at each other, then at me, and I know they're about to get involved, which is not a good thing for her job security at all, so I stop this quickly.

I say, Just get me some ice water instead.

"And water it is," Maggie says, grinning still, because she thinks she's gotten the better of me.

After she leaves to retrieve the drink, my father turns his attention back to me and asks what that exchange was all about.

I shrug.

I don't know, Dad. I guess she just sucks.

Maggie returns with my water and sets it in front of me. "Are you all ready to order now?" she asks.

My mother and father look at me and I tell them to go ahead, that I already know what I want, and then I pick up the water and it's warm. There are no ice cubes in the glass at all.

And I say, Excuse me. I ordered an ice water.

Maggie, who was jotting down my mother's order, looks at me and goes, "Huh?"

I ordered an ice water and there is no ice in this glass. This water is warm. I wanted ice in my water.

"You just said water," Maggie snorts, her cheeks turning red. "You ordered water."

And my mother says, "That's not correct at all. I heard him say ice water, and besides, I've never had a glass of water at a restaurant without ice in it. Did you do this on purpose?"

"No, I didn't," Maggie snaps. "He said water and I gave the kid water."

"Hey," my father jumps in. "Do you have a problem with my son?"

"No, I—"

But my father cuts her off. He says, "I want to see Jesse, your manager, right now."

"Fine," Maggie shrieks, then spins from our table and disappears into the kitchen.

My father empties the bottle of champagne into his glass and says, "That's too bad."

What is, Dad?

"It's too bad Maggie's about to lose her job."

I sit back and say, No, don't. Please don't get her fired.

"Are you kidding me?" my father snaps. "She was being a fucking bitch to my son and my wife."

But it's not her, Dad. It's me. I hung out with her one night and it did not go well at all.

"Did you sleep with her, Travis?" my mother asks.

"Scarlett," my father snorts, grabbing her arm. "Don't ask him that."

Leaning forward against the table, I say, Whatever, Dad. It's no biggie.

I look at my mother and think, Fuck it.

I say, I tried to have sex with her but I couldn't get it up. I was too high on cocaine.

"Jesus Christ," my mother snorts.

And my father lunges at me and backhands me across the face so hard that my neck snaps sharply to the right and bounces right back up like I'm some sort of bobblehead doll.

Fuck you, Dad.

"What?" my father snorts. "Fuck me?"

"Lance, Travis," my mother pleads, trying to stop us.

But my father goes, "No, Scarlett." He goes, "Did you just hear what came out of his goddamn mouth?"

And I say, I thought you'd be superstoked, Dad. Knowing that your son is hooking up and fucking hot girls. I fuck lots of hot girls, Dad. I don't hang out with ugly people. Ever.

And I'm saying this loud enough for all of the tables around us to hear it. Then the manager shows up.

Putting a hand on my father's shoulder, he asks, "Is there a problem with one of our waitresses, Mr. Wayne?"

No, I bark, before my father can answer. It's all me. It's my fault. Maggie is awesome. I'm not feeling well. I'm actually leaving.

"No you're not," my father snaps.

Yes I am.

I jump out of the chair and look at my mother, her face back in her hands, eyes covered, breathing very quickly and heavily.

Mom.

She doesn't look up.

I'm sorry about this.

"Travis, sit down," my father orders.

No, Dad. I'm leaving.

"Why?" he asks.

Because I'm already gone.

I shove the chair away from me and leave the Red Tie Restaurant.

I end up at Rawson Park. It's the only place I can think to go to avoid my parents for the rest of the night.

The park is empty and I sit on a tabletop and call Claire. She answers her phone and tells me she's working at the Inferno bar. It's superloud in the background and she's yelling, "I don't want to talk to you!"

I know you don't. I was just calling you to tell you that I'm going back to Hawaii to turn myself in.

"What?" she yells. "I can't hear you!"

I'm going back—

"What?" she yells again.

Somewhere nearby a dog is barking loudly. The owner comes out and tells the dog to shut up but it keeps barking, so the owner yells louder and louder and then I hear the dog make this horrible squealing noise and then I don't hear it bark again.

And Claire shouts, "Are you still there?"

Yes! I'm—

"Well, you shouldn't be. Don't ever call me again!"

Click.

Fuck!

My voice echoes.

"Fuck you!" I hear someone yell back.

I squeeze my phone as hard as I can. Then,

BAM!

I slam it against the top of the picnic table.

BAM! I do it again.

BAM! I do it and the phone face cracks.

BAM! I do it and everything breaks. I smash the phone into a billion fucking pieces and I pound the table with my fist repeatedly, stopping only when I notice that my knuckles are bleeding.

Turning around, I look at the tornado slide, then sprint to it, and climb up its ladder, sitting in the same spot where Laura and I had sex. I'm trying to cry, but nothing is coming out, and I lean back against the cool metal and imagine bugs, big black ones, like roaches and crickets, crawling around the inside of my brain.

I imagine red raindrops falling all around me.

Lying at the top of this tornado slide, imagining how this city would look in flames, I slip my bloody hand down my pants. I wrap my fingers around my penis and massage it until it gets hard. Then I begin sliding it furiously up and down. As fast as I can. Going at it at it at it.

Visions of Cliff jamming a rusted coat hanger between Laura's legs pound my head, and my eyes pop open.

My mouth dives for air.

I tilt my head forward, my body covered in sweat, and I slowly lift the crotch of my pants and pull my closed hand out.

I clench it as hard as I can, so hard that it looks like the veins are going to pop out of it, and when I open my hand again, a white and red stream of come slides past my wrist and down my forearm, and I sit up and find where Laura wrote our names and slosh the rosy red slime across the heart she drew.

WHEN I WAKE UP THE NEXT DAY, I FIND A NOTE FROM MY
father, stuck to my bedroom door. A note that goes:

> *Travis,*
> *Please take your car down to Rex's shop on Kennedy Street this*
> *afternoon. It needs to be fixed up before you leave so it can go*
> *back to the dealership.*
>
> > > *Thank you,*
> > > *Dad*
>
> *P.S.*
> *Don't worry about what happened at dinner last night. I'm*
> *sorry for slapping you. Your mother will be fine. Her recovery*
> *time is much quicker these days. The only thing you need to be*
> *thinking about is school. I'm proud of you. To see my only son*
> *carry on in my footsteps has always been a dream of mine and*
> *I couldn't be happier with the choice you made.*

I tear the letter from the door, crumple it into a ball, and
set it on fire in the bathroom sink.

☐ ☐ ☐

While the car is getting worked on, I leave Rex's shop to grab a bite to eat. I lurk down to Taco Bell and stuff a number six down my throat, and on my way back to the shop I see Michael emerge from a crappy basement apartment holding a fog machine, an old man by his side.

I shout Michael's name and wave an arm in the air and he gives me the rock horns. "Come over here!" he shouts.

I step into the street and wait for a break in the traffic, then jog over to him.

The old man smiles and walks away.

"I thought you were gone," Michael says.

Not for three days.

I look at the fog machine.

What's going on? What's up with the old dude and the machine?

Michael, who is wearing a pink V-neck T from American Apparel and a pair of dark blue jeans, and has a black rag wrapped around his left wrist, lifts his shades and sniffs, "That old dude was Gerry. He sells hot electrical equipment from his shit-hole apartment right there." Michael turns and points at the door he just walked out of. "The band needs a fog machine and I just scored us one."

I light a cigarette.

A fog machine, huh?

"Yeah. We're shooting a video next month for this song I'm working on right now. In the video, the four of us are gonna be in an unmarked black van, stuck in traffic.

Suddenly the back doors fly open, a shitload of fogs rolls out, and the band jumps out, one by one, on like the gayest fucking scooters we can find."

I start to laugh.

What's the song?

"Well, I've only written the first verse of it, but the title is 'Jewelry, Electronics, and Firearms.'"

Oh, wow. The David Crosby story, I say.

Michael smacks me in the arm, grinning. "Nice one," he says.

Pause.

"What do you got going right now, Trav? You got some time?"

I reach for my cell phone but remember I don't have one anymore. Fuck it.

Yeah, I got time.

"Come up to the pad with me. You can check the verse out. Kick it a little before you leave."

All right.

Michael and I head toward his place, but at the end of the block, he makes a left.

Where are you going?

Michael points to this dented, wine colored station wagon parked next to the curb. "We're taking this," he says.

Is it yours?

"Nope." He walks around to the passenger side door and unlocks it. "It's Rodney's." He climbs into the wagon and crawls to the driver's side.

I walk to the door and look inside. There are no real

seats. The driver-side seat is a small wooden stool that's been nailed to the floorboard. The passenger-side seat is a white lawn chair that's been bolted down. The backseat is a small iron bench that's been welded into the car floor.

Are you kiddin' me, Michael? Rodney drives this? You drove this?

Michael sets the fog machine behind the stool he's on. "Yeah, what's wrong? It runs."

I shrug. Toss my cigarette.

Sweet.

I plop into the lawn chair and close the door.

Why do you have it?

Turning the ignition, Michael goes, "I was at the Cheetah bar last night with a bunch of people and somehow I got left there by myself, so I walked to Rodney's apartment 'cause he only lives a block away. But he was all passed out when I showed up, and instead of assing out on his nasty sofa, I saw his car keys sitting on the table and I jacked them, then jacked his car."

The wagon finally starts.

Does he know?

"Of course," Michael snorts, looking at me. "I called him today. I told him. He wasn't happy, but hell, bullshit happens, ya know." Michael slowly turns the car out of the space and we loom down to the end of the block and make a left on Kennedy Street.

"Don't do anything to draw more attention to us," Michael warns, pulling up to a stop sign. "I'm pretty sure this ride isn't street legal."

You think?

Michael nods. Says, "I'm pretty sure," right as a cop rolls past us, both officers glaring at Michael and me.

"Shit," Michael snorts, then guns the car up a block, whipping it into the parking lot of a Burger King, and eking out the other end of it, stopping behind this large building.

We sit for about two minutes before Michael goes, "You think we're cool?"

Probably.

"Righteous," he barks, cranking up the volume of the Vaz CD we're listening to and gunning the wagon back onto the street, back to his pad.

We walk to the front of his building, me holding the fog machine and Michael fumbling with his keys. When he finally gets the right one in the lock, he looks at me and says, "You know I was just fucking around with you the other night, right?"

Were you?

"Of course I was, Trav. I mean, I was a little cranky and strung out, but shit, I got so many fuckin' things going on, ya know. I can't be expected to be rad all the time. You know that, Pony."

I know, Michael.

"So we're cool. Me and you. You understand that I wasn't being a dick, I was just being me with no sleep."

Yeah, man. I understand.

He winks. "That's why we're close, brah."

I follow him up to his place.

Inside he tells me to put the fog machine wherever. I set it next to one of the sofas and Michael turns his iTunes on and starts blasting some Mötley Crüe.

"Here," he says, walking at me.

What?

He hands me a wrinkled piece of paper with the words "Jewelry, Electronics, and Firearms" scratched at the top of it. "Read it," he says. "It's the first verse I was telling you about."

Nice.

"Take a seat, man. Stay awhile."

I jump over the back of the nearest sofa and sit down. Michael walks into the kitchen, returning like a second later with half a twelve pack of Budweiser. "Help yourself," he tells me, dropping them on the floor next to me, disappearing into his room.

I light a cigarette and start reading the song lyrics, which go:

When you've reached the breaking point,
Grown tired of despair,
When you've fallen through the cracks,
Spiral desperation's everywhere,
When your back's pushed to the wall,
When there's no one left to call,
When your soul's been set to burn,
And there's nowhere left to turn,
There's always jewelry, electronics, and firearms,
Jewelry, electronics, and firearms

A huge grin parts my lips as I fold the piece of paper and set it down on the coffee table. I hear the door to Michael's room open.

Taking a drag, I yell, I like it a lot, man!

"Like what?" a girl's voice answers.

I jump, startled. Look to my left. The lead singer from that band Patrick Bateman is walking into the living room, her hair pulled back, her awesome body stuck in a pair of tiny American Apparel running shorts and a faded Black Flag T-shirt.

She stops behind the couch across from me, sliding her purse strap over her shoulder. "What do you like?" she asks again.

I point at the piece of paper.

The song he's writing.

"Yeah, it's okay," she says. "You're the guy moving to LA soon."

That's the rumor.

"What's in LA?"

USC.

"Oh, shit," she snaps. "Look at you. Mr. Bigtime."

Are you trying to take a shot at me?

"No."

Then keep that "bigtime" shit to yourself.

She sticks her tongue out and Michael reappears holding a mirror with a pile of coke on it.

He looks at the girl looking at me, then looks at me looking at the girl, and smirks and nods his head like he's won some sort of a contest.

"Party time," he says, dropping into the couch next to me, setting the coke on the coffee table next to his song.

"You two know each other already, right?" he smiles, waving a finger back and forth between her and me.

Not really. But I saw her band play.

"Awesome."

The girl looks back at me and shrugs. She walks over to Michael and leans down and kisses him and tells him she has to get going. "But I'll see you later?" she asks.

"You'll see me later," he smiles. They kiss again and the girl says bye to me and leaves.

Michael leans forward and starts making lines on the mirror. "Damn, she's something else," he comments.

I light another cigarette.

When did you two start hooking up?

"A couple of weeks ago. After this party. She came back here and I slayed it. Finally."

Pause.

He looks up from the coke.

"You jealous?"

No.

"Maybe a little?"

I don't think so.

"Yeah, whatever, Trav." Michael lunges for the beer and grabs one. "She's a really awesome girl. I think I'm really into her."

So what, do you love her now?

He pops the can open. "Maybe."

I roll my eyes, think about leaving.

"Shit, man," he snaps. "It's almost three. *Saved by the Bell* is coming on. Will you shut off the tunes?"

I get up and walk over to the computer and shut the music off and sit back down, ashing into the tray.

Michael flips the channels until he finds TBS. He jacks the volume and racks up six lines of blow. "So you're moving again," he says, swinging his eyes on me. "You're heading for Los Angeles, huh?"

I am. So what?

He starts to hum along with the *Saved by the Bell* theme song, then stops. Says, "I can't believe you're actually going to leave again. I *cannot* believe you're going to leave all of this."

What is *this*, Michael?

I smudge my cig out.

He spreads his arms and says, "You know, Trav, this."

But the only things I see are piles of drugs, a stack of Kobe Tai porn, a fog machine, and a pair of supertight jeans.

Things that seemed so important like nine months ago.

Things I don't care if I ever see again.

Michael opens a small case full of short red straws while I look back at the TV.

Today's rerun of *Saved by the Bell* is the one where Slater's dad wants him to join the armed services just like he did, only the things is, that's not what AC wants. What AC wants is to continue his standout wrestling career at the University of Iowa, so he hatches a plan with Zack Morris. He gets Zack to impersonate him during a meeting with one of the military recruiters, the ultimate goal being to make it seem as though Slater is too crazy and too unfit for the military. The plan goes well until Dick Belding starts poking his nose around in things. He catches Zack red-handed in the act of Slater-impersonating, and all hell breaks loose and Slater is left with the daunting task of confronting his control-freak father.

Blowing two lines up his nose, Michael goes, "This shit is way too simple, man. Just tell your dad what's up, ya know? It's your dad. He should listen. If I was on the show, I'd smack Slater and tell him to quit being a fag about shit and go to Iowa and wrestle." Michael takes a swig of beer. "That's why I get mad when I watch this show," he says. "It's simple, dude. Everything is way too simple."

I don't really know what to say to that, so I don't say anything, and he pushes the mirror at me and holds the straw out.

"Your turn, Trav."

No thanks, man. I'm straight.

"It's your turn, man."

I don't want any, Michael, okay. I'm fucking over it.

"Oh *right*," Michael snorts, mocking me. "You're over it, man. You're just a step above all of us."

I didn't mean it like that.

Michael flips his hand, like he's waving me off. "Don't ever fucking try to explain yourself to me again. I don't care."

Why are you getting mad?

"Because," Michael snorts, sliding closer to me, "I think the least you could do is humor me now." He rubs his nose. "I've been really good to you."

I know you have.

"No, I don't think you do, but that's fine. It's fucking cool with me. Have a fucking blast in LA. I mean, it's not like this shit's going to go away from you out there."

And I'm like, It's not about getting away from this, so how about we just drop it.

He snorts another line. "It's dropped."

I dig out my last smoke and light it.

Have you heard anything from Cliff?

"Nope."

Nothing?

"Nothing, man. But he's around," Michael says, taking another drink. "I know he is. I don't believe the rumors."

Which ones?

He burps. Blows another rail. "I heard one from this guy who knows this broad from Springfield, who told him that Cliff was in Omaha, holed up in some motel, listening to Nine Inch Nails records backward."

Yeah, right.

"I'm dead serious, Trav. I also heard from some babe who knows this guy who supposedly saw Cliff in Mason City shooting heroin with Katie in the parking lot of a Kentucky Fried Chicken."

Inhale. Exhale.

Now that I can actually buy.

Michael slams the rest of his beer. Grabs another one. "No way, man. Cliff doesn't have the resources to do shit. Everyone he knows he either owes money or favors to, not the other way around."

I pinch the bridge of my nose.

And Michael's like, "He's a junkie. He doesn't have anywhere to go. The best thing that asshole could do for himself is shove a gun up his mouth and squeeze the trigger."

Pause.

"Bang!" Michael yells as Dave slams into the apartment holding a bottle of Jim Beam and a fistful of socks.

"I'm drunker than thirty old men in an Arkansas trailer park!" Dave stammers, barely able to stand in front of us.

"What's up with the socks?" Michael asks.

Dave points at him. "Bought 'em for you. They were selling them at the gas station I bought cigarettes from."

Dave tosses the socks at Michael, then turns and nods at me. "Travis."

Dave.

"Hey," Dave shrieks. "I gotta joke for you."

Cutting more lines, Michael's like, "What is it?"

And Dave slurs, "What's the best thing about twenty-eight-year-olds?"

What?

"What?"

"There's twenty of 'em," Dave chuckles, flopping onto the couch across from me.

Pause.

Then Michael's like, "Oh shit, I get it now. There's twenty of them." He starts laughing.

"Wait, man. Wait," Dave says, waving his arms in the air. "I got something I bought." He pulls a black DVD case out. "We have to watch this."

"What is it?" Michael asks.

"I don't know, but that dude Marco told me I had to go home and watch it. He said I wouldn't be disappointed."

Michael reaches over and takes the case from Dave. He pops the disc into the DVD player and hits play.

For like a minute, there's only fuzz and Michael starts laughing. "You got ripped off, man," he jokes.

But then the screen flashes and a kid, probably our age, appears on it, hanging from a ceiling beam with a rope tied around his neck, masturbating.

Think asphyxiation.

Dave tells Michael to turn the volume up, so Michael does, and with clarity, I can hear the kid moaning as he jacks his piece really hard.

And Michael's like, "I wonder what he's thinking about," right as the kid shoots off this monster fucking load. I mean, it fucking sprays.

Just think about mayonnaise bursting out of a garden hose.

Both Michael and Dave start clapping until the kid tries to untie himself, but can't do it. At first he puts both his hands around the rope and tries to pull himself up to the beam, but then one of his hands, the one with all the come on it, it slips, and the kid's neck snaps back.

He regroups for a moment, then tries to loosen the rope by tugging at it, but nothing is giving and then he really starts to panic. He starts ripping at the rope, like over and over and over again, but it's just not working.

His face turns all red.

His tongue is hanging out.

His legs are shaking violently.

And probably five seconds later, the kid stops moving altogether. The noises he was making quit coming.

He's totally dead.

And Dave goes, "Michael, play it again."

"I'm already there," Michael says.

Why? I ask.

"'Cause that was awesome," Dave says.

No it wasn't, man. Michael, don't play it again.

"Screw you, Trav. It was awesome." He does two more lines.

It was fucked up.

"Hey, man," Michael barks. "You can leave if you're not into it. I don't care."

You're serious?

"I'm dead serious," he snorts. "I'm completely over your self-righteous bullshit this summer. You're not better than anyone here, okay? So if you don't wanna watch the shit again, bail. Go home. Move to fucking LA. I don't care."

I stand up.

Fine.

"I've never seen anything this cool," I hear Dave say.

I walk to the door.

"Me neither," Michael laughs.

I open it and split.

53

IT'S TWO DAYS BEFORE I'M LEAVING FOR HAWAII. TWO days before I fly into Maui and take a cab to the police station and deal with whatever needs to be dealt with.

I swim laps all morning and finish in the early afternoon. When I go inside, my mother is just waking up. She's walking downstairs in her pajamas, barefoot, her face the color snow white.

She tries to smile at me but I don't think she can, and then she sits on one of the chairs in the living room and puts her face in her hands.

Mom.

She doesn't do anything.

I'm sorry about the restaurant.

Still not looking, she groans, "No you're not. But it's okay. I'm not mad. It was a stupid idea. Just like your father said it would be."

Mom.

This time she looks up.

Do you need anything?

"No," she whispers.

I'm going upstairs.

"Okay."

I start walking for my room.

"Wait," my mother suddenly snaps. "What are you doing this afternoon?"

Nothing.

"I made a care package for your sister but I don't think I can see her again today. Would you drive to Russdale and give it to her?"

I don't say anything.

"Please," my mother presses softly, a tear shimmering in each eye. "Would you do that for me, Travis?"

Yeah. I will.

"Thank you. And maybe you and I can have lunch before you go off to school. I'd like that."

I turn toward the door and walk away.

Russdale is a very small town, almost two hours away from the city.

I leave the house around three, and before I get on the highway, I stop for cigarettes and coffee at this gas station and run into Chris and April on my way out of the store.

Chris looks stiff and in pain and April looks timid in her huge shades, hugging herself.

"I heard you were gone," Chris says.

Soon.

Pause.

I don't know when I'll be back.

"At Christmas," Chris says. "Just like last year."

No. Probably not. Things are different this year.

"How?" April shoots. "How is anything different for you?"

It just is.

Silence.

I look at April and she looks at the ground and then I look at Chris and his face is bare and plain.

"Well, good luck," Chris says, clearly not meaning it.

Good luck with what, Chris?

"Leaving," he says. "Good luck with leaving, Travis."

54

I GET TO THE REHAB CLINIC, WHICH IS ACTUALLY ABOUT ten miles outside of Russdale, just after four. The building is old and gray and brick. There are park benches and tables and a bunch of recently planted trees dotting the clinic's lawn.

I walk through the front door, down a short hallway to the receptionist's desk, and ask to see Vanessa Wayne.

The receptionist, a chubby lady with brunette hair and glasses, asks me who I am.

I'm her older brother.

"You're here by yourself?"

Yes.

"Hold on," the lady says. She stands and leaves the desk and a moment later she returns with this younger-looking security guard rocking a handlebar mustache.

The guard checks my ID and asks to see the small bag of things my mother sent with me. I hand it to him and he looks through the items one at a time: A self-help book, an empty journal, a handful of *Us Weekly*s, a box of green tea.

He hands the bag back to me. "I had to make sure there were no drugs or drug-related content inside the bag," the guard says.

I understand.

The receptionist points down another hallway. "Walk all the way down and make a left. Your sister should be in the rec room."

Thank you.

I move past them, down the squeaky clean hallway, and find my sister right away. She's sitting on a green sofa, watching the television all by herself.

She looks tired and sad. She's in her pajamas and her hair is scrunched into a ball in the back.

Hey, Vanessa.

She looks at me. "Why are you here?"

Mom wanted me to bring you this care package.

"Where is she? Is she not coming?" My sister looks panicked.

She's sick. I saw her this morning and she looked wrecked.

I hand my sister the bag and sit down next to her and stare straight at the television, a rerun of the VH1 show *I Love the 80s* flashing by, while she rummages through the bag.

"Sweet," she says, holding the journal. "I've been writing a lot the last few days. Mom must've remembered me telling her that."

I force a smile and look back at the screen and nothing is said for a while. The show fades into this Sienna Miller hair care commercial, and I watch it with a certain amount of intensity because it's easier than talking to my sister and asking her about the huge bruise on her forehead and the cut underneath her left eye. It's easier than looking at her and asking her where the big gash on her neck came from and why two fingers on her left hand are swollen and taped together. Watching Sienna Miller and listening to her talk about a hair care product is easier than talking to my own sister and listening to her tell me how she got here. So I keep watching and staring until the next commercial break.

This is when my sister nudges me and asks me if I brought any cigarettes with me.

I did.

"Let's go smoke," she says.

Are you allowed to smoke? You're underage.

"It's rehab, dude. What are they gonna do, write me a fucking ticket and fine me?"

I shrug.

"Come on," she begs. "I'm dying. Look at me. I'm dying. I need a cigarette."

Fine.

We get up and we cross the room and we walk outside.

I hand her a smoke.

"Thank you so much."

I follow my sister across the yard and she sits down on the ground, under the shadow of a large tree, and I do the same.

So how is it in here?

"Fuck, man. How do you think?"

I don't know. I've never been in rehab before.

My sister takes a drag. "I know you haven't. That's what's weird."

I lean back against the grass.

What's that?

"Me hitting rehab before you. I mean, I learned how to do drugs by watching you and Cliff and the rest of your friends do them."

For a minute my mind flashes to that one antidrug commercial I remember seeing all the time while watching Saturday morning cartoons when I was a kid. The one that was about this father who discovers drugs under his teenage son's bed, and upon this totally shocking discovery, he confronts his son, asking him, "Where did you learn how to do this?"

Only to have his son come right back at him with, "I learned it from you, Dad. I learned it by watching you."

And I say to my sister, Yeah, but the difference is I didn't go into a fucking Gap store with any of my friends and start jacking shit.

I sit up.

I mean, the fucking Gap of all places. Why? Why were you even at the Gap? You're better than that.

My sister shrugs. Exhales. Says, "There's not even an answer to that, Travis." She pouts. "There's not even a good lie I could tell or a completely made-up explanation I could give." She presses a hand against her face. "It's all a big blur."

I light a cigarette.

"Nothing makes sense anymore."

I start sweating.

"Everything spun out of control."

My sister flicks her smoke away and she starts to cry. She covers her face. She cries. And her entire body shakes.

"I don't know what to do anymore," she sobs. "I don't, Travis. I have nothing."

That's not true. It's just rehab. You'll get better and you'll get out of here and you'll do rad fucking things.

My sister drops her hands. "No, I won't. You don't understand."

What don't I understand, Vanessa?

My sister punches the ground. Her fist thuds against the dirt. "When I was in the hospital the doctor ran some tests."

What kind of tests?

"Blood tests."

Inhale. Exhale.

And?

My sister wipes her face with the back of the same hand she plowed into the ground and leaves a streak of dirt on the side of it.

Did they find something wrong?

My sister doesn't say anything.

What did they find, Vanessa?

"I'm HIV positive."

Visions of my sister and me playing Marco Polo in a hotel swimming pool while we were on vacation in Aruba, when she was eight and I was twelve, smash through my head.

She covers her face again.

My first reaction: I scoot back. I slide myself farther away from my sister. I'm scared. I drop my cigarette.

Do Mom and Dad know?

My sister looks up from her wet hands. "No. I begged the doctor not to tell them. I begged him to let me tell Mom first."

Damn.

Mom will be destroyed.

She will lose it.

She will absolutely snap and she will lose it.

"Can I have another cigarette, Travis?"

Yes.

I toss the entire pack at her.

Take all of them.

"Thank you."

"Hey! I saw that!" A bald man in a pair of slacks and a short-sleeve shirt snorts.

He's walking toward us and my sister goes, "Shit, it's my counselor, Matt."

So?

"I'm not supposed to be smoking."

Matt stops and stands over the two of us with his hands on his hips.

"This is my brother, Travis," my sister tells him, snorting up some snot.

"I know who he is," Matt snaps. "I saw his name signed on the registry. And now he has to leave."

Why? My sister and I both spit at the same time.

"Because he gave you cigarettes, Vanessa. And I already told you that you're not allowed to smoke. You're not eighteen. We still abide by the law here."

Fuck you, man.

I stand up.

"Travis, don't," my sister says. "It's fine."

I step into Matt's bullshit face.

That's my sister. If she wants something from me, she'll get it.

And Matt says, "Not here. That won't happen here."

Hey, man, you're an asshole.

"And you're done here, sir. Leave now."

I look back at my sister.

A different security guard approaches quickly.

"Don't make things worse for your sister," Matt snorts. "She's here because of addiction. We have rules for a reason, so please leave now."

The guard closes in.

"Travis, please listen to him," my sister says. "Go if he wants you to go."

I shake my head.

Fine.

"Thank you," Matt says.

I nudge my way past the counselor and start back for my car. The security guard trails me all the way there. He stands atop the cement stairs, watching, as I pull away.

I'M LIKE THIRTY MILES OUTSIDE OF THE CITY AND POLICE
cars and ambulances and fire trucks are all over the place.

As I get closer to the massive clutter of bright sirens, it becomes obvious that there's been a major accident, and as I am cautiously directed through part of the scene, I see four cars completely totaled in a ditch, and another one halfway up a shallow hill that leads to a field.

Beer cans are scattered all around the scene. A baseball cap floats through the vacant breeze. Stuffed animals lie beside one of the ambulances, which is being loaded with a stretcher, and on the stretcher is a body closed up in a bag. A few feet away from that lies a crumpled-up sign that says JESUS LOVES YOU, and next to the sign, a suitcase and a cover to a board that says SORRY.

Everything in this car is in slow motion.

I light a cigarette.

MUCH LATER ON THAT NIGHT, WHILE I'M EATING A PLATE of reheated Chinese food, my mother walks into the kitchen holding the phone.

"Please take the call," she says.

Who is it?

"It's Laura. She's called four times for you today."

No.

"Please, Travis."

No.

My mother holds the phone against her chest. "Travis, just talk to her. You're leaving soon. She sounds like she really needs to talk to you."

I drop the plate of food onto the counter.

Fine.

I take the phone.

What do you want, Laura?

My mother stands there watching.

"Don't be mad that I'm calling you," Laura says.

Oh, I'm not. I just want to know why you're calling.

"Did you hear about the small riot that happened last night at Whiskey Red's during the Jack White show?"

No.

Pause.

It was true, then. Jack White was playing all along.

"Well, sorta. The dude who played, his name was Jack White, but he had Down syndrome, and dreadlocks, and sounded like a white version of Wesley Willis."

Shut up.

"I'm not lying," Laura laughs. "And when all the people who'd purchased the tickets and camped out for the shit saw it wasn't the 'real' Jack White, it was like a total hipster backlash and a fucking riot broke out inside the bar. The SWAT team got called in."

I don't say anything.

"Isn't that just hilarious? A guy named Jack White playing a solo show under the assumption that he's the 'real' Jack White."

It's hysterical, Laura.

I roll my eyes.

What do you really want?

"What do you mean?"

Come on. You didn't call me just to tell me about a hipster riot at Whiskey Red's. Be honest.

"I heard you're leaving again," she says. "I heard you're moving to LA and going to USC."

You heard right.

"Oh."

Pause.

"But I thought you wanted to stay here for good. That's what you told me."

Hey, Laura. Like you said, things change.

My mother leans against the counter, still staring.

"Do you think it would be possible to get together and talk before you leave? I think it could be constructive."

"Constructive"? I snort. What the fuck is that supposed to mean?

"You don't have to be such a dick about it, Travis."

I clear my throat.

Ya know, I'm just wondering, how do you do it, Laura?

"How do I do what?" she asks.

Ya know, how do you do it?

"Do what, Travis? What are you talking about?"

How do you suck so bad?

"What?"

Click.

I set the phone on the counter and my mother shakes her head. She takes the phone back, and I tell her, You told me to take the call, Mom. You should've known better than that.

57

IT'S THE DAY BEFORE I LEAVE AND I'M HOLDING THE
plane ticket in my hand—the ticket I bought when I finally
figured out that there was only one option, when I finally
decided that it was time to take some responsibility for the
first time in my life.

Setting the ticket on the nightstand beside me, I grab a
small bag and begin packing, and not long after I've begun,
I come across that same Polaroid of Laura and me on her
eighteenth birthday, and I never want to see it again. Ever. So
I dig a lighter from my jeans and roll into the bathroom and
light it on fire.

And as I stand over the sink and watch it burn into
smoke and ashes, I throw my arms above my head and yell,
Nothing! You're nothing!, then I run water over it and walk
downstairs to grab some orange juice and the front doorbell
of the house starts ringing.

Looking through the peephole, I see Claire standing on
the front steps, smoking a cigarette, and I open the door
halfway.

What are you doing here, Claire?

"I have to talk to you about something. Will you let me in?"

I don't know if I should.

"Please, Travis. This is important," she presses, smearing out the cigarette with her foot.

Fine. Come in.

I step to the side and Claire walks in wearing a Black Flag hoodie and a pink miniskirt and black socks pulled to her knees.

Shutting the door, I follow her into the kitchen and ask her what's so important.

"It's just . . . ," she starts, then stops. "Can I have some water?"

Yeah.

I grab a glass from the cupboard and fill it up and hand it to her, watching as she drinks the entire thing in one swig.

And I say, I didn't think I'd ever talk to you again.

Claire sets the glass on the counter. "I didn't either, but I've been thinking a ton about what happened and I realized some things and I figured I owed it to you, as someone I've known and adored for-fucking-ever, to bring it to your face first."

So . . . ?

"Basically," she starts, then stops once again, her head shaking, a hand on her forehead. "God, this is so hard."

Fucking spit it out, Claire.

"So what I've decided is that if you don't turn yourself in and at least make an attempt to see if you are responsible for that girl's death, then I'm going to cruise on down to the police station and drop your name and tell them what you told me. Everything little thing, Travis Wayne."

But, Claire, I—

"I'm dead serious, man!" she screams, making fists with her hands, cutting me right off. "I cannot let you get away with that. I can't live with myself knowing I didn't do a thing! I just can't! I don't care how much I care for you!"

Claire, just—

"How could you fucking do that to someone, Travis?" She grabs my shirt with both hands and goes, "Do you understand the hugeness of what you're involved in? It's fucking huge and now I feel dirty. You made me feel dirty, Travis. It's like you dug a hole and threw me into it with you, and this is the only way I can get out of it!" She pushes herself away from me. "You did this, Travis!"

Burying her face in her hands, Claire starts bawling, and I go, Are you finished?

She looks up with a face full of tears. "What?"

Because if you are, that means it's my turn, and if it's my turn, that means I get to tell you that I already bought a plane ticket to Hawaii.

"You have?" she sniffs.

I'm leaving tomorrow.

"Oh my god."

So there. You don't have to feel bad about it, all right? It's done. I'm leaving. I'm gonna deal with this shit.

Stepping into me, Claire wraps her arms around my neck and goes, "Thank you, Travis," but I push her off of me and say, Don't thank me for this. I'm doing what's right. People shouldn't have to be thanked for doing the right thing.

"What do you think will happen?"

I don't know.

"Are you scared?"

Yes.

Pause.

The two of us stare at each other and I can't deal with it. I can't deal with her being here, knowing that this may be the last time I see her, and I shut my eyes and I tell Claire to go home.

Please, I say. Leave.

"Okay, Travis," I hear her whisper, and then there're footsteps and the front door opening and closing, and when I open my eyes again, I fall against the kitchen counter and begin to cry.

58

IT'S LATE AND I'M SITTING AT THE DINING ROOM TABLE, smoking cigarettes, staring at the moon through the large window in front of me. The phone rings and I jump. It rings and it rings and it rings and my parents must not hear it 'cause it keeps ringing, so I answer it.

"Travis," I hear, the voice on the other end sending a hard chill up my spine. "Travis, is that you?"

It's Cliff.

I know his whine from anywhere.

"Travis," he groans. "Fucking answer me."

What do you want, Cliff?

I hear him rubbing his nose.

"I need you to meet me now."

No way. No fucking way.

"Travis!" His voice rips my ears and makes my stomach drop. "Listen to me. I need you to meet me."

Why should I?

"'Cause I'm asking you, man. I'm asking you as a friend since preschool. I'm asking you as someone who once cut their arm with you and traded blood."

Cliff, I can't.

"Bullshit, man. You can. I need your help. I need you to meet me. Please," he begs. "Please come meet me. I need you to."

It sounds like he's beginning to cry.

"I need your help," he whispers.

Fine, Cliff. I'll help you.

Pause.

He sniffs hard.

Where are you?

"The Last Chance."

Why are you at an abandoned motel, Cliff?

"Where else was I supposed to go?"

I don't know.

"I'm in room nine."

59.

I PULL INTO THE PARKING LOT OF THE LAST CHANCE A little bit after three in the morning. During the drive I wanted so badly to whip my car around and go back home and wait until sunrise and wait for my plane to leave.

But I couldn't.

Something deep down in the core of my body wouldn't let me. I kept thinking about Cliff and thinking about him being so helpless and thinking about him being alone and scared and not having anyone to turn to.

Like me after I left Hawaii.

I park my car.

Inhale. Exhale.

The building is in tatters and most of the windows are cracked or broken and some of the room doors are missing. Graffiti covers most of the crumbling structure.

I turn off the engine and cut the headlights.

Step outside.

There's almost complete silence, the only noise coming from the distant murmurs of occasional cars and trucks driving across the interstate, and the high-pitched shrieks of crickets coming from the tall grass surrounding the lot.

The air is still. It feels dead as I stand in front of room number nine and knock.

No answer.

Leave, I tell myself. Turn around right now and leave.

I knock again.

This time the door opens a crack and Cliff jams his face into it. "Travis. Is that really you?"

Yes.

"Is it?"

Yeah, Cliff. Let me in or I'm splitting. I'll leave right now.

"Okay," he moans. "I'm letting you in." He undoes the chain lock and pulls the door open.

I step inside and Cliff tosses his arms around me.

Don't even, Cliff.

I push him off me.

It's really dark and I can't see anything, only the dull outlines of objects, like the desk pushed against the wall to my right and a bed frame straight to my left.

Are there any lights, Cliff?

He shuts the door and locks it.

"There's an overhead one I jimmied in the bathroom and a ground one in the corner."

How long have you been here?

He snorts a glob of snot back. "Like two days, man."

Pause.

Cliff stands next to me.

Why am I here, Cliff?

"I need your help," he says. "You have to help me."

With what? I can't even see anything.

I feel the clammy palm of a hand wrap around my wrist and when I try to yank it out, my arm gets snapped straight.

Cliff, what's going on?

"If I turn on the lights," Cliff says firmly, "will you promise not to leave?"

No.

"Promise me, Travis. Please." His grip tightens around my wrist.

Cliff, I—

"Please," he begs. "You're my only friend. I've helped you out so many fucking times with some fucked-up shit." His voice is trembling and shaking. And he snaps, "Just tell me you won't freak out and split when I flip the lights on."

Okay. I won't freak out.

"Promise me."

I promise you, Cliff.

"Good." He lets go of my wrist and stumbles and falls his way toward the far corner of the room and flips on the light.

Blood is everywhere.

Big spots stain Cliff's white T-shirt.

There are these deep fresh wounds all around his neck, all up and down his arms, like someone's dug a blade into his skin and yanked through it.

Both of his lips are split open.

And I'm looking at a gun, the same gun Cliff showed off to me and Michael, poking from the waistline of the jeans he's wearing.

What the hell is this, Cliff?

He pulls the gun out and goes, "You said you wouldn't freak out. You promised, Trav."

Whoa. I'm not freaking out. Just put down the gun and tell me what happened.

"I don't know. I don't remember," Cliff stammers, a line of red spit dropping from his mouth. "But you have to help me out."

With what? Fuck.

Cliff points the gun at me. "Bathroom." He motions me toward the bathroom doorway with the gun. "Right now."

I choke down the lump in my throat.

I feel sick.

I walk slowly and carefully into the bathroom, but I can't see anything.

What's in here, Cliff?

"Her," he says, switching the light on.

I almost vomit. My stomach sucks back and my body thrusts forward and my eyes fill with water.

Lying in the bathtub, in a swimming pool of blood, is Katie. Her mouth is taped shut. Her right arm dangles over the edge of the tub. A knife sticks out of her chest.

Oh, Cliff. What did you do? What the hell did you do?

"I don't know," he barks.

You killed her, I rip, stepping at him.

But Cliff points the gun right at my face and I stop dead in my tracks. "Don't even think about it, Travis. You're not going anywhere until you help me."

With what? She's dead. You killed her.

Slamming the butt of the gun against his forehead, Cliff goes, "I know."

What do you want me to do about it?

"We have to move her. We can put her in your car and take her somewhere and bury her."

I raise my fist.

Fuck you.

Cliff cocks the gun. "Don't start evil, Travis."

Evil? There's a dead girl sitting in a bathtub and you want me to help you move her and I'm starting evil?

"Yes." His eyelids flicker and in that moment, I see something else in Cliff. I see the six-year-old kid who raised money for a sick classmate by going door-to-door and selling candy bars. I see the ten-year-old boy who saved every cent he earned on his paper route one year so he could buy his mother a necklace for her birthday, which she accused him of stealing at first.

Looking Cliff dead in the eyes, I see the thirteen-year-old boy who stepped in and stopped a small helpless kid from getting his ass kicked by a group of bigger boys. Staring right at him, I see the sixteen-year-old boy who was smashed in the face with a beer bottle by his father after taking the fall for me during a second pot bust.

Then Cliff's eyelids close again. But this time, when they open, the only thing I see is a scared kid with blood on his hands, pointing a gun at me.

I start for the door.

I'm leaving, Cliff.

But he steps in front of me. "No you're not."

What are you really gonna do, Cliff? Are you gonna shoot me?

"Yes."

Fuck you.

"Help me."

No. I'm going. I have to go and you're gonna have to shoot me if you don't like it.

And for a few long seconds that feel like hours, I stand there and I wait. I wait to hear the sound of a gunshot. I wait for Cliff to pull the trigger and end my life.

I wait to feel nothing ever again.

But it doesn't happen. Instead of Cliff shooting me, he begins to cry, and falls against the wall, sliding down it, sobbing, "What happened to me? Fuck. What happened?"

And overcome by this sudden burst of emotion, I walk over to Cliff and I kneel down beside him.

I say, You're gonna have to do the right thing, man. You're gonna have to turn yourself in.

"I can't," he sobs. "I can't go out like that."

Placing my hand on his shoulder, I tell him, Cliff, you have to.

"Why, Travis?"

'Cause if you don't, I will.

Cliff turns to me. "Leave," he orders, pointing the gun at me again, poking it right between my eyes. I stand up and I back away slowly.

"Get the fuck out of here!" he snaps.

I turn around and run my hands down my face and walk out of the door, back outside.

Halfway to my car, this is when I hear it—

BANG!

And Cliff, he's dead. And everything in this city, it's all fucking over.

But for real this time.

afterword.

I DROVE BACK TO MY PARENTS' HOUSE THAT MORNING AND walked into my room and grabbed my bag. I looked around the room one last time, the bed unmade, CDs still all over the floor, the top left corner of my Vincent Gallo poster undone from when the tack fell out of it, and I didn't feel anything, even though somewhere down inside of me I think I wanted to, so I walked out and headed back for my car. And as I moved slowly through the long hallway that connected the house to the garage, with my bag strapped to my back and my plane ticket in my pocket, I noticed that the family pictures that had been taken down at one point had been put back up, replacing the two odd-looking metallic pieces of art, and for a moment I thought about who might've hung them up, but none of that ended up mattering, because they'd been taken down in the first place, and I continued moving and drove away.

At the airport I parked my car and checked in for my flight, and when it was time to board the plane, I didn't hesitate at all, and I fell asleep right away and dreamed not about Autumn Hayes, and bathtubs full of blood, but instead, I dreamed of nothing, and when the stewardess woke me, telling me that we had arrived, I got my things and told her thank you, then walked off the plane and into the Maui airport, where I took a taxi straight to the nearest police station.

When I walked inside, I told the desk sergeant that I had information pertaining to the death of a girl in a motel room last December, and I was promptly placed under arrest and taken into an interrogation room, where I offered up everything I could remember to the police and was then left alone inside the room for almost an hour before finally being charged. Only I was not charged with first- or second-degree murder or even manslaughter. I was charged with criminal negligence and failure to report criminal activity, because in the end, I hadn't killed Autumn. Autumn Hayes died, the police said, of asphyxiation in her sleep due to an overdose of multiple drugs that made her vomit while she was passed out, which she ultimately choked on and died.

But even though I was cleared in the actual wrongdoing of her death, I still felt no better and I still felt no relief. Two people's lives had been destroyed, and her family had suffered. And even though I would never meet or talk to anyone in that family, it was relayed to me that they were grateful I had come forward and filled in the blanks of the final hours of her life.

As far as my own family was concerned, my father and a top criminal defense lawyer flew to the island and tried to talk me out of pleading guilty. They wanted me to fight the case instead, but after two days of my not going for it, my father looked at me and told me that I was never his son, and then he left Hawaii, and I plead guilty in a court of law, my mother seated in the front row of the courtroom in tears, and was sentenced to eighteen months in a state correctional facility, where I still sit today, writing this story the only way I know how to.

And I'm not sure what I will do when I do get out. The future, while not unlimited with possibilities as it once had been, will still hold many opportunities for me. But the thing is, my slate will never be *wiped clean—this will never fade into the background and become some sort of learning experience or bump in the road. The shit that happened in my life and this book is real. And because I finally woke up to that whole realization much too late—the realization that life really happens and there is always a consequence for your actions—I lost everything, in some sense, but in a weird kind of great way, if you flip it all around, I may have gained the most important thing of all: the truth. I can live with that.*

Travis Wayne
Hawaii State Correctional Facility
January 2007

about the author.

Jason Myers has lived the *exit here* life. This isn't a memoir, but Myers has lived close enough to guys like Travis to know how to tell this story right. This is his first novel. He lives in San Francisco.

UGLIES
SCOTT WESTERFELD

READ THE BRAIN-KICKING
NEW YORK TIMES BESTSELLERS:

AND DON'T MISS THE ULTIMATE INSIDER'S GUIDE TO THE SERIES:

From Simon Pulse | Published by Simon & Schuster

From the *New York Times* bestselling author

Ellen Hopkins

Crank
"The poems are masterpieces of word, shape,
and pacing . . . stunning." —*SLJ*

Burned
"Troubling but beautifully written." —*Booklist*

Impulse
"A fast, jagged, hypnotic read." —*Kirkus Reviews*

Glass
"Powerful, heart-wrenching,
and all too real." —*Teensreadtoo.com*

Published by Simon & Schuster